A Fleeting State of Mind

by Julia L. Mayer

A Fleeting State of Mind. Copyright © 2014 by Julia L. Mayer. All rights reserved. ISBN 978-0-9914677-0-9

Cover design by Alan Thomas

Acknowledgements

Thank you to the many good friends and family who have read, listened, supported, comforted, encouraged, and listened and supported some more over the way too many years. Thank you to Sara Taber for her guidance and encouragement and to The New Directions program for bolstering my confidence. Huge thanks to Reisa Mukamal for her expert and tireless editing. Special thanks to Barry Jacobs for his constant support in all ways.

June Gray, best-selling author, and expert on Depression, will be answering your questions and signing copies of <u>Be Happy</u> on May 15th at the Barnes and Noble Book Store on Omega Square. Plan to arrive early, as large crowds are expected.

Chapter I - Patience (patients)

Depression hits unexpectedly, descending upon us fog-like, settling in unnoticed, until its thickness becomes blinding and undeniable. Despite all manner of interventions, depression tends to linger, until finally, just as it arrived, it dissipates, and once again we see clear skies. Depression is a mood, a temporary state of mind, one we can observe and understand. This requires time and patience. Most importantly, it requires a degree of kindness toward the self, a comforting, loving, caring approach that is the greatest challenge to the depressed person. (Be Happy, by June Gray, Ph.D.)

Dr. June Gray took a deep breath and let it out slowly. Pushing the entire painful situation out of her head, she opened the door to her therapy room and let in her next patient.

"Dr. Gray, you wouldn't believe what happened Saturday night. It was amazing. I think I got maybe three hours of sleep!" Annabelle tossed her long blond hair and flashed her irresistible smile, pausing dramatically. "Jerome was at the Top of the Crown."

June swallowed hard, bracing herself. She made the face that indicated, "Oh no, that can't be good, but I can't imagine what unbelievably exciting things happened as a result and I am eager to hear." She had lots of practice using that particular expression with Annabelle.

"You wouldn't believe what happened. But I have to tell you in order." Annabelle kicked off her platform designer shoes and took a deep breath. "We were drinking champagne. Really good champagne. He kept buying me more. I had on my sexy silk blouse. I looked really good. He was complimenting me, gazing into my eyes, flirting shamelessly with me. So, of course, I was in heaven. We had our own table. Some of his friends and business acquaintances stopped over and chatted with us. It was like I was part of his world."

"Did you feel comfortable being part of that world?"

"Absolutely. I fit in perfectly. One of Jerome's friends, Louis, talked to me for a while. He kept saying how beautiful I was. He actually invited me to go home with him."

"He did?" June felt offended for Annabelle, although she clearly felt flattered. It sounded like she had men swarming around her. June did a quick little check-in with herself. Was she jealous?

"Yes. But, I'd never do that. First of all, I was with Jerome." She stretched out his name lovingly. "But secondly, Jerome told me that Louis is still married but just pretends that he isn't. I can't deal with that."

"But isn't Jerome still married?"

A look of irritation crossed Annabelle's face. "Yes, but it's completely different. He's in the process of getting a divorce. Don't you get it?"

June just nodded.

"So, it got to be about 1:00am and Jerome told me that he had to get home because he had to go into work the next day for an important meeting, even though it was a Sunday. He works very hard. But I didn't want the evening to end. It was so perfect. I asked if I could see his car, which is, of course, a very top of the top of the line Mercedes. When they brought out the car, we both got in and drove around a little. It was the most beautiful car I had ever been in. I'd rather live in it than in my apartment." Annabelle gave Dr. Gray a look to indicate that it was that amazing. "I was so attracted to him. I had my hand on his thigh. And I kept moving it up his leg." Annabelle laughed. "I guess I was a little drunk."

As June listened to Annabelle's tale, she tried not to show how nervous she felt for her. She wanted to stay with her emotionally in the session; Annabelle was excited and happy to be getting the attention of a handsome, wealthy man. Who was she to ruin that for her with concerns about the sincerity of his interest in her? She was having a dream date. Maybe it was June's own situation that was interfering with her ability to enjoy the ride.

"Ok, Dr. Gray, here's the amazing part. Jerome pulls the car into his office parking garage and parks in his spot." Annabelle stopped. "He has his own parking spot with his initials painted on it." She paused. "We made out in his car for a while. It was just so nice to be touched. I don't even know how much time went by. But then I had to use the bathroom. I told him and we got out of the car and went up into his office. We took the elevator up and it opened onto this unbelievably beautiful entry way that led into the offices. It was marble and wood, polished and gorgeous. We were laughing so hard and I was yelling that he had to stop making me laugh until after I peed. He showed me the way to the ladies room. It was amazing. Also nicer than my apartment. I really was in heaven."

Annabelle stopped to examine June's face. She was clearly looking for her disapproval. June worked hard to stay neutral but encouraging. She wanted to hear what happened next, frankly.

"When I came out of the ladies room, Jerome was standing there giving me that look. He took my hand and we walked down the hall. He opened a door and it was clearly the board room. There was a huge oval, unbelievably shiny wood table surrounded by comfortable looking swivel chairs. He pulled the door closed behind him and held me. He pressed his body up against mine. We kissed. He started to undress me. I was shocked. In the board room? Can you believe we were in the board room? We were laughing and kissing and undressing. The next thing I know, we were making love on the board room table."

June's mouth was hanging open, because Annabelle added, "Its true. We were having sex on the table. It went through my head that there might be cameras or a security guard but Jerome seemed perfectly fine. I still can't believe it. We made love on the board room table." She laughed. "It was not the most comfortable experience ever, but I knew that he'd be sitting at that table, probably on Monday with his coworkers if not in the morning, and he'd be remembering Saturday night. That made me feel really good."

"I'm in shock," came out of June's mouth. Annabelle seemed pleased to hear that. She let out a laugh.

"Dr. Gray, it was the best night of my life. He finally drove me home at 5:00am or something. Even then, we were kissing in the car for a while. He didn't want to drop me off but he had to. He is the greatest guy."

Four days later at her very next session, it all came crashing down. Annabelle was crying hysterically. June was trying extremely hard to prevent her own misery from bleeding over into this session.

"Annabelle, I know it's painful to feel such a huge disappointment. And I know it sets off your depression. But, if you can just be patient, your depression should lift by itself according to the latest research, regardless of medication or therapy, within six months."

June regretted it right after it left her mouth.

"Patient? I've been waiting for twenty years. How much more patient do you expect me to be?" Annabelle screamed, filled with years of rage and frustration. It took June's breath away.

"Well, I..."

Annabelle had been June's most challenging patient for several years. They'd been meeting twice weekly. June so badly wanted to be helpful to her. Annabelle was an accountant who felt bored with her career, was now in her early forties and was desperate to find a man. Desperate was an understatement. Yet she was unable to keep the attention of the men she wanted. June was considering getting a consultation from a colleague, referring her to someone more competent, quitting doing therapy altogether and opening a bakery. People are usually happy in bakeries.

"Dr. Gray, are you saying that this therapy is a waste of my time and money? If so, I'll just jump off the bridge right now. I'll walk out of here and jump off the Chambers Street Bridge. Is that what I should do? Just tell me now. You were my last hope and all you have to say for yourself is, 'be patient'? I'm a hopeless case. I have nothing to live for. Jerome probably wouldn't even notice. I should go jump off the bridge. Tell me what the point of my going on is?" Annabelle fell back in defeat, into the deep, old, stained, grimy couch.

June felt like crying. "I know how helpless you must feel. I wish there were something more I could do for you right now. I know you're suffering."

Fortunately the hour had ended. "This is obviously something we will need to discuss further. However, our time is up for now. You know I want to help you. If you like, we can start with it next time." June spoke with her hands folded in her lap, with the most calm therapist-like demeanor she could muster. Pure acting. She wanted to jump up, hug her and cry together. They both needed a good cry. But she'd been trained to remain calm, collected and to keep her hands off unless someone requested a hug.

"Start with what?" Annabelle retorted, "What to wear to a suicide attempt?" "Hang in there," June replied, knowing her threats were dramatic expressions of her desperation but not of sincere determination. She ushered her out as quickly as she could, shut the door behind her and was overcome by relief. Hang in there? Interesting choice of words. She had made it through another session with her. Barely. She wouldn't see her again for three days. She needed some air. She peered out the window and saw Annabelle get into her red two-door sports car, slam the door, and speed away. June walked down the flight of stairs to the first floor and out the door into the sunlight.

The time seemed ripe for some self-analysis. Her short wavy brown hair was turning gray. Strands of white with the texture of telephone wire popped up here and there. The premature gray hair made her seem a bit older and wiser than she deserved, counteracting her baby face with its pudgy cheeks, pointy chin and big brown eyes.

She found herself easily fatigued. Getting out of bed in the morning had become a bit like hauling a car out of a swamp. Even after one of her better nights of sleep, she just didn't have the energy to get out of bed and start a brand spanking new day.

It had begun to seem painfully obvious that she was depressed. She'd always avoided honestly considering it as a real possibility. She was a therapist; theoretically, she should have been beyond depression.

Here she was, a thirty-five year old, single, unhappy, psychologist experiencing early burnout. Once, she'd thought becoming a psychologist would fulfill her dreams. She'd always wanted to be one. But now she felt like she could crack open and crumble on the floor like a cartoon character if she continued on much longer.

She could picture that day: Annabelle would walk into her office demanding to begin immediately and she'd see on the slightly stained, neutral, industrial-strength carpeting in front of her a pile of little, crumbled pieces in the muted tones of one of Dr. Gray's outfits. She'd frown and say, "Another person in my life who's disappointed me. I should have known."

As June stood in the fading afternoon light, she scrounged up some other obvious symptoms that made a decent case for depression: under-eating at times, general lack of motivation, procrastination in many areas, crying a lot, dysthymic mood on a regular basis. She tried to make the case for PMS, but not many people have PMS twenty out of thirty days a month, and sometimes thirty out of thirty. She was also awkward, lonely, socially phobic and self-deprecatory. Your typical psychotherapist? Perhaps.

The main source of her sustained dysthymia, Phil, thought it ironic and amusing that every therapist he knew, June included, seemed severely neurotic. Phil was a computer analyst. He would say "businessman." Whenever June referred to Phil as her boyfriend, she'd chuckle in a resigned, sarcastic way to herself, because he was a forty-two year old man, especially un-boy-like and not so great in the friend department, either. He saw himself as the picture of mental health even when they were focusing their conversation, or as he would put it, June's distorting, magnifying circus mirror, on his trouble with commitment. He believed that they had reached the point of analysis paralysis on the subject. He was not ready, and had no idea when or if he ever would be.

June had been feeling lately that she was reaching the end of her rope. Phil thought that it was a pity. He hoped that she'd hang in there.

She had hung in there, through unmet longings, dashed wishes, disappointments, choked-back tears, self-blame and attempts to improve herself for Phil. She was in love, so she made allowances. However, their fourth Christmas and New Year's Eve as a couple tested her tolerance. June had spent years hearing from her patients about their Christmas gifts and New Year's celebrations. Even people struggling in difficult marriages had a better time than she did. Phil and she didn't exchange gifts. He declared that they weren't brainless conformists. They were above the media manipulation rampant in the country. Usually, after stopping by June's parents' house and bringing her brother's kids gifts, they'd visit Phil's parents for an austere, quiet Christmas meal. Then home. Or they'd skip Phil's family and just go home. And New Year's Eve dinner was always home cooked because Phil didn't want to deal with the crowds and high prices restaurants charged on that night.

Two weeks before their fourth Christmas, Phil announced that he would be attending a three-day seminar that would take him to Chicago, from December 19th to the 21st. Because travel at that time of year was so crazy, he informed June that he would be going on the 18th and staying in Chicago until December 26th. He had not thought to invite her and had no concern about what she would do on Christmas without him. He had left her so little time that she could hardly have found alternative plans for herself. She was too mortified to ask anyone to let her join them, anyway. Phil was back for New Year's Eve. They ate at his place. She spent the night fighting back tears. Phil insisted that she had PMS. He suggested she calm down.

If June had been her own patient, she would have forced herself to confront the denial and question the self-esteem of someone who would allow this type of treatment to continue on for so long. She, as patient, would realize that she deserved better and leave Phil and find true love with a terrific, devoted guy. Then she, as therapist, would be sending herself a big bill which she, as patient, would gratefully place in the mail the next day with a big check attached to it.

> *People often find their way into psychotherapy because, at a deep level, they are longing for love and unconditional acceptance. The outward complaint is usually anxiety, depression, marital strife, or low self-esteem. They have lived for so long fueled by their hopes and fantasies about what they might one day experience, that they find themselves in relationships that fall very short of their ideal and hardly know how they got there.*

Phil was tall and handsome with a distinguished graying head of hair. His emotional range was limited. He repeatedly told June to calm down, which had the polar opposite effect. Phil, however, continued to view the phrase as his most useful, sympathetic and logical intervention.

He used that phrase on Valentine's Day following their disappointing holiday season. It fell on a weekday so they had no plans. June had hoped at least to receive a phone call, if not a card or, God forbid, flowers. At 9:00 pm June called Phil to let him know she was disappointed, an unusual and big step. Her hand shook as she held the phone.

Phil accused her of being childish, needy and competitive with him such that she would want to make him feel like he had failed her. He refused to be pulled in to what he claimed was her ridiculous plot. She became angry and raised her voice, to which he replied with a robotic monotone that she should calm down.

> *Within the therapeutic situation, gift giving can hold great significance. A patient may believe she is giving the therapist a gift in gratitude, but she may also be longing for approval and gratitude in return from the therapist. Or hoping to win the therapist's love. The particular gift chosen may hold symbolic significance, relating to issues arising in the therapeutic process. A gift's meaning and purpose should never be neglected in therapy.*

Seven months later, June found herself dreading the upcoming holiday season. She was awakened in the morning by the blaring noise of her alarm clock. She stumbled into the shower and cried in time to the water pouring on her head. She looked in her closet for something to wear, finally picking a presentable, or at least not too shabby, outfit that she had not worn in several days. She was eager not to start from scratch. She just didn't have the stamina for that much decision-making.

She ate some tasteless breakfast cereal, and forced herself out the door of her studio apartment through the wet streets and into her rattling Japanese car and out onto the highway. She spent a great deal of time wondering why, exactly, she was on the planet. What was she waiting for? Where was her life going?

Her little car stalled at a traffic light in the rain. She started it three times before it gave in and turned over. Angry drivers all around her honked and gestured at her. If only she could get her life going again, like her car. She was totally stalled.

She made it to her office to meet with a new couple who had been referred to her by a colleague. George and Gina, a couple in their early thirties, sat on the couch in June's office with a huge space between them. George's face appeared to be frozen in a permanent glower beneath his close-cropped black hair. Gina, blond and attractive, smiled apologetically.

"George and I have been together for seven years. We got married one year ago, finally."

George interrupted, mumbling, "Finally."

Gina smiled at him and patted his leg. "I mean, we got married and things were going well. But lately, in the past few months, things have changed."

George interrupted again. "I don't know what you're talking about. You're imagining it, like I said. I don't know what we're doing here."

Gina looked at Dr. Gray, shrugged and said, "We just don't seem as close as we were."

George stared at her as if threatening her. "I'm under a lot of stress lately."

"He is. It's true," Gina conceded. "He has a lot of issues going on at work right now. But something has changed. George is very impatient with me. He doesn't like to spend time with me anymore."

"I said I'm under stress. Work's been crazy. I've told you that a hundred times. I get no support from you. All you do is accuse me." George gritted his teeth. "What about all of your problems?"

Before he could begin to list them, Gina said, "George and I haven't had sex since two weeks after we got married."

"That's bullshit." George looked rageful.

"But it's true." Gina looked unsure of what to say next.

There was silence. June had the urge to get up and run out of the room before George did something scary, but she sat still. She had to speak. "What happens when one of you brings up sex?"

In a low disgusted voice, George said, "I don't want to discuss this here." He turned to his wife. "You won't want me to discuss this."

June felt afraid to make eye contact with George. So she looked at Gina, too, who said, "He's never interested anymore. I've tried. It isn't easy for me to show him I'm interested. It's always been kind of hard for me. But I try."

"Why's it always up to me?" George snapped. "I have no problem with sex. How about we just agree to sleep together soon and be done with it?"

June felt confused. She wasn't entirely sure who had the problem. Because George seemed so angry, she sensed it was him. "George, you seem upset..." she began.

"Of course I am. I'm sitting here with an idiot and a lousy, useless therapist. Why wouldn't I be upset?"

June looked squarely at George and said, "I'm not comfortable with your calling me a lousy, useless therapist in such an angry tone." This was their first appointment. She felt sure he'd insulted his wife on many occasions, but a patient had never insulted her like that before. She couldn't allow it to stand unnoticed. She would have been behaving like Gina, trying to smooth things over.

George exploded, "You are. You suck. If you knew anything about what you were doing, you'd have asked me how I feel being here, whether I really want to be here, or if I felt forced into it. You'd be interested in why Gina and I are having problems instead of assuming it is all my fault."

"I never assumed it was all your fault."

"You are assuming I'm the one who's avoiding sex." George leaned forward and jabbed his index finger in the air in front of June's face.

Gina broke in, "George, the doctor is just trying to gather information. I'm sure she hasn't concluded anything yet. She knows that I have problems, too."

George stood up and towered over them. "I don't have any problems except you. You're the problem." He stormed out of the room, slamming the door. June and Gina heard the waiting room door slam next.

June looked at Gina and said, "I'm sorry this hasn't gone well."

"It's not your fault at all." Gina gave her a weak smile. Fighting back tears, she added, "I'm pretty sure he's having an affair. I followed him to work the other day and saw him meet a young woman after work at a restaurant. I sat in the parking lot calling his cell phone and he just let it ring. Then he called me back from the men's room all angry. I didn't let him know where I was. He thought I was at home. After they had dinner I saw them get in his car, and I followed them to a motel. The next day, I found the motel receipt in his pants pocket when I was hanging up his clothes." She suppressed a sob. "He didn't even bother to get rid of it."

"What were you hoping to achieve in therapy?" June asked cautiously.

"I guess I wanted him to admit it, break up with her and try with me."

"Do you think there is any chance of that happening?"

Gina began to cry quietly. "I guess not. He didn't even care enough to hide the motel receipt."

"What will you do?"

"I think I'm going to take a leave from work and go stay with my sister for a month." Gina's voice was hoarse. "That's what I've been thinking about doing. I think I need to be away from him for a while. Maybe he'll miss me."

June assured Gina that she could call her any time, come in by herself to work through either staying in the relationship with George or leaving him, or even get a referral from her for someone else if she would prefer. Gina was grateful, and seemed relieved to have a plan.

After Gina had left the office, June felt a mix of emotions. Was she a failure for not keeping George in the room? Could she have handled the situation any other way, or was it doomed from the start? Should she have felt ashamed for feeling relief that they wouldn't be returning? Also she hated it when referrals didn't work out. She hadn't been getting so many lately. The money issue was always there. She felt so sorry for Gina. What made her not only tolerate George, but love him?

> *When a patient reports a sexual problem in her relationship, the therapist should hypothesize larger ongoing issues within the couple. Often, a loss of interest in sex is an indicator of building anger and resentment affecting both members of the couple. The recommended treatment, if there are no other medical symptoms, is couples therapy.*

June's weekly Saturday night date with Phil, once a reward at the end of her often painfully difficult work week, had become intolerable. On Saturday night, the lamps in his living room gave off the usual harsh glare of a doctor's exam room. They sat side by side on the stiff, itchy couch that forced them to sit up straight. She disengaged herself from Phil to turn off the light right over her head, with the precious antique china base. She felt a reluctance that surprised her as she moved back toward him. One arm around June's back gripped her shoulder just a bit too tightly, the prelude to sex. A faintly bitter taste in the French kiss. In these weekly rituals June tended toward passivity, allowing Phil to orchestrate the proceedings. She had tried in the past to participate, to vary the activities, to add surprise, and it had not gone well. He'd become irritable and withdrawn. She'd feel his disapproval, and as usual, it crushed her into accommodation.

Phil needed to be in control and he needed a kind of regularity that reminded June of bathroom habits. The transition to phase two of their sex for the evening had now begun, because Phil stood up, reached ceremoniously for her hand and walked her into his bedroom. There, at least the lighting was less bright. Only one lamp by the bed was on. They removed their clothes separately, Phil folding each piece of his attire and creating an organized pile, in case a surprise inspection occurred during their passionate exchange. After disrobing, they entered his double bed on opposing sides, meeting in the middle.

In the past, this unwaveringly choreographed encounter had been an event June had looked forward to, mostly as evidence that Phil cared for her. His desire to have sex on a weekly basis was the best evidence she could find. She looked forward to the physical closeness. Tonight, however, she felt shocked that she was experiencing not just reluctance but actual revulsion at the thought of sex with Phil. Every touch felt like sandpaper. His breath got worse by the minute. She felt tense and realized that she would have preferred a fist fight with him to sex. Even if she were losing.

Since phase two had always progressed in the same manner, Phil evidently saw no reason to alter the ritual, despite June's rigid body. He pulled her toward him, ran his hands from her neck over her breasts to her hips and around the back over her ass and down her thighs. She felt herself shudder. She looked at his face. He had his eyes closed and looked relaxed in a kind of deep concentration.

"Phil, I'm not feeling well." June thought she might throw up. "I'm sorry." She began to pull away, a wave of relief washing over her. She realized she had been holding her breath.

His eyes were now opened. "You were fine at dinner. You seemed fine in the living room."

"Well, I'm not fine now. I need air." June's head was swimming with fears and possibilities. Would she never again want sex with Phil? Had she suddenly stopped loving him? How had she never before noticed all the repulsive features he had? She really did want to vomit, not so much because her stomach was upset but because she wanted to rid herself of some Phil-ness that had gotten inside of her. She got out of bed, found her strewn clothes and began to throw them on, her head spinning.

"I'm sorry you are unwell. Is there anything I can do?"

"No." June realized she was shaking. That made it difficult to get her underwear back on.

"Are we not having sex tonight, then?" he asked.

"No, we aren't."

"Should I drive you home?"

She was eager to go home and agreed that he should drive her. But she felt angry and hurt that he'd want to rid himself of her because she didn't feel well and he didn't get his weekly sex. He should have wanted to take care of her, not abandon her.

She wasn't about to cry in front of him and needed to get home. Her feelings were so confusing: disappointment and relief, frustration and longing. He never made her feel special. Should she even expect that? This was possibly the most unsatisfying date she'd ever had with him.

Back safely at home, after crying only briefly, she thought of her patient, Donald, whose wife, Kat, had left him six months before. He was tall and thin, in his early forties, with a crop of curly red hair and a crooked smile. He'd had his sixth session with her earlier in the week. They were struggling to work through his loss. Prior to leaving,

Kat had begun to make a habit of going out partying, spending money to the point of landing them in unwieldy debt, and ignoring Donald. He hung in there though. When she finally left him, after a year or more of bad behavior, he was surprised and crushed. They had been married for ten years. He loved her. Kat continued, even after leaving him, to lean on him, to ask him for money, to call him at night to complain about other men. He couldn't bring himself to feel angry with her. And he couldn't move on. In therapy, he had been working on anger issues, only to discover that he felt strongly that he needed to protect Kat, even from his own anger. He felt sorry for her and could see that she was troubled, and therefore couldn't blame her for hurting him.

With Dr. Gray's permission, he had begun allowing himself to feel some irritation with her. It actually did bother him that she'd gotten them into terrible debt. He'd worked hard to save his money. And it did bother him that she called drunk at 3:00 am to complain to him about another man. And he couldn't understand why she needed to go out so often. As he became more comfortable with these emotions, Donald was able to separate a little emotionally from his wife and consider finding another woman.

In their most recent session, Donald confided, "Dr. Gray, I met this woman at a bar, but it was a nice, classy bar. She was really interested in me. She's in sales. I think I like her. It's the first time in a while that I've been interested in anyone besides Kat."

"That's great, Donald. I'm glad you're meeting people."

"I'm worried that it'll make Kat angry."

"What if it does? She left you. Does she have the right to stop you from getting on with your life?" June had to watch her own tone, not to overwhelm him with her angry empathy.

"No. But I hate to upset her. She's got so many problems of her own. She still needs me to be there for her."

"Donald, don't you think you deserve someone who takes care of you, too?"

"I guess. This new woman's name is Pat. She's really cute. She wanted us to get together again tonight. I said I would take her out to dinner. I'm nervous. What if we have nothing to talk about?"

Kat and then Pat. June wondered if that could possibly be meaningful. "You were married for ten years. You aren't used to dating. You can always ask her questions about herself, her dating history, what she likes about her work, her family. Why don't you come up with a mental list of topics. People love to talk about themselves."

"*I* don't. I hope she doesn't ask me too many questions. I get all tongue-tied when people ask me a lot of questions. What if this gets serious?"

"Donald, it's only your second date. Please take your time and get to know her and see if she's a stable, caring person. See if the two of you can become friends, if you really can learn to understand each other. Don't rush into it just to replace Kat. You need to take your time."

Donald agreed after further expression of anxieties, comparisons to his relationship to Kat and admitted eagerness to have a new and better relationship in his life. He left feeling anxious and excited. June felt hopeful for him. She wanted him to have the experience of being with someone who could take care of him too. He deserved something positive in return.

June had been sitting on the couch in her apartment thinking for an hour since Phil had dropped her off. He hadn't bothered to walk her to the apartment building door, nor even given her a goodbye hug in the car. She supposed that her thoughts had turned to Donald because she was feeling a little like she deserved something positive in return too. She'd been patient and forgiving, at least with Phil if not with herself.

Donald was the kind of patient June loved to work with. He had a clear problem. They could discuss it and explore it and make progress. He worked hard, listened to what she had to say and thought about it between sessions. And, best of all, he wrote her out a check for her full fee each week.

Money had been an anxious theme that wove its way in and out of June's life. Phil had no money problems, but her income fluctuated because she was in private practice. In the current reality of managed care, she could never actually predict her annual income. She'd managed to accumulate very little in savings as well as very skimpy quantities of spending money. This was partly due to her expensive rent and partly due to the never ending pile of student loans for which she would have sold her first born had she had one to be rid of.

On the day after the failed sexual encounter, June was feeling stuck and tortured. She kept thinking about the research evidence that it takes six months for a depression to lift, to get to the light at the end of the tunnel.

It hit her that she could give Phil a six-month deadline on their relationship. A revolutionary and scary idea, but somehow that made sense to her. He'd have the next six months to make it into something serious or they'd part ways. Either way she might see some light.

It felt absolutely right. She had to try it.

He'd probably tell her three days before the deadline that he was farther along in his ability to commit than he'd ever been before, with anybody, but couldn't make any promises. He wouldn't want to be responsible for leading her on. She'd have to do what she needed to do...and of course, she would get sucked right in like dust to a vacuum cleaner, and give him more time.

It was her own fault. She loved him. The problem all along had been that she loved Phil. They had a good time together on occasion. She learned a lot from him. They rarely fought, except over commitment. She knew he cared about her. But not as much as she cared about him. She felt trapped. She might have liked the option of having children. When June brought up that issue with him, he'd become annoyed and accuse her of trying to manipulate him.

How would she feel without him? Five years seemed like such a long time. She didn't want to look back at five wasted years. She didn't want to look back at six or seven wasted years, either. She supposed if the relationship ended and she fell into a truly deep depression, she would have the comfort of knowing that if she waited another six months, she would feel better. Either that or she could consider jumping off the Chambers Street Bridge with Annabelle...

June next saw Phil over dinner at the Fish Platter on the following Saturday night. The chatter of voices and the clinking of utensils were bouncing off the charming tin ceiling and shaking the oyster plates that sat on a high shelf all around the perimeter of the little restaurant.

"Why don't we give our relationship six more months?" June yelled across the table. "If, at that point, you still cannot make a real commitment to me, we can just end it and go our separate ways."

Phil's mouth fell open, full of tuna steak with soy and ginger marinade. "June, how can you say that? Don't you care about me anymore?" Phil then closed his mouth and chewed and swallowed his food.

"Of course I do. Believe me, if I didn't, why would I be giving you six months?" June had been ready for him to appear injured, and felt proud of her preplanned response. However, from here on in, it was going to be improvised.

"You know I care about you," Phil said. "I take commitment very seriously. I have to really know deep in my heart if you and I should truly spend our whole lives together. I cannot take this important decision lightly. When I commit, it is for life. You know my history. You know how my brief marriage affected me, the pain and disappointment. I always hoped that you would be more sensitive to my issues. And, I have to tell you, I feel disheartened. We have been through this before, June. Why are you bringing all of this up again now?"

She shrugged. "I don't know. Do I need a new reason?"

Phil looked thoughtful for a moment, and said more confidently, "You know that six months will be just an arbitrary, intrusive pressure on our relationship. I cannot promise that I will know for sure at that point. However, I am sure that this game you are playing will not have a positive effect on our relationship. All I have ever wanted was for both of us to be happy."

June pondered whether she had ever before been this unhappy, and realized that she could be setting a new personal record. She looked Phil in the eye and asked the perpetually unanswered, waste-of-breath question once again, "What will make you know?"

"I don't know. I really wish I did." June could have said it for him. They finished their meals in a loud clattering silence. Her first few bites had tasted delicious. She love ginger and soy. They had ordered the same meal, their agreed favorite. For the rest of the meal she might as well have eaten the napkin and tablecloth.

"I need to have the deadline." June said, as Phil looked at her reproachfully. "I can't go on this way. I don't want to lose you. You know I love you. But I feel like my life has stalled and I can't get it restarted. I'm sorry."

There was a long pause. "Well, then," he said matter-of-factly, "we both have to do what we both have to do." He shared with her a tight-lipped smile and added, "Dessert?"

She told him that she needed to go home and be alone that night. He looked pained and asked if there was anything he could do to make her feel better. She said, with a fake little return smile, "No, I need to be alone. By the way, so that there is no confusion, the six months starts today. The deadline will be April first, as today is October first." June stood up, grabbed her sweater off the back of her chair and sped out of there. She left him with the check. It was his turn to pay, anyway. He always kept track of that.

Hours later, sitting in her dark apartment, she realized that her deadline for Phil to profess his commitment was April Fools' Day. She pictured Phil, on bended knee, smiling up at her, saying "Honey, let's get married...April Fools!" In her twisted way, she took it as a sign that this was exactly the deadline she was meant to have.

June lived in a studio apartment in a nice part of the city. She could not comfortably afford a larger place and was fearful of living anywhere but a nice neighborhood, as a single woman who frequently returned home late in the evening exhausted. Her studio was small. Its saving grace was the relatively large windows along one wall, and the somewhat high floor on which it was located. The building had an elevator and a door man who spoke little English. They waved at one another with knowing nods on a frequent basis. She suspected he had confused the terms psychologist and prostitute. But he might have approved of her all the more for it.

The bathroom had a tub which had been a near lifesaver on numerous occasions. The closet was fairly roomy and the kitchen was not decrepit. The Formica counter tops were an ugly burnt-orange, but there wasn't a whole lot of counter space in the kitchen to get her too worked up about it. There was a rectangle of speckled gray and peach linoleum in the kitchen, demarcating it, as though it were a separate room sans walls. The rest had a tightly woven wall-to-wall pale green and gray carpet. It was industrial strength, like at her office, but neat and fairly new looking. She didn't have many belongings. Everything in her life felt temporary. No real home, no boss, no real job, no real relationship, she feared, and no real plans for the future.

Years earlier she had sold most of her graduate school books, and had squeezed the maybe fifteen worthwhile ones onto her bookcase at her tiny office. Those special volumes she thought about a lot. She referred to them frequently and had memorized much of their contents. They were her dearest belongings.

June's clothes tended to be old and dark and plain. She wasn't much of a shopper, or especially interested in style. She never did receive many gifts, so she didn't have much to display. Upon reflection, she had very little to show for the thirty-five years of her life. Clearly, she could find her way into a depression in ten steps or less.

Phil was not a materialistic guy. This was true even outside of Christmas time and the influence of the media. It included June's birthday and every other special occasion. He didn't like to be wasteful. If she gently reminded him that her birthday was approaching, he resented the reminder, and insisted he was planning to get her something. Then reluctantly, and without much consideration, he'd get her a book, or a pair of sunglasses, or chocolate or flowers. If she was not truly overcome with joy about the gift, he was injured and couldn't understand what she wanted from him.

Was that what she wanted for the rest of her life? She supposed it was better than nothing. Maybe she could have met someone else. She wasn't unattractive, although she was certainly not beautiful. She didn't exactly put a lot of time into her appearance. Minimal make-up, minimal attention to dress and hair, minimal jewelry and a mood like the depths of a swamp. At least she knew that Phil was willing to put up with that.

June thought of Vivienne, a patient of hers, who was involved with a married man for three years. He paid her bills, saw her on a couple of week nights for a date (i.e., dinner and sex) and called her every day. When Vivienne and June began working together, she was impatiently expecting that her married lover would leave his wife and purportedly lousy marriage shortly. He developed a series of excuses: his wife was unstable, ill, about to inherit money and he deserved a piece of it, she needed him, and most significantly, she was not totally unbearable. So what was the rush?

Three years later, Vivienne agreed that he wouldn't be leaving his wife. She began to see him in a more realistic light. To her surprise, she discovered that if he'd turned up at her door single one day, she would not have found him especially appealing. It wasn't so surprising. She didn't really want to take care of him all the time--to deal with his moods, his stress, his dirty underwear on the floor. Each rendezvous could be special as long as Vivienne worked hard to stoke the romance. She hung on his every call, planned each date and arranged not to repeat the same outfit. For Vivienne, this was better than nothing.

Vivienne and her longing for the unattainable. The married man, unfulfilled in his marriage, but not wanting something truly meaningful. The duped wife.

After days full of sessions like that, June drove home from her office with rock and roll turned way up, practically making her car windows shatter. But she couldn't drown out all the noise inside her head.

One thing June usually looked forward to was a phone conversation with Emily, her roommate from freshman year in college. They tried to talk twice a week. They were both so busy in their completely different lives that they could only get to see each other here and there. But even June's small pleasures had turned sour. As things with Phil began to head downhill, she became ambivalent about talking to Emily, who didn't have relationship problems. This caused June comparison pain.

She and Ed had met right after college. They'd dated for two years, gotten engaged and gotten married at year three. June had been maid of honor and was overjoyed for them. Emily and Ed were made for each other. They were both organized, goal oriented, extremely bright, well educated and socially at ease. They were fun-loving, kind people whom you just couldn't help loving.

> *Therapist burn-out can be an unexpected and complex problem. Working with certain high-risk populations can cause stress. Stress can come from a therapist's personal life, preventing him from having enough rejuvenation outside of his practice to remain fully present for patients. He may feel overwhelmed by his patients' problems, and may feel inadequate, anxious or even unable to tolerate doing therapy. He may struggle to maintain the empathy necessary for therapy to proceed successfully. A therapist risks acting out in the therapy, providing less than therapeutic help to patients, if he does not remain on the alert for burn-out.*

They had three beautiful children, a boy and two girls. Both Emily and Ed worked in the computer industry, in unusually stable jobs. They planned to retire by age fifty and enjoy growing old together. When June was younger, she fantasized about being brilliant and important, making a contribution and striking it rich, and of course, meeting the right guy and living happily ever after. Sometimes it was just too painful to see Emily.

> *Envy is a primitive emotional response, related to poor separation during early childhood. If the child doesn't successfully separate from the parent, she will struggle with feelings of inadequacy and longing. The envious person wants what belongs to another. She would not crave what the other has, if only the other did not have it. It can be seen as a wish to take from another, yet also do away with or replace that person. Both admiration and aggression are present in this ambivalent state of emotion.*

Birthday parties were always a difficult time for June. In October, Emily asked her over for one of her children's celebrations.

"I'd much rather come to Nina's birthday party Sunday than go where I have to go," June told her, apologizing.

Emily responded cheerfully, "That's okay. I understand that family comes first."

"It's pure, unadulterated obligation. You know that."

"You'll come over another time to celebrate with us. It's going to be a madhouse here, anyway. I think there are fifty people coming, most of them screaming children."

"Thanks for trying to cheer me up." They chuckled and got off the phone.

Emily was probably relieved that June wouldn't be coming because she would just be dead weight. What did she know about real live children?

June's obligation was a rare visit to her parents' that weekend. They periodically pressured her to visit, pulling out the guilt artillery. They never invited her over, saying, "Honey, would you like us to make your favorite meal?" She had no favorite meal with them.

It was two tedious hours of super highway in her jalopy, pulling to the left and slow on the acceleration. Stuck in the car, she started thinking about her family. Her anger came to a slow boil midway through the ride, as she remembered past injustices and periods of neglect and disconnect. She was amazed that she made it to their little, expanded brick house without an accident.

She parked the car, tried to decrease her heart and breathing rate by taking deep breaths, counting to three, then releasing. Repeated forty times. She told herself she could handle this. She told herself that she was an adult, that she didn't need their love. She told herself that she could play family therapist with a crazy family. Somehow she got herself out of the car. She felt stiff from the workout of rage and worn out from the ride.

She got her bag of gifts out of the trunk, slowly marched up the path to their front door, willed herself to ring the bell and waited.

After a few moments, she rang the bell again. She had told them when she would be arriving. She tried to put the fantasy out of her head of running back to the car, getting in and peeling out of there.

Finally, her mother came to the door. She looked happy to see June for about a second, giving her one stiff, awkward hug. She cheerily announced that they hadn't heard the doorbell because they were all out back. June began to have a sinking feeling in her chest like a deflating balloon. She stood there wishing for that good solid rage to return. Then they walked out to the back patio.

The glare of the Indian summer sun hit her hard in the face as she stepped onto the back patio. Considering that she had lived there for most of her childhood, the disorientation she felt when she returned always took her by surprise. As her eyes watered and then began to adjust, she saw her brother Gerry and his wife sitting at the umbrella table drinking what looked like scotch, her brother swirling his glass in a lazy, repetitive way. His wife was looking out over the yard at their two young daughters, who were running and screaming in circles. June's dad sat across the patio on the recliner, feet up, drink in hand, in what seemed like solitude.

When no one noticed June's arrival after several moments, her mother put her arm around her shoulder and gave her a squeeze. She then announced loudly, in a singsong voice, "Guess who's here?"

June's brother looked over, reluctantly put down his drink and slowly lifted himself from his seat. June walked over, eager not to cause him any unnecessary exertion. They hugged without feeling. He smiled at her and asked how she was. She said, "Fine." She leaned over his wife, Paula, and gave her a kiss. She air kissed June and smiled for a millisecond, then turned back to watch her children. She'd never shown any interest in June, who felt like the nerdy, unpopular girl in junior high, trying to make contact with the head cheerleader. Of course, she'd given up some years back. She and June had tried to have conversations but they had absolutely nothing in common besides the bad luck of winding up attached to the same family. She was supremely focused on her social status and her impressive, married friends, many of whom were doctors and dentists. She made loud and clear that her husband the dentist was acceptable, but his family barely tolerable.

June had watched her mother fawn over Paula and the girls for years, buying ridiculous gifts for them all, in an attempt to win them over. The girls would unwrap sparkly shoes, sparkly make-up, sparkly dolls and party clothes. June could see Paula's disdain as the girls unwrapped her mother's gifts. It was painful and made her feel annoyed and impatient with her mother.

June looked toward her father. Was he lost in thought? Meditating on something meaningful? Or maybe his mind had been abducted by aliens, and all that was left was the shell of a man with hair sprouting from his ears. She walked over and gave him a quick kiss. He looked up and said, "Hi, Honey. How are you?"

It wasn't a real question. He was just saying what the aliens had programmed him to say in an effort to avert any suspicions that the essence of his humanity had been sucked out long ago by a vacuuming device.

June couldn't help feeling a little like a teenager.

They exchanged inanities briefly and then she gravitated, as if on auto pilot herself, into the yard to her nieces who'd probably been warned by their mother to avoid all eye contact with her. At least they were still young and maybe not completely prejudiced against her. June didn't have a clue as to what to do with them once she got near them, though. She tried to talk to them but they continued to run after one another. After she had been standing there for about five minutes trying to get their attention, she found their mother suddenly standing next to her frowning and ordering the girls to stop disturbing their aunt and to settle down.

At this point, fifteen or twenty minutes into the visit, June had nothing else to do. Her mother was anxiously flitting around, putting salads on the table, forgetting serving utensils, panicking over whether the chicken was cooked all the way through. She had another hour and a half before she could possibly escape. She needed a drink badly.

She'd told so many of her patients that getting over childhood hope is a huge challenge. She'd clearly not gotten over her own. She'd thought that maybe this time her parents finally would be interested in her. Instead, things were the same as always. Her own disappointment with her parents reminded her of Annabelle's disappointment with her.

Early the next week, June was back in her office. Annabelle came in a week after her last session. They had missed one appointment. She'd had a scheduling conflict, so June had given away her time. She called at the last minute to tell June that her plans had fallen through, and she would be coming in. June had to let her know that she had scheduled someone else in her time. It was not a pretty moment. Her emotional response was at a level that June would have expected if she had told her she had cancer. She was utterly distraught and outraged at her unbelievably bad fate: first her plans had fallen through, and then Dr. Gray had taken away the one thing that she absolutely required to get through the week. Never mind that she had cancelled first in order to go to some invitation-only event with someone who had an invitation, but who then had decided not to attend at the last moment. This left Annabelle high and dry, with no plans on her Thursday night, and now, not even therapy.

So when she finally came in for the following appointment, she sat down with a look on her face that said, "I'll forgive you because I need you, but you should be ashamed." June felt grateful that it wasn't pure hostility. Annabelle removed the long leather coat that she'd been wearing, and the leather cap that matched, and tossed them onto the couch next to her. Her keys followed with a thump.

"You are lucky that I didn't jump off the bridge. The only reason I didn't was that I was afraid it wouldn't really kill me. With my track record for bad luck, I'd end up maimed so badly that I wouldn't be able to make another attempt and I'd have to go on living for forty years or more in a wheel chair. You know that's exactly how it would work out."

June tried to make her face express support and encouragement with a small smile, and said, "I'm glad that you decided to stay and face your issues."

Annabelle gave her a glance that indicated, "yeah, whatever."

June forced herself to remain silent.

Annabelle spoke, "I still can't believe that you told me to be patient. I thought you knew me better than that. I don't know how to be patient. When I'm angry, I'll pick something up and throw it. I'm down to three plates from a set of eight. My main problem is impatience. You know that. How can you expect me to suddenly become patient? That's why I'm coming here, whatever good it's doing me."

She was still hurt and angry from the previous week. There was her feeling of abandonment, her threatened rejection of June. At last, some real feelings about a real interaction between them.

"You're right, Annabelle," June said, eager to respond. "I was quoting research results to you instead of truly hearing how trapped, sad and disappointed you felt. I suppose it was difficult, even for me, to hear how desperately depressed you've been. I'm sorry I seemed so insensitive. I'm glad you called me on it. It was my error."

Annabelle looked as though she had been struck by lightning. She seemed burdened and agitated by the apology. She floundered, "You might have been right. I do need to be patient. It is important to keep up with the research in the field. I'm sure your intentions were good. But you can see how I would feel like you were not helping me because I can't suddenly make myself patient when I've been impatient all my life." Now she was practically crying and hyperventilating.

"You are right. I apologize," June reiterated.

Annabelle suddenly eyed her suspiciously. "Are you pulling some psycho babble trick on me? I had a lot more anger to get out on this, and your apology made me unable to express it. Is that fair? What do I do now? I need to work on my anger issues. Anger is the main reason I'm in therapy after all, isn't it? You seem to think that apologizing negates the whole thing so that it no longer exists."

"No. Not at all. I would assume that you'd feel some anger even after I apologized for an error, because the error made you feel criticized and unsupported." June spoke calmly and slowly. She had the feeling that they had surreptitiously gotten to something important and she didn't want to ruin it.

"Oh," was all that Annabelle could eke out. She was shaking her leg nervously. She tried to indicate that she was more than just a little angry, but the wind had been taken out of her sails. She actually looked deflated. June felt truly sorry that her only choices were anger or defeat. She pointed it out and got a confused look in return, as though Annabelle were trying to figure out why she should now feel offended by this new remark.

When her hour finally ended, June was beaten down. The music was so loud in her car on the way home that she got angry looks from the driver in the next lane while sitting at a red light.

> *Patience is the therapist's most important tool. Knowing when to make an interpretation is as crucial as having recognized the conflict or observed a repeated behavior. Inexperienced therapists have a tendency to blurt out comments too soon, when the patient is not at the point in the process of therapy to accept a hard to hear comment. Patience, timing and a level of sensitivity to the patient's needs and capabilities are crucial.*

Most people who made it in to see Dr. Gray were suffering, and didn't want to face the fact that they needed to suffer more to actually reduce their suffering. Not just cover up the problem. Most people wanted a cure in five easy steps that they could control, as if mental health can be managed like a diet. If you followed this special menu for three weeks, the pounds will come pouring off, or the depression will fall away and you will experience bliss. If only it could be that easy. June knew that ridding oneself of depression could be an endless struggle with some success, but usually plenty of setbacks too.

Chapter II: Humor

When you are feeling hopelessly down, make a determined search for humor. Watch a silly sitcom, rent a funny movie, call a friend who can make you laugh, force yourself to smile. No matter how useless you feel it might be, smiling and laughing have been found to have an emotional releasing effect, which eases feelings of depression. Depression, in its heaviness, makes you more likely to deprive yourself of even the smallest pleasures. You must overcome this focus on deprivation, and search out a good, hearty, soul churning laugh. And then give in to it. (Be Happy, by June Gray, Ph.D.)

As October and November went by, June found herself focusing on the deadline for Phil. She thought about the six months that were really twenty-six weeks, which could be broken down further into days, hours, minutes, and ultimately seconds, ticking by one at a time, until it felt like a huge amount of time and she'd want to scream in frustration. At other times she viewed the whole thing as a small segment in a lifetime of approximately eighty years, one one-hundred-sixtieth of a life. A brief insignificant interlude. Big deal.

Either way, June had become increasingly convinced that she was actually serious about her ultimatum to Phil. She was having trouble spending time with him without thinking about her April 1st deadline. Knowing that he had until April 1st made being with him easier in some ways, although the thought of being without him was scary, if she let herself think about it. But if he couldn't love her enough to commit to her, then he'd be the reason for the end in April. Having set the deadline, June began to feel as if it were written in stone. She wouldn't have been able to forget it even if she'd decided to drop the whole thing. She began to feel like the date was not even of her own choosing. There was a Karmic inevitability to it.

Humor is frequently viewed as a reflection of ego strength. It is considered a higher level coping mechanism. In an initial clinical interview, the evaluation of a patient's access to humor is indicative of ability to self-observe, to gain perspective and distance from conflicts, and to sublimate aggression. Humorlessness, evidence of rigidity and concrete thinking, can be an indicator of challenging work ahead.

Poor Phil experienced the deadline as a form of torture and blamed June for inflicting him with it. He reasoned that it indicated that she actually wished to end their relationship, and that therefore she was clearly not in love with him enough to hang in there for as long as he needed. His lack of psychological mindedness and his tendency toward concrete, black-and-white thinking made June feel briefly superior to him for a change.

At times, she felt more at peace and a bit happier. The possibility of the relationship grinding to an end had finally become a reality in her mind. It wouldn't be the end of the world as she had feared it would be. Oddly, while she felt freer, Phil began to seem unhappier and needier. June took a secret pleasure in his increasingly insecure glances.

If he wanted security, he knew what to do. If he couldn't do it, they would both have to face the consequences. June, for one, planned to be prepared. She sometimes found herself hoping he wouldn't suddenly become capable of commitment. That had begun to feel like it would have interfered with her termination plans.

Even though she didn't have the spare money, June called Emily and asked her to make the time to go shopping with her. She could hear her jumping up and down over the phone. Emily loved shopping and would have liked to be June's personal shopper. She got a sitter for the kids for a few hours and showed up at June's place all excited. If June would have allowed it, Emily would have completely made her over in her own image, which in some ways was what June desperately wished for.

In the department store, Emily forced June to buy some items she was absolutely sure she'd never wear. She insisted that June needed some brighter colors in her wardrobe, especially red. Laughing, June told her that she should appreciate that she was willing to buy new clothes at all. The new tops, slacks and shoes she bought were mostly dark colors and plain in style, but at least updated. She felt a little better afterwards. And was glad to have spent the time with Emily, although she found herself avoiding talking about Phil. She didn't feel ready to field her questions about their relationship.

The therapist never analyzes positive transference. These emotional ties are the underpinnings of the patient's determination to proceed with difficult, emotionally-charged work. When painful conflicts and emotions arise, including negative feelings toward the therapist, these already existing positive feelings allow the patient to continue the work, despite resistance, and painful revelations. The positive attachment, although often consisting in part of unanalyzed early childhood object relations as well as fantasy, must remain unexamined, for the most part, for meaningful therapy to proceed.

June had gotten Phil a sweater on her little shopping spree. It made no logical sense, but she'd done it. If she had explained her ultimatum to Emily, she'd never have understood why June had spent her non-existent extra cash on a dark green wool v-neck sweater for Phil. June's unsatisfactory answer to her would have been that she thought it would look good with his grey eyes.

June was usually careful about what she told Emily when it came to Phil. Emily had a blessed life. She'd always gotten exactly what she wanted, handed to her on a gilded platter. She was sympathetic with the disappointments in June's life, and was a good listener, but she couldn't understand why June didn't just improve her life and get happy. June believed she bit her tongue a whole lot. She could often see in her eyes that she was dying to say to her, "June, be happy! Enjoy life."

While shopping with Emily, June had a sudden fantasy in which the phrase, "be happy" was used in the same way people tend to say, "calm down," as though it would actually have the desired effect rather than its opposite. "Be happy." "Oh, okay."

Isn't that what everyone wants to hear, thought June. Just be happy. Have all of the pleasures life can hold, no guilt, and no suffering. Don't think about why you are suffering, or why anyone else is suffering. Just get past it fast. Take a pill, get hypnotized, do some trendy brief therapy, especially if it is covered by insurance and there are no additional payments to make. In her reverie, June couldn't help thinking that simple solutions were all everyone seemed to want. It was the same thing with food: take a pill to lose weight, do some quick and painless diet in which you somehow get to eat as much as you want. No control, no deprivation, just continued pleasure and positive results. Magic. Her favorite miracle was 'lose weight while you sleep.' The person with the problem need make no effort whatsoever.

June thought about how so many people want the quick ten steps to a happy life, a good relationship, weight loss, a higher IQ, better emotional intelligence (whatever that is), speedy success, etc. Her mind was racing.

Periodically, when she wanted to drive herself nuts, she'd go to a bookstore and look in the pop-psych section. Shelves bursting with volumes that promised it all and delivered some silly little specks of wisdom or common sense, dressed up as books full of absolutely necessary information from reliable sources. She wondered if people made money from these crap-filled softcover books. She wondered how the authors lived with themselves, knowing that they were fooling and manipulating the ignorant public.

Often, she'd have to stop herself from ranting out loud and knocking the books off the shelves.

One early November afternoon June had a free hour between sessions. She grabbed her bag and walked over to the bookstore a couple blocks from her office. She had intended to browse only. Somehow she found herself in front of the psychology shelves. Typically, she aimed for literature, mysteries or new fiction. Though her strategy had been avoidance of the pop-psych section, there might have been a few worth reading, possibly enlightening in some small way.

As she examined the shelves, she thought about the magic pill idea. It got her angry all over again. She stood there quietly steaming. A young clerk approached her. He pulled a book off the shelf and handed it to her. "You might want to read this. It's a fantastic book. It really changed my life."

June took the book from him, because he handed it to her. She looked down at the title. Your Successful Life: How to Make the Right Friends, Influence Others and Reach the Top by Chester Weathers. She recognized the name from a random talk show she'd tuned in to while flipping the television channels. She stared at the book for a moment and then reached out to hand it back to the smiling, expectant man in front of her.

He resisted taking it back from her. "No, really. You should take a look at it."

June looked him in the eye and spoke slowly. "I'd rather not. I don't like books like this. I'm not interested. Thank you." Again, she tried to hand it back to him.

He pushed it at her again. "This one is different. You look like someone who would benefit from reading it." He shrugged his shoulders. "I'm good at helping people find the right book." He stressed the word "right."

"I didn't ask you for help selecting a book. Thanks anyway." The man would not take it back. June felt like a child whose mother was insisting she eat her vegetables.

"Just give it a try."

Had he written it? She wondered. Upon whom else was he pushing crap-filled books? Poor, innocent, vulnerable people. She looked down at the soft cover book. As if from a distance, she watched her arm let it fly like a frisbee. It sailed above two rows of shelves and crashed into a third.

"What do you think you're doing?" the clerk said. "You can't throw books here! I'm going to have to ask you to leave. I have to call for security. Someone could've gotten hurt." Then, much louder, "Security!"

"No need. I'll leave peacefully." June began walking toward the exit as quickly as she could.

She heard him say, "I was just trying to help her."

June could feel the stares. After she left the store she kept walking quickly all the way back to her office building. She was afraid to look back. Her breathing didn't slow down until she was safely inside her office. Clearly she'd lost control. She was not in a good state of mind. And now she was humiliated on top of being miserable. Plus, she couldn't ever return to that book store.

> *The risk of suicide actually rises as depression lifts, according to some studies. When a person is suffering from an overwhelming depression, she often has little energy to accomplish anything. She may have extensive suicidal fantasies, but feels paralyzed and unable to act. As the depression begins to lift, her energy level may increase so that she begins to feel more capable of achieving her escape to imagined peace.*

A couple of weeks after their shopping spree, and maybe a week or so after June's bookstore horror show, which she 'd never report to any friend whose friendship she was hoping to maintain, Emily, June's perfect friend, bought new living room furniture. June knew that she'd had no problem with the sales clerk. When she called to tell June, she was excited in what seemed a child-like way. So June had to go see it. She felt obligated because Emily was bubbling over and she so recently and joyfully had gone shopping with her. Much of what made Emily happy were the small satisfactions in her life that, typically, would bring June not the slightest pleasure. June felt like an alien from a planet without social graces. She didn't care about anyone's living room furniture. She just might have cared a bit if she'd had a real living room of her own that was not also the kitchen, bedroom, office, and storage area.

Even then, she would have found it a strain to get herself all worked up over what furniture to put in it. If she'd had plenty of money and could have chosen Italian leather, like Emily, she probably would have spent about five minutes shopping. "I'll take that black leather thing. No, I don't need to try it out. It looks comfortable enough. No, I don't want to see it in white, brown, or this year's latest color, sable. Just write up the order for the damn black one." Emily knew and partially accepted this limitation of June's. And June tried not to judge what she didn't understand. So she went to see her furniture.

Her home was large, suburban, and immaculate. The living room set-a sofa, overstuffed chair and some tables-looked tasteful, cheerful, fresh, clean, and welcoming. It was a feeling tone that June didn't have in her to project onto her surroundings. Her look was worn, spare, not especially comfortable or inviting. But she loved Emily, rocketship-sized, late model, gadget-filled vehicle and all. She understood how different their lives were and that she needed that monster to haul many children to all sorts of sporting events and activities.

June used to think she wanted to have children. She thought that if she'd met someone with whom she truly could have had a committed relationship, she would have had children. She supposed she would have been in a situation similar to Emily's, albeit not quite so magical. They would have been discussing the relative pros and cons of the various humongous family-sized vehicles. They would have been comparing school districts and soccer teams and showing one another family vacation photos. June had seen quite a few of Emily's. June didn't even have a working camera. But she had no children, and no committed relationship. So, instead they spent an inordinate amount of time trying to find ways to dig June out of her deep well. June appreciated Emily's desire to help her. She valued her friendship more than any other, and felt ashamed of her envious feelings. She was unsure as to what value their relationship held for Emily. Why did she bother to hold on to June who went through periods of time during which she stayed away from her. June would indicate to her that she was going through an especially busy time at the office, or she'd let her think that she wasn't feeling well, like she had a recalcitrant virus.

June did manage to get over her envy at times, though. She was not convinced that she truly would have been happy with the suburban life: the big shiny supermarkets, the immaculate lawn, the bales of laundry, the flood lights from the neighbor's house glaring in at night through her lace curtains. June was not cut out for a life of competitive shopping and schooling and sports. She wasn't sure she would have much of value to offer children. In observing Emily and her three children, she found the responsibility to be daunting. She believed that it was fortunate for the world that the limit of her experience testing her parenting skills had been on a very few babysitting favors, and visits with Emily.

She realized that she was angry with Phil for not even giving her the choice. He had never committed to her, so they couldn't even get to the concept of kids. He clearly was just as terrified of that whole mine field as she was. He was a big chicken hiding behind his entitlement to be indecisive. He'd been such a disappointment, June could have spit fire at him. Barbecued chicken.

That became her view of him. Sometimes when she thought about him, she imagined a big singed feathery mess. Other times, she just felt angry. However, the unfortunate truth of the matter was that deep down, in the core of her being, June believed that Phil could not commit to her, and could not even really love her, because she was not a lovable person. It wasn't even his fault that he'd been unmotivated to commit to her. Each time she recognized this core belief she felt so empty and sad that she became completely depleted and cried herself down a dark well. It was always late at night, when she was alone, and could have been dead and no one would have even known that she felt this heartache. She could not be loved. Why wasn't she a lovable person?

In the morning after such a tortured night, June usually could see more clearly. She was running out of patience with Phil. What exactly was she waiting for anyway? A reluctant guy to give her a reluctant, pressured consent to spend his life with her?

She had hung in longer than many might. She'd been willing to put up with less than she should have. She didn't expect love, so she didn't demand it, and therefore, she didn't receive it. That strengthened her belief that she was unlovable. The whole mess was sad, but at least logical in its repetition compulsion.

> *Our early relationships, filled with conflict, raw emotion, intense vulnerability and few defenses, tend to shape our adult relationships, even when we make Herculean efforts to avoid this outcome. We are drawn to repeat, to make efforts toward mastery, to expect, predict and relive old tragedy. We cannot avoid redoing what we have already done. Our only hope is to bring to consciousness these old fantasies, fears and wishes, and then, in the light of day, reduce them to the small, childish visions that they truly are, thereby stripping them of some of their power.*

Sometimes when June's patient Annabelle spoke in their sessions, her self-critical attitude was too much for June, who wanted her to go easier on herself. June believed she needed to learn to forgive herself, and have some sympathy for her suffering rather than anger, punishment, judgment and shame. And perhaps, June hoped, not quite to the same degree, so did she. June had to set the example for her.

She knew she could never be an Emily. But she thought of herself as a sensitive, caring person who could empathize with suffering even when it was packaged in rage. That has allowed her to help some people who other therapists would run from. She didn't think that Emily could do what she did for a living, for whatever that was worth. One thing Emily did have as a result of her solid marriage was financial security. Neither June nor poor Annabelle had enough of that.

Part of June's concern regarding Phil was financially related. Life would have been easier for her if they had shared their incomes, especially his. However, June knew that she would have resented him for it, and the inequity in income would have made her feel that she should have been grateful to him. And he would have used that to control her.

As November rolled along, she found herself feeling tired frequently. At first she thought it might be the colder weather and the increased darkness of late autumn. Increasingly, she had trouble falling asleep and she spent time late at night feeling exhausted, worrying about her life. It felt so permanently halted. She began to realize that her life was causing her fatigue, not the season. Eventually at night she'd fall asleep, but then she'd awaken again suddenly at about 2:00 AM practically every night. At that point she'd find herself wide awake, angry and full of energy. She'd feel as though she could go out for a run, if it weren't so dark, cold and dangerous. She'd toss and turn for about two hours, and finally she'd fall back to sleep. And, big surprise, when she woke up the next morning, she'd feel like a steam roller had flattened her.

She knew she needed to do something about this. She had no idea why she kept waking up at 2:00 AM, practically on the nose. She began to think about keeping a pen and a notebook nearby on her night table, so that she could write about what she was feeling in an attempt to get herself back to sleep. This was the kind of solution that she might have helplessly suggested to a patient with insomnia. So she tried to make herself take her own medicine.

> *Sleep disorders, like other psychosomatic symptoms, tend to be symbolic. Sleep and the fear of death are intricately intertwined for many children, as sleep may seem the closest thing to death in life. Trouble falling asleep is often related to difficulty relaxing, letting go of control, usually indicating high levels of anxiety. Early morning awakening is usually an indicator of depression. Sleep is interrupted and a foggy, frustrated, agitated feeling usually accompanies early awakening. Awakening in the middle of the night is thought to be the result of powerful or disturbing dreams.*

June began to theorize that this 2:00 AM awakening must have been some message her unconscious mind was sending her. She had not the vaguest idea what it was about. But at least this view was an optimistic one. She wasn't assuming that she had a brain tumor yet. She tried to believe that if she were patient and attentive she might get some idea of what her message to herself might be. She might find some clues as to how to get out of this gaping hole of a life she'd found herself in. Or not. First, she would have to convince herself that the whole idea of some inner self that you can listen to isn't just a pile of crap.

During June's period of poor sleep, Annabelle showed up at one of her appointments crying. She felt that her life was worthless, meaningless, unmitigated torture. Jerome, with whom she had become obsessed, hadn't called her in several weeks. She worried over whether to call him and actually came up with some pretty good excuses to do so. Still, she was afraid he'd be angry, so she couldn't call him and face his rejection directly. She felt as though she might as well not exist.

June sat quietly, feeling exhausted, trying to look empathic, but nervously worrying that as soon as she was finished lamenting, Annabelle would look expectantly at her to say something comforting or helpful. June dreaded that particular familiar moment. Inevitably, she'd fail at this impossible task, and Annabelle would turn her aggression toward June with the same vehemence with which she directed it inward. June wasn't sure she could handle it this time.

June also feared that if she didn't attempt to play the game Annabelle set up, she'd feel so dejected that she might try something suicidal in nature. But if June did play, Annabelle would use her to soak up some of her overwhelming rage, rather than take it out entirely on herself. Could June tolerate it? It felt like the blind leading the even more blind.

June's comment, when the crucial moment came, addressed the extreme and harsh view Annabelle held. All or nothing and relentless. She sat there listening attentively, allowing June to feel a false moment of success before she cut her off, stating, "Okay, I know that. How's that supposed to help me? What do I do with that?"

June checked the time and took a deep breath. How was she supposed to help Annabelle feel that life was worth living when she wasn't so sure about it herself? Thinking about Annabelle's family history and its lasting impact on her, sometimes made June think about her own family and its impact on her.

> *Those who go into the field of psychotherapy often are interested in the mind, the emotions, and the nature of human relationships. Some feel the work can be a challenging and even enjoyable career worth pursuing. Others are attracted to the ethical dilemmas, the responsibility, and the political issues that arise. But, underneath it all, at an unconscious level, most people who enter the field of psychotherapy do so as a means of attempting to master their own family problems.*

June's parents had always been opinionated and harsh. They were united in feeling that her decision to become a psychologist was foolish. The money wouldn't be good enough (compared to her brother the dentist), the work too unpleasant (who wants to hear other people's problems all day?), and somehow this choice of profession was a direct reflection of their childrearing abilities. So her career choice became an embarrassment to them. They were both reluctant to reveal to their friends what she was planning to do for a living. And they resented her for it. And the worst part was, in retrospect, June believed they were somewhat correct.

They had a supportive veneer: "We want you to be happy, dear. That's what really matters." Her mother would pronounce the words with a fake, but very white smile and clenched teeth. She would add, "Your happiness has always been important to us." June would watch her mother's eyebrows rise remarkably high while she made that last remark, to prove that she had always been a good mother.

June did not remember her as abusive or especially cruel. It was the omissions that affected her. She was not a confidant, or a friend, or even a warm, comforting hug. She was always a disappointed lecture, an irritated look, and a quick judgment. Never in June's favor.

June did the obligatory holidays and periodic phone calls, but there was really nothing more to do. And no one was asking for more. Her brother worked it out in a healthier way, was unquestioningly treated better because he was male, and was distant from his emotions. As a result, he was able to tolerate spending more time with the folks. This was beneficial to June.

She regretted that they were so distant. The saddest part was that she had no idea if he regretted it or was even aware of it. He seemed to be a very busy, contented guy. His wife and daughters were never especially interested in June, either. It sometimes felt as though her family members had all agreed that a safe distance from her was required. It was like June irritated them if they got too close. She was just too intense. She dealt in unpleasantness.

This was the bulk of the focus of her own five years of therapy. Her best solution was avoidance. The only other solution that came close was finding another, more accepting family. She liked Phil's family at first, although after a couple of years, when no progress occurred, they became wary and avoidant of her. It figured.

"So, what am I supposed to do about my depression?" Annabelle asked June impatiently, as though there were something she could say that would clean up that mess like a paper towel wiping a spill. June looked at her, speechless. This was not an uncommon interaction. June knew that Annabelle was convinced that no one could help her, and June felt paralyzed and unable to help her. She was certain that it had something to do with the way that Annabelle viewed the world as hostile and uncaring, and she came up with requests that were unanswerable to reinforce her belief.

June also believed that Annabelle was not so extremely different from most people in her eagerness for a quick fix. Something to latch onto, to cover up the pain, like a band aid on a cut. She tried to give Annabelle reassurance in the form of evidence that she had actually improved, but she didn't want to hear it. It tended to have an irritating impact on her. She disagreed with or belittled every sign of progress, while continuing to demand the impossible, i.e., something from June to make her feel all better, that she could take with her.

June had spent plenty of time exploring this issue with her, offering her interpretations, reflecting on feelings of neediness and emptiness. Annabelle didn't care. She just continued along her one-way track, clinging to some childhood fantasy, wanting more from June than was humanly possible to deliver.

June left the session feeling drained, sucked dry. And Annabelle left feeling frustrated, not having gotten her longed-for fantasy fix that would make everything all better, so she could live happily ever after. There were days in which June had the fantasy that she could actually provide it. Something no one else could provide. She'd fall into a reverie: What do so many people think they need? Love? Safety? Security? What would a quick fix actually look like? She strongly believed that there was no such thing. For her, thinking about it became an exercise in sarcasm or magical thinking. Or ideas for one of those stupid pop-psych books.

Happiness is a fleeting state of mind. If you were consistently happy, you would not recognize it as happiness after a while. It is always a feeling within a context. You must experience unpleasant feelings in order to appreciate happiness. Therefore, it cannot last. You can feel it temporarily, and then it is gone again, leaving you bereft and yearning. You long to regain it, but it is always bittersweet; its arrival indicating its pending departure.

June pondered. People just wanted to be happy, taken care of, well fed. It didn't really sound so farfetched. Why was it so unbearably difficult for people to achieve?

What does a depressed person want? To feel happy. What did Emily stop herself from saying to June? "Just be happy." What did Annabelle want June to give her the secret to? Being happy. June wouldn't have minded being a little happy herself. She couldn't remember the last time she'd felt happy. Perhaps she needed a refresher course. She wondered if they covered being happy in continuing education. Surely it would be broken down into easy, do-it-yourself steps. Maybe there'd be a little quiz at the end.

June thought about it. Some people believe that they can't be happy and then find ways to prove it. That was Annabelle. They had discussed her concern that if she let her guard down for some brief moments of happiness, she'd be taken by surprise by some horrible disappointment. Then she'd go and let her guard down with the wrong kind of guy and her expectations would be verified. And each time she wouldn't recognize what she was doing. She'd think that the new guy wouldn't disappoint her.

June's ultimatum to Phil had given her a strange sense of calm, which she enjoyed experiencing when she wasn't in a panic. Smiling at him for no apparent reason unnerved him, so she did it, and felt noticeably happier. Wearing her new clothes and accessories that Emily had helped her select had improved her mood a modicum as well. She considered making a list of the top ten things to do to improve one's mood, and handing it out to depressed patients.

The depressed person should not be left alone to wallow in her misery. Add structure to the depressed person's daily routine. Help her reengage with the world. Does she take vitamins? Exercise? Belong to a gym or running club? Does she work regularly at a job? Could she volunteer somewhere, especially in a people-helping capacity? Adding responsibilities and activities into the life of a depressed person often has the effect of pulling her out of her depression, and back into the meaningful workings of the world.

Chapter III: Appearance

Even when you feel dark and dismal on the inside, brighten up the outside. Wearing bright colors and flattering clothes changes your mood. If you wake up in the morning full of dread, put on a bright, colorful outfit. The reactions from others can't help but lift your spirits, as well. If you look colorful, others will react to you more colorfully. You will surely feel better. (Be Happy, By June Gray, Ph.D.)

June was fortunate to have Emily in her life, but she didn't want to lean on her too heavily. She had three children and worked a complex full-time job. But she was a generous person. She seemed to feel responsible for June, having gotten to know her family firsthand when she came home with her over college breaks. There was the one Thanksgiving dinner when everyone took turns saying what they were thankful for. June's parents mentioned their health and grandkids, her brother and his career. When it was Emily's turn, she said she was grateful for her friendship with June. The rest of the family looked shocked, said nothing, and acted like she hadn't spoken. It was an incredible gesture on her part. Since then, she'd become June's real family. June often wished that she could have offered her something of great value in return, but she had nothing except loyalty and admiration. Emily rarely needed June as a confidant. What could she possibly have offered her? June couldn't even give good advice to herself.

June had a panic attack in the middle of the night on a Friday night in early December, like she'd never experienced before. Her heart raced and she couldn't catch her breath. She was sweating and shivering. Certain that she was dying, she worried that no one would find out for days. Phil was away at a conference at the time, although she was certain that she'd rather die than call him for help. She had no weekend plans. She thought about calling 911, but felt too embarrassed. She still had enough oxygen going to her brain to know that people don't die from panic attacks. But she couldn't calm herself down. She tried for an hour, felt exhausted and then dialed Emily's number. The clock by the bed read 2:30 am. She put the phone down and tried to be calm. She joked with herself - what is the worst thing that could happen? She could die. Half the time she

found herself wishing that might happen, anyway. But her heart felt like it would
explode out of her chest.

She picked up the phone again and dialed Emily and let it ring. Ed answered, of
course. June loved Ed, but was already feeling so humiliated about calling that she was
hoping to get directly to Emily without having to explain herself to Ed. She apologized
over and over and asked for Emily. To his credit, he did not seem angry, exactly. Just
very sleepy. Either too sleepy to be angry or perhaps concerned that something really bad
had happened. He woke Emily and she took the phone into another room. She sounded
very concerned. June knew she shouldn't have called. She should have just gone on
suffering.

Emily said, "What's wrong?"

June apologized over and over, and told her finally that she was having a panic
attack and had no one else to call. The thought of an ambulance arriving and strange men
in her apartment taking her to an emergency room was unbearable. She didn't bother
mentioning her additional fear that they might laugh at her. She knew that if somehow
she were to end up in a psych unit at some hospital, she would have to kill herself in
shame and defeat, as soon as she got out, of course. June was self-preserving enough to
not end up there. It was possible that she didn't actually want to die, and that her greatest
fear in life was going crazy. She briefly believed in God long enough to beg him not to
let that happen. She begged him not to take away what little sanity she called her own or
to make her physically helpless.

June attempted to explain all of this to Emily that night on the phone. To her
credit, she listened patiently. June feared that she was dozing off, so she paused. Emily
hadn't been sleeping at all. She said calmly, as though they were sitting at some coffee
house together, "What is really on your mind, June? What is it that you're worried
about?"

Answering these obvious questions had not occurred to June until Emily asked
them. And she was supposed to be the therapist. She felt simultaneously grateful and
inadequate. Her panic had begun to abate, so she gave it a try. What was really on her
mind? At first she wasn't sure. She had not chosen to snap wide awake suddenly in a
panic. But she knew pretty quickly that it had to do with Phil. Of course it did. "I know
that my relationship with Phil is ending. It's been stagnant for so long that I've had to
come up with an ultimatum, and I'm going to have to enforce it. And it's approaching.
And it makes no difference to him. He doesn't love me. He never really has, in any way
useful to me. He never intended to marry me. I'll always be alone. I'm a failure in some
basic, core way. I feel worthless. I know that Phil will be out of my life soon and I'll
truly have nobody. I know now that I never had Phil really, but I've held on for too long
because I've been fooling myself and he's been better than nothing."

June was crying and shaking and at the same time observing herself as though she
were watching someone else. She was amazed at the extent of her feelings, which poured

out without thought. She had loved Phil. She was deeply disappointed in him. And so intensely angry. Also, scared and lonely. And embarrassed to be burdening Emily with all of this in the middle of the night. She was angry with herself for sinking so low and mortified by the shame she felt.

Emily listened quietly, and when June gave her a chance by pausing, she tried to reassure her that she would always be there for her. She hadn't been aware of June's feelings about Phil, or her ultimatum, because of course, June had to wait till the predawn hours on a Friday night to tell her. She was supportive, insisting that June would meet someone else. June felt painfully grateful to have her in her life and realized that she needed her as an audience for her intense feelings. She couldn't take in much that night, but Emily said one thing that June would always try to remember: "Life is always most painful before a big change." That made June feel a little glimmer of hope. Perhaps a big change was coming. She knew she couldn't continue on like this. But she had no idea what was next. Maybe this was her chance to turn something rotten into something better. Emily had found a bright side.

June thanked her a thousand times and they hung up. She felt tremendous relief, at least temporarily and went to bed and slept more soundly than she had in a long while.

The following night, she was up again for hours. Awakened at 2 a.m., as if a marching band had started playing. But this time there was no panic attack. She looked around her room calmly, and felt intensely aware of being alone, on her own, but not completely unhappy about it. She wrote a note to herself to remember to send Emily a fruit basket.

Then she grabbed a notebook and started writing and couldn't stop. Ideas were flowing. She was making herself laugh out loud. She came up with ten pop psych steps to pure happiness. There was pure happiness in the room. She was breathing it in. Completely down in the dumps one night, panicky beyond belief shortly thereafter, and finally deliriously happy. Sounds like a typical week, for a fast cycling manic-depressive. June decided that the manic part wasn't so bad.

She wrote and wrote until her hand was so cramped that the writing was illegible. This frantic spouting of ideas continued on strong for about two hours, at which point she became suddenly exhausted and had to go back to sleep. She capped her pen, closed her notebook, set them both carefully on the night table, lay back down and slept peacefully until morning.

The same pattern occurred Sunday night. On Monday morning, she awoke feeling some energy, no headache, and only the slightest bit of dread. This, for June, was the equivalent of a miracle. She decided to celebrate by wearing the bright red turtleneck her mother had sent her three years earlier for her birthday. She cut off the tags and put it on.

To her surprise, she received comments on it all day. The color seeped in through her skin and raised her spirits. She chuckled to herself here and there all day. Anyone observing her would have rightly decided that she'd lost her mind. She felt as though she had stepped through the mirror and had no plans for a return trip.

That night June again awoke at 2:00 am and wrote feverishly. She organized the book into ten chapters, each entitled with one of the ten steps. She felt unbelievably clever. But what if it were the mad scribblings of a maniac? She was actually afraid to read what she had written before. Keep plodding ahead, she told herself. She didn't have quite the same level of energy as the previous nights, but wrote for two hours, enjoying the ridiculous game. Once again, she capped her pen, shut her notebook, placed both beside the bed and fell asleep.

When she was eating her cereal the next morning, she began to consider her middle-of-the-night scribbling. What if it became a real book? Any person with an easy fix fantasy would become a part of her target audience. That would include almost everyone. She found herself organizing it, and imagining doing it. It would serve as a therapeutic task for her; it already had. It was something to focus on daily, to direct her aggression, resentment, disappointment, anxiety, etc. She thought she could do a little every day and have her private laugh.

She'd need some clever sayings. She thought about it and came up with, "make yourself smile when you feel like crying." She had to use tacky phraseology to capture quotable sound bites that had that cure-all feel to them. People would come away repeating little sayings to themselves.

She needed a title for this book of superficialities. "End Depression While You Sleep," or "Ten Days to Happiness." "You Too Can Be Happy," or finally, "Be Happy." A book on how to become happy. It would be some kind of twisted achievement if she could publish the book and get even one person to read it, eager for a quick cure and an easy path to happiness.

It wouldn't be good enough or bad enough, she didn't know which, to publish. Just writing it could be amusing enough to bring her a little relief from her constant depression and hopelessness. She had a project.

June had plans to see Phil that night for dinner. They rarely saw one another during the week, but had arranged a Tuesday evening date because Phil had been out of town over the weekend at a conference. For the first time, it felt like a burden to June. For years it had been the highlight of her day or even week. She decided to wear a very old and wrinkled but colorful dress of deep purple and cobalt and varying shades of blue. Years earlier she'd seen it at a street fair, loved the colors, bought it impulsively and then had been unable to bring herself to wear it. Luckily, she never discarded old clothes. She attempted to de-wrinkle it, short of ironing it. She tried to stretch it out, smoothed it with her hands, and hung it in the bathroom when she showered. She felt different wearing it, daring, brighter. She felt that people noticed her more as she walked to the restaurant.

June suddenly realized that she loved color. It had powerful mood-affecting properties. Lately she'd noticed that when she wore something colorful and attractive, and received compliments and looks, she felt better. She truly enjoyed the puzzled expression on Phil's face when he saw her, too.

His expression changed to irritation and he said, "What's the matter with you? Why are you wearing that old thing? You look ridiculous. Are you trying to send me some kind of mysterious message, like that you have no money for clothing?"

June's heart sank. She could have slapped her own face for still wishing and hoping that maybe he'd say something that she needed or longed for him to say. What was the matter with her? She felt embarrassed and ashamed. The phrase, "He doesn't love me," was ringing repeatedly in her head like a car alarm in the middle of the night. She considered turning around without a word and leaving, but couldn't do it. He would know that he'd hurt her. She couldn't permit that. She had to recover quickly.

His eyes scanned her face. June watched him looking at her and was struck hard by the knowledge that he hardly knew her. He had no spontaneity, and so little humor. He seemed smaller, more immature, so constricted, and just a little bit repulsive, although she couldn't help feeling some sympathy for him.

For him to behave in such a cutting, mean way, he must have felt threatened by her. And all she had to do was wear an old, colorful dress. Who would have imagined that she had that kind of power in her? They had always silently agreed that she was at his mercy. She supposed he could see that something in her had altered in some subtle, indefinable way. He wanted to squash it, humiliate her into retreat, and make her feel insecure so that she'd need his support.

He had nothing of which to accuse her. June had not been untrue or disloyal in any way. However, it was clear as day to them both that the cement of her loyalty to him had cracked. An irreparable pothole had formed, maybe even a sink hole. Perhaps they were both feeling sad and angry about it. June knew she was, and Phil, clearly, was feeling something.

June made herself smile a bit, sat down and said, "You seem upset." She was pleased with herself for coming up with such a psychologist's response in her own life.

"I am not upset" predictably left his lips before she had finished. "But I remember that dress when you showed it to me years ago and I gave you my opinion of it then. Knowing my view of it back then, why would you wear it with me now? What is going on? Is it a joke, or something else?"

That would explain why she never wore it. "It is definitely not a joke," She responded a little too seriously.

"Then what is it? What would you call it in your professional opinion? Regression?"

In psychoanalytic literature, regression is a defensive maneuver, chosen unconsciously as a means by which a developmental conflict might be sidestepped. Regression is a return to an earlier developmental stage in which the current conflict does not yet exist. Behaviorally, one might observe a lower maturity level, a reverting to more childish attitudes or activities that are likely to seem inappropriate. The regressed person has no awareness of this transformation.

"I would call it a dress." Clearly, he was looking to offend her. Just use a technical term, make sure you use it incorrectly, and watch the psychologist go ballistic. So June lost her control a bit. "What do you care what I wear? I have never seen this much emotion from you about anything having to do with me. Not in all five years that we were together." She hadn't wanted to make it sound like it was already over, but that was how it came out of her mouth.

Phil looked startled and paused, visibly calming himself down. June could read the mental message crossing his face, "Calm down now, Phil." Somehow it worked for him like it never had for her. He said, "I was surprised. I thought you had just gone shopping for new clothes and here you show up in an old rag. But of course, you can wear whatever you like. What would you like to order? I have to get home to do some work tonight."

The defense of isolation of affect involves the unconscious separation of memories from the emotion associated with them. The person can seem cut off from his feelings. He may easily discuss practically anything, even a traumatic event, with a sense of calm and logic. The emotion has not vanished, instead, it has been pushed into the unconscious such that the person has no awareness of it.

June was actually relieved, and silently agreed to drop a topic with so little surface meaning and too much deeper meaning. She needed to conserve her strength. Did he really deserve her efforts to explain her feelings, or needs, or even her experiments and efforts to save her own life?

She ordered broiled chicken with lemon and vegetables. They spoke about Phil's computer conference and other superficial topics, awkwardly, and she could see that Phil was out of sorts. It was an early night.

She went home and felt out of sorts herself. It wasn't even losing Phil that was so painful, it was all her hopes and fantasies that she had to give up. The plans for the rest of her life. The oil that kept her engine from dying. She had to start over and hardly knew how. This meant that on April 1, Phil and she would go their separate ways. She didn't think she really wanted to be his friend. She wasn't even clear about how much she actually liked him.

This was sounding a bit too familiar. Had Phil been just a repetition compulsion? She didn't want to think about it, but couldn't help comparing him to her mother. She had never had enough interest in June to bother developing their relationship into something more meaningful after June left home. They hadn't become friends.

> *Repetition Compulsion is the unconscious repeating of old object relations, relationships from infancy and childhood with parents and caretakers, for the purpose of attempting mastery over them. When a person finds that she is currently having a relationship with someone who has similar characteristics to one of her parents, especially if these characteristics make the relationship difficult and conflictual, she might begin to evaluate whether she is engaging in a repetition compulsion.*

June needed some new friends other than the few old college friends who called now and then, and a couple from graduate school. All of these could hardly be considered close friends. She did include them when counting her friends on her fingers, however. Developing new friends was not a task at which she naturally excelled. Actually, it was a course which she had repeatedly failed or from which she had needed to withdraw. She had painfully passed up on reaching out to new people time and time again. It felt so risky.

> *Social anxiety tends to be highly correlated with low self-esteem and difficult object relations. There are several typical expectations of the socially anxious person. One is that people will respond negatively, or angrily, rejecting any attempt to engage. Another is that he will be humiliated. Often the anxiety is so intense that social interactions will be avoided at all costs, giving the person with social anxiety little opportunity to overcome his fears.*

June regretted somewhat that part of this April Fools' Day deal was that she would have to cut off contact with Phil altogether. He was one of the people who had been close to her for the past few years. She worked alone in her office and befriending patients was a big no-no. She slept alone in her studio apartment, most of the time, especially lately. And she didn't have many opportunities to meet new friends or lovers.

She felt strongly about not befriending her patients. Books, papers, lectures, you name it, focused on the issue of boundaries between therapist and patient. To June, it had always been simple and obvious. If a therapist becomes a friend, then the therapy becomes impossible. Boundaries are lost and so the therapeutic relationship is lost. This is ultimately of no help to the patient or therapist. However others may feel, it was out of the question for her. Over the years, some of her patients had described fantasies that she would become a terrific friend - same relationship but no annoying fee, she presumed. But, in reality land, June did not behave as a therapist to her friends. Or at least, she tried not to, and succeeded most of the time. As a matter of fact, lately her closest friend had seemed something like a therapist to her. At least, she'd been trying her best to help June, who had even allowed her to do so, which was progress for her.

So, Phil was not going to work out. June was gradually letting that seep into her being. What made her feel panicky was her heartfelt belief that there was no one else out there for her to meet to take Phil's place. And if there were, she wouldn't have any way to be introduced to this person. And if she did have access to Prince Charming, it would be doubtful that he'd even notice her, not to mention actually be interested in talking with her and, big guffaw, dating her. No wonder she had tolerated Phil.

She'd have to force herself to believe that it was at least remotely possible for her to meet someone else, that there could be some sensitive, intelligent, super guy who could somehow, mysteriously, potentially become interested in her. She tried a little exercise she sometimes did to get some perspective on her life and problems. She became her own patient. She advised herself to see about arranging to try to meet new people. That advice was absolutely easy to give, rolling off the tongue. Following it was another story. If it were not so difficult to do, she would have done it already, as would her patients who always nodded politely, saying they'd try, except for Annabelle. She would just stare at June and then tell her how unhelpful she was.

Ways in which June might have met new people were limited. She could have gone to a bar. For her, this would have been like wearing a sign that reads "Almost Ready to Kill Herself from Loneliness." She was not a big drinker, and would not have wanted to be with someone who was a big drinker, or who hung out in bars looking to meet people. She found the whole bar scene overwhelming and lonely anyway, and was poor at making small talk. If it worked at all for anyone, it would have to be the college and early twenties crowd. But maybe she was just squirming and rationalizing her way out of going within twenty paces of a bar. She didn't know how to behave in a place like that. She could have lectured people on the drawbacks of drinking too much. They might have found that riveting.

She could have gone for some continuing education credits. Five hundred people in a room listening to a fascinating lecture on stress reduction by some self-claimed specialist. Slim possibility there. She could have attended an annual conference of some national group on Psychodynamic Psychotherapy, and met some guy only to learn that he lived on the other side of the country. And probably had plenty of hidden issues around control and anger. She could have taken a course at a local college. Art class, foreign language, photography? She didn't have a lot of fun money to spend on taking courses in order to meet the love of her life. Or energy, or patience for that matter.

Now and then Emily had offered to set her up, but it was always with computer guys, whose names might as well all have been Phil, because that was what she was surrounded by. June thought she might tell her to look around for her again, anyway. Maybe some of these guys had now been through their first marriage, couples counseling, divorce and individual psychotherapy, and were ready for her. In the past, when Emily had offered up a single guy from her office, June had always said "no thanks," out of loyalty to Phil. To Hell with Phil. At this point, she believed she would go out on a blind date with a muskrat, just to hone her dating skills. She'd been held back in dating school for years now. She needed to see the whole thing as a laugh, or for practicing her skills, like interviewing when you don't need a job.

She continued to write in her book in the middle of the night, religiously. Sometimes even before bed. When ideas came to her, she jotted them down. If she had given it a moment's thought, she wouldn't have, but the whole thing felt automatic, fueled by some hidden force. The book had become a part of her routine, as if she had always written every day. It was a concrete part of her life, like taking a shower or doing laundry, although she didn't do laundry more than every week or two. She had some laughs, albeit, alone. But a laugh for her was always a welcome event. So, she ruined it, of course, with her intellectualized interpretation about directing her aggression into her silly book on curing depression. She had been calling it, "Be Happy," and had drawn a big silly smiley face on the cover.

The first few lessons in the book were to practice patience, to have a sense of humor and to dress in bright clothes. Ridiculously simple minded. The depressed person was to practice patience, as though it were a religion, or the equivalent of learning another language. June had no idea what she actually even meant. The dressing in brightly colored clothes idea came to her after she began to wear her old colorful clothes. When she received that shocked reaction from Phil, by wearing her old dress, she realized that simple things can bring a sense of satisfaction. The small efforts are sometimes the most powerful. It was actually the greatest emotional reaction she had engendered in Phil in ages. That was depressing. Her advice in the book was, if depressed and angry, dress so that everyone notices.

Ridiculous, yes, but compelling and fun. Eventually, she thought she might show the book to Emily for a laugh. She had a good sense of humor. June thought she would appreciate the sarcasm, and the not so subtle attack on pop psychology.

At her usual mid-week appointment, Annabelle came into June's office, head in hands. She threw herself down onto the couch and folded over, head in lap. June sat quietly, hands folded in her lap, waiting for her to explain herself. She held the pose, dramatically, a few moments too long. Looking up, finally, she said, "I just want to die." Her eyes were ringed with red from crying. Her face looked puffy. "What's the point? I'm not allowed to have joy in my life. I can't win. Why even try? Why even get my hopes up for a moment? I just get burned. I'm destined for unhappiness. No one can help me." She let out a moan and folded forward again.

June waited for a signal as to what she wanted in return, or if there was more that she had to say and eventually figured out that she wanted her to ask what happened that had her feeling so hopeless. June asked. She gratefully looked up and declared that the man with whom she had been involved, who they had discussed ad nauseam and who June personally felt strongly was a user and loser, had informed her that he did not know what direction their relationship was taking. After repeating his comment, she added, "Can you believe that?" and looked closely at June for an empathic response.

June felt her own feelings come up and tried to push them aside.

Annabelle looked pleadingly at her. "What does his comment mean? How should I respond to that?" Her tone changed suddenly and her eyes brightened. She said, "I want to tell him that I have been asked out on a date by another guy, a doctor. Do you think that is a good idea?"

June felt truly sympathetic. Annabelle thought she could force him to appreciate her. The sad, painful truth was that no matter what she did, she wouldn't be able to make this guy love her. It's that looking to get blood from a stone thing. The session ended with a blanket of sadness hanging over both of them.

June needed to find ways to get out from under her own blanket and make some changes. She had been growing her hair long. It had been fairly short for years. Phil had always felt that she appeared more mature with a short, neat haircut. He appreciated how controlled it looked. Since they first met, June had wanted to do whatever it was that was most likely to please Phil. He had a hidden agenda about which they never spoke. Namely, it was that he was seven years older and self-conscious about it, and eager to have June appear closer to his age. He'd made no efforts to look younger, however. He had never considered coloring his hair or dressing in a younger style. He'd seemed older than his age from the first day she met him, and she had looked younger than her age. Of course, it had been her job to alter herself to please him.

She hadn't even thought about the inequity of it. Why give up her youth any more than she unwittingly already had? She was tired of unthinkingly striving to please Phil. So she stopped. Her hair was getting longer and more wild. She liked it.

When she looked in the mirror, she found fine wrinkles around her eyes. It was ironic that she'd made efforts to look older, and now she wanted to make some efforts to look a little younger, or at least her actual age. She'd been one of those women who lived to please some man. And she'd always loved long hair. It saved her from having to sit at hair salons, which made her uncomfortable. She didn't enjoy having a stranger's hands in her hair. She could never think of anything interesting to say to the hair dresser. She preferred to sit quietly and uncomfortably wait for the whole tedious thing to come to its final conclusion. After all the clipping, moussing and blow drying, her hair could have been standing straight up, and she would have gratefully looked in that little hand mirror and nodded her head up and down. She'd think, just let me pay and go. Anything to escape further torture.

Maybe she was fooling herself. Perhaps this was all about her depression and she was just letting herself go, not taking care of herself like she had done in the past. Phil would definitely believe that. She was at the point where she wasn't sure she even knew how long she'd been depressed. But she thought it started way back, and taking care of herself to please Phil hadn't made it go away. It was a good thing that she'd finally allowed herself to decide how her hair would be. That was progress that outweighed any grooming concerns.

The most interesting part of the whole hair thing was that Phil had not commented on it. Not even once. She supposed that after his shocked response to her colorful dress, he had vowed to redouble his efforts to control his emotional responses to her.

On a cold, wet Saturday in mid- December, June went down to the basement laundry room in her building. She was too cowardly to go to that dark, isolated, underground laundry room alone, so she usually dragged her huge duffel bag down the street to the well-lit, street level public laundromat two blocks away.

On this day, however, it was cold, windy, and raining, and she couldn't gather up the energy to get herself soaked while dragging that big, heavy bag down two blocks, and later back up two blocks. And her laundry couldn't wait. She had practically nothing left to wear. It was still quite early, so she assumed she would probably not be attacked, basing this hope on the assumption that most killers and rapists are asleep in the early morning hours, after being up traumatizing people all night. She entered the dusty, ancient-looking, lint-filled room, and to her surprise and horror, a good-looking guy was pulling his wash out of the washing machine and putting it into the working dryer. There were two washers and two dryers, but only one dryer was actually capable of drying clothes. The other broken one just completed the set.

He smiled at June, said "good morning," and announced that he was glad to see that he was not the only person who woke up early on a Saturday morning. June made some mumbling, self-deprecating remark along the lines of, "If you can call this awake."

She wanted to drop the laundry and run. She was unwashed, wearing sweats, and carrying an overstuffed basket of rancid laundry. She wanted to tell him that she can look a lot better than she did at that moment. He shouldn't be afraid. Then she wanted to cry. Instead she stood there staring at him like an idiot.

He smiled kindly, and generously told her that she looked comfortable, the way people should look on a Saturday. She assumed that he felt so at ease with her because he viewed her as a spinster, old maid type, oldly living alone in the old building. He looked young. He kept right on talking. This was a good thing, because June had turned into a mute. It turned out that he lived a few floors above her, off to the other side of the building, in a one bedroom. He had only lived there for a few months, but was finding it pleasant. He asked June if the doorman spoke any English at all.

She heard herself say, "Only if he really wants to." The entire time he spoke, she secretly did deep breathing relaxation exercises and told herself that his girlfriend was upstairs sitting in a skimpy negligee, in that roomy, one-bedroom awaiting his return. He had dark hair, striking bright green eyes, and a look of intelligence. It was difficult for June not to stare into his eyes, which were so lovely and intense. When would he mention his girlfriend, engagement, wife, gay partner? The sooner the better. Someone like this could not possibly be single. Not that it would have made any difference if he were.

She stuffed, as quickly and privately as she could, in the closet-sized room filled with large machinery, her underwear, bras, socks etc., into the washing machine that he had just emptied. He had left the lid open for her. Obviously, a gentleman. She did it as they spoke, becoming lightheaded, and mentally having a simultaneous second conversation inside her own head, and attempting to keep the two conversations separate. And she was trying to look relaxed and natural, like this was an everyday occurrence. She forced everything into one load, cramming it in like her life depended on it. She felt as if she had crammed herself into the washing machine, and it was running on the hot water cycle, warm water rinse, with too much bleach.

They talked for the entire wash cycle. He said at one point, that if she didn't mind, he would stay and talk with her until the dryer finished. June was so grateful, although she internally reminded herself that it was just a matter of convenience. Why should he leave, only to get to his apartment, and turn around and come back within a couple of minutes? Or maybe he didn't trust her alone there with his clothes. She only hoped that his remaining there would not overwhelm her, causing her to crack open and spill the contents of her pounding head all over the laundry room floor. Not that it would have had much of an impact on the laundry room: it was that dirty.

When June's wash cycle ended, he still had a few more minutes of dryer time left to go. She had no idea why they didn't make these two symbiotic machines have the same length cycles. It seemed like it would be so logical. Finally, his dryer did stop, he took all of his clothing out, put it in a big pile, and began to fold it neatly. She was impressed, although she couldn't help making a mental note about how that much neatness and organization could mean a compulsive personality organization.

June began to move her stuff to the dryer and was shocked to notice that her underwear and bras were all pink and scarlet. She owned all beige and white underthings. Gasping, she heard herself say, "Oh, no." He looked over. June had turned from light beige to scarlet herself by then. She wished that she hadn't said a thing, or even opened up the washing machine. She could have waited until he had left the room. Or she could have just continued on as if nothing were unusual. As if all of her underthings had always been that color. But it was too late. She felt like biting off her own tongue.

He looked so concerned, and said, "Oh, no. It's my fault. My new red shirt. I don't have it here. I must've left it in the washing machine. You must've used hot water. I am so sorry."

He didn't seem the least bit embarrassed, just truly sorry. He asked if he could pay her to replace everything that was ruined. She couldn't allow that. She tried to take responsibility for the whole thing by saying that she should have checked the machine before putting her things in. He insisted that he should have checked before leaving it free for her to use. June had begun to wish with all her might that she might dematerialize. He tried to insist on paying her, and she absolutely refused. They both laughed awkwardly. He finally claimed to need to get back to his apartment, and did leave, and did not ask for her number. Of course not. She probably wouldn't have been able to remember it anyway. Her head was full of lint. A little while after he left she began to breathe again.

Unfortunately for her, they had exchanged first names. It gave her something to cling to. He'd told her that he liked her name. So, she couldn't refrain from repeatedly thinking about that, as if it were some secret communication code that she had to break. His name was Michael. June had truly always liked that name. For the entire week that followed that Saturday morning, she walked around thinking about Michael, going over the minutiae of their conversation, and wearing red and scarlet underwear, under her drab, black clothing. No one else knew. It was their little secret. She was overcome by the intense pain of infatuation. He had changed the color of her underwear. She was sure that in some countries, it would be considered akin to a marriage proposal.

He'd brought his red shirt upstairs wet, so he had probably hung it in his bathroom to dry. June's imagination needed a muzzle. She had this extensive fantasy that he would think about her and their interaction, and what had happened to her underwear, and her underwear on her, each time he entered his bathroom and saw the shirt hanging there.

She couldn't stop thinking about him. Every single day, she hoped and feared anxiously that she would run into him. She hung around her building even more than usual. Of course, usually she was alone in her one room. He knew her floor number. He could find her if he wanted to. Why didn't he come down to visit her or to try to find her? She considered putting a little red flag on her door. She had lost her mind altogether.

She repeatedly attempted to snap out of it. She told herself that he must be with someone else. She tried to imagine what she looked like. She made her sexy and beautiful. But his laundry was clearly his alone. He could, June told herself, have a girlfriend who did not live with him. She tried to convince herself that she was experiencing a case of early rebound, in which the rebound was occurring before the relationship had officially ended. Not unheard of. She knew it was winding down with Phil. Maybe she was desperate. Maybe? Who was she kidding? What an understatement. She was looking for someone to save her. Did she have to choose the first guy she ran into in the laundry room who happened to turn all of her underwear red?

She was in a bad way. Why couldn't she get herself to stop thinking about this guy she barely knew, had spoken to on only one occasion, whose last name she didn't even know, who she really knew almost nothing about? This guy who knew the color of all of her underwear.

Chapter IV: Initiative

Passivity leads to feelings of helplessness and hopelessness. Change your life from passive to active. Take initiative whenever possible. Volunteer for the extra project at work, approach your boss for the raise, allow yourself to buy that great outfit, even if it's not in the budget. Reach out to others. Keep track of the interesting things in their lives. Find something about which you can compliment people whenever possible. You will find your unhappy mood lifting before you know it. (Be Happy, by June Gray, Ph.D.)

June tried to do her laundry every two weeks. She actually had fifteen pairs of panties so that she could make it that long. But the Saturday after the fateful red underwear day, she got up early to do her laundry a week before it was absolutely necessary. She carefully arranged to get down there at the same time that she had gone down on the previous Saturday. She was estimating of course, and obsessing over the length of washer and dryer cycles, and second guessing how crazy it might seem for her to show up at exactly the same time a week later. And she was recognizing that no matter what time she would show up, she'd be crazy. She managed to get herself out the door and down to the laundry room.

Wonderfully and terrifyingly, Michael was there doing his wash. June stopped breathing. He'd just put his things in the dryer. The room could have been a ballroom in a fantasy castle, with a minuet playing and chandeliers glimmering. It felt so lovely and welcoming. She suddenly had the fondest feelings for this basement hovel of a laundry room. Whatever illogical, mistaken fear she'd had about the room in the past fell away, and it was now the place she most wanted to be.

When Michael looked up and saw June, he smiled and gave her a big hello. He took a quick, but exaggerated look inside the washing machine and informed her that it was safe to proceed. Obviously, he had not forgotten about what had happened the previous week. The pounding of June's heart was so loud it seemed to rattle the tiny basement windows high up on the walls. She wondered how he could be so calm. Of course to him she was just some neighbor he had met in the laundry room. No minuets playing in his head. What was the matter with her? She had to try with all of her focused energy to be normal. She proceeded to put her laundry into the washing machine, after a quick hello. After only one week, she had a much easier time fitting all of her clothing into the machine. She suddenly felt self-conscious about being there, and needed to make him feel certain that their running into one another in the laundry room was a coincidence.

"I thought I was the only person who actually did my laundry every week."

He smiled. "I don't usually do my laundry this often, but I'm going out of town and I wanted to take care of it before I left."

June was eager to ask him when and where and why and for how long, but he didn't give her a chance. He kept talking and moved onto other subjects. It turned out that he was seven years younger than she was and worked for one of the big publishing companies as an editor for professional how-to books. He'd been an English major in college and also did some writing of his own. He seemed so young. June tried to calm down and continue to breathe, telling herself that there was no way he could possibly be interested in her. When he finally asked her what she did for a living, he paused for a while after she answered.

Over the years, June had noticed that people tended to have one of two reactions to her profession, either interested and looking for advice or suspicious and critical based on the assumption that she was judgmental. She hated telling people what she did for a living because she never knew which way they'd respond.

Michael wondered why anyone would want to hear other people's problems day after day and how in the world June felt capable of helping anyone with longstanding emotional instability. He made it clear that he was aware that there were plenty of people out there who needed help. But he had trouble understanding what could help them. June explained that this was the purpose of graduate school and years of supervision.

She tried to tell him a little about her work. He seemed impressed with how difficult the work appeared to be. Or he did a good job faking it. Most people would hear about what she did and, whether or not they admitted it, they'd believe anyone could do it. It was like helping a friend. June didn't often meet people who actually thought it sounded like hard work. She was flattered but suspicious. They talked a little more about the building, repairs or the lack thereof, and before she knew it the buzzer went off. His dryer cycle seemed to end in record time. For a moment she thought that perhaps this dryer was malfunctioning, and that it potentially could be another topic of conversation. She could even be sympathetic and comforting if his clothes came out still wet. She pictured them standing close together in his apartment, hanging his dripping underwear on the shower bar in his bathroom.

His clothes came out perfectly dry and adorable. This time June made sure to take her opportunity to carefully but secretly take a good look at his laundry. He wore the most relaxed-looking, comfortable, attractive tops and underwear. The briefs seemed to be a combination of boxer and brief, some in gray, some white and some with a subtle stripe. She realized that she'd been staring at his laundry for too long, and forced her eyes away. She'd become infatuated with his laundry, too.

> *Infatuation is an intensely positive feeling. Only a few facts are actually known about the target person at the time the infatuation occurs. It is often based primarily on appearance of the target person and need on the part of the infatuated person. Logical argument and rational discussion cannot cause a person to snap out of an infatuation. It is based for the most part in fantasy. Time alone determines whether infatuation will turn into real feelings.*

June's crush was out of control and she needed to rein it in. She felt embarrassed, not to mention completely vulnerable with a racing pulse. On his way out, as he slipped from her hungry eyes, Michael turned back for a second and again offered to pay for her ruined clothes. She was shocked that he had brought it up again. It meant that he remembered. Seeing her had at least reminded him of her scarlet underwear. Her pulse doubled and her face turned red, the same color as her underwear. No wonder she had not dated anyone besides Phil in five years.

She refused and assured him that she couldn't let him give her money. It was her pleasure that he dyed all of her underclothes red. She didn't exactly say that. She tried to make a joke. The temperature in the room felt like it had skyrocketed to 110 degrees. She said that she was actually enjoying the red family of colors for the first time in her life.

He smiled. What a beautiful smile. He seemed to like her joke. He turned to leave again. It had suddenly become extremely quiet. He stopped again and suggested that they should get together some time.

It was very casual. He might have meant that they should have coffee and talk about the building or the doorman. Maybe he didn't have the slightest idea that she was hearing him suggest they go out on a real date. But maybe he did.

June's brain became a blank jell-O, jiggling aimlessly in the breeze. She must have stared off into space, expressionless for a moment. A dejected looked crossed his face, and she came out of her trance in time to say that she would love to do something some time. She suggested that he call her and told him her phone number. To her dismay, he didn't write it down. He said something along the lines of "great" and left the room.

The remainder of June's weekend was spent in anxious fantasy, waiting for his call. She didn't do anything useful besides folding and putting away her clean laundry. By Monday, no call received, she was back in real life facing her patients once again.

Claudia sat across from her on the worn couch, her shoulders hunched forward, an apologetic expression on her face. In the nine months that she'd been coming in weekly to meet with June, she had always dressed in a crisply professional way, always with a personal touch, like a colorful scarf, a striking pair of shoes or a piece of artistic jewelry. At forty-four and married for seventeen years with four children, she'd long ago found a relatively comfortable juggle of career and family. She looked her usual neat and attractive self, but her expression reflected defeat.

"Dr. Gray, I can't do it right now. Too much is going on, between Christmas, Fred's cousin's wedding, and then his 45th birthday party. His mother won't stop bugging me about it. My brother keeps cornering me to give me a lecture about how marriage is for life. I can't do it now."

June had been expecting Claudia to delay setting her divorce in motion. She'd come in for the first time to say that she no longer loved her husband, and hadn't since she'd given birth to their third child. They'd had big, blow-up arguments over the decision to have a third. She'd wanted another child badly. When their third, a second son, was born, she felt overjoyed, but her loving feelings toward her husband had vanished. Their fourth, a rambunctious girl, now three, had been an accident.

Claudia, through the therapy process, had come to realize that she felt her husband, Fred, did not and never had respected her. He called her insulting names, never did anything to help around the house and was terrible in bed. He didn't see any need for foreplay and had no patience. Claudia was certain that she'd be happier without him. She'd planned what neighborhood to move to, considered who among her friends and family would function as her support network, and decided on the best time to let her children know.

As the months passed, she decided to stop having sex with her husband. That's when he noticed that something was up. At first he ordered her to have sex. When that didn't work, he asked. After two months he'd begun to beg. But Claudia didn't budge. It gradually became clear to Claudia that Fred had begun consulting his friends as to what to do to solve the sex problem. He'd begun to empty the dishwasher, bring her the random bouquet of flowers, get her actual gifts for major holidays. He'd managed for the most part to stop calling her names directly to her face. She'd come in to therapy and tell June how after a particularly frustrating discussion between them, he'd walk away and she'd hear him mumbling names under his breath.

His harsh treatment of their eldest, a fourteen year-old son, had upset Claudia for years. She began confronting Fred about it. He'd be defensive, but she could see that he'd begun to try to control himself.

Claudia spent sessions discussing how Fred's control over his behavior seemed directly related to the no sex status. She viewed his behavioral changes as an act, a manipulation, and while she appreciated the dishwasher being emptied, she had no faith that Fred was making any permanent changes.

So she'd planned to leave him. June offered her support through her emotional exploration of her marriage, the feelings of having settled, frustration with the years during which she'd tolerated Fred's poor treatment and the frightening prospect of drastically changing her life, as well as her kids' lives. She was afraid. She'd repeatedly cried about it.

When Claudia said, "I can't do it now," June had the feeling that she really meant that she'd made the decision to stay and not to leave Fred after all. June looked at her and said, "It's okay to do whatever you feel is best. That's all you can ever do."

"I want to leave him. But right now, it's just not possible."

"You don't have to leave him now." June was concerned that she thought that she wanted her to leave him, and that Claudia was worried about disappointing her.

"I don't know, Dr. Gray. I just don't know."

"Claudia, you need to do whatever is best for you and your family."

"I don't know what that is. I feel confused. I think I'm going to take a break from therapy for a while."

She left therapy instead. June understood, although she felt sad and disappointed. She also felt relieved. She wasn't eager to have to help someone decide whether or not to get a divorce. She couldn't possibly know what was really best for Claudia and her family for the remainder of their lives. So they parted ways.

Lately, June had been extra vigilant about not allowing her own feelings to get in the way. She had plenty of personal feelings about staying in relationships too long, resenting mistreatment from partners, and the challenges of ending relationships. She knew she had to allow Claudia to do whatever she felt was best for her. She never believed that her role was to tell others what to do. What a joke that would have been, considering the mess she'd made of her own life.

Chapter V: Attitude

An optimistic attitude, even when it begins as an uncomfortable acting job, can go a long way. Force the negative thoughts out of your head and focus on the outcomes that you want. Create a chain reaction. Think positively, and your body will respond with a positive mood. Others will gravitate toward you as a result, and before you know it, you won't need to act optimistic, you'll be feeling it. If you are having intrusive, negative thoughts, write them down in your 'dark thoughts' book, and leave them there. Without them weighing on you, the world will seem a brighter, more hopeful place. (Be Happy, by June Gray, Ph.D.)

That brief laundry room conversation had an unfortunate effect on June. She went over it repeatedly in her head for the remainder of the day and into the next week. She berated herself for not being more interesting, flirtatious, reassured, eager. She couldn't stop thinking about it. It interfered with everything she did. Finally, she decided that she would write down as much of it as she could recall in an attempt to get herself to stop going over it. This would be a kind of intervention that she would suggest to someone who ruminated and obsessed. Write it down so that you no longer need to repeat it in your head. You won't lose it, or forget it or even forget a part of it if it's written down. You can read it whenever you need. She would advise this and feel proud of herself for the clever and valuable suggestion. It helped a little.

Compulsive rituals and obsessive thinking reflect high levels of anxiety. The patient with magical thinking, a form of logic used in early childhood, unconsciously believes that by performing rituals and thinking obsessively about certain subjects, she will prevent something frightening from happening, or have control over an outcome. This is reinforced by the safe feeling that usually follows the rituals. The patient then believes that to maintain that safety, the rituals must occur repeatedly. Obsessive-compulsive behaviors allow a person who fears losing control, to have a sense of control, however false.

June was stuck on his not having written down her phone number. Did he have an exceptional memory? She had offered the phone number. Perhaps he hadn't really wanted it, or he would have asked for it. Had he felt compelled to ask her to get together with him but no real intention to follow through? Then her offering him her phone number might be reason for her to feel humiliated. She drove herself nuts.

June's phone rang midday on that following Sunday. She ran to answer it, stopped to take a deep breath and make herself sound calm and relaxed. She let it ring twice, and then answered expectantly. It was Phil. She was tremendously disappointed. He must have heard it in her voice although she did try to hide it. He asked, "Were you expecting a call from someone else?"

She wasn't about to go within a mile of that subject with him, so she tried to make a joke out of it. "I was sure that Publisher's Clearinghouse had honestly meant that I was a winner this time."

Phil did pretty well with it, saying, "Sorry to disappoint you. Can I offer you a consolation prize?"

It was an unusually cute response from Phil, the man with no sense of humor. It immediately made June feel guilty, sad, a little affectionate and a bit irritated. Not a comfortable mix of emotions. She couldn't just dump him after all this time, could she? She had Michael fever with a Phil cold tablet. It was difficult to swallow and not at all effective. She agreed to make plans, if only to have a time set to talk.

June saw Phil on the Tuesday before Christmas for dinner and still had not heard from Michael. He had said he'd be out of town. But she was becoming convinced that he had not remembered her phone number and had never intended to. She felt gullible and suspicious. Why did he get up so early to do his laundry? Why did he seem so eager to get to know her? Maybe there was something seriously wrong with him that she, as a trained and experienced psychologist, should have picked up on. But then she chastised herself and thought, "Who am I to talk?" There was plenty wrong with her. Look at how much obsessive thought she had given to a little impulsive, meaningless invitation. He was just being friendly, making conversation, being polite. She wished that she could get that into her head.

Phil walked into the diner where they had agreed to meet. June was already seated at their table. He looked good in his coat and suit. He had a familiar, comfortable feel about him. She was accustomed to him. He gave her a nice kiss, and smiled. He was obviously in a good mood. He said that he was glad to see her. June, to her great surprise, felt a little glad to see him too. They had a pleasant dinner together.

She left feeling confused. Could she make it work with Phil? That would be either the easiest thing to do, or it would be the most impossible. She hadn't agreed to go home with him, so she'd basically refused to sleep with him. She knew Phil didn't love her enough. She needed to make herself realize that. She had to face it. There was no way to make it work with Phil. He was pretty good for a dinner, especially if he paid, and that was it.

It was difficult for June to sort out how she felt about Phil because all of her positive feelings were shrouded in anger. Long-lasting anger of varying intensity topped off with a big dollop of disappointment. This was so much a part of her relationship with Phil that she couldn't imagine her feelings about him without the layers of negative feelings. As a matter of fact, she realized that if he were to have asked her to marry him, and had done it in a gentle, sensitive, caring, loving manner, with regrets and apologies for taking so long, she probably wouldn't actually have been able to bring herself to accept him. That would be after having revived from fainting, of course, and then making him convince her that his body had not become inhabited by kindhearted aliens.

She would have felt for the rest of her life, or the rest of her marriage to Phil anyway, that she'd pushed him into it, and that she truly cared for him in some way more than he could ever be capable of caring for her. A reluctant last-straw marriage proposal was the most realistic possibility, and even that was unlikely. But there was no way that she could accept that and feel good. It really wasn't so horrible to be single. She didn't think that she could bear being married to Phil. Even living with him would surely be hellish. Every chore would be done by exacting standards; even the dishwasher would get loaded in one particular way only. She would always have been the disorganized slob in his eyes.

> *When two people enter into a relationship, they bring their old issues, habits and abilities, which shift and adjust according to the needs of the relationship. Each member takes on characteristics of the other, each comes to accept imperfections in the other, and each grows and matures as a person because of the other. This is the road to intimacy: gradual understanding and appreciation of one's partner with increasing knowledge and acceptance of both the self and that partner.*

The sooner June disengaged, the better. She was wasting precious time waiting for someone who, amazingly, she no longer really wanted despite desperately waiting for the past five years. This was a revelation.

The unfortunate fact was that over the years there had been many experiences about which Phil and she had agreed or felt similarly. These included books and films and various foods. He knew her views and she knew his. This kind of knowledge can take a long time to develop. He knew how to order for her while she was in the ladies room at a restaurant, what kind of wine she liked, which movies she would never go to see. A new person would not know her habits, her flaws, her failings, wouldn't have come to accept her for who she was. There would be that hovering risk of rejection.

> *Early in a relationship, both partners are usually on good behavior, revealing only their best characteristics. They hide insecurities and anxieties so as to reduce how vulnerable they feel. Yet, they feel vulnerable anyway. Each cannot yet know how much the other cares for him or her, in part as a result of each not knowing the other fully. Inevitably, most relationships progress in stages, gradually moving to greater levels of intimacy, or failing to do so.*

Michael didn't call, and it wasn't as though a huge line was forming behind him. June had no plans to stoop to hanging out in the laundry room every Saturday morning yet. There was a very low likelihood that she would run into or even formally meet someone else who would be interested in her. She had to come to terms with the great, painful, terrifying probability of being single for the rest of her life. She had to face it head on, with determination and strength. Her weekends would be lonely. If she hung onto Phil, he would never leave, and she'd have this frustrating, somewhat insulting, humiliating but utterly predictable and reliable relationship. She would have weekend plans. Could she give up the glass with a few drops in it, for a perfectly empty glass with a tiny bit of potential?

> *The sociopath is notable for his lack of conscience. His goal is to get his own needs met regardless of the impact on others. He will do whatever it takes. Sociopaths are often highly social, charismatic, fun-loving, extroverted people. They may have many acquaintances but no intimate friends. Usually, they cannot maintain close relationships successfully. Generally, underneath a veneer of pleasant helpfulness, the sociopath is an angry, impatient, resentful, entitled person with no interest in self-examination.*

Someone more sophisticated than June might have continued the relationship with Phil, while looking around for someone else. She found that kind of thing to be very difficult to do. She was a bad liar. Even if she had tried, Phil would have seen it written on her face.

She felt as though she had no control over her life. And that she was probably not actually lovable. She could feel the waves of unhappiness overwhelming her again. She needed to stop this escalating landslide. She needed to get herself focused and organized. She had to get through another holiday season, in which there would be no romance, only family obligation and heartache.

> *Highly accommodating people feel unlovable. They believe that the only way to maintain relationships is to serve the needs of others, always putting them before themselves. They often blame themselves for not being accommodating enough. It is most important to get to the source of the feeling of being unlovable, and to help patients use judgment about the people with whom they are in relationships, in order to help them to change their behavior and feel that their needs are important too.*

Several days after June's dinner with Phil, she had her next session with Annabelle. She came in to June's office, threw herself on the couch and said, "Which antidepressant do you think I should take?"

June sensed that some sort of trap was being set before her. "Why do you ask?"

She sighed impatiently. "Do you think I have a typical depression or an atypical depression?"

Again, June could see that she was being led down a path. She had no idea of the intended destination, but it didn't seem like any place she was eager to go. "Have you been to a psychiatrist recently?"

Another dramatic sigh, and Annabelle said, "Dr. Zeigler gave me a new one to try. He says I have atypical depression. I couldn't understand what he was talking about. But it would figure: leave it to me to have something unusual, worse than everyone else. He never has enough time to talk to me. I didn't get to tell him all of my symptoms. He cut me off. I haven't been on any antidepressants for two years. I'm not so sure that I want to get started with that circus again."

"Did you discuss it with Dr. Ziegler?"

"I told you there was no time." Annabelle sounded irritable. She continued to pressure June to tell her what to do. "So, what is your opinion? You know me well. Am I atypical?"

June's view, generally, was that the person who prescribed a neurotransmitter-altering medication should spend adequate time with the patient for whom he or she is prescribing. It seemed unethical to leave all the discussing up to the non-medical therapists. Wasn't that why she paid the psychiatrist so much for the appointment? To be fair though, the doctor could have given her two hours, and for Annabelle, that would have been too little time.

June began slowly, "You know that antidepressant medications are not my specialty. I'm sure that's why you met with Dr. Zeigler. Maybe you'd feel more comfortable if you called him to discuss it further."

Annabelle reacted to her response as if she had abandoned her. She became silent and moody, and next spoke emphatically about how suicidal she felt and how she really would do it at some point, so that it really didn't matter which antidepressant she took. Nothing worked for her, anyway.

June attempted to point out the sequence of her thoughts and found her completely nonplussed, but she did seem to brighten up a bit, perhaps from receiving attention. At least June had been listening to her.

She spent most of the remainder of the session discussing how her latest boyfriend had stayed up with her until 4:00 am the night before and how he'd promised her a weekend vacation all expenses paid. They were to discuss when and where next time they got together. Annabelle was unsure of when that would be and could barely contain her impatience.

She had in mind a trip to an island for four days and three nights which was longer than he'd promised. She wanted him to fly them first class. June could predict that she would overwhelm him with an endless stream of demands and entitlements, eventually forcing him to abandon the whole idea of the vacation, if not her.

Certain patients suffer from feelings of desperate neediness. They have a deep well of painful longing, never to be filled, never to be truly satisfied. Attempts to fill the deep neediness are met with more neediness, more demands, more longing. Of course, as time passes, the therapeutic relationship grows, and as a result, the rage felt by the patient over her frustrated longing begins to show itself within the therapeutic relationship. It is at this point that the real challenges to the therapist begin.

After a boring New Year's Eve with Phil that ended with an early bed time in their separate apartments, June was feeling particularly in tune with the cold, lifeless weather of early January. Phil called a week later to tell her that he had been doing some very hard, serious thinking. He was feeling good about their relationship. He was feeling trust and confidence in her. "I feel a bit further along in the direction you want me to be heading," he said.

She hadn't seen this train coming. It took her a moment to gather her composure again. "Which direction are you referring to?"

He laughed uncomfortably, as though he had rehearsed and said his lines and there was no more that he could think of to say. He fumbled, "You know, the, uh...future...uh." There was a long silence. Finally he added, "You know, in thinking about the future potential for a possible official commitment."

He spoke so haltingly and sounded so ambivalent that she realized, with relief, that this was probably a false alarm. His claim that he was further along left him several years behind her and meant virtually nothing. He was buying time. She felt a stinging hurt, but knew there was no point in expressing that. He'd never understand why. He was proud of himself. So she said that she was glad to hear it. And changed the subject quickly. Maybe he had somehow finally picked up on his radar that she was on the verge of giving it all up if only because she had stopped sleeping with him.

It hurt because it was too little, too late. June knew it did her no good. But her heart leapt a tiny leap when he said that he was further along. It was a positive comment, approving of her. She couldn't help eating it up. This was something that she'd wanted from him for so long that she couldn't stop herself from responding. Of course, immediately following the warmth was shame and humiliation that he could still get to her. She got off the phone as quickly as she could and cried for a while. Phil wasn't good for her. She knew that. She needed to stay away from him.

June needed to move on. And it couldn't just be to Michael, the fantasy who never called or reappeared again. By the end of January she'd decided to ask Emily to set her up with a colleague. The whole idea made her cringe, but options were limited. As soon as the request left her lips, Emily was on it. She had two guys in mind and would speak to them both that day. There was no going back. She knew she'd hear from at least one of them shortly.

She focused on writing her book more than ever, took the notebook to the office and worked whenever she had a cancellation, during her lunch breaks, or if she had a bit of time between patients. And then took it home after work and wrote in the evening. When she awoke at 2:00 am, she wrote some more. It had become her best friend and good luck charm. She kept it near her at all times. It was a silly thing, but she felt exhilarated writing in the book and organizing the ideas. She became attached to the notebook and the particular pen she was using to write in it. It was a black felt tip. It was her secret. She was too embarrassed to tell anyone about it, anyway.

The writing made her feel stronger, more focused, and less like she had no life, although nothing had really changed. She fleshed out the ten steps on note cards, making them up out of thin air. They weren't based on the slightest bit of scientific evidence that she was aware of. As she wrote about each one, she found herself following it to some small extent, not always consciously at first. She'd notice and have her own little laugh. She wore bright colors, smiled more, and forced herself to be more patient with people. The book grew quickly. It was the only thing in her life that brought enjoyment. It was a way to escape from her utter loneliness.

It was an unusually warm week in early February. There were even a few days that felt like spring. A few ill-informed crocuses were appearing through the melting snow. June had a couple of cancellations, probably the result of people preferring to relax outdoors than dig up painful emotions in her dingy office.

She sat outside on the plaza surrounding the building and wrote in her notebook. She watched people walk by, alone, in pairs, in groups. She saw people in uniforms, jeans, designer outfits. There was so much life to watch, so many people, each so different, all going various places at varying speeds. She felt more alive than she had in ages. Apparently, the weather can be a great determiner of mood.

Seasonal Affective Disorder (SADS) is a form of depression impacted by availability of sunlight. Research has shown that levels of depression rise when the weather is colder and daylight is briefer. Many people admit to feeling a greater degree of depression during the winter months. Treatment takes the form of exposure to sunlight and warmth. Lamps closely duplicating the wavelength spectrum of true sunlight are utilized.

Maybe June was hypomanic. She felt like she'd had a blood transfusion. She had so much to write. "Even if you are depressed, it is important to put yourself out there. Be among people. Surround yourself with life energy. Remember how precious life is." And, "Put yourself center stage now and then." Ridiculous, but she giggled to herself and watched people go by. She became eager for spring.

Her moods fluctuated like spring weather. She couldn't help wondering why Michael hadn't called. It had been almost two months. Most normal people would interpret that as evidence that he wouldn't be calling, and move on. She should have put him out of her mind. But she had the useless tenacity of a small dog chasing its tail. Why hadn't he written down her phone number? Why couldn't she forget about him? What was wrong with her? Was she so special that she deserved to have some excitement and happiness in her life? He probably saw: desperate female approaching midlife. It was as obvious as if she'd had neon signs with flashing arrows pointing at her. Maybe he thought he wouldn't be able to escape from the laundry room alive unless he showed some sign of interest in the gargoyle posted there. She must have seemed pathetic.

Patients who come to treatment feeling that others look down on them, feel disgust toward them or just disregard them, are usually projecting their own self-judgments, self-hatred, and disappointment onto others. This is, of course, an unconscious process. Convincing these patients that others do not have such extremely harsh opinions of them is one of the challenges for the treating therapist. Another is to discover why they suffer with such severely negative self views. Early object relations are usually the cause.

June wasn't so far gone that she couldn't recognize projection when she happened to be the culprit. She just couldn't help it. She had no idea why he suggested they get together and then chose not to follow up. She kept wishing that he would call and she feared that he still could. She didn't know which would have made her more agitated, worrying over why he hadn't called, or his actually calling and wanting to get to know her.

She awoke early on the following Saturday morning and had plenty of laundry to do. She had the usual clothing from the week, but also added her sheets and towels, and anything else made of cloth that was lying around. She contemplated dragging it down the street to the laundromat like she had always done in the past. She packed it up, knowing full well that no matter what she told herself to do she would end up going down to the basement laundry room with her laundry bag, hoping to see Michael at the usual approximately 8:15am time. Why lie to herself?

She hoped that she might have the self-control to avoid the humiliation she'd feel while throwing herself at a stranger. But at that moment, that level of control was out of the question. She had obsessed over which relaxed sweats and tee shirt to wear, and was on her way down to the basement. It could have been flooded with three feet of raw sewage and she'd still be dragging her laundry down there.

The room was deserted and dusty. It felt a bit scary, reminding her of why she had always gone to the place down the street. She stuffed all of her laundry into the washing machine, barely able to fit it all in. She didn't care if she never saw any of her clothes again, except maybe the red bras and panties. She could have cried from frustration. She should have headed down the street. She was putting herself in danger. There was something seriously wrong with her. She should have stuffed herself into the washing machine on the superwash cycle on the off chance of agitating some sense into herself.

In the early stages of a relationship, fantasy allows a person to attempt to know and attach to another person. The relationship is more likely to contain primitive object relations early on as a result. As with any defense, fantasy can function rigidly and ineffectively as well, as in the case of compulsive fantasy. Reality needs to supplant fantasy for a relationship to thrive.

June tried to reason with herself. For the most part, he was a figment of her imagination. She hardly knew him. She needed to pull herself together and stop thinking about him. It was extremely distasteful to contemplate her level of desperation. It gave her a sick feeling in the pit of her stomach. She moved her wash to the dryer after an interminable wash cycle, still alone, practically in tears.

On Sunday she awoke feeling especially badly and could not get out of bed. The phone rang at 10:00 am. She let it ring. She listened to each ring, and heard her answering machine pick up. She couldn't move. She heard Phil's voice on the machine, hesitating and awkward after all this time. She didn't get up. She listened in a removed, distant way, and felt completely disconnected from him. Who was this guy? Why was he calling? He finally stopped talking and hung up. There were clicking sounds as her answering machine reset itself. Then silence. She realized she hadn't even listened to what Phil had said. About a minute later, she was in tears, crying, and feeling overwhelmed by her own unhappiness and the pointlessness of her life. She cried so hard, she couldn't catch her breath. She felt as if she were seeing her life clearly for the first time.

She must have cried for an hour before she was able to calm herself down. She had exhausted herself. It felt familiar; She'd done the same thing in childhood. She fell asleep. When she finally awoke, it was early afternoon and she felt sad, but also hopeful. The image in her head was a faint rainbow after a rainstorm. She realized that the only way she could possibly escape from her predicament aside from killing herself, which she truly didn't want to do, was to change her attitude. She needed to pull herself together and take action.

She tried to rethink her view. She attempted to look at the brighter side of the situations that upset her. She started with Phil. Five years was better than six or ten years. She didn't regret all of it. But now she needed to move on. Phil was not a bad person. She couldn't hate him. He was just limited. She had to accept that. She had to stop wishing that he would change. He was who he was. She made herself a nice dinner and spent the evening taking care of herself.

That night the phone rang. She tried to have no expectations whatsoever, but failed. She answered the phone in as neutral a voice as possible. It was a guy named Pete. Emily had given him her number. He was eager to meet right away. He sounded friendly, laid back and fun on the phone, telling June about his longstanding friendship with Emily and Ed. He went on about Emily like she was perfection made flesh. June couldn't disagree with him, but felt a little anxiety that she'd disappoint him. They made casual dinner plans for the next evening. June didn't make a habit of going out on Monday nights, but he seemed so eager. It wasn't as if she had any other plans.

Monday, she woke up determined to make it a good day. She looked in the mirror, suppressed the usual sigh of disappointment, and focused on the positives. She had nice warm, expressive eyes, and despite the small wrinkles, a nice face. It was a friendly face, although somewhat sad looking.

> *Research indicates that smiling actually makes people feel happier. The movement of the particular facial muscles that cause the smile apparently sends the message to the brain that a feeling of happiness should occur. When subjects were asked to smile, whether after viewing a happy image (child's birthday party) or an unhappy image (flat tire on a car), they were found to reveal on a questionnaire that they felt subjectively happier than the frown group (who were asked to frown at both images) as well as the control group.*

June put on a nice outfit. Weight had never been an issue, but she had gotten thinner lately, probably as a result of feeling depressed and not completely caring for herself. She decided that she looked good in her suit. She tried to taste her breakfast.

She smiled as she left the building and headed toward her car. A couple of people smiled back.

Despite feeling a bit fragile in her sessions, June remained calm and wasn't as nervous as usual. She let the patients do the talking, without the usual pressure she felt to be responsible for making brilliant interpretations or filling up the silences. She appreciated the fact that her patients had turned to her for help, or to listen to or witness their difficulties. She knew that it wasn't an easy thing to do. There was a certain amount of confidence, trust and hope placed in her as a therapist. This felt valuable.

> *How, what, and when we eat is both a reflection of our primary object relations as well as a reaction to current societal pressures. When we gorge ourselves, we are desperately eager for emotional fulfillment and eager to quiet powerful unacceptable feelings. Purging is in part an ambivalent rejection of the primary object, allowed in and then violently removed. It is also a rejection of aspects of a current relationship. When eating is rejected altogether, often an intrusive, early object relation and a current difficult relationship are being steadfastly and stubbornly refused. Each of these eating related solutions to difficult early object relations, as well as to current stressors, are challenging to work with because of the patient's lack of flexible control over impulses.*

Every now and then people thanked June for helping them. In those rare instances, she felt tremendous gratitude toward them for choosing her as the person they turned to in their moments of greatest emotional pain. And she felt proud that she could make her office a safe and supportive environment. It was an honor. She began to realize that it remained an honor, even when people were not thanking her for it. She felt like she had opened a window in her stuffy office. The real windows did not actually open.

Monday evening at 7:00 p.m. began to roll around before she was ready. She walked over to the restaurant Pete had chosen, one within walking distance of her office. It was a small café that served light meals. She got to the café first, a couple of minutes early. The sun was setting, turning the sky orange and pink and there was a chill in the air.

Pete arrived five minutes late, which was still perfectly acceptable. June watched him walk toward her as she stood in front of the cafe's big plate glass window. He was tall, athletic looking and definitely handsome, with sandy blond, neatly trimmed hair, and he was wearing a long camel hair coat. He gave her a big smile, one that seemed comfortable and confident, and he waved as he approached. June smiled back, thinking that maybe she should trust that Emily could set her up with someone great.

He was still smiling when he stuck out his hand and said, "Hi, I'm Pete. You must be June. I recognized you right away from Emily's description."

"Hi." June replied, continuing to smile back and shake his hand.

A sudden look of concern swept across his attractive face, "I hope you haven't been waiting long."

"No. I got here a little early. I was enjoying the sunset."

Pete gave the sky a glance, turned back to June and said, "Should we go in?" He opened the door and led them to a small table by the window. After they sat down, he looked her in the eye and said, "So, tell me about yourself."

June wasn't expecting such a direct question, the kind people asked in interviews. She immediately thought of all the things that she definitely didn't want to tell him. She tried not to be nervous. It was a good sign that he was asking about her. It probably eliminated a diagnosis of Narcissistic Personality Disorder. She had to keep things positive. She smiled again, "What do you want to know?"

"Emily told me you are a psychologist. What other interests do you have?"

June was a little taken aback because he skipped right over her career and she realized with horror that she didn't have any other interests except maybe trying to control her feelings of depression and desperation. She definitely wasn't ready to discuss those interests. "My work as a psychologist keeps me pretty busy."

"How so?"

"I do therapy for hours each day. Then there are the notes, phone calls and of course all of the insurance headaches."

"Insurance headaches?"

"They sometimes don't approve sessions, or pay properly or pay at all."

"That sounds annoying." Pete was looking around the restaurant. He began to read the chalk board.

"It is annoying." June could feel herself getting worked up over the whole insurance issue. "They don't care about patient welfare. They only care about money."

Pete leaned in across the table and said, "They have a really good grilled vegetable sandwich here. You should try it."

Just then the waitress came by. She was college age, dressed all in black with many piercings on her face. She pulled a little pad out of the back pocket of her very tight black jeans. June looked at the chalk board and picked a sandwich that was not the grilled vegetable. Pete ordered it, saying he'd let her try his.

"Pete," June said, "You don't really want to hear about my insurance woes. It's bad enough that I have to deal with it when I'm at work."

Pete gave her a little smile and said, "Shouldn't people who need therapy pay for it themselves anyway?"

Maybe he knew nothing about therapy or its costs. She needed to enlighten him. "Well, there are quite a few people who cannot afford therapy without their insurance paying a portion of it. Therapy isn't cheap."

"Of course." Pete looked concerned. "It's tough. There are so many things we all do without because they just aren't in the budget."

That seemed like the perfect opportunity to turn the spotlight on him and away from herself, so June said, "Tell me about your work."

Pete looked thoughtful for a moment, and then said, "I'm sure it would bore you. Computer engineering is a complex field."

"Oh. Ok." She tried to smile. "What else do you do? For fun?"

Pete leaned back in his seat and put his hands up behind his head. "I like to socialize with some of the people at work. Right now I am in this terrific work group. We have a blast. Sometimes we'll go to happy hours after work. Great, great people."

"That's terrific," June said, thinking it sounded ok. He liked to be social. Nothing wrong with that. Although she wasn't particularly social. What if he liked to be more social than she did?

"So how long have you known Emily?" Pete looked very interested.

"Years. We've been best friends since before she even met Ed." June was trying to think of the number of years it was, and she was wondering why she found the question to be irritating.

Pete, with too much enthusiasm, said, "She's terrific. A really, smart, great, lady."

He called her a lady. June had no idea what to do with that. "She's a great friend."

"You're lucky to be such good friends with her."

"Yes. I am. Emily is a great friend. I feel fortunate to have her in my life."

"You are. She's got a great, upbeat personality. Everyone thinks she's terrific. I'd do anything for her."

June had this sudden sinking feeling. Sinking through the wooden chair she was sitting on, through the dingy linoleum floor tiles, through the cement and then the dirt underneath. Pete was sitting here with no interest in her whatsoever. He'd come as a favor to Emily. June couldn't just get up and walk out on him after she'd set them up. She knew Emily had done it in good faith. She'd probably asked if he were interested in meeting her friend. He'd agreed. He probably would have agreed to anything she'd asked.

June had to get a grip. "Well Pete, it sounds like you really think highly of Emily. That's great."

Pete stared at her for a moment. He started to speak, then stopped. The sandwiches and drinks arrived. June picked up her sandwich and took a bite. It was definitely his turn to talk. Her turkey, goat cheese and roasted pepper sandwich on whole wheat artisan bread was tasty. She watched as Pete took a bite too. She watched him chewing thoughtfully.

"June, you don't have to tell me, but I was wondering, just out of curiosity. I was wondering how Emily's marriage is going?"

June must have looked shocked.

More quickly, Pete added, "I'm only asking because, you know gossip at the work place. I'm sure that's all it is. You don't have to tell me if it's private or something." He jammed another bite into his mouth and chewed aggressively.

"I'm not sure what you're asking me. As far as I know Emily's marriage is one of the best I've ever seen, and I am a psychologist."

"Right. Of course." Pete could have left the table at that point, and as June sat there looking at him, she wished he would have. Instead they ate in an awkward silence. As soon as the last bite of his sandwich was in his mouth, not even yet chewed, Pete was pulling out his wallet. He laid a twenty on the table, swallowed his chewed up bite and gave June that big smile again. "It was so great to meet you. It's been really interesting. Unfortunately, I have to run. Hey, say hi to Emily for me."

"It was great meeting you, too." June didn't get up. As soon as his wallet came out she decided that she would stay and sit there for a while after he left, as if she weren't totally humiliated.

> *Flashbacks are a complex phenomenon. They can include distinct imagery without emotion, imagery with strong feelings, or no imagery at all, only strong emotion. This last form is most disconcerting, as the strong feelings seem to arise from nowhere, and are attached to no image, leaving the subject wondering why she is feeling so intensely anxious, fearful, or angry. She is also left feeling helpless to rectify the situation, as it cannot be logically explained away, until it is understood to be a flashback.*

June rationalized that it was just a blind date. Hardly anyone came out of them unscathed. Why would it be any different for her? It wasn't personal. He hadn't really wanted to date her. It had all been about Emily. And she'd tried to be a good friend. June couldn't complain. She wasn't going to let the whole thing bring her further down. He wasn't really her type anyway, whatever that was. She knew who her type was and she was trying not to think about him.

The next day, as she stared out the dingy window over the beat-up desk in her office she noticed the striking whiteness of the winter sky. No distinct clouds, no perspective, not a sign of the sun. She felt insignificant. A familiar feeling. She had to get back to the drudgery of paperwork and reluctantly opened up the file that she had been avoiding. She'd managed to delay this particular chore for too long because it made her want to leave the field and do something more fun like trash collection.

She read the record. Twenty sessions completed. Only twenty allowed for the entire year. They'd had several weeks in which they'd met twice because the patient was in such distress. The frustration pounded in her temples. Out the window, she saw a small bird land on a leafless tree branch. What was it doing there alone?

June picked up the phone, dialed the 800 number while taking deep yoga breaths and trying to relax her clenched jaw and stop the familiar pounding. An extremely upbeat recorded voice on the phone requested a slew of personal information to be typed into the phone key pad. After June revealed her private life to a computer, the voice told her that because of heavy call volume her call might not be answered anytime soon. However, she could hold and they'd respond to her and her fellow prisoners in the order in which they had dialed in. And, in extra special language, the voice also told her that someone might be listening in to her conversation for educational purposes. And the icing on the cake was that she was informed that even though sessions might be approved, which meant that she would spend hours with the patient trying to help her, she was not guaranteed payment for those approved and already utilized sessions.

June waited. She looked up and saw that the branch was empty again, the tree deserted. She had 45 minutes of her one hour break remaining. Loud static-laced Musak was playing in her left ear. The Musak stopped and the phone rang twice, her hopes rising. There was a loud click, and the happy, informative recorded voice repeated its entire message. Her heart sank and then practically stopped.

She doodled on the inside cover of the file. Her patient, Eva, was in her early thirties, clearly bipolar, single and in desperate need of more sessions. She seemed to be entering a manic stage. Ideally, she'd be coming in twice a week on a regular basis. Instead, recently they'd made it once a week, even skipping a few to spread out the twenty sessions. She could hardly afford her co-pay. June had to keep seeing her whether the insurance company agreed to more sessions or not. Her patient had offered in lieu of payment, to illegally record movies onto DVDs. June thanked her but couldn't possibly agree to that.

The phone rang again and this time what sounded like a live voice answered. Live yet not lively. June tried to sound impressive, "This is Dr. June Gray. I am calling with regard to..."

"ID number." The bland, deep, monotone, possibly female voice cut in.

She recited the ID number.

"Name of patient and date of birth." Not even a please. June began to wish she were talking to the upbeat recorded voice. After more data gathering, they finally got to her reason for calling.

"We've used up her allotted twenty sessions but she's doing quite poorly and requires more in my clinical opinion."

"If she's used up all twenty, she has to wait until her year is up which is July."

"I am aware of that but I am concerned about her. She cannot wait. She needs therapy now. She seems to be entering a manic phase and might require hospitalization."

"Please hold." Loud Musak in June's ear again. No comment about how long she'd have to wait or why. But at least she said please. June looked at the clock. She now had one half hour left. She waited and waited, almost giving up, losing track of how much time had gone by, stared at the white sky, the bare tree, felt like crying, pulled herself together, doodled, tried to make her headache go away by relaxing her clenched face, felt like crying again, and then, surprise, her connection to the un-dead was back.

"You'll have to speak to a supervisor to get permission to convert inpatient time to outpatient. I'll need your name and phone number so the supervisor can call you back."

June knew this trick. It was the black hole trick. "You can't put me through now?" She felt desperate. "I've been waiting on the phone for a long time. I need to get these sessions approved as quickly as possible. I'm sure you understand. If this very troubled person were a relative of yours, you'd want to help her right away."

"Name and number."

There was no way to get through to someone who could actually help at the insurance company. For years June had tried to find short cuts through the obstacle course. Every now and then she'd accidently speak to an intelligent, capable human voice. She'd be so grateful for the help she would feel pathetic. The whole system was huge, bureaucratic, and suffocating.

After hanging up, she checked the clock again. Twenty more minutes and she would be back in session for several hours in a row. Even if the supervisor weren't an imaginary person, he or she would have a hard time getting her on the phone, if he or she actually even tried to call. She knew the game. Eva could suffer for weeks before this might get resolved. She'd see her anyway and gamble on whether she'd ever get paid.

From one frustration to another, June had an obligatory visit near the end of February with her family. Of course, her brother the dentist, his lovely wife and their children were the focus of the weekend, despite her much less frequent appearances. She'd bought expensive gifts for everyone, baked cookies and blondies, and driven herself the two hours to her parents' home. They all thanked her for the gifts, complimented her on the baked goods, and made superficial small talk.

However, as usual, following each compliment from her mother was a criticism, or a suggestion on how June could make an improvement. These mixed messages had been her mother's modus operandi her entire life. But it was more painful than usual when she found her sister-in-law falling in step behind her mom. She complimented June's colorful spring outfit, only to follow it with, "It seems so unlike you." She was not technically incorrect. But June wondered why she couldn't have stopped with the compliment.

And what possible response could she have to that comment? "So true. I have changed. I am not as depressed as I used to be." Instead she just smiled and mumbled a thank you.

June's mother told her how thoughtful she'd been to choose such lovely gifts for her nieces, although they already had more than enough toys. And didn't June need a haircut rather badly? Her mother stared at the top of her head a bit too long and added that her hair seemed so flat on top.

June never quite got the space to acknowledge the compliment before the attack came. Then she was trapped looking for a way to welcome the compliment and ignore the criticism. Often, she was forced only to respond to the attack and behave as if there had been no compliment, or visa versa.

Perhaps meaningless, but still overwhelming and familiar. She entered that confused, upset, swirling world of neurotic ignition. She made great efforts to step outside of the intense winds, but the tornado pulled her right back in. She felt injured, rageful, misunderstood. Much more than the situation called for.

June knew these kinds of trigger reactions made it difficult for her to spend much time with family. Rather than leaving with a warm feeling of love, she left with a burning feeling of anger and disappointment. She wished she could have gotten past it. She didn't really care what her mother thought of her hair, or gifts or cooking or anything else. She'd worked long and hard to shut off that reaction switch that turned on when her mother did what should have been predictable by then. She wasn't a specialist on hair, or dress, or anything else about which she criticized her. Fortunately, she practically never visited June, and didn't ask about her home, her personal life or work. These topics could have been potential mine fields for criticisms. But for the most part, they were of no interest to her. So, June was relatively safe from attack. Unless she chose to interpret her family's complete lack of interest in her as an attack. She was more inclined to see it as a fortunate relief and to try not to think too much about it at all.

After a weekend with them, despite her efforts at shielding herself, she felt down and dejected and in need of some recovery time. She wished that someone understood that. In the past, Phil had served as a support with regard to her family. He was completely disconnected from them, and although he'd always felt that June had been too sensitive about what they said and did, he'd been able to support her in her efforts to disconnect from them, to not care what they thought. He preferred to have her efforts put toward pleasing him instead of them. As she was trying to free herself from him, she couldn't exactly look to Phil for support. She didn't want to rely on him in any way for any reason at this point. She was alone again. Maybe it was the safest place to be anyway.

Chapter VI: Integration

Keep your thoughts positive. When a negative thought enters your mind, toss it out. Why make your life more difficult with self doubt, self criticism and pessimistic thinking? Look at the big picture. You are unable to appreciate the great gift that life is because you focus your attention on minute, unimportant issues and turn them into obstacles to happiness and satisfaction. You question yourself and others. You look for loss, not gain. You seek out disappointment, not pleasure. You must decide to make the changes necessary to let happiness into your life. No one else can do that for you. Change your perspective and look at the bigger picture. Remain observant and conscious of the joys of life. (Be Happy, by June Gray, Ph.D.)

The weather was slowly changing into chilly instead of freezing and spring was approaching. There were some buds on the trees and a few flowers beginning to pop up from the muddy ground. June should have felt hopeful. There were only so many times she could call Emily without feeling self-conscious about being dependent and annoying. She'd spoken to Emily so many times about her family that she was convinced that, despite the fact that she would never say so, she must have wondered why June didn't just get over her disappointment and anger. She seemed to understand her mother so well, and had the ability to predict her behavior so accurately. Emily couldn't understand why June didn't just let go of her tortured emotional response. June appreciated Emily's restraint in not asking that question.

> *Progress takes time because newly learned patterns of behavior and acquired insights must be integrated into the already existing array of behaviors, thoughts, and emotions. There is a gradual expansion into new and improved interactions with the world. These experiences build upon one another, increasing growth through more behavioral variations and adaptations and continual development of insight and self-knowledge. The process feels slow, yet real change is occurring. Patience is required.*

The more distant June was from her family, the better protected she was from the pain and disappointment, but the less her family was involved with her. She felt like she couldn't win. This was the point in thinking about her family at which she began to wish that she had never been born, particularly when she was feeling depressed. Something about it felt unfair. Life never was fair though.

> *Our earliest object relations set the tone for the ways in which we relate to others throughout our lives. The child takes in the attitudes, judgments, love, and anger that the parents direct her way. As the child grows to maturity, these same attitudes come to be expected from others outside of the family unit. If the parental treatment of the child has been harsh, the child will grow to expect harshness from others, and will carry with her an internalized version of her parents' harsh attitude toward herself and others.*

June could have contacted other professionals, and made friends and connections if she hadn't been shy and fearful of judgment. It was all so frustrating. She somehow remained trapped in her behaviors and in her uncomfortable neurotic reactions to things. And this was after a lot of therapy.

Strangely enough, she could help other people. Even though she was incompetent to perform some of life's most simple tasks, she was a sensitive and adept therapist. She did understand what it was like to suffer. Being a therapist might have been the only career in which she could possibly have had success. It did take its toll, though. She got yelled at, cried to, complained to, and whined to. Not to mention the stress she felt trying to help people deal with huge issues like death, infertility, cancer, trauma, and abuse. She didn't understand everything, couldn't always accommodate, didn't always pass tests set up for her, didn't always sympathize enough for some, and of course, she charged too much.

Sometimes it was extremely rewarding work. She helped people feel hopeful about the future, improve their social lives, their jobs, their relationships. She even helped prepare people for healthy relationships and commitment. She worked with quite a few people who began treatment in a miserable, dissatisfying, disappointing relationship and ended treatment in a happy, committed, satisfying, healthy relationship.

What was wrong with her? She could help others to do exactly what she wanted more than anything else for herself. She wished there were some pill she could take, or some exercise she could do to fix up her life, or some chant to repeat at bedtime, so she could get cured in her sleep.

She needed to find a way to meet new people. She needed to feel better about herself and not fear judgment so much that it paralyzed her. She needed to be more outgoing and friendly and less depressed. She needed that magic pill. Or a brain transplant.

Dissociation, a temporary feeling of distance from the self, is caused by such extreme levels of anxiety that the emotional system shuts down. The sufferer feels as though she is watching the scene she is in, rather than experiencing it. She feels emotionally detached and strangely calm. This can, at times, be so powerful that the person actually loses consciousness of her surroundings temporarily. This intensity of dissociation is associated with flash backs from trauma. Milder levels of dissociation are more common, and indicate that the sufferer is struggling with more anxiety than she can comfortably manage.

There she was again in the laundry room, feeling miserable. Rain was pouring outside in huge, noisy sheets, crashing to the pavement outside the prison cell-sized windows near the ceiling. June was concerned that the basement might flood because there had been so much rain lately, but she wasn't about to drag her laundry down the block in this weather. She felt on the verge of tears. She was premenstrual, retaining water like a sponge and feeling out of control. "Nobody cares about me, and why should they?" kept reverberating in her head. It was her responsibility and her's alone to care for herself, and she just wasn't up to the task.

June felt angry. The world had disappointed her. She felt hopeless. At the peak moment of experiencing hopelessness, into the laundry room walked Michael. He looked pleased to see her at first. She stared at him in shock for a moment. Perhaps she had truly lost her mind and was now hallucinating. She'd completely given up on him to the degree that she had practically believed that he no longer existed, and perhaps never had. But there he was. How awkward for them both. His initial smile had left his face and he was looking uncomfortable. Now he would need to create a quick explanation for having dangled a carrot in front of desperate June, and then having ripped it away. She'd actually offered him, a total stranger she had met in a semi-subterranean laundry room, her number. How foolish. And she'd gotten her just desserts.

She tried to say hello, squeaked it out, and went back to emptying out the dryer. Her face would not stop burning. Michael cleared his throat. She felt a strong urge to leave the room quickly before the heat from her face created a spark, ignited some stray lint and caused the place to go up in flames. She took her things out of the dryer, focusing on the task as if she had never seen socks this fascinating before.

Finally, Michael spoke. "It's been a while. Sorry I didn't get a chance to call you."

June shrugged. "Call me? Had you planned to do that?" She looked at the freshly laundered tee shirt she was attempting to fold as the words fell with false innocence from her lips.

"Yes. You gave me your number. Remember? I guess it really has been a while." He looked dejected. As if he had any right to be. As if she didn't remember. He continued, "I originally went to visit my cousins for a couple of weeks in December. But almost immediately afterward I was sent out of town unexpectedly for a two-week book tour. I think it was only two days after I got back. And that got extended unexpectedly to more than three weeks. Things have been really crazy at work for me. Anyway, I'm sorry I didn't get a chance to call you."

June's head felt like a big empty beach ball. She was able, with great effort, to mumble. "That's okay."

Michael continued, "I guess I felt awkward calling you while I was travelling. I, uh, guess I could have. I wasn't sure what to do. I just felt like we hardly knew each other. I didn't want to be presumptuous. And then when I got back, it seemed like so much time had already passed that I guess I felt awkward calling you."

The room reverberated with his words, as did June's hollow head. Her whole mistaken view of the universe swam around in her head, making her dizzy. She said, "Oh."

"You must have thought I was playing games with you, taking your number and then not calling you. I should have called. I'm sorry." Michael was looking inquiringly into June's eyes, which she could barely keep on his.

She felt like crying. She could not under any circumstances allow that to happen. "Oh, well, no. I didn't think that." She managed to force the words through her lips. She no longer had any sensation in her arms and legs and her head felt as if it would spin off her body and go into orbit. His green eyes were the most beautiful eyes she had even seen.

"I would still like to get together. I don't know if you have the time. I would understand if you can't."

June heard Michael speaking as if from far away. She felt upset with herself for assuming the worst, and then she felt ashamed and the blushing began again. That made her angry and more embarrassed. She was drowning in a whirlpool of neurosis, standing in a dank laundry room, with the one guy in whom she had been interested in the last five years, as her attentive, too attentive audience.

She choked out, "Please stop."

He looked surprised, and repeated questioningly, "Stop?"

"Yes. Why don't we just make plans for lunch or something right now, forget the whole misunderstanding and move on." She heard the words coming from her as if from a distant land.

Michael's eyebrows raised slightly. "Good idea," he said. "How about later today? I'll come by and get you at your apartment. We can go somewhere nearby. Unless today is no good."

At this point, in her state of near total dissociation, June calmly said, "No, that sounds fine." She put her remaining clothes into her basket, told him her apartment number and said, "I'll see you around noon then?" He nodded and she left, clean clothes in shaking hands. She would have several hours in which to recover. She hoped that would be enough. She felt extremely embarrassed, anxious, shocked, a virtual rainbow of feelings. She could hardly believe that she had basically invited him to lunch, told him what time to pick her up and left the room. And he had agreed. He even seemed relieved. Too bad she was not on any medication. It would have been a good time for a big dose.

June sat in her apartment unable to put away her laundry, much less even gather her thoughts. She stared in shock, at nothing in particular, realizing in a Eureka! kind of way that she had brought this whole messy neurotic reaction of embarrassment on herself. She felt ashamed of her assumption that the greater part of the world in general, and Michael, as a specific example, were selfish, unreliable, uncaring and thoughtless.

She still felt suspicious of him, but determined to stop herself from thinking that way. There had been a logical explanation, and it had sounded painfully sincere. She decided she would always assume there was before assuming anything else. She had to stop thinking that she was inconsequential and worthless, and that there was some other reason for the behavior of others that happened to affect her. She was able to recognize that when she was in session with her patients. She would try, starting then, to look on the brighter side and to think more positively.

What she was thinking seemed corny and stupid, and therefore, she immediately jotted down notes for her book. It could not be a good thing that her brain was thinking in stereotyped one-liners. Even scarier, these ideas were holding powerful meaning for her. They allowed her to hope and gave her the capacity to recover from her state of intense anxiety, deal with the laundry, get herself dressed without too much obsessing, and prepare for her date. Her date! No, she'd think of it as only a lunch with a nice guy. No pressure or expectations.

He showed up on time and seemed pleased to see June. His wavy dark hair was neater than she'd seen previously. Clearly, he'd made some effort to look good. She felt and suppressed an urge to reach her hand up into his hair and mess it up again. Not so much in order to mess it up as to feel it in her hand, between her fingers. He was dressed casually but neatly: a tucked in, short-sleeved, cotton shirt, jeans that fit beautifully, not too old or faded, but also not stiff and brand-new looking, and a clean pair of sneakers. In addition to all of that he still had his sparkling green eyes.

June's attraction to him should have melted her into a puddle on the floor, but he was so kind and gentle and friendly, in such an unassuming way, that instead she felt almost comfortable. She was nervous but not ashamed. She had repeated to herself that there would be nothing to be ashamed of. Maybe he was interested in her, too. Hard to believe, but there he was in her apartment. She had also repeated to herself that he was just a neighbor. It's good to get to know your neighbors. Nothing to be ashamed of.

Luckily, he did most of the talking at first, because June's head was swimming with her self-affirming, anxiety-reducing phrases. She tried to smile, listen and nod without looking like an automaton. She only took in bits of what he was saying. After they rode down the elevator and walked out into what was thankfully now sunlight, June began to relax a little and actually hear what he was saying.

"...Valentine. She thinks she's a movie star, but I guess she does have mobs of fans. We'd get out of the car and people would run up waving her book at her. She loved it. We were late for every reading and every appearance. I began to think that was how she wanted it. And she saw me as her servant. Very demanding and rude. But no matter what I did for her it wasn't quite right. She took out all of her frustration on me. If she weren't the company's hot seller right now, my life would be a lot easier."

He continued to talk of the promotional tour he'd returned from a month earlier, relaying awkward moments and mix-ups with the author and her fans. He spoke well, had a good sense of humor and made June laugh.

They walked into a little, casual lunch place a block from their building, and found a booth near the back. The place wasn't crowded and looked pretty clean. June was in heaven, except for the nagging concern about what would happen when it was her turn to talk. What could she tell him that would not be utterly boring?

She picked up the great big plastic-coated menu and briefly blocked her view of him, hoping something would jump out of it that she could order, eat a little of, and not get caught in her teeth or drop on herself. She had read somewhere that spaghetti with tomato sauce on a first date was the worst possible selection. But avoiding tomato sauce seemed like an obvious thing to do. And this was not a date. She felt the need for more guidance. She couldn't ask Michael what he was ordering. She would seem so wishy-washy. She couldn't take too long to decide either, or the silence would become uncomfortable. Not egg salad, nothing with spinach, no sauces, nothing requiring coordination. She wished she could just get a soda with a straw and a lid, and not order food.

June was mid-dilemma when the waitress came by. She heard Michael order a sandwich and a soda. She heard herself order a salad, dressing on the side, and a soda. That sounded pretty good. Too bad she felt so detached from it. They had an awkward moment when the menus were removed since they had formed a temporary boundary between them. "I've been doing a lot of talking," Michael said, looking chagrinned. I tend to do that when I'm nervous, I guess. I'm sorry. I don't want you to think I'm some nonstop talking, ego maniac or something."

June smiled. "That's exactly what I was thinking."

"You must get that a lot, being a psychologist." June looked at him blankly. He continued, "People thinking that you might see something in them that you don't like, that maybe they don't even know is there." As she continued to stare at him, he added, "Is that crediting you with just a little more magical power than you have?"

"If you only knew the bureaucratic red tape I have to go through in order to access my magical powers, you'd realize that you are perfectly safe."

"You just want to disarm me, so you can catch me off guard."

"I don't use my magical powers unless someone is paying me for it. So, you don't have to worry. My tremendously incisive, analytical powers are turned off at this time. It's safe to proceed."

"But they could kick back in at any time?"

"Well, of course." June listened to herself, shocked that she was actually pretty amusing. She had no idea what would come flying out of her mouth next.

He seemed legitimately interested in her career and what little stories she managed to muster up. She ate some of the salad without incident and watched him eat his sandwich. She laughed because he was funny. He laughed when she tried to be funny. It felt to June like they were old college friends, except for her nagging guilt about Phil and her nagging attraction to Michael that felt like the Earth's gravitational pull. He insisted on paying, which made it all the more like a date for her.

After lunch they walked around the neighborhood a little, talking about various stores and restaurants. Because they walked right by it, June pointed out her favorite earring store to Michael, who had never been inside it. She didn't tell him that she went in there for little rewards when she felt down and hopeless. She thought she would save that for never. The weather was perfect. June felt like she was in a dream, from which she would give her all not to awaken.

Michael did finally say that he had work he had to do and needed to get back. June was hurt, grateful, relieved, overwhelmed, and basically needed to go home, unscrew her head, and relieve some of the pressure. She knew that once she was alone, she'd think over every moment, analyze it, obsess over it, and worry about what would happen next. She needed a lot of time to do all of that.

He was so easy to be with, which said a whole lot coming from June. She wasn't even comfortable alone with herself, not to mention other people. They had an immediate rapport. Now she understood what people meant when they talked about chemistry. She'd never felt it before. They had a definite connection. He felt familiar and necessary to her. She physically ached, wondering if he felt it too.

When he dropped her off, he said, "I'll talk to you soon."

For those who have thoughts that spiral out of control, intrude at inappropriate times and feel burdensome, thought stopping is the interventional tool of choice. As the patient first notices the intrusive thought, he is instructed to shout "Stop!" internally. The patient is instructed to then replace the negative or anxious thought with a positive or calming thought. This process requires practice, both in halting the negative, intrusive thoughts and in making the successful positive replacement.

June told Michael that she had a great time. She made sure to smile. She had a sudden urge to give him a big hug. She didn't. They stood awkwardly for a moment and then he waved and turned to head up the stairs to his place. She felt like crying suddenly and got inside her place and shut the door as quickly as she could. After about twenty minutes of obsessing over it, she decided that a big hug after lunch on a casual first date would have been inappropriate. She felt proud of herself for that. Normally, she would have obsessed over something like that for entire days. Her comfort was that if she had taken the risk and gone for the hug, she would have had plenty more to mull over afterward. She would have felt much more vulnerable. If he knew how she felt, he could have taken advantage of her that much more easily. Or rejected her, knowing how badly she would feel. Or he could think she was some needy nut case, hugging him midday after a first lunch together. So, ultimately, and after much deliberation, June concluded that she had made the right choice.

She'd managed to tell him that she'd had a great time. She worried and picked that one apart. Was she too eager, too revealing? Should she have been cooler, more aloof? She could not judge her behavior properly. Life would have been much easier if she could have shut off her brain at times. Or at least turned down the volume.

She noticed the light flashing on her office line answering machine after about a half an hour. Reluctantly, she played back an hysterical message from Annabelle, begging her to call. June was forced to escape from the prison of her own creation, and to enter Annabelle's for a while.

She tearfully informed June that she was now more depressed than ever before, though June found that hard to imagine. The man she had been somewhat involved with, but thought she was thoroughly involved with, had ended it, claiming to be going back to his wife to try again for real this time. But he said he would always have a warm spot in his heart for his little Annabelle.

She screamed into the phone, and therefore June's ear. "I want to kill him. He's an asshole. He used me. Fuck him. I wish he would die." Then she caught her breath and began loudly wailing. "Why doesn't he love me? I am not lovable. No one will ever love me. I will always be alone. I should just end it now." Then there was more crying and cursing over the phone line. After she began to calm down, and was again able to speak, she informed June that she had broken a vase and two dishes already.

June forced herself, painfully, to sympathize. She attempted supportive comments and offered her an appointment time earlier in the week. She told Annabelle that she thought it would take time to get over him but that she would and could, and might even look back on the whole relationship from a different perspective. He didn't deserve her grief. He'd never cared enough for her. June told her that she had confidence that she would get past this, and she promised to help. As she spoke, Annabelle seemed to calm down some and she thanked June. She also eagerly agreed to the earlier appointment time. They hung up and June realized that she was speaking from her own experience. She saw Phil as a mistake from which she was glad to be extricating herself. She had found it difficult to tolerate Annabelle's pain, though. And was relieved that she had not kept her on the phone for as long as she had with other crises.

The call had interrupted June's obsessive thoughts, and though it was a disturbing interruption on the whole, it seemed to drain the energy out of her own self-torture. And it put Phil into her mind. This brought her back down to earth quickly.

> *Rebound can be seen as the narcissistic replacement of the lost object. The extent to which fantasy plays a role in the new relationship, and reality takes a secondary role, results in the large number of relationship failures that tend to occur. When a love object is lost, the narcissistic injury and primitive longing felt can interfere with the ego's ability to test reality adequately. The replacement object is viewed as better than the lost object, idealized, to compensate for the pain of the loss.*

April first was approaching. It was less than a month away and June had forgotten to have the countdown she had imagined would traumatize her every day. Her natural tendency was to deal with things ahead of schedule, and it looked like that had happened here. She'd also received some unexpected assistance from a very nice guy she had met in the laundry room. He helped her break free. She should have just been grateful, even if she never heard from him again.

She didn't hear from him on Sunday. She didn't expect to. But she hoped he might call, although she couldn't think for what reason. If he had, she would have been at a loss for words. Unless he had a specific reason to call, it would have been an awkward conversation in which she would have struggled to find something interesting to say while attempting to hide her intense anxiety and excitement at his having called. The thought of it alone was exhausting. Unfortunately, despite June's attempts to argue logically with herself, she couldn't bring herself to leave her apartment all day Sunday on the off chance that he would call. She couldn't get herself out of orbit around the strong pull emanating from the telephone. As the days passed, though, the gravity weakened. She told herself that Michael was a busy guy. He had seemed to have a good time on the date. He'd told her he would speak to her soon. She tried not to think about it.

Two weeks later, it was a typical Monday morning and June was back to work after another quiet, disappointing weekend in which she hadn't heard from Michael. She had a full day, with Annabelle in the mix. She felt distracted in her sessions, and kept having trouble snapping out of it. She would try to bring herself back to reality with thoughts like, "You are making too much of this, you idiot. He may never call you again. Why should he? You're crazy. Or maybe he's traveling again for several weeks and didn't bother to tell you. Calm down; he's not the only guy in the world." These words of wisdom were disregarded and could barely be heard over June's loud and rapidly beating heart. She only wanted to hear his lovely, charming voice, look at his sparkling green eyes and wavy brown hair. Her diagnosis: infatuation, severe and intractable. She couldn't cut through the thick fantasy swirling in her head.

The phone rang late Monday night. June had been in a dreamy fog, and the ringing shook her out of it. She tripped over herself to get it. And then it was just Phil. He seemed irritated with her. June noticed that tone in his voice, as she tried to hide her own disappointed tone. Normally, his ire would have had the power to bring on a panic attack in her. Instead, she felt her own irritation rise up and slap his in the face. She tried to hide it, and calmed her voice to ask what was wrong.

He replied, clearly speaking down to her. "Oh, nothing."

June chose to play along. "That's good." She was not especially interested in Phil and his feelings, or even her feelings about Phil. There was a silent pause. But it didn't last long.

"It's just that I didn't hear from you all weekend." He accused her. "I was concerned that something might have happened to you."

June was floored. She hadn't called him and hadn't even realized it. She couldn't stop a tiny sarcastic laugh from emerging. "That's funny. You didn't call me, either. If you were so concerned about me, why didn't you call, or run over and bang on my door?" She had a sudden clarity of thought. It occurred to her that Phil was behaving a little like her mother on a bad day. Control and accusations of guilt from him in an attempt to create shame and remorse in her as well as passive compliance with whatever he wanted.

Ignoring her comment, Phil stated, like a lawyer finishing up his closing statement, "You have called me every weekend for years now. Suddenly you stopped. What is going on?"

"I guess I stopped." He was correct. It was shocking, actually. Whether or not they had made plans, she'd called him every weekend. She'd been afraid not to call for fear that she'd learn that he wouldn't bother to call her. It had turned out to be true. For the first time since she'd met him, she'd forgotten to call. And he'd waited until Monday night to call her in irritation. Her fears had been well founded. He would be so rigid that even if he were concerned about her, he wouldn't spontaneously step out of his rules and regulations to save her life, so to speak. June felt like someone had just knocked the wind out of her. This is what she'd spent five years waiting for?

Particularly in men, low self-esteem can be revealed by a pattern of over-compensation, in the form of excessive pride and confidence. As with the reaction formation defense, excessive confidence can disguise and compensate for the extreme lack of confidence, forcing the negative feelings into the unconscious. The over-confident person may be unaware of his underlying lack of confidence.

There they were on the phone, Phil triumphant in his argument, and June shocked to learn once again how shaky the foundation of their relationship had been. She still had to give Phil some sort of explanation. She knew the lack of her call this weekend had meant a great deal to him. She gently said, "I've had a lot on my mind lately, and I truly forgot to call you. Sorry." She didn't know why she said that, but there it was. She chose not to make waves just then. Chicken.

She wasn't sorry at all. She would never call him again on a weekend. But she was afraid to confront him with that. She wanted him to quietly fade away.

"Well," he sniped. "You're the psychologist. All accidents have underlying meaning. So, why did you forget, Doctor Freud?" The word doctor was said as though June, and Freud, were offensive, small rodents.

Phil had never believed her when she had tried to explain Freud's theory of parapraxis to him - that there is a deeper meaning to slips of the tongue, or forgetting a name, or even, in this case, forgetting to make a phone call. But with the chance to use her own words against her, he didn't hesitate.

"I suppose I have to interpret it as my not wanting to call you, at an unconscious level, of course. Perhaps there is some unexplored anger that has revealed itself in this inconvenient way."

There was a long silence after she spoke. It crossed her mind that she could have just said he was right as usual and not pushed his face in it so hard.

"You must be joking. What do you have to be angry with me about? I have been utterly honest with you all along. And, if you were angry with me, why not just tell me, rather than play childish games with the telephone. Of course, this is exactly what you were doing. I have always told you exactly how I feel. I expect you to do the same. Don't test me to see if I'll notice. That should be beneath you."

People who tend to be exceptionally good at care-giving, who help others in need, often unknowingly hide a hidden layer of suppressed resentment, disappointment and frustration beneath a thick veneer of caring. These are compensated for by their acts of kindness. Their solution is to give to others as they wish they could have someone else give to them. Then they can have the vicarious enjoyment of needs being met, as well as feel good about their own generosity, while maintaining some control over their own unacceptable feelings.

June could see that there would be no way out of this and certainly no way to win, or even make her point satisfactorily because Phil would never allow himself to lose. He didn't realize he had already lost everything. June had struggled with him in conversations for years, trying to put forth her expectations, her rights in a relationship, only to be informed that his rights, rules and limits were always supreme. He was so convincing that for years she'd felt that she was demanding, selfish, and overly needy. He was always more logical, more sensible, and more right. And certainly more calm. That would not change now, in his mind, no matter what she said. And she was tired of these futile arguments.

"Phil, I must not be as mature as you are. I don't always know my feelings as clearly as you seem to. Nor can I always convey them to you in logical little sound bites. Please excuse me for having caused you any moments of mild concern over my wellbeing. You shouldn't have to be bothered by this kind of thing. It has never been part of our relationship. And I do not intend to cause you to begin to worry about me now that our relationship is all but over. I need to write notes and do some chores tonight, so I can't stay on the phone."

June couldn't believe what just came out of her mouth. There was a long silence. Had she left him speechless? It suddenly hit her that he hadn't actually believed her six month deadline. And, as she hadn't mentioned it lately, he'd either forgotten about it or assumed she couldn't go through with it and the matter was moot. He'd seen it as another stupid little game that she was playing. Not worth mentioning. He hadn't expected her to say what she'd said. In all of their previous conversations of this nature, she'd always been contrite and nervous and not at all sarcastic.

"I am not sure that I understand what you are saying, June," Phil finally faltered. "You do seem tired and overworked. Perhaps before either of us says anything we may regret, we should plan to meet in person, after we are well rested, and then talk further."

June wanted to say, "No way. It's finally over. Goodbye." But she couldn't bring herself to do that to him. She didn't really want to hurt him. They set their date for the upcoming Friday night for dinner at their usual place, which she had believed would always be their favorite.

Or maybe it was just his favorite place. More and more June was noticing how she'd followed his lead in so many ways. He seemed as though he had so much self-esteem that anyone who really wanted to get to know him could do the hard work of getting to the interior of that perfectly reasonable and naturally handsome outward appearance. He was worth knowing, from his perspective, so others could do the work. His views were so logical that his preferences or decisions should be followed by all. It was always a poor reflection on you if you dared to reveal that you disagreed with Phil.

June began to believe that Phil's self-esteem might not have been so amazingly healthy. He was opinionated and rigid and compulsive. Maybe he was actually anxious and unsure of himself and hiding behind appearances, too. He seemed so shut down most of the time. His affection for her was controlled and limited. For so long, she'd been grateful for any of his attention, and so flattered by it, that she had no way to judge that it was inadequate. What did she have to compare it to?

It was Wednesday late afternoon when June came home to a message from Michael. The world transformed from black and white to intense Technicolor hues as soon as she heard his voice. He called to ask if she would be interested in attending a book party on Friday night. An author whose book he had edited was celebrating its publication. The call seemed so friendly and casual. June wanted to hug the phone and scream. He ended the call with, "Give me a call and let me know." And he left his phone number on her machine. She grabbed the phone. But put it down again so she could stop shaking, take in some oxygen, and plan out what to say.

He called! June knew she would tell him that she would love to go. Or should she ask what the book is about, so she could read up on the subject area? "How-to" books were his field. How to what? What would she wear to this thing? Would it look desperate to call him right back? He was giving her only two days notice. Maybe she should say she's busy. She couldn't possibly do that. She wanted to go.

She looked down at her date book to check the date, and there she had written, "Dinner with Phil." She had completely forgotten. She would have to lie to Phil. That was a terrifying thought. He'd know that she was on a date with someone else. She couldn't let him know that.

June decided quickly, desperately, to lie to Phil. She would tell him that she'd forgotten about a Society meeting and ask if he could change their dinner to Saturday night. Would he even know that she hadn't been attending the monthly Psychology Society meetings for nearly a year now, ever since a crazy, trendy-therapy promoter had become the president? The meetings had become unbearable, even if it was one of her few opportunities to socialize a little.

June was not a liar by nature. She realized that many people would find this lie to be a tiny, mild, acceptable one that served the purpose of preserving feelings while allowing her to do exactly what she was burning to do. But it was so much more. It was obvious to June that Michael was winning by a landslide and Phil was stuck in the starting gate.

She called Michael first and to her relief, got his answering machine. She said that she would love to go and would he call her back to tell her what time to be ready, and how to dress for a book party as she had never been to one before.

The next call would be far more challenging and anxiety-provoking. She had Phil's work number. She would have to talk to him.

When June heard Phil's voice on the phone, she suppressed a feeling of revulsion. He sounded surprised to hear from her and immediately asked what was wrong. She began to say that nothing was wrong, but he interrupted her in an irritable voice. "We're seeing each other on Friday, so I'm surprised that you'd interrupt me in the middle of my work day rather than wait until Friday. You must have something important to say."

He spoke in a forceful, logical way that June was beginning to realize was also nervous. He sounded puzzled but not really angry. That voice had always felt so rejecting to June, like she was a little child and he was her impatient father. After five years of dating, he should be happy to talk to her on an unplanned occasion. She wanted to say, "Never mind" and hang up. But those five years also told her that this wasn't about her. It was about Phil and his work compulsions. He hated to be interrupted.

So she just jumped in. She told him her little lie. It was much easier to do than she had expected. She heard herself ask if they could switch to Saturday, although she wished she hadn't. She could have just cancelled without rescheduling.

He silently considered the pros and cons of her request and finally agreed that Saturday would be acceptable. They hung up. June hated him. She wondered why, if he had been free on both Friday and Saturday nights, that he hadn't wanted to see her both nights in the first place.

After a moment or two, she breathed freely. She wouldn't have to think about Phil for a while. She could focus all her thoughts and feelings on Michael. Immediately, the phone rang. She thought it might be Michael. But it could also have been Phil calling back, having figured out that she was lying. Or it could be a telemarketer or June's mother. Sometimes she wished she had Caller ID on her ancient phone.

She reluctantly picked up the phone and said, "Hello."

"Hi, June. I am so glad you can make it on Friday."

June felt relieved, nervous, and unable to breathe or speak. She finally blurted out, "What do I wear? I have never been to anything like this before."

"You'll look great in anything. It's no big deal. Just make sure your underwear is red."

At first she did not understand his comment. She was shocked that he actually mentioned her underwear. "Oh my God, I can't believe you said that!" she practically screamed. Then paused. She had to say something so he'd know she wasn't offended. "All my underwear is red. That should be easy."

"Then you're all set," he laughed.

"No, you have to give me a better idea than that. Do I wear a business suit, all black, a dress? If you don't give me a little more guidance, I'll obsess about this for two days."

He thought for a moment and said, "It's a cocktail party. People dress up a little. But I am not a very formal dresser, and we probably won't want to stay all that long."

"We won't?" June felt a pang of nervousness, like he was about to tell her it would have to be a short and early night.

"No. They're so boring and the hors d'oeuvres are bad. I was hoping we could go long enough for me to make my required appearance, shake the hands that I have to, and then I could take you to dinner."

"Oh. That sounds great." He wanted to be alone with her. Joy and terror.

"Then I'll come by your place at 7 on Friday."

"Great." June didn't want to get off the phone, but it seemed awkward to try to continue a conversation. So they had a moment of silence and then both said goodbye at about the same time and hung up. Her heart was racing. She felt a little dissociated, definitely not enough oxygen making its way to her overwrought brain. He wanted to see her, take her to a party with him, sit with her through dinner. He remembered her red underwear. She found the whole thing so hard to believe. What was wrong with this picture?

June began to wonder if he was a sociopath, that he could see how vulnerable she was. Maybe he just wanted to get her into bed. Why would he show so much interest in her? What about her could have made him so eager to get to know her? He must have wanted to take advantage of her. But he seemed so nice. She could see that if he planned to use and discard her, she would just willingly go with the program, like a lemming off a cliff.

She felt like a teenager trying to pick her outfit. She could not recall the last time she had been so concerned about what to wear. She called Emily in desperation, knowing that if anyone could help, she could. Plus, June had to tell her all about it.

She was only too happy to comply. This sort of thing was her specialty. She arrived an hour after June had put in the call on her hotline, bursting through the door.

"Ok. Let's get a look at that closet and see what we can scrape together. You know I don't have a lot to work with here." She pushed her way through June's little closet. "And I only have an hour. They'll all throw a joint tantrum if I am not back by bedtime. But you know, this is what life is all about." She barreled through hangers drooping with old, drab clothes, pushed and moved things while making comments like, "This has got to go," and recalling certain items from college. She mumbled something about changes in style through the decades.

June watched in awe, fully confident that she would find something. She was a master. In the end she came up with three possible cocktail party outfits. June couldn't have done it herself. She couldn't even recall when or how she'd gotten one of the outfits Emily came up with. The next was a mix-and-match that only Emily could have arranged, given the slim pickings of June's wardrobe. It was in shades of blue. The third was a red dress that she had purchased with her recently, under duress. June had seen no use for it, but Emily had insisted that having a little red dress in her closet would come in handy as she was attempting to change her life. June would have chosen black, but Emily wouldn't let her. As it turned out, June already had a little black dress. That was the first of the three choices.

She modeled all three and obsessed over each, although she knew immediately, as soon as Emily had pulled it out, that she would wear the red dress. She had felt a wave of destiny, or karma or something.

The second outfit was a skirt and top set from opposite ends of the closet, never having met before, and not having seen the light of day for years. June made a mental note to wear it on some other occasion, and tried it on. But there was no contest. She also needed Emily to help her accessorize, so she tried to rush it along, and put the red dress back on.

"You look great!"

June looked in the mirror. She did look good. She wasn't sure how it happened.

"You're glad I made you buy that."

"I am. You are a shopping goddess. I will never doubt you again. Now, help me pick out shoes and jewelry."

"That's why I ran over here. You can't be trusted to do this on your own."

Ignoring the insulting but true comment, June asked, "How should I do my hair?" It was a little like getting ready for the prom.

Emily meticulously went through all of her things and came up with everything she needed. As she did, June told her a little about Michael. She didn't want to say too much and Emily was kind enough not to push. She interrupted June only to make her try on shoes or a necklace. They decided to go without jewelry, but put her hair up a little. Somehow they got it all done and June sent her on her way with a little time to spare before her kids' bedtime. Once again, June felt grateful to have her in her life.

> *In helping the patient to recognize her own role in her repeated relationship failures, the therapist must gently build the case for repetition compulsion. The patient begins to see a pattern of similar occurrences, men with similar characteristics, the same feelings arising. She plays a complex role involving her choice of partner, overly eager attitude, ignoring problem signs, and clinging to a fantasy of the relationship, rather than seeing the relationship for what it is in reality. The patient can then begin to do the work of understanding why she would need to sabotage her own happiness. This is no easy task.*

That Thursday, June was aware that Annabelle's appointment was scheduled to be the last appointment before she was to leave to do an in-service at a social service agency with the staff there, on group process. For Annabelle, it was her typical midday time, convenient for her because she worked a half day. June, however, was concerned because she had trouble getting her out of the office on time. June had recently become tired of the way she constantly tested her limits. She was tired of her tirades and tantrums. They all made June wonder why she did what she did for a living. Who would choose to be alone in a room with someone having an angry tantrum? She obviously needed to address this issue with Annabelle. The fact that she hadn't was a reflection of her own issues with confrontation. She knew she needed to do it, but confronting her was one of the least pleasant parts of her job. So she delayed, hoping the problem would just disappear.

June had a responsibility to treat Annabelle, part of which entailed helping her to see where her behavior was out of control, inappropriate, destructive, or self-destructive. And she had to help her see what responses she brought up in others, including June. In thinking over her strategy, June began to realize how little she actually had to lose. If Annabelle left treatment as a result of her limit setting, June would feel bad, but it might be a bit of a relief. She was having a difficult time bearing her grief and despair week after week lately. She realized that she was eager to move away from those feelings and get on with her own life. Annabelle seemed so painfully trapped in it all with no relief in sight. It was hard for June to tolerate. Plus, she knew she felt over-identified with Annabelle.

June's needs had to be set aside so she could help Annabelle with hers. Perhaps her increased negative acting out was in direct response to her sensing June's impatience and detachment from her in their sessions.

June felt relieved that she had taken a moment to think about it. It would definitely be helpful in their work.

Somehow, June managed to get through her day and to arrive home where she could safely and peacefully obsess over her preparation for the next evening. She felt a sudden, dangerous urge to call her mother. She stopped herself. She knew full well from plenty of experience that it would be nothing but disappointing. On those rare occasions when she actually felt good, she found herself mysteriously longing to share it with her mother. Of course, she must have actually meant her fantasy of a terrific mother. When she did go against her better judgment, the phone call often ended with her feeling completely deflated and saying to herself, "I told you so."

Maybe she needed deflating. She held off for a while, but finally gave in to her irresistible urge.

"June, dear."

Her mother was always happy to hear from her initially. She asked what was new, as always. Usually, June had nothing to report, and her mother would get bored quickly.

But she reported that she had a date with someone new. This bit of information held her attention, as June knew it would. She wanted details. Suddenly, mid-sentence, she realized that she'd called her because she still longed for her approval. June felt disgusted with herself.

June reported that he lived in her building and was a book editor. To her mother, this only meant a loser with not much financial future. That was about it for her. She lost interest. Her mother knew nothing really about what would potentially make June happy. To her own surprise, June hardly cared. Her quick dismissal did not have the usual sobering effect on her. When she began to ask questions about Phil and report on his financial prospects and what a nice guy he was, June felt all the more ridiculous for having called her.

June thanked her for her concern and said something about keeping her updated. She got off the phone quickly with a work excuse. She could tell that her mother was dissatisfied. She hadn't torn June down.

June worked as usual on Friday, although she had some dead time and some cancellations. She felt distracted and nervous, just counting the hours until she could go home and get ready. She tried to make herself feel more realistically about the date, but she couldn't get her feet to stay on the ground.

Finally, by 3:30 p.m., after an hour with nothing to do but drive herself up the wall, she'd gotten herself stirred up into a major frenzy. She called Michael at work. She was terrified doing it. Her hands shook, her heart beat so hard that her body shook and she could barely punch in the numbers on the phone. But she had to do it. She decided to get it over with. Let him cancel now rather than after she got home that evening.

As June hit the numbers she was overcome with doubts. What if he resented her call, or actually had planned to call her to cancel, or had not planned to but then decided to when he heard her sounding so excessively nervous? The phone rang twice. She almost hung up, but knew she would only end up calling back and looking like a loser when he guessed she had hung up the first time.

Michael answered the phone. June was shocked. She had no idea what she had been expecting. She forced herself to speak, "Uh, hi, Michael?"

He said, "Yes," obviously not yet recognizing her voice.

June remembered her name, "Hi, this is June. I, uh..." She was a blank. She couldn't remember why she'd called.

"Oh, I'm glad you called," he cut in, sounding upbeat. "I've been wanting to call you all day, but I didn't want to seem neurotic to a psychologist." He paused. June laughed. Then he added, "Unless something is wrong and you're calling to cancel."

June heard herself answering him, "No, I'm not." She felt embarrassed. Why was she calling him? Who made that decision? She heard herself add, "I'm calling because I'm nervous, a neurotic psychologist actually, and I wanted...I am actually not sure why I'm calling." They both laughed.

They talked briefly about how their days had been so far, and he reiterated at what time he would come by her place to pick her up and they got off the phone pretty quickly. He did still want to see her. As a matter of fact, he was eager to see her and nervous about their date, too. She felt excited and impatient. The rest of the day dragged on like never before.

Finally, she left her office and drove home. She had two hours to get ready. It seemed like too little and too much at once. She hadn't felt so happy in years. It was a scary feeling. Too good to be true. Was she actually ready to get involved with someone who showed interest in her? Would she need to run screaming, or sabotage it in some way, or learn to her dismay that she had unknowingly sabotaged it? Or perhaps she wasn't seeing something glaringly wrong with him that she would eventually recognize and feel like an idiot for having overlooked.

Why had she spent the last five years with someone as unbelievably unavailable as Phil? She'd kept hoping for more, but all the red flags were there, waving in the breeze. Five years was much too long for the obvious to sink in. Maybe she was comfortable with the distance. By the end she was most certainly depressed and frustrated. But for quite a while, she'd put up with it. Did that mean she sought it out, and would again, in the typical repetition compulsion, straight out of Freud?

Did June analyze things until she no longer knew who she was? Of course she did. That was what she did best. She was a psychologist. It suddenly occurred to her to call her old therapist and ask for a few adjustment sessions, just on the off chance that it might prevent any unconscious sabotaging she might try. She planned to call first thing in the morning. She no longer had to worry about it. She could not imagine that it would require a whole lot of therapy, just a small refresher. First time in a relationship that actually may have potential. Needed to know how not to completely destroy it. Yep. That sounded like six to ten sessions. At least it would to her insurance company. She wondered if she could still get the reduced fee she had gotten as a student. Fat chance.

June dressed and attempted make-up and hair style. Pretty good. When she looked in the mirror, she actually saw a happy, glowing, eager face that looked more attractive than she had remembered. As she was giving up on perfection and determining to walk away from the mirror, her doorbell rang. For an instant, she saw a look of horror on her face in the mirror. She felt her heart stop. She felt weak in the legs and lightheaded. Could she make it to the door?

She finally did, and there he was looking at her. They both stood staring into one another's eyes for a moment. June knew that this was the man she'd been longing for, probably since puberty. As they stared, it seemed that they made a quick non-verbal acknowledgment of what seemed so obvious: they were meant for each other.

It felt like time had stopped. June wanted to leap into his arms and kiss him. Instead, she choked out, "Hello. Why don't you come in?" And he did.

He smiled and said, "You look stunning. You look great in red."

She returned the smile. "Thank you." And then she couldn't help herself from blushing, thinking about her red underwear and how silly and exciting the whole red thing was.

He seemed to notice her face change and must have realized what she was thinking. He said, "I'm glad the shirt in the wash wasn't brown or green." They both smiled more.

As they left the building, they waved to the doorman who winked back. It was a silly little thing, but June felt as though the doorman, and perhaps the entire world, the stars and sun, the whole universe was approving and smiling and winking at them.

Michael put his arm gently around her as they walked down the street. It was a simple, sweet thing to do. It overwhelmed her. She had always wished that someone would want to be close to her, that it wouldn't be awkward, self-conscious or forced. This was so natural that it shocked her. They were only a few blocks from the cocktail party. She luxuriated in the closeness. His aftershave smelled unbelievable. She felt so completely happy, safe, and comfortable, as if she were learning for the first time what it meant to be held. She would have been happy to keep on walking for hours.

They stopped at a corner and waited for a light. He looked down at her and asked, "Is it ok that I have my arm around you?"

"I love it." June immediately felt embarrassed for having blurted that out with such forcefulness. And she used the word 'love' with a guy she hardly knew. Was she trying to scare him off? How vulnerable did she plan to make herself? Why didn't she just reveal how clingy and eager and deprived she truly felt, while she was at it? Then she could watch as he turned and ran away at top speed before the end of the evening. She felt so foolish. There was nothing she could do. She was literally dumb. They had a few moments of silence, and then crossed the street.

Michael broke the silence. "I need to warn you: I'm not very good with names. And it is going to be especially hard for me to remember anyone's name or even care who they are when I am standing next to you."

June couldn't believe what she was hearing. Was she being manipulated somehow? She couldn't handle the compliments. "I don't remember names very well, either." Her head was spinning. How could she be more interesting than his work? This was shocking. How could he be so attracted to her? She couldn't imagine that the person she had been looking at in the mirror earlier warranted all of these compliments. His attraction was shocking. How gloriously, wonderful it felt to have his arm around her was shocking. Would she actually survive the evening?

They reached the entrance to the building. Michael stopped and faced her. He took her by the hands, looked her in the eye and said, "Am I making you uncomfortable, by saying so much? I often speak before I think. I don't mean to overwhelm you. You look a little overwhelmed. I don't want to scare you away. Just tell me to back off."

"No. I'm fine. I'm, uh, not used to anyone complimenting me, I guess."

"I can't believe that."

"God's honest truth."

"Well, if you want to know what I'm thinking, it's that you must be formulating a diagnosis for me based on my behavior. Can you tell I feel a little intimidated being on a date with a psychologist?"

All June heard was 'a date!' "You have nothing to worry about."

"I'll wait till I've read the clinical report you've written before I believe that."

June couldn't help smiling. "I'll have it to you in two weeks. Things are backed up at work."

"That's what everyone is always saying to me. Could we possibly make it a priority?"

"Well, there's a big report due before that one."

"Oh really? Who are you evaluating?"

"I'll be judging and second guessing myself. Psychologists are just as neurotic as everyone else, if not more so."

Michael said with relief, "Thank God for that." They both laughed. And then they were staring at one another again. It was the strangest feeling, a magnetic attraction, but at the same time a sense of mutual understanding, as though they knew a lot more about each other than they actually did.

They finally got onto the elevator. June felt a little dissociated, like she was moving in a dream, or on the moon, gently floating. She was blown away by Michael's expression of feeling, by her own feelings, by suddenly arriving at a cocktail party and having everyone know Michael and seem glad to see him and have him actually capably introduce her to an array of faces, outfits, and hairstyles. They all saw her as his date. She kept trying to wrap her mind around that idea.

June gulped down a glass of wine that she somehow found she had been holding. She couldn't remember anyone's name or face except the author for whom the cocktail party was being held. Despite her whirling head, meeting him had impressed her. Jonathan Price was a lanky, arty looking man in his fifties, with silvery hair, a narrow face and an intense look. While still feeling oddly separated from herself, June found that she was asking him a series of questions about writing. As he was a writer of 'how-to books," he seemed glad to answer. She asked him how much time he spent writing and what time of day he did his best writing. She asked if he worried about offending anyone with his ideas, or revealing too much personal information. And, aware that Michael was his editor, she asked what it was like to work with an editor. His answers were not unusual, and he raved about working with Michael. Finally, he asked June if she had an interest in writing, since she'd asked him so many questions. She felt unsure what to say.

She said that she was a psychologist in private practice, and started to digress about health care and how it had been going through many changes as a result of managed care. And that mental health care had changed in basic fundamental ways as a result of managed care. She went on about ethics and confidentiality and poor treatment. Once June was up on her soap box, it wasn't easy to get her off. Poor Jonathan began to look fidgety as though he regretted asking, and was thinking that he had a lot of other people to meet and hands to shake. It was his night to be celebrated. Perhaps he'd only humored June so long because Michael was his editor and she was the editor's date.

So she wrapped it up and said that she'd been trying to write about how to treat depression given the frustrations of managed care. After a quick and slightly encouraging comment, he managed to escape and move on to bigger and more important contacts.

Michael, who had been nearby, but in and out of conversation with other people, leaned over to June and whispered, "I had no idea that you were a writer. I want to see what you've written."

She'd had no idea that he'd heard any of their conversation. She didn't want to mislead him. She didn't consider herself to be a writer. And she wasn't about to show Michael what she'd written. She felt alarmed. "No. I'm not a writer. It's nothing really. Just something I do to make myself feel better."

"That is what a lot of writing is, among other things." He added, "You don't have to show it to me. But I am an editor; it's what I do for a living."

"We'll see." June smiled. "I'd have to know you a lot better and trust you completely to gently and kindly let me know that my writing isn't very good."

Michael introduced her to more people. They had some bland cheese and crackers and carrot sticks and then he took her hand and said, "It's time to leave."

The next thing June knew, they were on the elevator heading down to the street. She was grateful to be out of there. She looked over at Michael, who was smiling. He said, "You look relieved. Either you are, or I am feeling so relieved that I think you are too."

"We call that projection."

"So, there's a word for everything, huh?"

"Yeah. I do feel relieved. I don't intend to point out my every weakness, but meeting fifty people in an hour is not a task at which I feel very competent."

"I wouldn't expect you to remember any of those people. And right now, I don't care who any of them are. I just want to go get some dinner." The elevator landed and Michael took June's arm and they began walking.

He named an Italian place nearby that she'd never been to, which he'd been told was great. He hadn't been there, either. They agreed to try it. A strange momentary thought sped through June's brain: what if she ran into Phil there? But he was such a creature of habit that this likelihood was miniscule. She felt a bit guilty. But it passed quickly. The restaurant was a few blocks away, and once again, as they walked, Michael put his arm around her. And once again, the world melted away, and June didn't care if they ever made it to a restaurant, or ever ate again, or if Phil were to appear right in front of her on the sidewalk. She had never felt so wonderful.

They arrived at the restaurant. It was a small, low-lit, romantic little place, with candles on the tables and fresh pasta and seafood. They ordered some wine. The food was very good, but June could barely eat. And she broke the pasta and tomato sauce rule. They talked pretty comfortably about many topics, mentioned their families and how neither of them spent much time with theirs. His childhood memories seemed better than June's on the whole, though. But most of his family lived far away.

They avoided certain topics. Michael didn't ask about June's dating or relationship history and she didn't feel comfortable asking about his. June wasn't eager to bring memories of other people into their conversation. She felt relieved about it anyway, not being so eager to talk about Phil. If they were there together, it probably meant that they were free to see one another.

> *Those who did not receive adequate love and positive attention in childhood, dream of finding it forever after. Although many are capable of managing without much care from others, the yearning for the missing love of childhood can be so intense that it leads to feelings of extreme vulnerability. As adults, they may actually find themselves anxious and uncomfortable when that love is finally offered and fear its sudden termination. True caring from another may even bring up sadness that comes with the recognition of what was lacking for so long.*

After dinner they walked all over the city and ended up near the river. They stopped to look out over the water and Michael turned to face June. He looked into her eyes and whispered, "You are so beautiful." Leaning forward, he put his hands on her shoulders and kissed her on the lips. His lips felt so soft, and the kiss so gentle, that June thought she might faint. Afterward, he stepped back a little and she watched as his eyes searched her face. He asked, "Was that all right? I should have asked you first."

"It was very nice," June said, a little embarrassed to be assessing the kiss. She was reeling from it, as it had somehow taken over her entire body.

"I'm glad. That was our first kiss. We'll always remember that we had our first kiss here, looking out over the water, on this night."

It seemed as if Michael believed that they would be old together, reminiscing back about their first kiss. Everything would have been wonderful, except for that persistent voice in June's head. The voice of the psychologist, the character assessor, who kept doubting. Why had that damn voice been so quiet all those years with Phil? She wanted to relax. She wanted to enjoy the moment and the man before her, and not have a running commentary in her head, as if she were at a baseball game.

June felt a strange combination of ecstasy and anxiety, longing and detachment. They began to walk back to their building. He had put his arm around her again. She was shivering a little because it had gotten cooler as the night had progressed.

He gave her a squeeze and said, "You're shivering. We had better get you home." June felt a plunge of disappointment, and then shock at how disappointed she felt. What had she been expecting? She didn't want him to drop her off. She wanted the evening to go on forever. She was afraid that if they parted ways, the fairytale would end. The spell would wear off.

As they entered the building June heard herself say, to her horror, "You aren't just going to drop me off, are you?"

Michael looked surprised and said, "I was hoping you'd want to come over and spend some more time with me. You can leave anytime you want, since we're neighbors."

"Oh good." June couldn't help herself. She laughed. "I guess I'm not ready for the evening to end yet."

"Me neither," he replied.

> *Early on in relationships, there is a tendency toward premature, and therefore, false intimacy. Unconsciously, the partners avoid anxiety through the idealization of one another, and through a belief that they have found something so unusual and special that it defies the normal progression relationships usually follow. Ultimately, if the partners do not gradually get to know one another in more realistic ways, therefore experiencing the anxiety, the relationship will fail.*

His apartment was spare like June's, except that it was larger with better views because it was higher up. The bedroom was actually a separate room, and he had a separate kitchen and living room. The living room had large windows on two sides, and a brown leather couch, some large pillows, a stereo and a television. Something about it felt like Michael--warm and comfortable, not pretentious.

They had some wine, sat down on the couch, and talked. They discussed their careers. He'd never been to a psychologist, or any other kind of therapist and he'd never had much contact with any in his everyday life, although he had known a few people who'd gone to therapists regularly. He had taken some psychology classes in college and had always found the subject interesting. June didn't know many people who had not been to a therapist at least once, outside of her own family. She didn't know how to interpret it. His lack of familiarity with therapy made him seem so well adjusted, or innocent or naive. Or was he denying deep-seated problems? Phil was one of the only other people June knew who'd never been to a therapist, and this was because he strongly believed that they were crackpots. Probably including herself. Did Michael also have that opinion? She felt so eager to avoid disappointment that she couldn't bring herself to ask him.

He talked about how he had become interested in his field. It had started with a love of reading and a college internship. They had an animated conversation. So different from what she'd become used to with Phil over the years. They could have kept talking all night. But they both noticed that they'd become tired, and looking at the clock, saw, to their complete amazement, that it was 4:00 am.

June didn't want to leave, despite having stayed far too long. She looked up at Michael and saw him looking intently at her with his beautiful green eyes shining. He said, "May I kiss you?"

She instantly realized that she'd been waiting for hours for him to kiss her. He put his hand on her hair, and her face. He was so gentle. They were swept away. At some point they stopped for a moment, looked at one another and laughed. And then they were kissing again. Somehow they ended up in his bedroom.

The thought went through June's head that they should not have sex, although she wanted it desperately. She really hardly knew him, although she felt as though she'd known him for years. There was such an intense connection. She spontaneously decided that the very worst thing that could happen would be his dumping her afterward and her becoming angry, depressed, and hopeless. She'd already been down that road. She'd survived it before. But at that moment she couldn't believe that he would ever hurt her.

Would he think she was cheap, or desperate? Did most of the girls he dated get in bed with him on the second date? Was that how he operated? Why would he think she'd just agree to it? She knew it was a very bad idea. She had warned patients against getting sexually involved too quickly. She knew it could only lead to hurt and pain.

However, she was so infatuated that she didn't think that she could have stopped even if she'd chosen to. It felt too good. So emotional and passionate. His body was warm and soft and muscular. He was so gentle and considerate with her. She had never experienced such caring during love-making before. She didn't know that it could be as wonderful as this. Afterward, he held her and they both fell asleep.

June awoke in early morning light, Michael's arm still around her. He slept so peacefully. She had her opportunity to look at him closely. Objectively speaking, he was probably not everyone's idea of the most handsome man. His face was angular, with a somewhat large nose, and looked so kind and patient. His hair was dark and a little wavy, and looked adorably messy to June.

She suddenly felt strange. How had she ended up here? This relationship had progressed at lightning speed. She felt a pang of fear that he might hurt her after all, now that she was in the early light of day.

She strained to look over at Michael's digital clock, trying not to wake him. It was just after 8:00 am. She had probably had three hours of sleep. No wonder she felt shaky. She couldn't go back to sleep. But she was afraid to move for fear of waking Michael. She looked at him again. He still looked absolutely beautiful.

She needed to use the bathroom. She got up very slowly and gently and tiptoed to the bathroom. After using it, she washed up a little. She looked at herself in the mirror over the sink. Not great but not absolutely terrible, either. She opened the medicine cabinet. No secrets to be found.

When she came out wrapped in a bath towel, he was sitting up, in a tee shirt and shorts and smiling at her. "I can't believe that you're here!" He looked so glad to see her. "This is so great. Can I make you breakfast?"

June knew that there was no way that she could eat after three hours of sleep, and she suddenly felt shy. "You don't have to go to any trouble. I can just go back to my place. You must be tired."

He looked disappointed. "You need to try my French toast. It's my specialty. If you really want to go home, how about waiting until after breakfast?"

She felt stuck and uncomfortable. Why would he want her to stay there? Was he feeling obliged to prove that it wasn't a one-night stand? She felt anxiety washing over her and finally said, "Ok." He looked relieved. She gathered up her clothes.

She had no idea of proper etiquette for this kind of situation. Does one stay for breakfast and leave right afterward? How and when would she put on her clothes? She couldn't tell what he actually wanted, and didn't want to disappoint him. This wasn't her typical weekend experience, or typical experience ever. Totally unknown territory. No one had ever wanted to spend this much time with her before.

June looked questioningly at Michael's face for some kind of a sign. "I don't want you to go to any trouble. You must be very tired. I think we got about three hours of sleep." She stepped back into the bathroom, and found his robe hanging on the back of the door, pushed the door mostly closed and quickly dropped the towel and pulled on the robe. She came back out and he was still sitting on the bed. "I could just get dressed and we could have breakfast another time. I don't want you to feel like I'm the date who wouldn't leave." She was feeling extremely self-conscious.

As she spoke, Michael jumped up, threw the comforter back over the bed and straightened up. When she was done speaking, he said, "You look adorable in my robe." As he headed out of the room, leaving her standing awkwardly by his bathroom door, he added, "I would really like you to stay. Please try my French toast."

June was not hungry in the least, but he seemed so eager for her to have breakfast with him. She wasn't eager to go; she just didn't want to out-stay her welcome. She threw her underwear and dress on, stuffed her stockings in her bag next to her shoes, brushed her hair with his brush, hung his robe back on its hook and walked out of his room. She felt ridiculous in her dress.

June walked into the kitchen to find him leaning over a big frying pan, looking too charming for her swirling head. He looked up and laughed, "You really didn't have to get all dressed up for breakfast. I like to keep it informal."

"I was under the impression that you were making French toast, so I got dressed to honor the French and their sense of style." She scrounged up what little wit she could after only a couple of hours of sleep and no coffee.

Michael asked her to watch the toast and to flip them over in a couple of minutes, once they were beginning to brown. Then he was gone, back to his bedroom and she was alone with the French toast. She had never made it before. The toast started to brown, smoke was risking from them. What if she burned the French toast? Would he send her on down to her apartment with no breakfast? Was this some kind of absurd test? She flipped the yellow, soggy looking bread over and waited. She wondered out loud, "What do I do now?"

Just then Michael called in, "Put them on the plates in another two minutes." She stood there feeling odd, wondering if she would ruin breakfast. What would he think of her if she couldn't even make French toast. She wasn't confident that she could judge when they would be ready, although she knew she'd recognize it once they had turned to little burnt, black rocks. Just then they started to smoke again. She quickly began to put them on plates, thinking that if they were undercooked, at least he could put them back in the pan.

As June was struggling to get them out of the frying pan onto plates, Michael walked in, dressed in jeans, cleaned up, shaved, brushed and looking like he had gotten eight solid hours of shut eye. "Perfectly done. You probably make a lot of French toast."

June stared at him. "I have never even eaten French toast before. I don't know what it's supposed to look like. I've just never been much of a breakfast person." She kept thinking: I need a cup of coffee and no food right now in order to prevent collapse.

Michael eyes seemed to light up. "You've never had French toast before in your life? Then I get to introduce you to it."

June felt a little pressure then, when she finally bit into a piece of it. Luckily she did not find it repulsive. It would have been a lot better with coffee, though. While they ate, as he was telling her his recipe, he interrupted himself to ask if she would like to do something that day. He had no plans, but was thinking it might be nice to go to the new contemporary art exhibit at the museum.

June had been eager to see it as well. She agreed to go. She was thinking about how bizarre it was that they were having a marathon of a date. She agreed only on the condition that she could go home briefly, shower, and change her clothes. After insisting that she should just wear the dress, Michael finally agreed that they could meet back at his place in an hour.

> *The rare phenomenon of "folie a deux" is truly fascinating to*
> *observe. Two people, who may each otherwise be relatively high*
> *functioning with regard to reality testing, form a relationship in which*
> *they share a delusion. Each reinforces the other's acceptance of the*
> *delusional beliefs. At times, this can lead to unrealistic or dangerous*
> *behavior patterns, that each alone would never have considered.*

As June entered her apartment, she felt a strange mixture of relief and longing. She'd almost invited him to come down to her place with her, but had quickly judged that to be insane. And she felt that she should have a little time alone, just to get her bearings. Professionally speaking, this was not normal. Despite her ecstatic mood and lack of sleep, she couldn't help but notice that she had gone from a five-year relationship with such measured time together and such limited intimacy to the date that would not end. The danger signs were flashing in red neon. And June just smiled up at them. She liked red.

Despite the addition of a cup of black coffee, she was done a little earlier than they had planned and paced around the apartment impatiently. She found herself opening her front door and heading back up, ten minutes early. She had evidently lost her mind. As she reached his apartment, the door opened and Michael came out. When he saw her he looked surprised. He said, "I was finished early, so I decided that I would head down to your place. I guess you decided the same thing." They smiled at each other and the term "folie a deux" leapt into June's mind.

They headed out into the sunshine, and had a great day at the museum. The exhibit was fascinating. The main artist was one whose work June had never seen before, but who had been in the news lately. The theme of his work in this show was communication difficulties and confusion, a theme that turned out to be meaningful to both of them. The time flew by. By mid-afternoon, they were both completely exhausted. They headed back to their building. As they entered the elevator, Michael looked sleepily at June and said, "At the risk of sounding completely crazy to a psychologist, I was wondering if you would like to come back to my place to take a nap."

A thought flickered through her tired mind that perhaps she had been brainwashed to want to be wherever he was from then on. She must have looked uncomfortable or alarmed because Michael tried to reassure her.

"I would understand if you need some time apart. I just hate to leave you. But I don't want you to feel any pressure. I can wait to see you another time if I have to." Michael gave her a tired but very sweet smile.

She was a lost cause. "There's nothing wrong with an innocent nap, I suppose."

Michael looked happy that she'd agreed to nap with him. Still, in the back of her head, sleep-deprived as she was, thoughts were spinning. Why did he want me to nap with him? Why did he want to be with me at all? What did he see in me? Was something wrong with him? Something major? Was he obsessed? Did I remind him of his mother, or an ex-girlfriend? June didn't know anything about his relationship history. Was she just passively doing everything he suggested because she was so lonely and desperate? Had she lost her sense of self and merged with this relative stranger overnight? Her brain was in a throbbing, murky knot.

June looked up in the elevator to find Michael staring hard at her. He spoke softly, "I have never before spent this much time with someone I've known so briefly. But I don't want our date to end. Does it have to? Is that okay? Should we part ways? Do you think we have a problem, Doctor?"

June smiled. They were so much on the same wavelength, it was frightening. "I have not had an experience such as this before, either, and am therefore, unable to make a determination at this time. Also, I'm so tired I can barely stand up. This exhaustion has impacted my judgment such that I am not confident that any opinion I might currently hold would be valid and reliable."

He stared at her in mock surprise. "You must be a psychologist or something."

"An unbelievably sleepy one."

"At least I feel competent to help alleviate that problem," he replied as they stepped off the elevator onto his floor.

They entered his apartment, kicked off their shoes and made their way over to his bedroom, and fell into bed. June took a brief moment to look around, noticing that she felt both excited and perplexed. She glanced over at Michael before closing her eyes and he appeared to be sound asleep, looking calm and peaceful.

> *The psychoanalyst asks, "What is love?" Is it an attempt to reconstruct the original love object relationship? Is it a repetition compulsion serving the wish to master failure? Is it a longing to bolster a weak sense of self, find a mirror for the ego, meet narcissistic needs? Much has been written, but love remains one of the deepest mysteries of the psyche.*

June awoke disoriented and confused. What day was it? What time was it? Where was she? She even wondered "who am I?" for a moment. It hadn't all been a dream. They'd spent the morning at the art museum, and the night before it together, and the evening before that. She recalled that it was Saturday, guessing that it was late afternoon. She didn't want to wake Michael again, so she didn't move to get a look at the clock. What did it matter, anyway? She closed her eyes again and rested a little more. She kept drifting in and out of sleep for a while longer and finally woke up fully, feeling extremely happy, even giddy. She felt like she finally knew what it was to be in love. In the past, it had never felt so clear. This time the feeling defined itself. How had she gotten so lucky when she had been so unlucky for so long? How could it be that this wonderful guy who she felt so attracted to in every way, seemed to feel the same way about her?

Just then, as if she had spoken her thoughts aloud, hands were gently on her shoulders wrapping themselves around her. June opened her eyes, and saw a smiling Michael moving over to hug her. He said, "Did you sleep well?"

She smiled back and reported, "Very deeply."

"I'm so glad." He leaned toward her and kissed her. She longed for him to hold her and then he was. She wanted his lips on hers, and then they were. Every touch, every caress pulled her in deeper. She wanted him.

They gently removed each other's clothes in bed, laughing when an item was uncooperative. By the time they finally made love, she wanted him so badly she could not have waited another moment. His beautiful, strong, lean body on top of hers, felt like the only thing she'd ever wanted. He kissed her over and over on the lips, neck, and even eyelids, and caressed her hair. She felt ecstatic.

Afterward, they both drifted back to sleep in one another's arms. The last thought June had before she fell asleep was that it felt like she was living someone else's happy life.

June awoke suddenly to the sun setting outside the big window in Michael's bedroom. She must have jumped and looked horrified because she saw him open his eyes, and a look of concern come over his face.

"You look upset about something."

"What time is it?"

He leaned over to the clock, "7:30. Why?"

June didn't respond right away. She was supposed to have dinner with Phil. Normally, she called him on the afternoon of their date to confirm a time and place. She'd completely forgotten. And normally, they'd meet around 7:00 p.m. and it was already past that time. She felt panicky about how to handle it with Phil, and she had to hide that from Michael.

"You look unhappy. What's the matter?" June could feel Michael's concern for her. She hadn't the slightest idea how to explain the mess her life had been before she met him. And of course it still was that mess. How would she tell him she had a date planned with Phil, or even who Phil was? She wished Phil didn't exist, or that she'd been stronger and braver and had totally ended it with him already. She couldn't just lay there panicking, though. Time was passing. She sat up and quickly got herself dressed. She attempted an explanation.

"I totally forgot that I had plans with someone tonight. I was having such a great time with you that I completely forgot."

"Call them. Here." He handed her the phone.

She put it down. "I had better go home and call."

He looked at her for a moment, clearly realizing that it must be a guy. "Okay."

"I want to explain it to you, but I don't have time now. I'm sorry." June faltered. He looked hurt. She could see that he was trying to allow her some privacy and trying not to look hurt. She wanted to tell him she loved him. But it was so extremely too soon in their relationship that she couldn't find anything to say to describe even a little bit of what she felt. She blurted out as she headed for the door, "I had the greatest time ever. I am so sorry to leave, but I have to go."

Michael, who had thrown on his clothes when she did, and had walked her to the door, smiled a little. He replied, "This was the best time ever for me too, and the only marathon date I've ever had. I suppose it had to end at some point." He reached for her hand as she was reaching for the door. June stopped and turned around and he put his arms around her and kissed her on the lips passionately. They could not get enough of each other. She couldn't believe how amazing it felt to kiss him, even then. She didn't want his arms and hands to let go. But they did. He opened the door and said, "I hope I'll see you very soon."

As June walked away, she heard Michael's phone ring. She turned to see him standing in his doorway watching her, and wondered why he hadn't gone to answer the phone. She opened the door to the stairway, and looked back again quickly, to find that he was still standing there with the phone ringing in the background.

> *The fear of causing disappointment and the strong desire to please both come from old object relations in early stages of development. The relationship between these takes on gradually increasing complexity with regard to the control and management of anger. It is crucial to achieve a level of mastery over the conflict between the need for expression of anger and the desire to avoid disappointing another as well as the desire to please and therefore maintain the love of the desired object. If a level of homeostasis is not achieved between these conflicting needs, anxiety will result.*

June ran down the stairs with her head spinning. She didn't have time for the elevator. The closer she got to her apartment, the more her panic increased. She fumbled for her keys and entered her apartment, her eyes immediately zeroing in on the flashing red answering machine light. She punched in Phil's number without bothering to listen to his messages. There were two, and she assumed both were his. When he answered the phone, she blurted out, "I'm sorry, Phil. I have been running late today. Do you still want to meet?"

In his ultra-calm voice he slowly inquired, "Did you get my messages? I have never known you to be late like this."

She explained that she'd rushed in and had not had a chance to listen to them yet. She told Phil that it had been an unusual day. She was wracking her brain to try to come up with a reason for being so late.

"It is nearly 8:00 p.m. You usually call me by 3:00."

He was getting on her nerves with all of his exactness. Did he need to inform her of the obvious? She wanted to scream at him and hang up. So what? Who cares what the pre-approved routine was supposed to be? A tsunami of resentment came over her. Why was she bothering? She'd jumped out of heaven and flung herself down the stairs to make a date, albeit late, with someone who irritated the hell out of her, not to mention she no longer found desirable or interesting. She was feeling mostly repulsed by him. And now he was punishing her with detailed attention to routine and time instead of meeting for the dreaded, damned dinner and letting her get the breakup over with.

He was droning on in his superior monotone about how important it was that they meet that night. He seemed not even to care about why June was so late. She interrupted him, something he usually hated and lectured her about, to get them to the meeting. "Where and when, Phil? Let's get there already, then talk."

"Well, after being so late, you are suddenly in such a hurry." Phil couldn't help himself.

"I'm eager to make up for lost time." An understatement.

He named one of the typical places they had always gone to, with the explanation that he had determined that they could both arrive there in fifteen minutes if they left right away. They hung up their phones. June glanced in the mirror. She looked like she had just had sex and a long nap. She was a mess. She made the decision to stop and brush her hair and wash up, despite the risk of being late that it involved and the possibility of a boring lecture being inflicted upon her.

> *Lying can be seen as an attempt at separation during adolescence. The lie creates a sometimes necessary barrier between parents and teen that reassures the teen that his parents are indeed not omnipotent and that they cannot read his mind. A recapitulation of this can be observed in some adult relationships as well, where fear of intimacy is an issue. When one member of a couple begins an affair, a forced separation occurs because one member in the couple is lying to the other. Getting away with it is an important aspect of the affair, making it at once exciting and also reassuring. The person having the affair is comforted by the knowledge that his partner in the couple is not all-powerful and all-knowing.*

The idea of telling Phil that she'd been ill and had slept through the afternoon occurred to June, although she could have said that on the phone. She could say that she went to the doctor's office and had been delayed there due to the long wait to see the doctor, it being Saturday and all. That probably would have worked. She could then say that the doctor had found nothing wrong or that it might have been food poisoning. But that might have gotten them into a conversation about where and what she had eaten. She felt extremely reluctant to tell Phil anything about her time with Michael. If she said food poisoning, she'd have to hear some judgmental comment about how she never should have ordered whatever she had claimed to have eaten. She decided that simple was best. The doctor found nothing. Possible stomach virus.

June had reached the dreaded destination. There was Phil, waiting for her, apparently controlling his emotions as usual. He took her hand and led her to a table. They sat down, but he wouldn't let go of her hand. This was highly unusual. She managed to yank her hand free. The irony that this was the one time she didn't want her hand held tightly in his was too much. He also had an eager expression on his face that made June feel that she had a brief glimpse of Phil as a child looking to his mother for a sign of approval. He was smiling at her, clearly looking for a return smile from her. She was, at that moment, feeling a little like she had just returned to the North Pole from a long stay on a tropical island. She gave him a flicker of a smile. She felt obliged. Fortunately, that was enough for him. It all came out of his mouth like an avalanche.

"I have been eager for us to meet tonight because I wanted to let you know something that I think will make you very happy." Phil was actually gushing.

It nauseated June.

The idea that he thought that he could make her happy alarmed her. There was nothing he could possibly say to make her happy except that he'd met someone else. She somehow knew he wasn't going to say that. "What?" managed to leave her lips.

"I have given it great thought, and I have determined that we should go into couples therapy as a way to prepare for a future commitment." Encountering her silent stare, Phil added, "I have agreed with your suggestion."

This floored June. She gasped. She had mentioned the idea a year or more before. This was long before the ultimatum. He'd brushed it aside at the time, expressing confidence that if they were meant to stay together, all could be worked out through greater efforts on both their parts, especially hers. She'd felt insulted at the time, seeing his dismissal of the idea as just more evidence of his belief in the total uselessness of her profession. She would have cheered to hear his change of heart a year ago. Now it felt ridiculous. She felt detached and irritated. He wasn't even saying that he could commit to a future with her. Only that he was willing to see a professional to explore if it could be pushed along.

There was no point to this discussion now. June had to get out. She was in love, she felt, with someone else. She had gotten off his bus several stops back and he hadn't even noticed.

He continued eagerly, "I kept the names you gave me when we last discussed it. We could make an appointment for next week. I feel that there are some issues that you and I need to clarify, having to do in particular with dependency needs and expectations on your part, and then I will know better how to proceed. I know that you have been waiting a long time and I do appreciate your patience. To me, commitment is a serious issue, requiring a great deal of thinking. But I want you to know that I am closer to being ready to really commit than ever before. I cannot promise you anything, of course. But I am grateful to you for standing by me. It means a lot to me."

"Listen, Phil," June interjected. "I need to talk to you about something." She had to say it. Her head was going to explode. She was feeling so trapped and couldn't listen to his blather for another minute. She had to find a way to let him know that it was all over. "Of course I do remember suggesting that," she began cautiously, "but that was at least a year ago. I don't think it's a very good idea, anymore."

Phil's face fell. "Why not? You spend years attempting to convince me of the value of therapy. I am finally willing to give you the benefit of the doubt, and you need to disagree with me. Who is ambivalent now?"

The satisfaction in his face as he spoke impelled her to continue. "I've been wanting to tell you that..." She took a deep breath. She had dated Phil for five years. For most of that time she'd idealized him, and had hoped, sometimes desperately, that he would become more devoted to her. Here he was, doing his best to do that, but it was too little, too late. "I have been dating someone else." She managed to get it out.

Phil looked momentarily shocked, like June had just unexpectedly captured his queen in a game of chess in which he had felt comfortably in control of the board. She watched him pull himself together again quickly and rethink his approach. He looked at her kindly and said, "I don't blame you. I know I have delayed things a long time. I did not realize that you were feeling so frustrated with me that you would need to date someone else. I suppose when I consider it, certain behaviors of yours make more sense now. But I do understand. I forgive you. Don't worry. I appreciate your honesty. I understand if you have had a few dates with other people. Of course, you are entitled."

"I want to keep dating this person," June faltered. Her face was burning beet red. She felt like a teenager talking to her authoritarian dad. But, she had to keep the momentum going.

Phil looked pensive in response to this bomb. "I see," he finally said. There was a long moment in which they sat silently. June was so eager to get up and leave, but she felt glued to her chair. The waitress came by and Phil ordered the usual as he had on so many other occasions as if this were an ordinary date. Phil finally smiled down at her again and said, "I want to work this out with you. I can see that you feel as though I have slighted you. And you are slighting me back. But look at it this way: we have had five years together. I think I deserve at least a few couples therapy sessions. At least we could see what there is left between us and sort out our feelings. It's only fair."

June looked at Phil closely. He looked the same as always on the outside. But it seemed that something had changed inside. The look in his eyes had a desperation she'd never seen before. He was eager as he had never been before, as she had wished for constantly, and now it felt like the worst kind of burden. June said finally, "What's the point, Phil? Therapy cannot perform miracles. In the past five years, you were never ready to commit to me. Maybe there's a good reason for that. Perhaps it means that we aren't meant to be together."

"No," Phil quickly cut in. That's not true." Phil's face reddened and he looked upset. "I think we are meant to be together. We have known each other for five years. That is a long time. I could not bear to let it go to waste. I am certain that some couples therapy will make the difference. You always said it would. Don't you believe in therapy anymore?"

June ignored the low blow. "I told you that I'm seeing someone else." She felt that, at this point, blunt would be most effective.

"I know. But you can't possibly know him like you do me. And I know you far better than he possibly could. We have years of history together. At least come to a few sessions. You owe me that."

This made June feel both angry and guilty. She didn't owe him anything. Then why was she feeling like she did? Anger alone would have been a healthier reaction. Until not very long ago, she had looked up to Phil. She'd yearned for his attention. She couldn't even have imagined the conversation they were having, his begging and her refusing. She'd dreamed of being in couples therapy with him. Could she just walk away now?

Phil was pleading. This in itself was so difficult to bear that June found herself agreeing to go to a few sessions. Her inner rationale was that therapy might actually make it easier for them to part ways. There would be a witness, and she'd know he would be cared for by a therapist and make her exit. She would not pretend that she wanted a relationship with Phil. Maybe they could even end up as friends. Perhaps then she wouldn't feel so intensely that five years of her life had been for naught.

She buckled. They agreed that Phil would call and set up the first appointment. She told him the times that worked best. She also told him that she had no plans to stop dating this other guy. Phil demanded to know his name. June felt reluctant to tell him. She said, feeling self-conscious about how immature it sounded, "I would rather not talk to you about him."

"If you are really going to do this for me, you can't keep secrets from me. I need a name, just so I can refer to him if necessary."

"Michael," she said against her will and immediately regretted it. She should have made up a name. Just saying his name brought up so much feeling in her that she felt ashamed in front of Phil. She could tell that Phil noticed her discomfort. After an awkward silence, Phil said softly, "Michael does not know you like I do. Just remember that I have stood by you through many ups and downs. I have always been there for you, listened, helped you. You know how I feel about you."

He made a good point. June felt guilty and somewhat responsible for Phil's feelings. She also felt trapped and repulsed and angry.

Phil pressured her after dinner to go home with him, but she repeatedly refused. He kept saying, "I don't understand," as if the change in her behavior were out of the blue. He finally accused her of punishing him by withholding sex, and seemed to have worked out something in his head because he let the issue drop.

When she reached her apartment June took a deep breath and let it out slowly. She'd already done the most difficult part: blurted out that she was dating Michael and planned to continue. It suddenly struck her that she couldn't be sure whether Michael actually planned to see her again or not. Maybe it was just a one-weekend stand to him. Or maybe he misunderstood her running out, thinking she was involved with another guy. That would be ironic.

She had no idea what to do. Call Michael? Wait? Their time together had been so intimate, but Phil was technically correct: Michael did not know her very well. But Phil didn't either.

The phone rang. June jumped a mile. She immediately assumed it was Michael and ran for it, her heart pounding. When she picked it up and eagerly said hello, she heard, "Tuesday night at seven p.m. I'll meet you at the entrance to your building at quarter of." Phil had worked quickly. Her heart sank. She agreed to meet him. She realized after hanging up that she hadn't thought to ask who the therapist was, and he hadn't bothered to tell her. She'd wait to find out on Tuesday, rather than speak to him again. Her phone sat silent the remainder of the night.

June's head was spinning. She'd been wanting, in her usual compulsive style, to go over the entire weekend with Michael in her mind. She wanted to remember how she felt each moment, how he looked at her, how he looked, exactly what he said word for word. She wanted it captured, so that no matter what happened she would always have it.

But thoughts of Phil kept intruding, along with fears about Michael's intentions. Could Phil suddenly really be so interested in her? Was it just that she'd finally done the withdrawing? Was Phil sincere, or was this his way of holding onto a relationship because he happened to be more comfortable continuing status quo?

Was Michael going to hurt her? She felt like she was in the middle of open heart surgery and had just learned that the surgeon's reputation was questionable. Could she trust him? Could anyone be that attracted to her? Why would anyone want to spend an entire weekend with her? She didn't even want to do that, but she had no choice. Was it just some twisted, male kind of challenge to him to see if he could get her into bed with him twice in one weekend? How could she have done that? She felt out of control and confused and a little ashamed of herself. And fearful and alone.

Chapter VII: Commitment

You will always be the person who can take care of you the best, even if you are busily wishing that someone else would do it. Take responsibility and do something about it. Buy yourself something that you have wanted for ages. Give yourself a special treat. Make plans with a friend for dinner or just drinks at some special spot. Sign up for a class, buy yourself a new outfit, get a new haircut, get a manicure. Do whatever it takes to feel cared for. Having plans lifts your spirits so easily. Why not give yourself something to look forward to? (Be Happy, by June Gray, Ph.D.)

Monday, June dragged herself out of bed to go to work. She instinctively wore black and felt depressed. She dreaded going to the office. She had a day full of people who were feeling especially troubled lately, most severely, Annabelle. Her recent on-again off-again relationship, if it could even qualify to be called that, had reached a new level of masochism. The boyfriend had cancelled plans with her and rescheduled. On the night of the cancellation, Annabelle chose to go out alone rather than stay home. To her horror, she happened upon the boyfriend out with another woman at their favorite spot. Annabelle was so shocked, she stood there and stared. He got up, came over to her at the bar and begged her not to make a scene, insisting that there was a perfectly good explanation, but that he would have to call her with it in the morning and that she needed to leave the premises immediately. He returned to his table and proceeded to ignore Annabelle until she finally made herself leave. She didn't know what else to do.

To make matters worse, he never did call the next day or even the one after that. He just never called. So here was Annabelle in June's office, obsessed with the question of whether she should call him or wait for him to call her. Tonight was supposed to be their rescheduled dinner date. She needed June to tell her what to do, immediately. Her attempt to point out to Annabelle that he had clearly lied and manipulated her irritated her.

She was focused on finding a way to get an explanation from him, argue away her rage and disappointment, and get on with the dinner dates. This painfully slow session ended with her deciding to call this guy if only to accuse him of cowardly avoidance of her. She would force him to face her anger and offer an apology, if not a proper explanation. Short of openly suggesting that she dump him, June had little to offer except support. At least this plan was active rather than passive. June recognized the plan for what it really was, a thin veil for the true plan, which was to reconnect with the boyfriend in any way possible, at any cost, and punish and then forgive him. There would be no expectation that he would even examine, not to mention, change his behavior.

This made June sad. What had she put up with for five long years? Had she been as desperate as Annabelle, in her own way? Is that why she found her situation intolerable and her solution pitiful? What had changed for her that she'd found a way to escape and Annabelle hadn't? What if there were no Michael? Could June have escaped from Phil on her own? Would a therapist have expected her to?

> *To make progress in psychotherapy, the therapist must build a strong enough therapeutic alliance with the patient to allow for exploration of painful and frightening subject matter from the patient's past and its integration into the present understanding of self. The patient may test the therapist's commitment to the work, which, when handled properly by the therapist over time, will lead to the development of trust. The patient must feel dedicated to the effort as well, in order to persist. He will want to improve his own life experience, as well as please the therapist with his efforts.*

June came home to no messages. Darkness. Inside her heart and all around her. How could she be so worthless and so special all at once? Obviously, she was mistaken about being special. She'd doubted it, anyway. Michael hadn't called. Again. He couldn't possibly really care about her. He barely knew her. He hadn't lived through anything more than a weird, isolated weekend with her. If he were to get to know her, the depressive, empty, fearful, worthless June, there'd be no reason for him to stick around. She suddenly felt as though the cartoon cloud she had been floating along on had dissipated, and she was looking down at the sky she was about to fall through on her way to a crash landing.

Even Phil had been able to hang in there only because he'd maintained a level of distance in which he was able to have her in small doses. Maybe he knew best. Had she been just as much at fault for the stagnation of their relationship as he had? Perhaps she should have left things as they were with Phil.

She felt herself spiraling down quickly into familiar terrain. The idea of couples therapy the next day seemed laughable, and June might have laughed over it, if not for how completely humiliating, shaming, useless, and depressing she knew it would be. She feared that somehow it could get worse. She couldn't even bring herself to eat dinner.

She crawled into her bed and hid from the world and herself until she fell gratefully asleep.

Suddenly, it was Tuesday. June had to get up and help people. She wondered, as she did every now and then, "If my patients knew what I actually felt like, would they be afraid to come back? Perhaps they'd keep seeing me, knowing that I truly did understand what they were going through. Or, perhaps, they would think that if I couldn't get my shit together, what hope was there for them?"

She downed her coffee, ate some tasteless flakes of cereal, and climbed into the jalopy while fighting off a fantasy of brake failure, working hard to get her mind into the proper state to help others. At least focusing on that prevented her from thinking about her evening.

Later, when she arrived home after a tedious day at work, there was a friendly reminder message from Phil. That was all. She had been hoping for a message from Michael as much as Annabelle ever had hoped for a call from her lying guy.

June managed to eat a little dinner, encouraging herself by thinking about the benefits of being alert and able to think clearly. She had no hunger for food, although she had a desperate hunger gnawing at her. She absolutely didn't want to see Phil, or his therapist of choice. She couldn't pretend to have forgotten. She kept telling herself, "How bad can one session be? Therapy, in principle, is a good thing."

She feared going for that very reason. She knew that therapy does get to the heart of the matter, when it is done right. And the heart of the matter was that it was over with Phil. Even if Michael didn't pan out. She was terrified of really finalizing it with Phil and being alone. And she was afraid to hurt Phil with the utter truth spoken before a witness who would hear it. She knew she would feel out of control, overwhelmed by her own sadness, as soon as a sympathetic ear was turned her way. She didn't want that to happen.

It was quarter to seven. June was outside the building, right on time. And of course, there was Phil, right on time. He gave her a warm welcome and took her hand and held it as they walked. It seemed so strange: in the past, up until a couple of months ago, June had longed for small gestures. Now these actions repelled her. She also felt nervous. What if Michael saw her holding Phil's hand and misunderstood? She let go of Phil's hand and looked up at him and said, "I'd rather not hold hands."

He frowned and was silent as he let her hand drop. He looked hurt, and finally said, "You have told me in the past that holding hands was something that you really liked."

June could have responded in so many ways, but felt that she needed to deliver a simple, consistent message. "That was the past. Things have changed."

"That is not really fair." Phil said pedantically. "You aren't giving me a chance. You can't just withdraw after five years without trying at all. These therapy sessions are for us to try, not throw away our time together. I am telling you that I'm now ready to work things out. I know that is what you have always wanted. Don't you believe me?" He gave June a desperate and pleading look. It was not at all attractive. But she felt sorry for him. In part, this was because she could see how pathetic his attempts to manipulate her had become.

The truth was that she didn't believe him at all. But if she'd said that, he would have had carte blanche to prove to her that he really was ready to work things out. So, instead of arguing about something that she no longer wanted to win anyway, she made it easier for herself. She nodded that she did believe him, and sighed and said, "Let's wait to talk it over in the session, since that's where we're going." They silently walked another five minutes, to the office. Phil looked over at her every few moments as though he were eager to convince her of how ready he really was.

He had chosen June's old supervisor, Dorothy Miller. June thought she was the greatest, one of the very few mentors in her life. She was so glad to see her, yet embarrassed beyond belief. She knew she had to tell her the truth, that the relationship with Phil was going to end that night, for good. She would see how June felt, anyway. And it was less embarrassing to reveal to her that she was moving on from Phil, than to have her believe she wanted to work things out with this limited, stilted, over-controlled and controlling guy. She was still embarrassed that she would know that June had been involved with him, and after this session, he'd probably continue to see Dorothy and badmouth her. Or by telling Dorothy about their relationship, he'd be letting her see what June had been willing to put up with for five years. Either way, she wasn't going to end up looking great. The least she could do was to show her how much better she was doing now. What a real laugh that was, after she had earlier considered her car's potential for brake failure.

June had to bite the bullet. At least she knew Dorothy would make a good therapist for Phil. She'd be leaving him in good hands. That would alleviate about half of her guilt. Overall, she was glad he'd chosen Dorothy.

There they were, in her waiting room. And soon enough, there was Dorothy coming out of her office to welcome them. It had been years. Her hair was much grayer and she had gained some weight. But she was still a calming presence. She greeted them both warmly, and asked June how she'd been. This was to acknowledge that she knew her, not to truly hear anything. So June obliged her by saying a quick "fine."

They entered her office area that still looked as June remembered it: big windows with Venetian blinds, shelves of books, stylish furnishings, an overall feeling of safety and comfort. They sat on the leather couch, June all the way to one side, Phil in the middle, too close to her. He reached for her hand again and got it before she could move it away. He was playing to the audience now. June realized that he could not care less about holding her hand, or he would have held it at least a few times in the last five years. He squeezed her hand and smiled at her pleadingly. June felt as though her hand were caught in a meat grinder.

Dorothy sat across from them in her big darkly upholstered chair, under the track lighting. Behind her was her dark wooden desk, with various objects and small sculptures upon it. The horizontal blinds were mostly shut, to keep the setting sun from hitting them directly in the eyes. In her welcoming, yet reassuring, yet friendly, yet confidential, yet wise, yet empathic yet whatever else you were looking for way, Dorothy spread her arms outward and said, "What brings you here today?"

She looked at June during the everlasting silence that ensued, and June realized that she believed that she had wanted the couples sessions.

Phil found his voice eventually, and spoke as though he represented them both. "We would like to work toward a commitment in our relationship. We have been together for five years, and it seems, we require some assistance regarding our communication skills. We have had some trouble telling each other how much we care for and appreciate one another. I suppose after five years, we have begun to take one another for granted. That does occur in couples, I have heard..."

Finally, Dorothy interrupted him. June thought she never would. She'd felt unable to, although she desperately wanted him to stop. He sounded so foolish. Knowing Phil as well as she did, she knew he needed to get his speech out, and she wasn't going to be the one to try to stop him. When Dorothy did interrupt him, he looked startled and then irritated and then suddenly calm. June watched with a sense of deja vu. She could have predicted the entire process. It was a little frightening.

Dorothy looked at June and said, "I would like to know how you feel about all of this, June." Looking back at Phil, she added, "I appreciate hearing your view of the needs in your relationship, and I think this gives us a place to begin."

Again, it was silent. June took a deep breath, and said, "From my perspective, the relationship between Phil and myself is over and has been ending for the last six months. I don't want to work it out at this point. For me, it's just too late."

The silence this time was enormous. It filled up the entire room, pushing out against the windows and the door, threatening to make the place explode. Even Dorothy looked surprised. Phil looked as though this had come as a complete shock to him, as if he hadn't heard it before. He cleared his throat and said, "I am sure she does not mean that. She is hurt and angry and understandably so. It has taken me a long time to get to this point, uh, where I can work toward a commitment between us. That is one reason we are here, for June to work through these feelings. I really do understand..."

At this point June interrupted him, "You're wrong, Phil. I'm here because you begged me to come. Let me make this perfectly clear: I no longer want to negotiate our relationship. I have moved on." She had not intended to mention Michael at all. She meant that she had moved on from wanting Phil in her life. But Phil used her wording as an opportunity to bring up Michael. She hadn't wanted Dorothy to think that she had jumped out of one relationship to be in another. Although, clearly she had, or she was at least desperately hoping she had. But she was here to sort things out between Phil and herself, not discuss the rest of her life.

"June met some other guy and has apparently transferred her feelings onto him temporarily, I feel, as a result of the negative feelings that have built up inside her toward me. I am not a therapist myself, but it seems fairly clear. I would like her to commit to working here, on her feelings, and I am sure that she will find..."

Again, June interrupted him, feeling like he was tattling on her to mom. She felt embarrassed for him and for herself, imagining judgments from Dorothy about her ever having been involved with Phil. "Phil, I am sitting right here. You aren't even talking to me. You're attempting to bully me into attending therapy sessions with you. Even if I hadn't met anyone else, it would be over between us. I just don't want to be with you anymore. I don't know how to make it any clearer to you."

Phil looked at Dorothy as though she were the relationship police, and he expected her to make an immediate arrest. June felt mortified that they had exposed her to this silliness. He began in a pathetic voice, "Don't you think she owes me this?"

Dorothy took a deep breath and let it out slowly. June absolutely regretted coming to the appointment. She felt humiliated and began to sink into that void where her emotions began to suffocate her and her judgment became murky. Why had she agreed to come with him to a therapy session? How could she have allowed him to choose the therapist? Why in the world had she thought that this could be the least bit productive in any way? Now she had lost the respect of a respected peer. Dorothy would see her as the neurotic crazy that she was. Thanks again, Phil.

Dorothy began to speak slowly, "It is not for me to make that determination. All I can tell you is that for two people to make a relationship work, they both have to want it to work and that requires..."

"She doesn't know what she wants," he whined. "She is confused. I understand and accept that. Can't you make her see it?"

June felt irritated by the way he spoke of her, as though she were a child in need of behavioral control, or a good lesson, or better parenting. She said, "I don't really see the value in my coming to any more sessions with Phil, or even staying for this one. Although I'm glad to have seen you again, Dr. Miller, I wish it were under different circumstances." She felt satisfied with her attempt to regain composure and appear professional to Dr. Miller as she rose to leave.

"You can't let her leave!" Phil practically yelled.

Dorothy put up her hand to stop all movement. She began calmly, "It sounds like I will need to meet with you separately before we will really know the best way to proceed. Why don't we plan to do that next week, and for now, use the remainder of the session to fill me in on your history together."

So June stayed, and they managed together to give her the basic facts of their history: dates, time lines, activities they had enjoyed together, or had routinely engaged in. Beyond that, there was very little that they agreed about. And even with regard to the facts, they viewed the five years of their relationship very differently. There had been events and dates that had been so important to June because they seemed to be meaningful, or had been painfully disappointing to her because they had not been meaningful to Phil. He barely remembered the specifics of those occasions, except that she had been highly emotional or moody. His sense of time lines was completely different from June's. Their anniversaries meant nothing to him because they'd only been dating. To him, it was logical to celebrate a wedding anniversary, but not a dating anniversary. He didn't remember when it was, or feel any desire to celebrate the day with June. He viewed himself as generous and sensitive. He'd viewed her over the years as needy, dependent, in dire need of reassurance and guidance, and claimed that these issues were some of the reasons that he'd had trouble committing to her.

The process of dragging out five years' worth of relationship into the light of day had June struggling through most of the session to remain calm, aloof, and blunt. She succeeded pretty well, until they got onto the topic of her hopes, expectations, and disappointments. A huge tidal wave of mixed feelings washed over her. She had felt, during most of their relationship, like a failure. She hadn't felt special, beautiful, bright, talented, or whatever else enough to be loved by Phil, no matter how she'd wished for it. Looking back now, with Dorothy's peaceful, understanding face before her, June could see that Phil had never loved her, not with a definition of love that was of any value to her.

> *With character disordered patients, there is the tendency for the characterological features to be ego-syntonic. The patient is unaware of the effect his behaviors and attitudes have on others, or feels justified and believes that others should accommodate him. He feels no need to make changes, and sees nothing wrong with his functioning. To him, when something goes wrong, the blame belongs with anyone but himself.*

June knew even now, despite how he might protest, that he still did not and never would love her. This experience felt like a Phil power play. Force June to do one last double flip through the flaming hoop, and then show her how she failed.

> *When a rat is trained to press a lever for food, he learns to expect food with each press. When the reward schedule is switched to a variable schedule, the rat may press many times and receive no food pellet, or he may press a few times and receive a pellet. Eventually, if he presses enough, he will get his reward. As a result, he continually presses the lever. When the lever is no longer associated with food, the rat may continue to press it for a very long time, still expecting the eventual pellet, demonstrating how difficult the behavior is to extinguish.*

June felt ashamed that her dependency, neediness, and low self-esteem had kept her in that relationship for so long. All relationships require some dependency to satisfy basic human needs. She had almost consistently been unsatisfied and disappointed. She'd continued to try, anyway. Every now and then she was successful. So, she hung in there.

June hoped that Dorothy was bright and sensitive enough to see Phil's character style the way June now saw it. He wasn't attempting to hide or alter it. One of his main problems had always been that he thought of himself as perfect. June had actually believed him for so long. He had been convincing to her, in part because she'd wanted to believe it. She'd desperately hoped that he was the one for her, more desperately as the years passed.

Even through their fact-finding mission, Phil and June had complete disagreements that were painful and upsetting. Apparently, he'd never believed during their second through fifth years together, that he would be spending his life with her. She had too many imperfections. He believed that she didn't know herself well enough to know that she wanted to be committed to him. He'd found it necessary to play the role of the adult who limits the child.

In retrospect, and June hated to admit it, it looked as though Phil had been correct about that.

Finally, the time ran out. June felt a wave of relief crash over her. She'd been perspiring as though she'd been in a sauna. She wanted to run out, go home, and cry in her bed. But she sat and patiently waited to be dismissed. They set up their individual sessions, both thanked her, and turned to go. With her hand on the doorknob, Dorothy paused and intently looking each of them in the eye in turn, said, "I suggest in situations like this, that you spend as little time together as possible. If you can avoid each other altogether, that would be best." Phil looked shocked. June felt a joyful singing in her heart. She really is good, June thought. She made a mental note to refer people to her.

They each shook her hand and thanked her again, and were soon out in the fresh air. The sun was setting and there was a slight breeze. June was ecstatic and in pain. She was devastated, ashamed, embarrassed, and most of all, relieved.

She had no intention of spending even one irritating moment with Phil, starting right then. He actually reached for her hand again. This time she pulled it away and said to him, "Look Phil, can't you see that it's over? Stop grabbing my hand. We have nothing together. I need to get away from you." She was surprised to hear herself blurt all of that out. Maybe the session had already had an impact on her.

He paled and looked like he was choking. "But it had gone so well," he faltered. "I thought that we made progress. I saw you get upset. I could see that you care."

"I was upset. I am upset. But it's not about you now." She felt triumphant, until she looked up at him and saw him standing there with tears running down his face. She'd not once before seen him cry. She could see the shame and rage he felt about losing control, too. She had a moment, like a flashback, in which she felt for him intensely. She felt like she wanted to hold and comfort him, something she would have loved to have had the chance to do in the past. She had loved him. His real pain was painful for her to see, and it did still mean something to her. But almost as quickly, she lost the feelings. She looked up at him with curiosity. Here was this handsome, super controlled man, reduced to tears, over her. She could barely believe it.

She reached up, patted his arm, and said in as comforting, non-hostile a way as she could muster, "I am sorry. Dorothy recommended that we stay away from each other. I intend to follow her advice." She walked away quickly without looking back.

June found herself walking faster and faster. She needed to get home. She could hardly believe what she'd just been through. She was overwhelmed and could not process all of it. Had she actually just left Phil standing in the street crying? Was that real?

She noticed that her speed walking had graduated into a jog home. Gratefully, she reached her building and, purposely looking away from the doorman, she sped over to the elevator. The heavy metal door closed before her. She got to her apartment door, fumbled with her keys, realizing she was experiencing a panic attack of sorts. As her apartment door closed behind her, she tried to calm down but she couldn't stop shaking and hyperventilating. And she couldn't stop the pounding in her chest. She felt like the world was crumbling around her. It really was over with Phil. She was alone. She had wasted five years of her life, with wishes and poor judgment, and had gotten nowhere but older. Why did she think she could help other people with their relationship problems? She didn't know what a relationship actually looked like. She'd been in some insane mock-up of one for five years. Just then she realized with a shocked sort of amusement what the date was. It seemed impossible. She ran over and checked her date book. She found April first, and written at the bottom of the page was a reminder of her appointment with Phil to see Dorothy. It really was April first. She'd been waiting for it with anticipation and dread, only to have it creep up on her at the worst possible moment. And it really had ended with Phil. It was over.

June landed on her broken down old couch and just cried and cried. She poured out what felt like an endless well of sadness, hugging her one throw pillow.

She had no idea how long she cried like that. It became dark outside. It was dark inside, too. She began to feel numb, even a little dissociated. She sat without moving for a long time. There was a soft knocking sound on her apartment door. She heard it, but thought it was nothing. She didn't move. Then she heard it again, a little louder, and realized that it was someone knocking on her door. She felt sudden panic rise up through her body again. She didn't want Phil there ever again. She would not let him in. She was so entirely convinced that it was Phil, that she neglected to look through the little peep hole, and just opened the door a little.

It was not Phil. It was Michael. Oh God. Here she was, beside herself, puffy as a helium balloon, standing in front of the guy she most wanted to impress.

June gave him a weak smile, realizing that this would be the end for them, now that her secret craziness and misery had been exposed. "Hi," she whispered. He immediately looked concerned and unsure of what to do. There was no hiding it now. If she'd known it was him, she would not have answered the door. Her apartment was totally dark. He'd never have known that she was there. Why hadn't she checked the peep hole?

He walked in and pushed the door closed behind him, and hugged her. He stood there and held her silently. She felt his hand on her hair. And he waited for her like that. The gentle weight of his fingers on the strands of her hair felt so comforting and reviving she was afraid to move. It was like oxygen and sunlight had poured into an airless, dark room. She breathed in all she could.

June stood, held by him, paralyzed, and silent. She could sense that he was waiting. She couldn't help but feel convinced, in the deepest recesses of her heart and mind, that Michael wouldn't want her. Who would? Basically, she had turned out to be nobody with nothing. She could continue to live as nobody or she could die and have it go unnoticed and unregretted. "Well, she had no life, and nothing to hope for anyway." Or "Who was she really? I never got to know her." How can one get to know nobody? An empty shell of a human being is not knowable. She had fooled Michael briefly into believing that there was more than there really was or ever could be. Perhaps Phil always knew that she was nothing, and that was just fine with him. He actually wanted nothing.

June knew Phil hadn't really wanted her. All the crap with the therapist and the hand holding and sniffling was only because he could not tolerate her loss of interest in him. It was a narcissistic injury to him. He'd never really wanted her. Perhaps no one had ever really wanted her.

She felt limp. She found that she had been leaning on Michael. He still held her against him, one arm on her back and the other hand on her hair. She felt unable to move because she was certain that this would be the last time she would be held so softly. She waited for him to become impatient. Why didn't he move?

Finally, June moved her head back and looked up at him. She knew she was red and puffy, ridiculous looking, an unrecognizable mess, the real June. He looked sad and concerned. She felt embarrassed again. She decided that she'd better let him have his visit and go. She couldn't keep him hostage out of pity.

She smiled a little. "Hi." She coughed out a pathetic laugh. "I'm sorry I seem like such a wreck. I am such a wreck. Thank you for holding me. I feel better. But please don't feel like you need to stay. I'll be fine."

Now Michael's eyes widened. He looked surprised. "You want me to leave? I just got here. Do you really want to be alone?"

"I'm assuming that you'd be more comfortable leaving."

"Why would I want to leave now? You don't want to tell me about it?" Michael was scanning her red, puffy, ugly face closely.

Masochism is a complex condition in which a person gains gratification from suffering. Consciously she believes that she despises the pain she feels, and wishes she could find a way to escape it. But there is unconscious satisfaction derived from the suffering and punishment. Masochistic tendencies usually develop as one outcome of a difficult and punishing relationship experienced early in development.

June sighed. Why was he making her spell it out for him? Wasn't it obvious? "I don't want you to leave, but I don't want to burden you. I would completely understand if you would prefer to go. We could see each other another time." She tried to pretend that she believed that he would want to get together another time so that she wouldn't begin crying loudly again. She could play the game. She assumed that he would leave, run as soon as the door was fully closed behind him, and never look back, breathing a huge sigh of relief on his way. She wanted to make it easy for him to get out.

However, the thought of his leaving was so painful to her that she didn't think she'd actually be able to recover from it. She might suffocate. But she didn't want him to feel trapped, suffocating with her. That would have been even worse.

Michael looked down at her with his penetrating eyes. At this point they were standing a little further apart and he was holding her hands in his. He said, "I don't want to leave. I feel so bad seeing you so unhappy. I want to understand what you are feeling and why. Will you let me get to know you better? I don't want you to feel that you have to hide your feelings from me. I'm not judging them. Everyone feels upset sometimes."

He sounded so sweet and innocent that June began to get lightheaded. Why wasn't he just leaving? She knew that he had no clue of the vast terrain of her craziness. Somehow she still had him fooled. He thought that this was just a bad day. An unusual event. Maybe he'd just never seen anything like it before. It seemed unfair to let it continue. June said, "I appreciate your concern. But I actually don't think you understand what you are dealing with here. Do you have experience with explosives? You don't want to get to know me better. I am a mess. This is me. You deserve better. Please don't feel obligated." She worried that he felt more obligated the more she told him not to. But she didn't know what else to do.

Michael was still looking at her very intently, like he was trying to see past her words and into her soul, like those green eyes had some kind of superpower. June didn't understand. Why would he want to do that? Just turn and save yourself for 's sake. What was in this for him? Could he be a masochist?

He said, "Can we sit down? Can you try to believe for a minute that I mean what I say?"

"Maybe for a minute." His voice was so soothing and gentle that June was not sure that he could be real. Perhaps this was a dream. She led him over to the couch. He said, "Wouldn't you like to tell me about it?"

Why couldn't he see that telling him would seal away any remote chance that he would want to keep seeing her? He was her dream guy: attractive, caring, attentive. She felt entirely too vulnerable to him. She recalled suddenly the many occasions in her therapy in which they had talked about her expectations, what she deserved in a relationship. Her therapist kept telling her what she deserved. June had tried to take it in, plaster it to the inside of her head as a reminder to refer back to if she forgot it, but she couldn't get it to stick. Here it was, though, in front of her. She deserved a man who was caring and attentive. She could hardly bear it.

There was Michael next to her on the old, wet-from-crying, dusty, dirty couch, the picture of attentiveness. June was terrified out of her mind. Could she handle the inevitable rejection? Should she take a leap of faith? Were there truly men out there like this? Was she delirious? He had asked her to try to believe him. What did she have to lose? She suddenly thought of a frustrated patient she had seen for several years who used to refer to all of the men who had rejected her as bottom feeders. Like certain undesirable fish at the bottom of the ocean. To her, this was the absolute worst insult imaginable. Michael could not be a bottom feeder, could he?

June was unsure how to behave with someone like him. How would she start? How would she know when to stop? Would she recognize when he'd had enough? He hadn't left yet. He'd seen the surface of the wreck and had not yet averted his eyes. She had given him as many outs as she could.

"You really do want to stay?" June blurted out, having allowed herself the minute of belief.

"Of course I do." He finally smiled at her, and then put his arm around her and said, "I want to know what is making you so upset and I want to try to help you feel better. I hope you'll let me."

June found herself starting at the beginning, five years ago, and giving him an overview. It flowed pretty well, given that she'd just gone through it all in the therapy session. There were awkward moments, but she felt relief that she could open up and be honest with Michael about what she'd been through, and was obviously still dealing with. She was able to explain then why she had run out of his apartment after their marathon date. She felt relieved about that.

As she spoke, she checked Michael's face for boredom, judgment, irritation, rejection or any other sign that might make her question or regret what she was saying. He just kept looking sympathetic and encouraging. He did not look especially unhappy.

June finished her explanation with a description of the therapy session and how it had brought up so many feelings and so much regret and self-criticism. As she said it all, her view felt clearer. It was true: These were old feelings, not especially related to the present. She felt her heart lift a little. Through telling her tale to Michael she had gotten a little bit of objectivity, enough for her own training to help her see what she had been doing. She was reliving old feelings about herself. They were so powerful because they were so old. Ending her connection with Phil was not the same as feeling inadequately cared for by her parents and feeling unlovable. The rejections involved in this situation were very different from the rejections she had experienced as a child.

Michael said, "It sounds like you have finally gotten yourself free. You should feel good about that. I can see it wasn't easy."

"I actually do feel good about that," June blurted out, and realized that she was proud of herself. She had done it, by herself, significantly, before any couples sessions had occurred. She had left Phil behind months ago really. She was proud of that. It was the emotional cart full of heavy baggage that she had trouble leaving behind so easily.

Michael smiled at her again and said, "You look like you feel a little better." June nodded. "I'm glad." he added. "I'm also glad that you got yourself out of that relationship with Phil. But I can't help wondering if maybe you aren't really ready to get involved with anyone else just yet." He looked at her expectantly.

June felt like a sixteen-ton weight had fallen on her chest. So that was his plan. He would escape from her, after all. Objectively speaking, it was too soon to begin a new relationship. But it was, subjectively speaking, too late. There was no doubt in her mind: She knew she wanted Michael, like she had never wanted another person before. She'd had other boyfriends before Phil, with whom there had been some passion. And even early on with Phil, when she'd been hopeful, there had been some passion, although she'd always felt a subtle judgment from him that passion meant loss of control and therefore weakness.

There had never been anyone before who pulled her in like a magnet the way Michael did. She felt like she had to control herself just to keep her hands off of him. She could stare at his face forever. She felt crazy and out of control. Phil would not have been proud of her, for so many reasons. It felt like something at a chemical level, it was so intense. Michael had actually just now said the word, 'relationship' and had been referring to them. Did he mean it?

She looked up to see Michael watching her closely. He pointed to her head and said with mock seriousness, "You seem to have a lot going on in there."

"What do you think would be best for me?" June heard herself ask.

Michael thought for a moment and said slowly, "I want you to do what's best for you, but I'm having trouble seeing exactly what that would be because I also want what I think is best for me."

"Maybe the same thing will be best for us both," she responded. She held her breath.

"I hope so." Michael paused. "There are some things I should probably tell you too, although I don't think that tonight is the best time." He looked at his watch and practically jumped out of his seat. It was four in the morning. Michael stood up suddenly and said that he had to run upstairs to take a shower and put on a suit because he had an important meeting to attend at 8 a.m. June felt terrible for having kept him up all night. Her mind automatically jumped to imagining him in the shower.

Michael took her face in his hands and kissed her on the lips so softly. He put his arms around her, hugged her and said, "I really do have to leave to get ready for a meeting. I have no regret about staying up with you all night talking. I loved it, except for the beginning part when you were so unhappy. But it got better. I would stay up with you all night anytime you like. Just let me know."

> *Often people who have not had unconditional regard growing up find that they are more comfortable in the role of caregiver, in which they have the primary responsibility and control. They are uncomfortable being taken care of, or relying on others. The feeling of powerlessness and potential for disappointment is excruciating. The feeling of gratefulness that is experienced when another person has done something for them, leads them to want to respond immediately in kind. They feel tremendous discomfort and indebtedness.*

His words were so comforting to June. He had her figured out well enough to know she would need reassurance about this visit. He knew she'd feel guilty. No one had ever bothered to know her well enough to predict her needs before. And it seemed so easy and natural for him. It was wonderful. She thanked him for reassuring her and added, "I would do the same for you anytime, too."

He smiled and said, "You may have to sooner than you think, if my meeting goes badly."

He left. The door closed behind him. June felt guilty, anyway, and worried that she might have caused him to have a bad meeting. Was that what he was saying as he left?

She sat still. He was gone. She had no idea when she would see or hear from him again. He was too good to be true, and she had shown him how scary she was. He'd have time to process it. She had a strong feeling that it was going to have to come to a crashing, burning end.

What was in it for him? There were plenty of more attractive, lower maintenance women out there, many of whom were younger than June, even younger than Michael. Why her?

What was wrong with him?

June took a shower, dressed and somehow got to work. She had six appointments to get through. She was deliriously tired and fixated on every word that she could recall having left Michael's lips. Why did he stay and comfort her all night?Somehow she got through her appointments. She made it home. She hadn't been able to eat much all day. She lay on the couch, thought about all the notes she needed to write, and fell asleep.

She was startled awake by the phone ringing. She went to get it, all jumpy and breathless, and let it ring again while she took a deep breath and tried to ground herself by checking the clock. It was 6:30 p.m. She had slept two hours. She couldn't get herself fully oriented. She answered the phone with a tentative, "Hello," fearing Phil or her mother. Surprisingly, it was Michael.

"Oh, hi," June gasped. "I feel so bad about last night. I am so sorry and embarrassed. I hope it didn't interfere with your meeting today. I'm not usually like that. I hope you don't think..."

Michael interrupted her and said, "I called to see how you are. Please don't be embarrassed. It was fine. I don't think you're upset all the time, and you certainly had some serious things to be upset about. I'm sorry that you were upset, but I am glad you talked to me about it. That made me feel closer to you."

June wondered whether she was still sleeping. She said, "Have I become completely delusional, totally lost touch with reality and made up this wonderful, great guy in my head? And now I think he's on the telephone telling me he can handle my freaking out? That he feels closer to me as a result? This could not possibly be reality. I must have had a psychotic break. It actually doesn't feel as bad as I'd always feared."

Michael laughed. "I hope this isn't how you diagnose your patients. Maybe I should come down there so that you can see for yourself that I am flesh and blood."

"Sounds like a good intervention to me." June responded. "I would like to make up for last night in some way..."

"You don't have anything to make up for. I didn't do anything I didn't want to do. I hope that when I freak out, you'll be there for me, too."

"Of course. At this very moment, I am actually wishing that you would freak out so that I could comfort you."

"How about if I come over and we can think together about how you might comfort me." Michael laughed.

He was at her door about ten minutes later. In that interim she had raced around like a headless chicken, trying to brush her teeth and hair, change into jeans, and rein in her overblown feelings of exaltation all at the same time. She attempted to shame herself into a sense of calm. It was useless. She was just plain too happy. She managed to bring herself down a tiny bit by insisting that she didn't deserve to be this happy, and by reminding herself of her certainty that inevitably, it would be short-lived. The whole thing really seemed dangerous. The higher she got, the harder the fall, or something along those gravitational dimensions.

June wanted him so badly, and felt so out of control, that she tried relaxation exercises on herself. Her worst area of study in graduate school was behavioral treatments. They had always seemed worthy of the magazine shelf in the supermarket. She never mastered the techniques. Here she was now, trying to do deep breathing and visualize a beach, warm sun, relaxing waves breaking in the distance. All she managed to visualize was the beach, the warm sun, distant waves and Michael making love to her. When her hopes of breathing in the proper amount of oxygen were getting dim, there was Michael's knock on the door.

She tried one more deep breath, but she was getting light-headed. She pulled the door open and there he was, smiling beautifully at her. She felt weak, like her legs might give out. Somehow she managed to get him into her apartment and close the door behind him.

He grinned. "Here I am in the flesh. Do you need more proof that I am real? Because I feel prepared to do whatever it takes."

As they sat down on the couch, June said, "I think I do. I'm afraid that now I suspect that I'm having a dream, rather than a delusion, and that I might wake up at any time and find you gone. Poof."

"What can I do to prove that this is reality and that you are awake?" Michael looked innocently concerned, but had moved very close to her on the couch.

"Well," she pretended to think hard. "We could do things that might make me wake up, and when I don't, I might believe that I am not asleep."

"Okay." Michael said. "I have a few thoughts about how we might accomplish that. Have you had any dinner yet?"

"No, I'm very hungry." She realized this as she heard herself say it.

"Then let's go get a quick dinner somewhere nearby. Eating might make you realize you are awake."

"No. Not necessarily." June responded in psychologist mode. "Many people dream of eating. It would be inconclusive at best."

"This is going to be a real challenge." Michael moved closer still and kissed her hard on the lips. "Does that help?"

"No. That feels like pure dream."

"Then we had better start with food."

They went down to a nearby coffee shop. June realized that she hadn't eaten practically at all since the night before. She was really hungry, but still so anxious with

Michael that she had trouble deciding what to order. She finally settled on a sandwich and so did he.

As they were eating, Michael told June about his morning meeting. He said that editors come and go and move around a lot. June had an instant flash that he was about to tell her that he was being transferred across the country. She held her breath and stopped chewing. Instead, he said that he was being considered for a promotion to be the top editor of his division. Her bite of sandwich almost fell out of her mouth. He said that he felt eager to move up, but nervous about the increased responsibility and accountability. He knew he'd be busier and probably have to dress up more often. They were interviewing other people, so he wouldn't find out for another week or so. He added that he was pretty certain he'd get the offer.

June felt proud of him, and excited and nervous for him, despite not comprehending anything about what the job change would really mean. He'd acknowledged his fears and anxieties about the promotion so easily.

They walked around a little after dinner, and after a while he said, "Do you still think that I am not real?"

June smiled and whispered, "I am afraid you aren't. That somehow I'm being fooled."

He took her hand in his and said, "Let's walk back. Obviously we have an intractable problem on our hands. We're going to have to do some hard work."

"What do you have in mind?" she asked. She was hoping, as she had all evening, that he would come back to her apartment, kiss her, hold her and make love to her. She felt ashamed of herself for being so out of control, although it felt good. She had to bite her tongue not to directly proposition him.

Michael smiled and said, "I think we need to go back to your apartment and come up with a game plan."

June had the sense that Michael had more to tell her. That he was holding something back, too. When he told her at dinner about his meeting and potential promotion, she at first thought that might be it, but even after that, she felt that there was something he wasn't saying. On the other hand, since there was so much on her mind that she wasn't saying, so much that she could have exploded from the pressure, she wondered whether she was just projecting onto him.

When they got into her apartment, he closed the door, she dropped her bag on the floor, and they immediately began kissing passionately. He began to undress her. He pulled her shirt off and then looked down and smiled, and said, "Your red underwear."

June smiled, "That's all I have now, you know." And then he was kissing it and her and then the red bra was on the carpet, and then they were on the carpet.

Afterward, they were still laying on the carpet in June's living room. It was beginning to get dark outside, with little glimmers of light coming in through her horizontal blinds. He held her and said, "I'm so attracted to you. I hope that's okay."

She said, "It's the best thing that's ever happened to me in my entire life." And then she panicked. She really did fear scaring him away. She looked at him in the fading light, his beautiful, lean, graceful body. She tried to relax and be with him in the moment.

He squeezed her closer to him and said, "I've never felt this way about anyone before." June could hear the emotion in his voice. "I want you to know that I'm real, and the way I feel is real. From the moment I met you, I knew you were someone special. I didn't know what to do. I was afraid I'd make a mistake or scare you away. I still fear that." He looked into her eyes. "I was so grateful to be able to be there for you last night. I..." Michael stopped himself. He took a breath and his tone changed a little. He said, "I've spent a lot of time thinking about you."

"I guess you must actually be real, because I never could have dreamt this. It's better than I could ever imagine." June looked into his green eyes, "I'm afraid that you will vanish as mysteriously and unexpectedly as you appeared." She whispered, "Please don't."

With his voice full of emotion, he replied, "I'm not going anywhere. And you had better not, either."

He did go back to his apartment, and June got her first fully restful night of sleep in months, maybe years. She slept so deeply, as though some agitated part of her was finally at peace. She felt maniacally happy the next day, and anxious beyond belief. She could not sit still or concentrate on anything.

No one is perfect. June needed to understand Michael better, get a more objective view, a better idea of his character style, as if he were a patient. She was repeatedly stuck on the fact that he seemed to want her, was attracted to her, and said he thought about her. How could that be?

Chapter VIII: Reinforcement

To counteract the stresses of everyday life, set aside your daily activities and take time for meditation. Twenty minutes a day of focused time will cut into the stress cycle, give your body the rejuvenation it needs, and provide strength to better tolerate the unending battles of life. Daily meditation allows you to be in the moment, to notice the frequently overlooked but important details that make life meaningful. Mindful attention to activities helps you to focus and ease stress. (Be Happy, by June Gray, Ph.D.)

June had her individual appointment with Dorothy that evening. Even though she was supposed to talk about her relationship with Phil, she decided that she'd use it to deal with her feelings about Michael. She needed to sort out her anxieties into neater piles: Michael, Phil, her family. She was so afraid she'd sabotage the relationship with Michael unconsciously, because she felt so undeserving. Perhaps a few sessions with Dorothy was just what she needed.

It was a relatively light day at her office. June managed to get some paperwork done but she caught herself daydreaming repeatedly. She went over and over every moment of intimacy. She thought about everything Michael said that she could recall. She questioned and judged most of what she had said and done. She repeatedly attempted to snap herself out of her reveries, only to find herself lost in them again only moments later.

On her way home she thought about meeting with Dorothy. What would she want to say to her? First, she'd have to explain how far from Phil she'd gotten and then she'd try to carefully approach what she actually needed help with. She'd always believed her to be an impressive and sensitive supervisor, but June had no idea what she was like as a therapist. How invested was she in helping Phil rebuild something with her?

Why did June put herself through all of this worrying and second guessing? If Dorothy wasn't helpful, then she wouldn't go back to see her again. It certainly wouldn't crush her. It was so annoying when she had to remind herself that she was an adult.

She feared she would question Michael's interest in her. Or point out something about his personality that June hadn't previously seen but that was undeniable and made him unacceptable. Or even worse, something that was a repetition of Phil.

This perspective assumed tremendous brilliance and insight on Dorothy's part. Why should she have such power over June's life? She was just as likely to be wrong. June would never assume such a degree of power or knowledge as a therapist. She'd never even want to influence anyone in such a way. And, to Dorothy's credit, June was sure she wasn't that manipulative. June realized she was projecting her feelings and fears about someone else onto Dorothy. Her mother, of course. This was the positive payoff for the years of therapy she'd had. At least she could sort out her irrational anxieties a little.

June felt ready to see Dorothy. Luckily, too, because the time was quickly approaching. She took the walk to her office, feeling optimistic. That should have set off June's alarms, but she strolled happily along with less than her usual hypervigilance. As she walked, she noticed tiny buds on the trees hesitantly beginning to open up. Young, lightly green leaves were beginning to unfurl. There were daffodil and tulip leaves popping up in spots around the trees that had been planted along the sidewalk. Early spring was always such a hopeful time.

She got to within a block of the office when Phil appeared before her, feigning surprise at having run into her. She made herself say hello and smile for a nanosecond. She reminded him that she had her appointment with Dorothy and he pretended to recall it. It was pathetic, but she let him have his game. She didn't have the heart, interest or energy to confront him.

He told her how much he missed her, and babbled on about wanting to call her several times, but June was able to get away from him. She walked in to her appointment feeling irritated and angry. He'd succeeded in getting her to focus on him in her session, for a while, anyway.

In Dorothy's office, usually a soothing place, she reminded herself that she had nothing to lose. She could leave and never return. But Dorothy's opinion was important to her. What if she revealed how irrational and poor June's judgment has been? What if she were convinced that Phil was the one for her? June's self-preserving response was that she'd have to reconsider her view of Dorothy. She knew that Phil wasn't for her and that she was desperately in love with Michael. What could Dorothy possibly say to contradict these facts?

As it turned out, Dorothy was warm and welcoming and seemed not the least bit surprised to hear that June had moved on from Phil months ago. She was curious about how she'd managed to be persuaded to go to the couples counseling session, which was how they began to recognize June's guilt regarding Phil. They discussed what had been valuable and beneficial to her in the five years that they'd been involved, and how she'd been so grateful for the attention and caring she had received, however sparse in retrospect. And Dorothy was able to spur June on to recognize the ways in which this was related to her wishes and disappointments regarding her parents, and how this was the deeper source of the guilt she felt.

June realized that her self-preserving distance from her parents made her feel guilty. A part of her believed that she should have been a more attentive and caring daughter, and that she would always be a disappointment to them. She recognized a deeper, older wish to win their love and approval that she thought she had analyzed away. She cried and felt tremendous relief. Dorothy was the superior therapist she had hoped she would be. And she claimed to be impressed with June's readiness for quick insight and comprehension.

They discussed Michael only insofar as June needed to understand her anxiety as intense fear that she'd disappoint him, and that he'd ultimately abandon her. And it became painfully obvious how that fear was connected to her relationship with her parents, and then later on, with Phil.

She also realized for what felt like the millionth time that she didn't need her parents' approval. They had their limits and probably didn't understand her adequately enough to make their approval truly meaningful anyway. She needed to focus on the fact that she had approval from Emily, Michael, Dorothy, many past patients whose lives she had helped to improve, and deep down, she did have approval from herself, at least some of the time. It just got buried in doubt so frequently.

By session's end June wanted to hug and kiss Dorothy and adopt her as her new mother. She felt tremendously relieved and hopeful. She realized that she'd been very close to understanding these forces within herself, but that she'd benefited from having the chance to go over it all with Dorothy. And, ironically, she had Phil to thank for that. She felt freed, moreso than she had ever before felt. Life was looking up. Maybe she could even focus on getting to know Michael better to see if he really could be someone she wanted to share her life with. She felt like she had a temporary (she was not a complete fool) grip on things. Dorothy was a minor miracle worker.

Phil was waiting outside for June. She was able to smile at him and thank him for the opportunity to talk to someone so helpful. He looked encouraged by this, so she quickly added that she needed to get home and would appreciate no further contact with him. And she walked away. She didn't stick around to study his face and feel concern that it was crestfallen. Not her problem.

June crossed the street and nearly danced home. She felt like a good, decent person who deserved a good, decent life. She felt energized. She returned to her building, smiled at the doorman and rode up the elevator.

Michael called around 8:00 p.m. to say he was working late and that it did look good for his promotion. But it meant a lot more work. He asked about June's day and she filled him in on general stuff about her practice. She didn't mention Dorothy or her amazing therapy session. He told her that she sounded happy. She said it was because she was thinking about him. She could tell he was glad to hear that. He asked her, "What specifically about me?"

June replied, "Your beautiful eyes and your smile and how you are the sweetest, most caring, sensitive person and how you also happen to be unbelievably sexy, too."

"Okay, that'll do." He added, "I don't want to lose control and have to come running over to your place right now. It would probably jeopardize my chances of ever getting somewhere in the world of publishing. Oh, who cares about that? I'll be right over."

June laughed. "Stay where you are and finish your work. I'm not going anywhere. I can wait."

Michael said seriously, "I feel very lucky."

"Me too," she added, her heart aching.

"I'd better go," Michael said slowly. "I have to finish up something for a deadline, so I don't know how late I'll be. I'll call you tomorrow evening, okay?"

June agreed to it but felt a stab of disappointment. Why didn't he tell her earlier in the conversation that there was no chance of seeing him that night? She felt misled. She wanted him to come over and stay with her. She knew that this was important work to him and that he was eager to be successful. She wanted that for him too, but didn't see why he couldn't come over later anyway. She hung up trying to see it from his perspective. He would be happier and more relaxed about work once he got that promotion. He would earn more money. That would be a good thing, too. "Try to control yourself," she told herself. Of course, the thought passed through her mind that he actually didn't love her or want to see her. That perhaps it was just the sex. She tried to force these thoughts out of her mind. She had felt his love and attraction before. She had even felt it over the telephone. "Please have some confidence. For more than ten minutes."

June was so full of nervous energy, with the whole night alone ahead of her, that she decided to do some more writing in her book. Now that she felt more happy more of the time, she thought that maybe she could come up with more ideas about how one goes about getting that way.

One way was to leave old baggage at the curb. But you had to recognize it before you could sort through it and differentiate it from your current and desirable luggage. You can't just drop it and run, as if it didn't really belong to you. It'll follow you wherever you go. You have to keep on sorting and tossing out the things that are getting old. For June, Phil was an example of baggage that wasn't very old, but was old enough to be sorted out and left behind. What had started out as new luggage had gradually gotten old and worn out, and had turned into old baggage.

She did manage to get quite a bit of writing done that evening. It was fun. Would she finish the book? She was feeling happier than when she had first started writing it. But it had become an enjoyment in its own right. She still believed that it was silly and ridiculous, but it was also therapeutic. She added a section about telling oneself supportive, encouraging messages and reframing things positively. She came up with the idea to leave notes all around one's home and car to find at a later date and then feel inspired after reading them. She made up some suggestions for these notes:

In the end, I alone must approve of myself.

My opinion is just as important as anyone else's.

I have just as much right as anyone else to be happy.

I am a good, caring person, and I deserve to be loved.

And so on. She suggested writing them all down on separate bits of paper, folding them up and leaving them all over. Then, when accidentally finding one of these strips of paper, one should read it and take it to heart, and refold it and put it somewhere else, to find on another occasion.

June could picture it: people filling their homes, cars, closets, drawers, etc., with little scraps of paper. It seemed very silly. They were like good fortunes from a Chinese fortune cookie.

The next day, she found herself taking her notebook to work with her again, and using time between patients, or cancellations as occasions to do some writing. She had no idea how she'd finish it. She figured that eventually she'd put it away somewhere. She felt a little like she was doing a book of crossword puzzles. There was no real intrinsic value to it except the pleasure gotten in doing it - a small challenge.

She also spent plenty of time worrying about Michael and his promotion, and also fantasizing about kissing him and feeling his body against her own, and just seeing him smiling at her. She thought about some of the comments he'd made to her and occasions when she knew he was clearly attracted to her. After a long stretch of darkness, the sun had finally come out.

Michael came over to June's place after work the very next evening, and seemed nervous. As soon as she saw him, she knew something was irreparably wrong. She immediately responded with panic. She had finally let her guard down and now he was going to destroy her. She knew it. He didn't sit down, or even move close to her. He stood and paced and then stood still again.

"What's the matter?" June gently probed.

"I, uh, I have to talk to you about something."

"Something?"

"Someone."

"Someone?"

"Yeah."

June could feel her heart rate increase. She asked, "What do you mean, someone?"

"I've been wanting to talk to you about this for a little while now, and I haven't been able to. I want to explain it so that you'll understand."

"What is it?"

"I'm hoping you'll understand. I'm in a difficult situation."

"Michael, please just explain it."

"I've been struggling with, well, I think because you're a therapist, you'll understand what, uh, I have to deal with."

June decided not to say another word and just let him get to it. She knew there was no way to hurry him and she believed that he was about to tell her that this was the end. She just held her breath and sat very still. She couldn't believe that he'd imagine her being a therapist should make him feel less guilty about what he was about to do.

"I wasn't actually working late last night. I had to, well, I felt responsible for taking care of someone."

"Who?" June couldn't keep quiet. He had lied to her.

"Amber."

The name just hung in the air for a while. If it could have turned the room a dark, glowing, shade of orange, it would have. Images flashed through June's mind. His actual girlfriend. What did he mean by "taking care of her"? She needs him. June's worst nightmare had arrived. It was Amber. Despite her efforts to be motionless, she couldn't prevent tears from slowly escaping from her eyes and running down her face. Phil flashed through her mind.

"It wasn't just last night. There have been other nights. But, you have to understand, she's troubled."

She's troubled. He lied. And June felt like a fool. She'd rather be troubled. Actually, she qualified for membership in that category as well. She wanted to speak in order to tell Michael to get out, but she couldn't make a sound. She sat there, dumb and dumbstruck. Michael looked miserable. It was obvious that he didn't want to tell her about Amber, but felt that he had to; the charade had gone on long enough. June wondered what it must feel like to have two people madly in love with you. Would it feel good, or burdensome? She began to realize that she was a bit dissociated. He seemed to be standing at a great distance, although the living room wasn't large by any standard. His voice seemed far off, too; muffled.

"...three years and she's having a hard time. I feel responsible.....first great love.....problems I don't completely understand.....cries....cut her wrist."

June wasn't able to follow what he was saying. She felt far away and her own mind was racing at such speed that it interfered with her ability to hear him.

"...says no one cares....can't trust her....desperate..."

June felt betrayed and helpless. The light in the room seemed dim, and she felt faint.

"...took her to St. Johns for an evaluation...."

June began to realize that this was indeed a troubled person. He took her to the mental hospital. She felt her mind begin to return to the room.

"What?"

"She had made her arm bleed and I didn't know what else to do. She's been doing this kind of thing to me for six months now. But I can't just ignore it. She could kill herself."

June found herself staring at Michael. "What are you talking about? I don't understand. You have another girlfriend who you take to the emergency room?"

"We were in a relationship for almost three years, but I knew she had problems after about four months. I thought I could help her. And I couldn't just leave her. I'm sure you think I'm an idiot."

"The jury requires a lot more information."

"I officially ended it six months ago. But she acts like we're still together. She tricks me. I know that sounds lame. I don't know how to explain it."

June's vision, hearing, and voice had fully returned and she realized that the conclusions she had jumped to were probably not completely accurate. She needed to be a therapist. She couldn't be his jealous, crazed girlfriend right now. Save that for later. She had to help him, if that's what he was asking her for. Amber was starting to sound like a problem more difficult than Phil. She had to focus on Michael right now, not herself. She was actually trained to do that.

"Michael," she couldn't help relishing saying his name, despite everything. "You need to sit down and tell me the whole story. Then I can help you."

He looked completely surprised and then absolutely relieved. "Oh, thank God. I was afraid you would hate me for deceiving you."

"Could still happen." June felt a strength that was so out of character that it seemed alien.

"Where should I start?"

"At the beginning, of course."

CLINICAL INTERVIEW AND REPORT BASED ON FINDINGS REGARDING AMBER

Amber is described as an exceptionally beautiful, petite, 25 year old female, with thick, wavy auburn hair and a somewhat underweight, though well-proportioned body. She presents as outgoing and talkative and has a radiant smile. She tends to dress with care, wears clingy, suggestive clothing, and frequently behaves flirtatiously.

Usually, her affect tends toward the happy, upbeat side, although she can change moods suddenly, transforming into an angry, helpless child. This mood shift tends to occur when Amber encounters frustration. When a frustrating event occurs, Amber becomes enraged in a matter of moments. She has sudden angry outbursts, filled with loud cursing, accusations, and, on many occasions, violent, physical behavior. She has been known to throw and break objects and even hit, scratch, slap, and punch people while in an angry tantrum. She seems to believe that her behavior is fully justified. On other occasions, Amber has been known to turn her anger upon herself, and cut or burn her arms and legs. She has also made several serious suicidal gestures. These are of grave concern to those few who have managed to continue to care about her.

Amber is the only child of the union between her currently divorced parents. For both Madeline (Maddie) and Terence ("T"), this was their first marriage. They fell madly in love as teenagers, had a wild wedding at the local Veteran's Hall that ran late into the night and resulted in much drunkenness, and had Amber in their early twenties. Neither had attended college. T worked in an auto body shop, and Maddie was a hair dresser. Both made good money and had plenty of fun. Both freely enjoyed the use of marijuana, occasional cocaine, and frequent alcohol.

When Amber was born, life changed for the couple. Maddie and T began to have disagreements. Neither wanted to be in charge of Amber, although Maddie did, by default, become the primary parent. Resentments developed, and T became less available. He would stay out late with friends, leaving Maddie home in their small, lonely apartment with Amber. On occasion, when Maddie couldn't stand it, she would go out, leaving the baby alone. T apparently began to see other women, and Maddie made herself available to other men. But Amber was a hindrance. At times, Maddie would lose her temper and blame Amber for her troubles, especially with T. It was not unusual for Maddie to scream at Amber, to hit her, or to lock her in a dark closet for an hour. Amber has memories of many of these experiences occurring throughout the years of her childhood, although in general her memory is spotty.

Early on, T played only a peripheral role with her, although he did become more involved as she reached grade school age. By the time Amber was in first grade, her parents had been divorced for four years. She had irregular visitation with her father and whichever girlfriend was over at the time. On the occasions when no girlfriend was over, Amber would be extremely eager to return home to her mother as soon as possible. This was often not an option, however, as Maddie usually had plans for herself during her brief reprieves. She would be partying at a boyfriend's place for the weekend, in an attempt to recapture a bit of her lost youth.

As the years of Amber's childhood passed, she developed symptoms of anxiety, including school phobia and panic attacks. She also developed bulimia during her transition through puberty, sometimes throwing up fifteen times a day. It would turn into anorexia as Amber's teen years progressed, when she found almost complete restriction of food to be her most effective tactic, giving her a feeling of intense power. By age 15, Amber's relationship with her father had waned significantly as he had remarried and his new wife had begun quickly to have babies in sequence. Three in total. It had become clear to Amber that her stepmother found her to be an annoyance and her father was completely invested in his new, stable family. Amber frequently found that even visiting her father's home would throw her into an inexplicable panic attack. Her stepmother accused her of being jealous of her step-siblings and trying to take the attention away from them. Amber became avoidant, making up excuses not to go there. As the three children, two girls and a boy, grew into toddlerhood, Amber only had to think about them, and her ability to breathe would be compromised. On the rare occasions when she did visit her father's home, she found that she could not tolerate kissing or hugging him, and she absolutely hated the children. She felt only rage toward her stepmother. She could barely tolerate being there, could not eat anything while there, and felt nauseated for several days after a visit.

Amber's increasingly frequent panic attacks and increasingly worsening anorexia began to interfere with her ability to get herself to school on a regular basis. As she began to look more skeletal, her few friends made comments at first, and then avoided her. Her teachers looked at her with alarm, but none felt that it was their place to interfere. At age fifteen, Amber was doing poorly in school and seemed to have an eating disorder. On an occasion when Amber did make it in to school, the guidance counselor finally contacted Maddie after Amber had a fainting spell in the cafeteria.

Upon hearing from the guidance counselor, Maddie was irritated. Amber always wanted more attention. Didn't she understand that she had freedom that Maddie never had at her age? Maddie wouldn't have cared if Amber stayed out all night, slept with boys, or even experimented with drugs. Instead, she was fainting at school on the days when she wasn't too afraid to go. When Maddie was her age, her father would have beaten her up if she'd come in after midnight, or had been smoking. Especially when he had been drinking. But she'd do it anyway. Amber should have felt completely safe. She had the life.

Maddie believed that what Amber really needed was a boyfriend. She felt that skinny was Amber's natural tendency and not a problem. Maddie went out and bought her some suggestive clothing and set her up with the boy, Hank, who cut their grass here and there. He was 19. He'd show her a good time.

Amber wore a halter top and short shorts on the night of the date. She felt like she was in a daze. She knew that Maddie wanted her to be a normal teenager, and she wanted to please her mother. Hank came to pick her up in his truck, and Maddie waved them out the door.

When Maddie had approached Hank about showing Amber a good time, he'd looked at her with a lack of comprehension. Maddie, while maintaining her temper, had to explain that her daughter didn't get out much and needed to go on a date. Hank had still looked perplexed, so Maddie reiterated that he should show her a good time. She smiled, hoping she wouldn't have to explain it one more time to the idiot boy. A lightbulb seemed to go on in Hank's head and he grinned. He then reassured Maddie that he'd show Amber a good time. The date was set.

When Amber and Hank got into his pickup, Amber looked over at Hank and asked where they were going to go. Hank smiled and told her

that they were going to have a good time. Amber sat back, trying
not to have a panic attack.

Hank drove the truck to a secluded spot, a barely paved road into
the woods behind the factory. When he parked and turned to Amber,
she was staring ahead of her. Hank tried to get her attention,
leaned over to kiss her, but she was staring like a statue. Hank
asked her what was going on and she didn't answer him. Amber's
mother had given him twenty bucks to show her a good time. He
wasn't about to give the money back. Hank took her face in his
hands and kissed her hard on the lips. She gasped for air and
closed her eyes. Hank took that as a sign that she wanted more. He
undressed her. She didn't stop him, she must have wanted it. She
had a really skinny body. Not much to hold onto. He leaned his
seat all the way back and showed Amber a good time. He had heard
that the first time wasn't much fun for the girl, and assumed that
this was true for Amber. She didn't make much noise at all. When
it was over, they put their clothes back on and sat for a while in
silence. Hank thought it was relaxing to look at the trees around
them. Finally, Amber told him to take her home.

Amber walked into her mother's house, went directly up to the
bathroom, stepped into the shower and turned on the water full
blast. She was fully dressed. She needed to wash it all off. She
knew that she couldn't continue living. When Hank had been forcing
his penis inside her, Amber had experienced her first flashback. It
was her father, not Hank, putting all that weight on her, hurting
her insides, breathing his hot breath in her face. Amber stood in
the shower, water blasting on her head, and realized that her life
was ruined.

Amber's first hospitalization was a real shock to her. She wasn't
allowed to smoke whenever she wanted, she wasn't allowed to throw
up, or even not eat. She had to go to asinine group therapy
meetings, and take little cupfuls of pills every day. Immediately,
her goal became clear. She needed to get herself the hell out of
there. The more she demanded her release, or refused to cooperate,
the more she got smug looks from the nurses and stern looks from the
psychiatrists who were constantly breezing through the unit. Not
one of them was smart enough to understand her. It was like she was
in prison. She spent days two through six in a state of nearly
constant rage, breaking anything she could get her hands on,
overturning trays, pounding the walls. She ended up alone in a
small padded room after banging her head repeatedly on the wall.
While sitting in there, Amber finally calmed down enough to realize
that all she had to do was play their game and she'd have her best
chance of release. Then she'd be free to kill herself as planned.

When they opened the door to the seclusion room, Amber walked out
smiling and apologizing. From then on she was a model patient,
helping others, sharing in group, following all of the rules. She
was released by day eight. The insurance company had only approved
the eight days, anyway.

Maddie came to pick her up and they drove silently home. As they got out of Maddie's car, she turned to Amber and said through gritted teeth, "All better now?"

Amber still felt that killing herself was ultimately the best plan, and she had decided that it would be best done with pills. No messy blood to give it away this time. It was truly amazing how the scars on her wrists had practically disappeared already. She knew that this overdose plan would take time. She would need to amass enough pills. She went back to school and was biding her time.

She met a girl named Sierra soon after, in gym class. They'd both been at the school for a couple of years already, but had never talked before. Sierra was taller, with tan skin and long black hair. She wore cool jewelry. Sierra asked Amber for a cigarette while they were changing in the girls' locker room. Soon they were doing everything together, and calling each other constantly. They'd become soul mates. They practically knew what the other was thinking. They'd come to school wearing the same thing without having planned it. They went out together to parties. Amber felt terrific for the first time in her life. Someone cared about her. Sierra gave her bracelets and earrings, and Amber gave her clothes to wear. After a while they didn't know what belonged to whom.

Soon boys became an issue. Sierra was boy crazy. So, Amber became boy crazy, too. One Saturday night they were talking in Sierra's bedroom around midnight, and Sierra brought up the problem of being a virgin. She didn't want to be one anymore. Amber, after a moment's thought, realized that she was not a virgin. At first, she cried. Sierra made her tell the story. She told the Hank story, and left her dad out of it. Afterward, Sierra told her that it was really cool that she had sex so young and didn't have to worry about not being a virgin. Sierra was determined to have sex too, so they'd both not be virgins. Amber was so grateful to have such a good friend. Sierra immediately called up some boys to come over for sex.

This began a new phase in Amber's life, in which the sport of luring boys into thinking she was infatuated with them, sleeping with them, and then tossing them aside when she knew it would hurt them, became her main fixation. Sierra joined in the fun. The two girls reaffirmed their bond to one another each time one or the other tossed a boy aside. Amber actually attended school and ate enough to maintain a minimum body weight.

After about eight months Sierra met a boy for whom she actually developed feelings and did not want to toss aside. Paul seemed to have feelings for Sierra, as well. Amber was devastated. She tried to lure Paul away from Sierra, to show her that he was no better than the others. But he wouldn't respond. And he told Sierra, who promptly cut all ties to Amber.

Amber's depression reappeared. Ultimately, Amber became a high school drop out with a track record of serial hospitalizations. She was given multiple diagnoses, from Borderline to Bipolar, and sampled just about every mental health medication on the market.

She was able to hold a series of low-level jobs, losing each one when her ability to suppress her rage gave out.

At age 23 Amber was working at a diner. She waitressed with an attitude. Her boss was sympathetic enough to let her, in good weather, do the deliveries at lunch time, when she was most likely to lose her temper. Getting out in the fresh air helped keep her calm. As a result, she had been able to keep the job for almost a year.

The diner was two blocks away from the publishing house of Sheffield-Jacobs, where Michael had been working for several months as an assistant editor. His job required that, in addition to the hack editing work he had to do, he take the lunch orders from the more senior people around him and bring them their sandwiches and salads. It was only a matter of time before Amber arrived on the 37th floor with three salads and two turkey clubs. At first, Michael and Amber chatted and flirted a little. He seemed to Amber to be like the guys in high school she had been able to have such power over: nice, innocent, caring in a way she did not fully comprehend, and easily made to feel guilty and responsible. She liked him. He was pleasant and seemed eager to please. She flirted with him until he had to ask her out. She played on his sympathy, let him pay for her, made it clear that he should buy her gifts, and rewarded him with sex. He thought she was beautiful and delicate, and needed protecting.

When Michael showed signs of becoming overwhelmed by her demands, both emotionally and financially, Amber's rage would become unmanageable. The tantrums, screaming, crying, accusing, and violence would wear Michael down and he would concede.

Early on in the relationship, Michael tried to help Amber to reach her potential. He supported her emotionally when she took a nursing class in the evening, although she ultimately dropped out. He encouraged her to make friends, to tolerate others better, to be respectful to her boss. Amber would try to please Michael by trying, but would eventually resent him, along with everyone else, for not accepting her just the way she was. It was clear to her that he wanted to change her. Who the hell was he? But, she needed him. She didn't want to be alone.

Slowly Michael realized that he was trapped in a hopeless, unhappy situation. As he tried to pull away, he realized that he'd had no idea how trapped he really was. Amber became desperate and pathetic. Her bulimia reoccurred, she began putting cigarette burns on her arms and threatening that if anything were to happen to their relationship, she would kill herself. She had no other reason to live.

Michael found that in order to maintain his own sanity, he had to lie to Amber and spend much less time with her. He attributed his limited time to work. Of course, as time passed, Amber figured out that he was avoiding her. He wouldn't tell her where he was most of the time, didn't always answer her calls right away like he used to, and wasn't especially happy to hear from her. Their relationship became strained. She would find reasons to fight with him, just to maintain the emotional hold on him. At first he'd be sucked into the fights, trying to defend himself. But she'd made him pay so dearly with her threats and suicidal acts that he learned to remain calm. No matter what she said or did, he acted nonplussed. This enraged her as well, but was less likely to cause her to injure herself.

The distance between them grew, and Michael tried to let Amber know that he was not capable of being what she wanted; maybe he wasn't capable of being in a relationship at all. Despite her disappointment she hung on. She continued to hope that she could reignite his passion. He put an end to their sleeping together. This was fine with her, except it tended to make her suspicious that there was someone else. He would reassure her that there was no one else. Until, finally there was.

Michael agreed that this was a lot for June to have to digest. He understood if she felt angry or disappointed in him, but he wanted her to see the situation from his perspective. He didn't believe that he'd been in a relationship with Amber for quite some time. However, he did feel responsible for her and worried about her. He wanted June's help to finally extricate himself from all ties to her. However, he understood if June wanted no part in it. He'd been very nervous about telling her because he was afraid she'd just end the relationship with him.

June couldn't stay angry at him. It would have been hypocritical. However different her situation with Phil had been, there were parallels. And she knew that her relationship with Michael was nothing like it had been with Phil. She needed time. It was late into the night when she told Michael that she wasn't breaking up with him, but that she needed time to think about the Amber situation and how to handle it. He was relieved.

> *By six months, most couples reach the end of the honeymoon period of dating, because they begin to see the relationship as a potential long-term commitment. At this point, if either person has serious doubts, the relationship may end. If it continues, both members begin to reveal more of their inner conflicts and anxieties. Each partner tests the ability of the other to tolerate him or her in a real way. Relationship difficulties can arise causing the couple to struggle. Either they will work through this phase, or real intimacy will not develop.*

June took two days, during which her mind flipped back and forth from thoughts of Amber and Michael to Phil and herself, to Michael and herself, like some insane minuet. She knew she didn't want to end the one thing that seemed to have made her life worth living, that even helped her overcome the bitterness of five wasted years with Phil. But she had no intention of wasting another five minutes if the relationship with Michael was not the real thing. She knew she was going to give Michael the benefit of the doubt. She had to deal with the existence of Amber and decide what role she'd be playing in that ugly little nightmare. She didn't know how she'd manage it all, but she knew that in the end untangling all of this would make or break her relationship with Michael. This was only a test.

She had to tell Emily about Amber because she'd been happily keeping her up to date on how the relationship was progressing. Now June wanted her advice about Amber. Up until then, Emily had been extremely supportive and encouraging and eager to meet Michael. But once she heard the whole story she made it pretty clear that she thought June should steer clear of Michael until he was completely rid of Amber. She thought he had too much of his own baggage. She insisted that he'd lied to her and that she shouldn't trust him. June had wanted her to meet him, but now felt nervous about it. She couldn't bring herself to take Emily's advice. She wasn't going to break up with him. Emily didn't understand.

June had called her, knowing that she would say what she didn't want to hear.

"June, you just got yourself out of a long relationship with a man who you say couldn't commit. You're the psychologist. Are you getting yourself into another one? This guy is stuck with his crazy ex-girlfriend, and he can't separate from her. Don't you think that means he isn't available for you? Not to mention what it says about him and his judgment."

"Well," June floundered. "He seems to think he's available and just wants my help."

"Come on, June. I know you thought that he was the one for you. But maybe he's not. And if he is, then setting a limit and making him take care of this by himself will be a good test. If he cares enough about you, he'll prove it."

June immediately thought, what if he can't prove it and I lose him forever? "But, she's really crazy. I've had patients like that. It sounds like he's really trapped."

"Then it was irresponsible of him to get involved with you, and mislead you."

"I guess so." June was starting to feel like she wanted to get off the phone lickity-split.

"You know I'm telling you this because I don't want to see you get hurt again."

"I know."

"Please consider at least taking time away from the relationship so that he gets the message. Will you promise me you'll think about it?"

"I will," she lied.

"Good. Now, I have to drive the kids to soccer practice."

Thank God, thought June. "Okay. Thanks for listening," she lied again, feeling that Emily really hadn't listened at all.

"Anytime."

After they hung up, June couldn't decide if she felt strong and determined or weak and fearful. And she decided she couldn't talk to Emily about it for a while.

She woke up in the middle of the night with a compromise. She would tell Michael that she would advise him but wouldn't get personally involved. She didn't want to meet Amber and, keeping Emily's annoying warning in mind, she wanted to set things up so that Michael did the work.

HOW TO GET RID OF A BORDERLINE AS QUICKLY AS POSSIBLE

1) Be swift and decisive.

2) Do not show sympathy.

3) Speak in concrete language. (E.g., "It is over. I don't want to have anything to do with you again.")

4) Do not respond to begging, pleading, anger, threats or invitations to argue.

5) Pay no attention to reminiscing, recounting fond memories, and past promises.

6) Outwardly blame yourself, not the borderline.

7) Make it clear that you have moved on, so that she knows really is over.

8) Do not hug or hold her. Do not give her one last kiss.

9) Do not answer your phone. Block your e-mails. Return unopened mail.

10) Avoid going places where she might look for you. Make sure your secretary knows not to put her through to you on the phone or let her into your office. When she finally traps you, be prepared to get away as quickly as possible. Do not show any emotion.

When June spoke to Michael the next day, she was filled with determination. She told him she had devised a plan for him. He was grateful and eager to see the plan. They arranged to see each other that evening.

That night, June gave him a copy of her 10 steps and he glanced at it and blanched. They spent the evening discussing how he feared that she might kill herself if he did what June was suggesting, and that he didn't want to go through his life carrying that burden. She'd guessed that he would be concerned about that and was prepared to discuss boundary management with him.

Progress Notes on the Case of Amber

Day 1: Michael calls Amber to arrange for a meeting. She neither answers her phone nor returns his call. Clearly, she is avoiding him because she suspects it's to reiterate that the relationship is over. Michael plays

Amber's answering machine message for June, because she insists. In a breathy voice, Amber whispers, "Hello. I am unable to answer my phone just now, but your call is very important to me. Sit by the phone 'til I call you back." June struggles with intense feelings of jealousy that she tries to hide from Michael.

Day 2: Amber has returned Michael's call at his home number during the work day when he is not there to answer it. He is required to play the message she left for June to hear. "Michael," same breathy, sexy voice, "I wish I had been here to talk to you. I am so busy lately. But I miss you intensely. Call me later." He calls her that evening, and she once again does not answer the phone. In his message, Michael states that it is important that they speak. June finds herself almost hoping that they never do speak to one another.

Day 3: Amber calls Michael in the evening at home, while June is over at his place. Amber immediately suspects that Michael is not alone based on his tone of voice. Michael does not handle it well, not immediately saying whether someone else is there or not. He decides finally to deny that someone is there. Amber becomes agitated and threatens to come over. Michael agrees that she should and Amber changes her mind. She pressures him to tell her what the big deal is over the phone. He pushes for them to meet in person. She says she is very busy. He finally convinces her to meet with him the following evening. He hangs up the phone and is a wreck. He finds her intimidating and is afraid of what her reaction will be. June tries to give him support and suggestions as to how to handle Amber. Michael worries through the rest of the night that she could show up while June is there and fears a confrontation. June finally goes to her own apartment to sleep. She feels highly irritated.

Day 4: The meeting. Amber takes the news that her relationship with Michael is over extremely badly. She yells and screams and cries a lot. She says she doesn't want to see him ever again. She repeatedly accuses him of lying to her and asks him if there is someone else. Michael dodges the issue by claiming that it is irrelevant. But she wears him down. He finally admits that he has a new girlfriend. Amber wants to know who it is. Again, Michael resists by saying that they do not know each other. Amber persists. Michael refuses to tell Amber the name of his new girlfriend, just as he has been instructed to do. Amber gives up suddenly and says, "Fine." She storms away. Michael returns to June, feeling anxious and relieved at once.

Day 7: June's phone rings. She answers and the phone is slammed down. This happens four times, the last time at 3:00am.

Day 9: At 4:00 p.m., June is about to enter her building after a difficult day at work. A young woman approaches her and asks, "Are you a therapist?"

Bewildered, June answers, "Yes."

The young woman, speaking quickly, says, "Good. I need to make an appointment. My boyfriend is cheating on me."

June suddenly realizes that the young woman must be Amber. She checks her watch and says, "I'm sorry. I have to go." She enters her building with her heart racing.

Later that night, she receives more hang-ups.

Day 10: Michael receives a card with hearts pasted all over the front, inside of which is an old picture of Amber and Michael laying on a sunny beach together. Both are smiling. Amber has written in the card, "Remember how good it was." She signs it "Love, Amber." Later that evening, June and Michael discuss all that has occurred and decide that Michael must meet with Amber again, to make her put a halt to all of the acting out.

Day 12: Michael and Amber meet again. Amber cries and then suddenly smiles and tells Michael that she has met someone else. They part ways.

Amber disappeared after that. The plan seemed to be successful. June worked her regular hours with a couple of late nights every week. Michael's work tended to come in waves. He traveled a little, calling her a couple of times a day when he did. They spent most nights at one or the other's apartment, depending on their schedules, keeping certain items in each other's places, like toothbrushes, a change of clothes, shampoo, and hairbrushes. They exchanged keys. If June worked late, frequently Michael would have dinner waiting for her at her place. Weeks went happily by.

June began not to remember what life had been like without him. How had she managed? She seemed to have become a "we" without seeing it happen. She was still an "I," but also a "we". And she loved it. She felt anxiety about the future, but she also experienced a sense of security and belonging. She lived to be with Michael.

They spent their weekends together as much as possible. June now looked forward to weekends like she never had before. She loved Friday afternoons because they meant a block of time with Michael, from Friday night till Sunday night. Mixed in with her happiness, were some negative moments with other people. She received periodic calls from her mother.

"June, how are things with Phil?"

"With Phil? I told you we broke up."

"I was so sorry to hear that. Have you tried talking to him? You've had a long relationship. Is there any chance he'll take you back?"

"I broke up with him, Mom. I told you that. I don't want him back. I'm seeing someone else now. I told you..."

"Phil was good for you. He's such a mature, stable fellow with a good career. I'm only asking because I'd hate to see you regret a rash decision."

"It wasn't rash. I'm much happier with..."

"Had he cheated on you?"

"Cheated on me? Why are you so suddenly focused on Phil? I had no idea you thought so highly of him. You were so neutral while I was with him. Why are you all concerned about him now? You won't even let me tell you about Michael."

"I didn't mean to upset you, dear. It's not such a terrible thing to show interest in someone who's practically been part of the family for years. You seem to be oversensitive about it. I know you don't want to hear it, but as your mother, I feel obligated to say it. Maybe you are making a mistake."

"I'm not."

"You say that so quickly. Dare I say it, defensively."

"Oh, listen to that. My office phone is ringing. I have to run. Love you. Bye."

"I don't hear anything."

The thought flashed through her head that her mother might actually call Phil or maybe she had talked to him already. He could have called her. June was fuming, pacing around the apartment, beside herself. She needed to calm down. She decided a cup of tea might do it. She got the tea bag, opened the cabinet with the mugs in it, and dropped the tea bag behind her. She bent down to pick it up, stood up and smashed her head into the open cabinet door. Then she was grabbing her head and cursing. She went to sit down on the couch and rub her head until the searing pain stopped.

Gradually the pain and her emotions subsided. June tried to think rationally, get some perspective. Phil had probably called her mother. He knew what her relationship with her was like, but he'd been feeling desperate. It made logical sense to him, to look to her as an ally, when after a month or so June hadn't come running back to him claiming she'd made a mistake. What mother wouldn't want to help her crazy, irrational daughter? June should have handled the phone call better, stayed calm, thanked her for her input. Now she'd probably report back to Phil that June did seem unstable, like an adolescent acting out, and that she was obviously going through something. And that he shouldn't give up hope. Maybe her mother even enjoyed being helpful to him. June knew that he'd feel encouraged by that and increase his attempts to connect with her.

As if she had psychic powers, within a day she received a phone message from Phil. "I've written you a letter, poured out my heart into it."

She could hear the crying and shaking in his voice.

"Please read it carefully and get back to me as soon as possible. It's very important. I hate to beg."

As it turned out, there were five letters from Phil over a two week period:

SUMMARY OF LETTERS FROM PHIL

1) I love you. I see it clearly now. Your plan worked. I appreciate you all the more. I know you love me too, even if you won't admit it. You don't need to keep playing this game. You won.

2) You could at least have the courtesy to respond to me. How can you be so cold? I would very much like to talk to you. I'm not certain that this therapy is helping me or us. I think Dorothy is wrong about keeping us apart. I found a behavioral guy who I really like. I need to discuss this with you.

3) I can't hang on to nothing. Though your mother tells me to be patient, I have pride too. I'm starting to feel like you might not be the person I thought you were. The good, honest, caring person with integrity. You know I don't like game players.

4) I've begun to hate you. I hate you. I hate you. (Repeated approximately 50 times in red ink) p.s. I really like the new therapist I chose. Did I mention that he was a behaviorist? He's helping me. I'm feeling better.

5) You've made the mistake. You're a fool. We'll be back together in five years. You'll see.

Mostly, June felt relieved that Phil seemed to have backed off. She was much more focused on her life with Michael.

Eventually, June met some of Michael's friends and he met Emily. Although Emily was perfectly pleasant in Michael's company, she began to make phone calls to June that were very anti-Michael. Much more negative about him than she ever expressed with regard to Phil. She would insist it was to protect June.

"June, he'll hurt you. You can't trust him. You need someone more like Ed. He's the first guy you've been with since Phil. It's rebound. You know it. Let it go."

"I don't think you're giving Michael a chance."

"June, think about it. He's so young. His last girlfriend was crazy. What does that say about him?"

"What does it say about me that I was with a non-committal stick in the mud for five years?"

"He isn't non-committal now. You've had five years with him. At least he's not crazy."

"No? Neither is Michael."

"Then why would he date someone who is busy cutting herself?"

"People make mistakes."

"Do you hear how you're rationalizing for him?"

"He was young."

"He still is young. Too young."

"Emily, I don't want to have to defend him to you."

"Why should you feel like you have to?"

"I don't."

"But you are."

"Because you're attacking him."

"I am not. I'm trying to prevent you from getting hurt."

"But I've been hurt by the guy you're saying isn't crazy."

"Are you trying to get back at Phil?"

"Have you spoken to my mother lately?"

"June, we've been best friends for years. I know you. It doesn't sound like this Michael guy is good for you."

"What are you basing that on?"

"All the trouble he's brought to your life."

"What trouble? I was totally depressed when I was with Phil."

"And now you're an anxious wreck. You've been stalked by a lunatic."

"Do you mean Phil or Amber?"

"I feel like you're taking your frustration out on me, June, rather than looking at your situation. Your relationship with Phil had problems, but it was stable and predictable. He had a good career, cared about you."

"Have you been talking to him?"

Emily paused.

June had guessed it. He was so intrusive.

"He did call me once. I listened but told him he'll have to deal with you directly."

"Have you been working on your Masters in counseling without telling me?"

"Funny. I'm trying to help you. You seem to forget that."

"I'm not asking for your help."

"Because you can't see clearly right now. But I have to tell you what I know is true. Even if you can't hear it right now. I wouldn't be a real friend to you if I didn't. It is better to stay with the guy you've known for years and work things out. No one is perfect. At least you know what you have."

"Listen Emily, you're making me feel like you don't trust my judgment, even that you think I've gone crazy. You haven't gotten to know Michael at all. You're being very judgmental. My feelings are getting hurt."

"Well. Maybe I don't understand everything. You know I'm not a therapist. I work in computers and I pay attention to facts. Ever since you started seeing Michael, your moods have fluctuated, you're really happy, then miserable, then anxious, then fearful, then excited. You've been all over the map. You've changed. I'm worried about you."

"I'm sorry you can't be happy for me, Emily. I'll try not to share my moods with you in the future."

"You're taking everything I say and twisting it to the worst possible interpretation. I have to go out to wait for the school bus now. I'll call you soon to continue this conversation."

"Ok. Bye."

"Bye."

June knew she'd be screening her calls. If she'd had a written list of friends to call, she would have crossed off Emily's name in thick black ink. Phil was getting pity from everyone June thought cared about her. What was he doing calling her friends? They were all suspicious of Michael. A feeling of doubt crept over her now that she no longer was defending him on the phone to Emily. Was she not seeing something in him? Was she missing something with Phil? After hearing about Amber, Emily had done a 180 degree flip. It was painful to contemplate, but she'd have to stop talking to her. She couldn't understand her vehemence. Why would she be so eager to have June back together with Phil?

The inevitable eventually happened. June's brother Gerry was forced to call her. She knew it was a matter of time before she'd hear from him, considering the insane war path her mother seemed to be on, and the horrifying acting-out behavior that now defined Phil. Her mother would have asked Gerry, then reminded him, badgered him, urged him, pushed him, shoved him until he good-naturedly gave June the call. He wouldn't think to call her on his own. Why would he? It wasn't as if they were in touch. Her sense was that he saw her as distastefully weird, and a bit of a social failure. He and his wife avoided her so as to protect their children and themselves from the spread of a sort of symbolically oozing infection that clearly emanated from her.

Fortunately, June didn't answer her phone. She sat in the darkened living room portion of her studio apartment and watched the phone ring. The loud, alarming noise echoed around the sparse room. It silenced after four rings and the silence hung in the air, in anticipation of the message. It could have been Phil, June's mother, Emily, any number of people who she was now avoiding, causing her tiny world to shrink even smaller. But, it was Gerry, her successful, happy, normal, well-adjusted brother. A tidal wave of relief swept over her as she listened to his message. She had successfully avoided him and his generous, caring advice, which secretly concealed their mother's cruel judgment.

His message:

> Hi June. I guess you're out at work. Uh, I hope you aren't working
> too hard.....or anything. Ha ha. Actually, Mom asked me to call you.

Um. I hope you are doing well. Everything here is great. The kids are growing up really fast. They're playing soccer and keeping us busy. Paula's juggling work and being a great mom. We'd love to see you. Anyway, uh, and my practice is too busy to manage, which I guess is a good thing. Ha ha. Plenty of people with bad teeth, and all. So, uh, I don't like to get into other people's business, so I'm sure you can imagine how awkward this is, but Mom really pressured me, and she's getting older, so I told her I'd do it. So, don't get angry, but she wanted me to talk to you about this new boyfriend you have. Mom thinks he's not good for you. So, I thought I'd call and see what all the fuss is about. We always liked Phil. Mom seems to think you should go back to him. Now, I don't know all the details and I'm not telling you what to do or anything. But why don't you give it some thought. Phil is a really good, stable guy. A good provider, I'd say. I hope he's doing well. He really seemed like a good match for you, ha ha. You know, I can tell you from my own experience that sometimes relationships get dull. Not really anything serious. But maybe you find yourself looking around a bit. That doesn't mean you throw away everything you have. So, like I said, don't get mad. Mom made me do it. Ha ha. I just want you to be happy and all. Anyway, call when you have the chance, if you feel like it. No rush. We'd love to hear from you. Bye, June.

June found that to be so irritating on so many levels, she erased it immediately. Thank goodness she'd pretended not to be home for it. Now she would work at pretending not to remember any of it. The combination of rage and numbness she felt settled, amazingly, into a strange feeling of good humor. June could see that he was such a good son. No wonder Mom vastly preferred him. He called despite not wanting to talk to June, or caring about who she dated. It was such an obviously lame attempt to carry out their mother's wishes. He liked Phil. Their mother had probably told him, in a near hysterical voice, to convince June to go back to Phil. June imagined that he was a really nice dentist. Eventually, she'd call him back, and avoid the topic altogether. He wouldn't really like to hear what all the fuss was about, anyway.

She contemplated her unusual reaction to her brother, with some surprise and relief. She began making comparisons between dentists and psychologists. Maybe they weren't mortal enemies, after all. They both had to deal with managed care and malpractice insurance. At times, they both aimed to extract something, a tooth, an emotion, from their patients. They both wanted to help people, although the degree of sublimated sadism required to extract someone's tooth made June gag in horror. Perhaps the idea of digging into someone's emotional muck nauseated him. Certainly, like the rest of the family, Gerry believed that her career was at best a kind of manipulative medicine show, without the medicine.

The messages on June's answering machine were a breezy walk in the park in comparison to those Michael was receiving on his machine.

Series of messages from Amber to Michael:

1) Hi, Michael. You aren't answering your phone. I wonder whether you're home and avoiding me. If you are, I can't blame you. Things have been really rough here lately. I could have used you to talk to. But I know you no longer care about me. What happened, Michael? If I could only understand what happened. One minute we were happy together, and the next, you drop out of my life. What went wrong? I just don't understand. Call me.

2) Hi Honey. I miss you. I know you miss me too. Remember my peach teddy. I have it here. It makes me think of you. I could put it on for you again. It's okay if you've made a mistake. You can always come back to me. I'm here waiting for you. I love you. I'll always love you. I'll never, ever stop loving you. We were meant to be together. Call me.

3) I know you don't care about me. No one cares about me. I'm worthless, a worthless piece of shit. I realize you don't care, but I just thought you should know that this is goodbye. I won't be bothering you anymore. You can forget that you ever knew me, or cared about me, or fucked me or promised me your love. You can pretend that none of that ever happened, and go on with your happy, goddamn life with Miss Doctor Perfect.

4) Michael, I need you. I just cut my wrist and there's blood everywhere. I feel weak. I think I am dying...Please know: I always loved you. I can't live without you....

When June got the panicked call from Michael, she was actually ready. She had heard the first three messages and could tell things were escalating. She told him to call the police and send them over to her place to get her. He was very tempted to go there himself and save her, which was, of course, exactly what she wanted. But he took June's advice and sent the cops. Somehow, neither of them felt very good about it. Amber was hospitalized briefly.

At least they had their work to distract them from the mess their relationships with everyone else in their lives had become. Michael was plenty busy, and June had her usual appointments.

Annabelle threw herself onto June's couch, dropping her leather bag and matching key chain onto the couch next to her. She looked excited. Excited in an over-the-top, agitated, frightening way.

"I had the most glorious night." Long pause. Annabelle always left spaces when telling a good story, to get the listener's anticipation cooking. "He took me to the Top of the Crown. We had the seven-course wine-tasting menu. It had to be a $500 meal. It was divine. He held my hand, told me I was beautiful, looked into my eyes. Everyone around us could see what an amazing couple we were. The waiters brought us special treats, fawned all over me. One waiter flirted with me a little, helping me learn how to use the sauce spoon. But Guy wanted all my attention. He was so cute. I wanted to run my fingers through his hair. His suit was impeccable. I just wanted to touch it, the fabric was so fine. I really think he has feelings for me."

When she finally paused, June was able to interrupt her. "Who is Guy?"

Annabelle laughed. "Oh. I forgot to tell you. I met him at the Ritz Bar a few days ago. We just hit it off. And he invited me to dinner. He's so terrific, and not cheap like so many guys." She laughed again. "I met a guy named Guy."

June nodded, smiled, tried to appear happy for her. But she knew the pattern. She guessed that the next thing that happened was he had gotten them a room, they'd had sex and then he'd taken her home. She probably wouldn't ever hear from him again. And June would have to weather the fallout. Like she didn't have enough of her own fallout to weather.

"After dessert, he was holding my hand. He asked me if I wanted to go sit and have a quiet after dinner drink. He's so romantic. I said yes, of course, thinking we would sit in the lounge. But he led me up the elevator to a room. He had planned ahead and gotten us a room. I couldn't believe it. He is so thoughtful. And, of course, I couldn't control myself. I was so attracted to him. We ended up in bed."

June was still nodding, still trying to be neutral, supportive, inquiring, anything but horrified and disgusted. She couldn't help thinking: Was she intentionally naive or in denial or what? How did this keep happening to her with no learning on her part? Was she so desperately needy?

"The only thing I didn't love was that we didn't stay over. He said that he had a really early meeting, and needed to drive me home. I got him to stay an extra couple of hours, and he finally got me home by around 4:30am. I don't know why we couldn't just sleep there. It was so comfortable. Really high quality cotton sheets and down pillows. The room was just beautiful."

"We sat in his top-of-the-line BMW in front of my apartment, making out, for a good half hour. Then he made me go up to my apartment. I didn't want to leave him. I feel so upset now."

"Upset?" June thought that this might be a good sign.

"I miss him. Why isn't my life always like that? When will I hear from him again?"

"Well, Annabelle, it does sound like you had a wonderful evening for the most part, but..."

"You are going to try to ruin it for me, aren't you?" She glared at June.

"No. I don't want to ruin anything. I know you feel you've missed out on so much in your life. But, since this is therapy, we should take a look at anything that comes up. You just said you were upset."

"Because I miss him now. That's all."

"There have been other occasions on which you've had a terrific time with a guy, but then he vanishes for awhile."

Annabelle looked irritated with June now. "Well, I can't predict what will happen with Guy. Should I just go out with nobody, so I avoid all guys who don't call me again?"

"That's not what I'm saying."

"Guy told me he is really busy with work. Obviously, he's a high-powered guy."

"Do you think that's all there is to it?"

"He told me his divorce hasn't gone through yet. He has to be careful. There's a lot of money at stake. He can't just spend all his time out dating. I have so little joy in my life. Don't ruin my one happy memory."

"You know I don't want to ruin anything for you. I want to help you to protect yourself."

"I don't care about that."

June was wishing that the minutes would tick by faster. She knew it would be a few more sessions before her disappointment would overwhelm her like a tidal wave, before they could address this pattern of behavior. She didn't want to be there for it, but she knew she would be.

Unfortunately for both Annabelle and June, her prediction came true in a manner of speaking. Instead of a tidal wave, though, it would be a series of small, soaking storms. They began in the next session.

"I haven't heard from Guy. He doesn't return my calls. I was thinking it would be cute to bring him a little box of chocolates from Top of the Crown. I could just leave it on his desk if he's not in his office. I'm not sure, though. I don't want to look suspicious or get him in trouble. But, it could look like I am a client. He gave me his business card when we met, so I know exactly where his office is. No one has to know why I'm dropping off a little package. I mean he's busy. It would just be a little reminder."

"What are you hoping he'll do in response?"

"He'll call me to say thank you. I found the perfect card to put in, too."

"You're trying very hard to get his attention."

"I just know that there's something special between us. I can't stop thinking about him. I know he feels it, too. We are just so perfect together. I deserve to be loved. That's all I want. Is that too much to ask?"

"It would be nicer if he called you without the reminder."

"No kidding." Annabelle paused and stared at June. Then she suddenly started to cry in loud, wailing bursts. "No one cares about me. I can't let it go. I know he doesn't care. But I need him. It's not fair. Why does everyone else get what they want in life and I never get anything? All I ever get is shit."

"Why do you need him?"

"My life is nothing. Empty. Worthless crap. I need something to look forward to, or I may as well just die." Annabelle continued to cry loudly.

June tried to maintain a neutral demeanor.

"I know that look," Annabelle accused. "You are thinking something stupid like, "Annabelle should go out and meet a nice, normal guy who's available, and they'll live happily ever after," as if that could happen. There's no one out there. No one. I'll never meet anyone. You have no idea what that feels like."

It was a moment in therapy in which there was nothing for June to say. She definitely did know that fear. Anyway, Annabelle always needed to be the least fortunate person in the room, with the most pain and in the most pathetic circumstances. June didn't want to outshine her. She sat there trying to look sympathetic.

Annabelle's final angry and hopeless words to June before the session ended were, "You have it together, the perfect life. You have no idea what it's like to be me. You can't possibly empathize."

June had her own session with Dorothy that same evening and found herself eagerly anticipating it. She wanted to have Dorothy witness the fact that everyone but Michael had turned on her. She was healthier, she felt, and the outcome was that the entire system had stopped working. That was her theory, anyway. Everyone wanted June to be back the way she had been for years: depressed and stuck. Now that she had become hopeful and happier, they were all attacking her. She couldn't wait to let Dorothy in on it.

Dorothy seemed skeptical at best about all the hysteria that was being aimed June's way. She began asking how June might be contributing to everyone else's reaction to her. Why would so many people be turning on her now? Was she feeling guilty about something and reacting in a hostile or defensive way? Were they judging her on her current behavior with them, rather than the issue of who she should be dating? What were her true feelings about Michael having lied to her? How did June actually feel about Amber and her intrusions? Did she see Michael as weak?

June left that session with a pounding headache and a feeling like she could vomit. She felt a little like she had been playing the role of Annabelle somehow. She was grateful that Phil was nowhere in sight. She felt suspicious of everyone including Michael. How could he have been so stupid? Why was he so weak and easily manipulated? Did she too have disdain for him? Who did she think she was, having disdain for anyone? She needed a hole to climb into. Dorothy made her see that everyone had been worried about her and that her reactions to them, hostility, sarcasm, and avoidance, had made them all the more worried. They must have been thinking that Michael was some kind of a crazy cult leader and June had signed up for a long-term membership. Why would she be so defensive otherwise? Why couldn't she discuss her concerns with them in a mature way? Maybe because she was a pathetic, immature, obnoxious, self-centered loser?

June got to her apartment, grateful that Michael was out of town. She needed to hide alone. She reached for the door just as she was concluding that there could be no such thing as June, happy and in love. She had completely forgotten why she'd been eager to meet with Dorothy. Had she actually hoped to accomplish something? If one is, by definition, a loser, not much can be done.

The next day she had a session with a patient, who after two years, was terminating her therapy. A success story. June wasn't completely useless.

At the beginning of their final session, June took a long look at Sarah. She was mildly surprised to note that she looked different from when they had begun their work together two years earlier. More mature, more sure of herself, brighter. She had come in at age 25, having had repeated brief relationships that had felt shaky from the start, but about which she denied any problems until she was taken by surprise when each guy suddenly broke it off. After the fourth repetition, she wisely decided that she needed some help.

She'd been June's favorite kind of patient ever since: intelligent, hard-working, eager to understand, and considerate. She didn't miss appointments, or call between sessions, except once or twice early on when another guy had broken things off with her. He was the last one. They'd explored her need to accommodate others excessively, her need to avoid confrontation at all costs, and her underlying low self-esteem. She had worked hard between their sessions, trying to notice her behavior patterns and alter them, trying to hold back on the accommodating and to be more direct. She'd done a good job, and it had paid off for her. She got a promotion and raise at her job in finance, at which she'd been at the same level and salary for four years. She'd also met a nice guy who was willing to let her practice her confronting skills on him. June felt proud, triumphant and sad that this would be their final appointment.

Sarah looked back at June, squinted and smiled. "I can't tell how you're feeling, Dr. Gray."

"How do you think I'm feeling?" June felt ashamed. Definitely a Psych 101 response, and in a termination session.

But Sarah smiled "I knew you'd ask me that. Well, I think you're going to miss me. I think you've found me interesting." She paused, eyeing June closely for affirmation or encouragement.

"You are interesting." June had begun to feel a sadness seeping into her veins.

"And I think you'd like to stay in contact with me."

Here was an awkward moment. Sarah had become increasingly perceptive over those two years in which she had come to weekly appointments. She'd become more empathic with others, something that occurs naturally in good therapy. June didn't really want to terminate treatment with her. She had pretty well accomplished her goals, and as a result, their sessions had become enjoyable. She'd arrive with plenty to discuss, reach her own conclusions, draw her own insights and make the connections to old patterns. She no longer needed June there, even to witness her self-examination. She was bright, funny, entertaining and June felt sad that she would no longer have the inside scoop on her inner life. But she had to set a boundary. It would not be good or ethical to befriend a patient for many reasons.

"Dr. Gray," She interrupted June's thoughts. "I have a fantasy that I'll be walking through the town you live in, with my future husband and a new baby, maybe a couple of years from now, and we'll run into you. You'll be so excited to see my baby for the first time. I'll let you hold her. I guess if we run into each other, it's unplanned, isn't it, Dr. Gray?"

"Yes. I see what you mean." June felt an aching in her heart. "I'd love to get an announcement if you do have a baby." As she spoke she pictured her foot stepping over a line but she couldn't pull it back. "I will definitely miss our meetings."

Sarah began to cry softly. "I'm afraid I won't be able to handle everything without you."

June looked at her, 27, bright eyes, always in a neat, trim outfit. June had believed she'd prepared herself for this moment, but she was taken by surprise by the emotions she was feeling. She needed to pull herself together. This was Sarah's last session. June smiled at her, having heard the same concern repeatedly over the years in which she had practiced. "Once you stop putting up with inadequate treatment from others, you find it difficult to go back. And you've already noticed that, right?"

"Yeah. I can't let anyone get away with anything. But I still get anxious when I have to confront someone about how they've treated me." June could see that she had relaxed.

"I think that's natural. You gain more confidence with practice and probably with age, as well."

"When I think back to the guys I was with before, I almost can't believe it. They were so selfish. I was working so hard to keep the relationships going that I didn't notice that I got nothing out of them."

As June looked at Sarah, sitting across from her, reviewing how she'd changed, reassuring herself that it was real, she felt the pain in her heart transform into a knot in her stomach. She recognized herself in Sarah and felt a tinge of jealousy. She had moved past June. She felt capable and confident about managing her relationships for the most part, and here June was, still struggling. Her entire circle of family and acquaintances were happy for her and supportive of her new relationship. They could see her growth and approved of it. She'd told June so repeatedly. Her mother had been wary of her seeing a therapist at first, but had become completely reassured once Sarah had gotten her raise at work. Sarah had joked that since then her mother had become the biggest supporter of therapy. Her family and friends had also let her know how much they approved of the new guy she was with, using that acknowledgment to also let her know how much they had disapproved of all the others. The grip on June's stomach twisted more tightly. She wasn't sitting there to compare her life with Sarah's. She was there to help her celebrate the changes she'd made, and bring some closure to their therapy.

"Sarah, you've worked very hard and it has paid off. You're far more self-aware than you were when we first met two years ago. So you are more aware of others, too. And that awareness helps you in all areas of your life."

"My mother says that she can't count on me to do things for her before she even asks anymore."

"That sounds like a good thing."

"It is. I told her those days are over. It's her responsibility to tell me or ask me if she needs something from me."

"How did she react to that?"

"She agreed that it was for the best, but I could hear a little regret in her voice."

"How did you feel about that?"

"FINE. I don't care. I can't be responsible for everyone else, or even just for my mother. I need to take care of me. I told her I'd still do just about anything for her, though. Her response was that I used to say I'd do anything for her, not just about anything."

"Progress!" June laughed.

"Dr. Gray, it's meant a lot to me to be able to come here and face stuff. It's been so helpful." Sarah's eyes started to fill again.

"I'm glad you feel it's been valuable." June told herself that she needed to be on her own, encouraged to be on her own. She needed June's confidence in her ability. They could not stay in touch.

When their final session finally ended, they both stood up and hugged each other awkwardly. June let her out of the office and closed the door behind her. She felt sad, relieved, jealous all at once. And she knew that she'd miss her and miss hearing about her life. She'd probably never hear from her again. Success.

Obsessive Compulsive Personality Disorder is a defensive character style in which a fear of losing control over unconscious aggression and fearfulness is quelled by the substitution of ritualized thoughts and behaviors. Isolation of affect, magical thinking, and intellectualization are the constellation of defenses employed to avoid the unacceptable impulses. Inflexible, black-and-white thinking is also a common indicator. Obsessive-Compulsive Disorder, a distinctly different disorder, is not integrated into the personality, but consists of isolated rituals and compulsions that feel as though they must be performed to maintain safety.

Despite the various challenges Michael and June were facing, they were spending time together and feeling closer. It seemed natural that the time came for June to meet Michael's mother, Penelope. A luncheon was arranged at her request. Michael had delayed the event for as long as possible. He repeatedly informed June that this was a luncheon, not just lunch, as if there were some secret message she was to decode from that. He offered little other information.

They met at the tea room in the Masterman's Department Store, where Penelope evidently lunched with frequency. It was so precious June wanted to laugh out loud. There were bird cages hanging from the ceiling, chandeliers dripping with glass, green and white striped wallpaper interspersed with wallpaper covered with huge pink tea roses. The chairs had white twirled metal backs with green and white striped cushions. Michael and June were by far the youngest people in the vicinity by about 30 years.

Of course June was having a nervous day of more than usual proportions. She'd slept poorly the night before and had been distracted in the office while with her patients. This was Michael's mother she was meeting for the first time. Of course, she wanted to make a good impression. She needed it to go well. It would even out the chess game that was still being played in June's head, in which all of her family and friends were being lured over to Phil's side of the board.

Penelope and Michael were waiting at the entrance to the restaurant when June stepped off the elevator. For a very brief moment, nothing happened. She could see out of the corner of her eye that off in the other direction were brightly colored clothes hanging on racks in the shopping part of the department store. Michael smiled nervously. June smiled back, trying to look relaxed and calm. Penelope blinked about forty times as she gave June a tight little smile. She was dressed meticulously in a fitted blue suit, and a frilly blouse. She clutched her overly large handbag to her chest with both hands and looked very proper. Her hair was in a short, blondish-grey colored bob, she was about the same height as June and she had a small, pointy nose and bright blue eyes. Neat and organized. They said their hellos. June shook a limp, tiny little hand, and they were led to their table. June felt like they were birds in one of the cages and she was heading toward her perch. She wanted to order a little bowl of seeds. She had the very strong feeling that Penelope would not enjoy her humor at all.

The silence between them was an awkward one. June reminded herself that she'd come equipped with her skills as a psychologist and could put them to use rather than sit there looking stupid. She expressed her extreme pleasure at finally having the opportunity to meet, to which Penelope gave her a quick nod while continuing to scrutinize her with what was beginning to occur to June was apparent displeasure. Michael looked like the pain he was experiencing was causing irreversible internal damage. No wonder he had avoided this moment so persistently. June decided to rise to the challenge.

"I've heard so much about you from Michael. He says that you are interested in decorating."

The annoyed look she'd received in response led June to begin forming her hypothesis about the exact nature of Penelope's craziness. But she needed more information, which Penelope soon began to provide. She leaned toward June and shook her head as though she were talking to a hopeless idiot. "I am afraid that there must be a misunderstanding. I do not work in the field of interior design. I employ designers when I feel that a room requires an update."

Michael interrupted, "I may not have explained it to June in a very clear way...."

Ignoring him, Penelope continued, glaring at June, "I have never worked a day in my life." She said this so triumphantly that June assumed she wanted to be congratulated.

"That's wonderful. I didn't mean to suggest that...."

Interrupting June, she continued, "Is it?" More glaring. "Don't you believe women should work? You have a job, I assume?"

"Yes." This was June's chance to tell her something about herself. "I do work. I'm a psychologist..."

Michael's mother snorted through her nose. June was shocked. Even her own family members had yet to actually snort at her about her career.

Michael interrupted with sudden intensity. "Let's look at the menu. What do you like to order, Mom?

His mother, clearly not at all interested in June's career, anyway, smiled warmly at Michael. "I like to order the tea sandwiches. They really do bring out a lovely selection." His mother's nasty mood seemed to vanish as she spoke to Michael.

June tried to join in. "Should we all order the tea sandwiches?" She looked at them both and smiled.

"You can have whatever you want." Penelope gave June a brief, tight little smile. "There is no need for you to try to please me by ordering exactly what I am ordering. Do you always do what others do, or do you think for yourself?" Apparently, Penelope's good mood was unidirectional.

"Now and then I do manage to think for myself. Why don't you order for me today, though. I'm going to find the ladies room." June got up and walked toward the elevator, only to discover that she had to go in the opposite direction and walk past them again to find the bathroom. Michael tried to look sympathetic as she walked by.

By the time she'd composed herself in the ladies room, and mulled over the fact that Michael hadn't adequately prepared her for this meeting with his crazy mother (Did he realize how crazy she was?), the food was being served. She sat down.

Michael's mother made no effort to talk. June was eager to choke down a few delicate, crustless, rectangles of bread smeared in yellow or green paste, suck up her glass of water and be done with the nightmare.

Between thumb and forefinger, Michael's mother lifted the daisy-patterned napkin off her little rose-covered china plate, shook it three times, and lowered it with a flourish to her lap. June leaned over to reach for one of the sandwiches when she saw her lift the napkin off her lap and shake it with a flick of her wrist, three more times, and then settle it back down.

June looked carefully over at Michael, who was drinking from a tiny flowered tea cup as if nothing unusual were occurring. She saw the whole thing start up again with the napkin and couldn't stop herself. She blurted out, "Is everything ok?"

Penelope looked at June and with a challenge in her voice, said, "Of course it is."

June had a moment of paralyzed shock, from which she resurfaced as Michael reached for a sandwich. She silently watched as the napkin routine occurred four more times, totaling seven. After the napkin settled a seventh time, Michael's mother took a sandwich. June wanted to laugh or shout out loud or kick Michael. Instead they ate in silence. Except that out of the corner of her eye June saw his mother nibble three tiny bites from one end of her sandwich and then flip it around and nibble three more bites.

Their eyes met and locked. June shoved the remainder of her sandwich into her mouth. Michael's mother watched her with an air of superiority, and purposely nibbled three bites on each end repeatedly until all that was left was a thin sliver of tea sandwich. That she folded gently in half and popped into her mouth.

June did not count her chews, but had a hunch there was a pattern to that as well. She took a few slow deep breaths to calm down. She had already been to the ladies room. If she returned so soon, Penelope would assume that June had some sort of bladder problem, not that it could even compare to whatever she was suffering from.

After Michael's mother finished her tiny sandwich she lifted her napkin and patted her lips three times on each side. The napkin ritual began again. It was flicked three times and then floated back to the lap. June couldn't stand it. She made herself speak. "This is a nice place. I had no idea that there was a restaurant inside Masterman's. The sandwiches are very good." She knew she was sounding insincere and lame.

The ritual stopped suddenly, and Michael's mother eyed June and smiled that tight, little smile. She practically spit, "So, how did you meet my son?"

Michael jumped in, "We live in the same apartment building."

June added, "We actually met in the laundry room."

Michael's mother turned to him and smiled sweetly. "Perhaps there are other people you might meet in your building, as well."

Answering her seriously, he replied, "Well, I have met a few other people, but you know I have long work hours so it isn't easy."

"I know, Honey." She kept smiling at him.

This woman was like a patient. June decided to do something, speak, confront, act-something. She said, "I noticed that you have a little ritual with your napkin." She tried to say it sweetly and smile. She had to force her face to act against its better judgment.

Beady eyes glared at her. "What do you want with my son?"

She felt small again. "We're dating."

"What do you want from him? Don't you think you should be dating someone your own age?"

June looked over at Michael. He shook his head as if to say, "Don't take it seriously."

June did the only thing she could do. "Please excuse me." Back to the safety of the ladies room. Inside the green and yellow, prettified but still dingy department store ladies room, June looked at herself closely in the mirror. Michael must have told her that she was older than him. Did he say seven years? Is that why the napkin ritual was seven times? Should she be angry with him? How did he not notice that the awful woman he calls his mother was torturing her? He actually loved Her Royal Craziness?

June had to go back out there, but she needed a game plan. She shouldn't let a little old crazy woman intimidate her, even if she was in love with her son. How unfair was it that her own family was so disappointing, and then she meets someone whose family appears to be even worse?

She left the ladies room to return to the table. She could see as she approached that the two of them were having a friendly conversation. As June neared the table, they both looked up. Michael asked, his face all concern, "Are you all right?"

"I'm fine." June smiled hard. She grabbed another sandwich and bit hard. It was all fluff, like eating a marshmallow. The thought crossed her mind to take three nibbles from each end.

Michael's mother gave her a fake smile and sweetly asked, "So, I suppose it isn't that unusual for a woman to find younger men attractive?"

June looked over at Michael who just happened to be entirely focused on his cute little tea cup again. "I've never dated a younger man before. Do you like younger men?" June heard herself say it and was shocked at her own audacity.

"My husband was ten years older than I. He was a wonderful, dear man. We miss him every day. Don't we, Michael?"

Michael looked at June. Was it defeat, anger, restraint? She couldn't read the look. He answered his mother. "He was a great man. I do miss him."

After Michael had walked his mother to the elevator and had returned to their charming little table, June gave him a long look. Finally, she said it. "You never told me your mother was crazy."

"Crazy? Oh, come on. She's not that bad. Definitely overprotective."

Now June had confirmation that she had entered some alternate universe. And the red flashing DO NOT ENTER lights were blinking brightly. She ignored them and continued. "She has OCD and is narcissistic."

Michael blinked twice.

"She's got borderline features. She's definitely a personality disorder with compulsions." June watched Michael's changing expression. He was getting upset. With her. But she couldn't contain herself. "Can't you see it?" Suddenly it hit her. This was how he had ended up with Amber. He had grown up accommodating a lunatic. He definitely needed to know this. They had to discuss it so that he would see how much sense it made from a psychological perspective. June felt a wave of relief. At least she understood now. She looked up at him, wild with eagerness to bring some clarity to the situation, probably looking a bit like a lunatic herself.

"June, I don't understand the terms you're throwing out haphazardly about my mother. She's a good caring person. I'm not saying she doesn't have a few quirks. She's overprotective. I'm her only son. Why do you need to diagnose everyone? What's your diagnosis for me?"

June was dumbstruck. "I don't actually diagnose everyone." She hadn't even given much thought to diagnosing Michael. She felt confused and dismayed. Was there anyone else she hadn't diagnosed? Dorothy? She had secretly concluded that she was overly intellectualized, and as a result of isolation of affect, artificially calm. Perhaps an "as-if" personality with obsessive-compulsive features. She'd certainly diagnosed Phil many times over. Forget about her parents. There was her overly perfect, people-pleasing brother and his eating disordered-with-compulsive-exercise wife.

Michael was staring at June in a way she didn't like. She had to defend herself. "I can't help it if I see personality disorder and mental illness in general, so readily. That's what I am trained to do. I think I'm pretty good at it."

"So, now you're saying my mother is mentally ill."

"Michael, I'm not trying to attack your mother. But I realized something very important. It helps me to understand how you ended up with Amber. I..."

Interrupting her, Michael practically yelled, "Would you turn it off? Just stop it."

June felt afraid suddenly. She had overstepped the boundary. Never go after your boyfriend's mother. She should have known that. A beginner's level lesson. Why had she done it? Was she angry with Michael? He hadn't protected her like she'd wanted him to at lunch. Old feelings of having no one on her side had come up. "I'm sorry. I got carried away. I didn't mean to be insulting, Michael. I'm really sorry." June felt her eyes fill with tears but she controlled it. This was her fault. Who the hell did she think she was, commenting on everyone else's flaws, when she was just one big flaw? "I can see that your mother really cares about you. I'm glad I had the chance to meet her." June tried to be mature and not to lie. She definitely did not like her, but she was glad to learn about her influence on Michael.

"I don't believe you. Why should I believe that you were glad to meet her when you're telling me she's mentally ill? Sometimes you are impossible, June. You think you know everything, you jump to conclusions, make accusations and you always believe you're right. If you're such a great psychologist, why didn't you know how upset I might get if you started diagnosing my mother?"

"Um. That's a good question. I guess I mistakenly thought you had a kind of separation and distance from her that I have from my mother..."

"So now you're saying I'm not adequately separated?"

"Well, no, but..." She was saying that.

"If I were like you, and not respectful toward my mother, I'd be healthier?"

They'd reached an ugly impasse. He'd cornered her. She was now feeling like a personality disorder herself. Had she not realized what a terrible person she really was? Was she stuck in an adolescent rebellion with her parents? Was she then the unseparated one? Did separation mean acceptance, allowances, some level of flexibility with one's parents that she didn't have? June felt light-headed and dizzy. She needed time to think. She felt a strong urge to call her own mother and be nice to her. She felt an equally strong surge of humiliation and sudden thoughts of suicide. She tried to get a grip. She didn't want to argue with Michael. He had definitely won this one.

June tried to smile. "I think you're right and I'm wrong and I need to do some serious thinking, alone."

Michael looked at her with just a touch of curiosity in his annoyed face. "Okay. Fine. I'll call you later." He got up and walked away.

June needed to cry badly. She sat still, hardly breathing until he left. When she saw him get on the elevator she got up and ran back to the ladies room. She knew if she just spent a little time in there, her new second home, she'd get herself pulled together enough to get herself back to her real home before losing it altogether. She felt dissociated. She couldn't decide if she was really as awful a person as she seemed to be at that moment.

Back home in her darkening apartment, she felt some deja vu. She threw herself on the couch face down and had a good cry. How many times had she done this before?

Michael did call her that night and they had a brief, awkward conversation in which she apologized one more time. She avoided all further discussion of his mother. Within the next few days, they had moved on enough to be comfortable with one another again. But they did not discuss the luncheon again.

One afternoon June was in her office, in between sessions. It was an hour during which Michael might normally call because she usually made it a break in her schedule to eat, do notes, make any calls she had to make, and of course, talk to him. She had let her 11:00 patient out of the office, and left the door between the office and waiting room open while she wrote notes. She began to sense that someone was in the waiting room. She got up and peeked through the doorway and was shocked to see Michael standing there looking around the room. He'd never been in her office before. She suddenly became panicky. Why had he come here? What had been happening that she'd been blind to? Was it the lunch? Was he like Phil, unable to be intimate past a certain point, and was going to give her some excuse now? Had it gotten to be too much for him? Had his infatuation faded? Was Amber back in the picture? They hadn't said "I love you" yet. He would have to say it first. She wasn't brave enough. She could see it in his eyes sometimes. Unless he was there to let her know that he never would say it because it wasn't true.

June took a deep breath and acted surprised although she had been secretly watching him for about ten seconds. "Michael, what are you doing here?"

"I wanted to see your office and surprise you." He looked and sounded nervous, which made her feel extremely nervous. "I knew that you keep this hour open, and I had some free time today. I hope its okay that I'm here." He came over and kissed her on the cheek.

That calmed her down a bit. Who would kiss someone and then tell her it's over? Why even kiss her? "Of course it's okay. I've wanted to show you my office. I'm glad to see you." She felt shaky. He was quiet. It seemed that he had something to say. She waited a moment and then invited him to come into the office from the waiting room. After he sat down, he was still quietly looking around. June couldn't stand it. After a couple of moments, she said, "What's the matter?"

She sat in her therapist chair, and he sat on the couch. Pretty symbolic. She saw Michael take a deep breath and then he said, his eyes looking down at the gray industrial-strength rug in her office, " I care about you very much. These past five months have been some of the best in my life..."

June interrupted him before she knew it. "You mean it's over?"

Michael looked surprised, "No. I'm not saying it's over. But I've been feeling bad about something. I don't know if I can say it very well. And I'm afraid that you'll think badly of me."

June felt her heart land on the ground and splat in a heap. Something had to go wrong. She was, after all, supposed to lead a miserable life full of unrelenting pain, suffering, and loneliness. What was it, a prison record? He'd killed someone? Had he lied to her in some huge way? He already had a wife? Or a child? Or he's gay? Or he still loved Amber?

"Just tell me what the problem is before I have a brain hemorrhage. I have four more people to see after you leave." June was sweating and felt like she could barely catch her breath. She was on the verge of tears. Why was he doing this to her? And, worst of all, Michael didn't seem to notice. He was so wrapped up in his big secret that he had finally decided to reveal, after misleading her all this time. Why couldn't she have just walked in the rain back in January to the laundromat, rather than meet him that Saturday morning in the basement laundry of the building?

Michael opened his mouth to speak and the words came out slowly. "I've been feeling that, well, my job, I got my promotion, you know, because I was very good at my previous job..."

She was getting frustrated and angry with him. He came to her office in the middle of the day to ramble on about his job and make her so upset that she would hardly be able to work with her patients for the rest of the day. She heard herself say, in an irritated voice, "Spit it out."

Michael looked surprised again, and said, "I'm sorry. I guess it's about manipulation. I was good at selling my clients and that's why I got a promotion. And now I'm doing even more selling and I am good at it. But I feel very bad. Maybe I have been selling you, too. I don't know. I am starting to not like my work. I'm not sure if you really even know me or I'm just such a good salesman that you think you do. But if you really did know me, maybe you wouldn't like me so much. I mean, I, uh, knew that you wanted attention and time with me and I wanted to make you happy..."

"But you aren't sure that you are making yourself happy? Is that it?" June tried to speak calmly. But she had to say it, get it over with. She saw where this was going. He would have to find himself, get his life organized, and have time away from her.

"No," said Michael, "I'm happy with you, but I just don't want to mess things up between us. I don't want you to think less of me, or find out that I'm not as terrific as you thought I was. I feel like I disappointed you when we were out with my mother. It was hard for me. I'm thinking that maybe I should, um. I wanted your opinion on this, but, I, uh, I'm not sure. I've never done anything like this before, you know...I..."

"What is it, Michael?" June practically screeched.

"Maybe I should see a therapist," he mumbled.

When a relationship becomes passionate, an assumption is made that both parties have found something that resonates, both at a conscious and an unconscious level. People find partners at the same level of separation and emotional maturity which makes for emotional understanding and empathy between them, but can also cause problems. This is especially true when both people are unconsciously looking for the relationship to serve as a way to resolve old conflict-laden issues.

June was stunned. She could barely believe what she had heard. "You want to go to a therapist? For therapy?" she choked.

"Uh, maybe. I don't think I'm totally crazy or anything. I just think..." Michael fumbled, searching her face for a reaction. "I don't want you to feel like you have to be a therapist to me."

"You're crazy," June cried out, jumped up, grabbed him, and gave him a big hug. "I would never judge you for wanting to see a therapist. It doesn't make me unhappy at all. As long as you aren't breaking up with me, I'm glad you want help. I'm sorry you're feeling confused and unhappy about your work. And I don't think you've hidden your true self from me. I am a therapist myself, you know. Not that you've used me as a therapist for yourself, but I like to think that I'm a pretty good judge of character. Although, sometimes I can get carried away..." She was so relieved that she couldn't shut up.

Michael's body had relaxed and he seemed very relieved, too. He stepped back from her and said, "That's why I thought maybe you could suggest someone."

"Sure. Let me think about it and give you some names later." June paused and looked into Michael's eyes, "I was sure that you were telling me that it's all over. Are you actually saying that?"

"No." Michael paused, then continued. "You are definitely the best thing that has ever happened to me. I'm afraid of ruining it. It makes me nervous sometimes. Maybe I don't deserve to be with someone like you."

"I feel the same way, Michael, and I've had five years of therapy." She smiled, feeling such relief that she had tears in her eyes. She hugged him again and said, "To me, this is like you saying you are considering converting to my religion." Michael laughed. She continued, "Therapy is supposed to help you know how you really feel and to feel free to do what you believe is best."

"I'm not sure I want to stay at my job, either, and that makes me feel like a failure. I worked hard to get there, and now I'm not sure." Michael spoke anxiously.

June could certainly relate to that feeling: four years of college, five years of graduate school, huge debt, and a constant nagging doubt about her career. "I know what that feels like," she said.

June could see the relief in Michael's face. He smiled at her and said, "I feel kind of silly. I think I made a big deal out of this whole thing. I made you upset, and I'm interfering with your work day because I couldn't wait until later..."

"I'm glad you felt you could come here. I'm glad to see you." She wanted to say 'I love you' but she stopped herself as usual.

June asked Michael if he wanted to take a quick walk around the neighborhood, after she showed him around her office. She watched him recover completely, making jokes about her couch and whether she hid candy in her desk. He actually found an old package of crackers in her top desk drawer. She couldn't remember how long they'd been in there, or where she'd gotten them.

As they walked in the sunny daylight, Michael put his arm around June and she felt him kiss the hair on top of her head. She felt a strange mixture of relief, sadness, empathy, lingering anxiety over the expectation of bad news, and joy. She was touched that he'd revealed his insecurity. It made her heart go out to him. She felt she loved him even more, and felt more vulnerable to him, especially while he was feeling unsure of himself.

Despite her own faith in the benefits of psychotherapy, she wondered whether he might realize that he was enacting something with her, or wasn't really getting what he needed in a relationship. She felt closer to him, yet somehow more nervous than she had an hour earlier. She also found herself scanning the people around them as they walked, looking for Amber, fearful that she'd suddenly appear before them while they were together, and that Michael would be nice to her. That he wouldn't be able to not be nice. June had worked with people like her and knew that Amber was more likely to injure herself than anyone else, but she worried that she seemed to have just given up suddenly. Fortunately, they didn't run into her.

June had trouble concentrating on her sessions that afternoon, because of a gnawing insecurity about the future and the fragility of all things, no matter how solid it may feel at any one moment. That feeling of empathy and awe regarding her patients' struggles kept coming up for her, threatening to make her too emotional. She worked hard not to lose her boundaries.

When she arrived home at her apartment that night, she walked in to find Michael sitting on the couch waiting for her. He apologized again for seeming to be out of control. She sat down with him, held his hands, looked him in the eye, and reiterated to him that she felt good that he'd shared his feelings with her. It made her feel closer to him. She told him that she had come up with a couple of excellent therapists. She gave him two names, a male and a female, both experienced, well educated, sensitive, and impressive therapists. She didn't know either one except as a distant acquaintance.

Michael took the names and informed her that he'd be calling tomorrow, and that he'd probably try the male first although he had no idea whom he'd feel more comfortable with. He took the piece of paper she had written the names and numbers on, folded it up, and put it in his back pocket, as if to bring the whole discussion of it to an end.

June looked at this beautiful, anxious guy sitting on her couch, trying to make his nervousness disappear, and she felt utterly drawn to him. She knew she'd fallen for him because of his sensitivity and at a deeper level even still because of similar issues regarding self-esteem and guilt. He was not as in touch with his as she was with hers, but he'd never gotten this involved with anyone else before and he'd never had psychotherapy. He did care about her, or his old, deeper level of anxieties would not be coming to the surface.

June knew she loved him and it would devastate her to lose him. She couldn't protect herself from being vulnerable to him. She'd have to take her chances. She leaned over and kissed him, and put her hand in his hair. He immediately responded to her with intense passion. They were kissing and caressing and undressing each other like they hadn't seen each other in weeks. They lay back on June's couch, with clothes strewn all around them, swept away.

Afterward, Michael held her in his arms on the couch. He ran his fingers through her hair. He said, "How did I get so lucky?" They were quiet for a few moments, and she sensed that he had more to say, so she remained quiet and hopeful. He leaned very close so that his lips touched her ear, and he whispered, "I love you."

Tears came to her eyes and her heart melted. She turned to him, looked into his expectant eyes, and whispered back, "I love you, Michael." They kissed and held each other tightly. She was in heaven. His words rang in her head.

Finally, Michael broke the silence. "I've wanted to tell you for a while, but I was afraid. Saying it makes it seem more real somehow and I guess I wasn't sure if you really felt the same way."

"Me, too. It means so much to me."

Michael put his mouth next to her ear again and whispered, "I love you," over and over. Tears rolled down her cheeks. She couldn't stop them. Michael held her face up and kissed the tears. He said, "I'll do anything to make it work between us."

"I will, too," she quickly added. "Then there's no reason why it shouldn't."

Finally, they stood up, threw on some pajamas and climbed into her small bed. They fell asleep in one another's arms. June slept deeply.

She awoke to a beautiful sunrise shining in on them through her window. She was happy and hopeful. The previous night had been a fairy tale. Things were definitely going better than she had imagined they ever could. She looked at Michael sleeping peacefully. He was real.

Not long after that, June came home one night after working late, expecting to drop off her things and run up to Michael's apartment. He was supposed to have his first psychotherapy appointment with Dave Cohen and she planned to wait for him at his place. She'd planned only to ask if it had gone well, and that was it. It would be up to him as to how much of his actual session he divulged to her. This was all on her mind when she opened her apartment door to find Michael sitting on her couch with a very strange expression on his face. He looked pained and excited at once, like he was in a sort of state of shock. He had a crooked smile on his face and his eyebrows were up like he had discovered a great secret in life. He had his arms folded across his chest. He said nothing when June came in.

She felt immediately upset seeing him that way. They looked at each other silently for a moment, and finally June said, "Well?"

He said, in a tightly controlled way, "Hi, how was your day?" but he wasn't really asking.

"What's the matter?" You hate Dave? He charged too much? What is it?"

"No, that went fine," Michael laughed stiffly a bit. "I liked him. He seemed intelligent and I felt pretty comfortable talking to him."

"Okay. That's great," June responded. "You know, you don't have to tell me anything about it unless you want to. Therapy is supposed to be confidential, your time, so..."

"Yeah. I know." He interrupted her rambling. "It went fine." Michael smiled strangely at her again. "I went to my appointment at five o'clock and got back here by around six thirty. So, I thought I'd come down here to wait for you, since tonight is your late night. So, here I sat, with nothing to do for a couple of hours. I noticed this notebook sitting on the coffee table..."

"Oh God." June gasped. She'd been writing in her book that morning and was actually finishing up all she had to say. She didn't need it so much anymore and was planning to put it away somewhere. He had read it. "I'm embarrassed. It's nothing. Just a joke, something to fill up my free time. I was planning on putting it away..."

"It's terrific. You're a very good writer. It needs editing, but it's a great book. Why didn't you tell me you were working on a book? You could have showed it to me. You know I'm in the publishing business," Michael said excitedly.

"No," June responded. "That's ridiculous. It's not a serious book. I'd never publish that. It's embarrassing. It's a joke. It is not a professional book. It would be embarrassing to publish. It would destroy my career. You can't be serious." She was getting more and more upset. She kept going because he kept sitting there with that stupid knowing smile on his face ignoring everything she said.

"Of course I'm serious. This could be a bestseller. I can spot one from a mile away. It would be a big boost to your career. You'd have people lined up waiting to see you." Michael seemed upset too, and was speaking in a pressured way. Not his usual gentle self.

"I wouldn't want my colleagues to believe that I'd written anything as superficial and simplistic as this stupid book." June felt angry, and leaned down to pick up the book. He grabbed it before she could.

"Look," Michael said slowly, "I thought you would be glad to hear that I think it's great and has a lot of potential."

June stared at Michael. "I see what's going on." She paused. Maybe it was just that he loved her. She quickly said, "You think it's good because it's mine. I wrote it. You aren't objective about it. That's very sweet of you."

Michael looked insulted and said, "Look, if you wrote a piece of shit book, I wouldn't be sitting here telling you that you are sitting on a gold mine. This book will be a top seller. I'll show it to a couple of my colleagues if you'll let me, and get their views on it, if that would convince you."

"I don't like how you're acting about this," June practically cried. "You're scaring me. You don't understand. You won't listen to me. It's a joke. I don't take any of the advice seriously. I was making fun of that kind of advice, of the twelve step theories and the ten ways to improve kinds of advice books. I can't publish that under my name. It really would destroy my career."

"A pseudonym. That's a great idea." June could see Michael's mind going like she'd never before seen. "But, to be honest about it, you'll receive requests for appearances and readings, and it would be best if you could do them." Michael stopped and looked at her.

June started to cry. He stood up and hugged her and said, "I'm sorry. This is what work is like. If you don't want to publish it you don't have to." As he said this, he handed her the book.

She took it and said, "Good. I don't want to publish it."

Michael's face fell. This was not the response he wanted, which is probably why she said it. She felt angry and confused. She was actually not sure at all what she wanted to do, and fairly flattered by his saying the book was great. But she was afraid to jump into this. And maybe he was wrong. How could he truly be unbiased? What if she published it, and people didn't understand that it was written as a joke and she became a laughing stock? He could just go on with his career, and hers would be over. "I really need to think about this, okay?" She looked up at him and tried to smile.

"Of course," Michael responded. He had backed down. "You would need to get an agent first, and negotiate a contract and have it edited." Michael paused. "It would be for a lot of money, you know," he said slowly.

What did he mean? Around $40,000? A year's salary? June would have loved to have that, but not in exchange for her entire earning potential for the remainder of her career.

"How much could I get for this piece of junk, Michael, realistically, in your opinion?"

"Well," he considered, "with a good agent, I think you might be able to negotiate with a publisher for around one hundred thousand dollars, plus the usual royalties. It is a first book. There might be other income involved too, lectures, a workbook. Who knows?"

"That's ridiculous," June yelled. "You're in fantasy land. This whole thing seems totally unrealistic. Look, you haven't been happy at work. You think that this book is a quick way out. You..."

Michael interrupted her, "You don't have to believe me, if that's so hard for you. If you'll let me, I'll show it to..."

"I'm not ready for you to show it to anybody." June felt panicky. She hugged the book to her chest. "I'll think about it. That's all I'll promise you." Michael and June stared at one another, as she clutched the book. They kept standing there and staring at each other. It became awkward.

"I'm sorry, Michael," June faltered. "I don't know what else to say about it."

"I can't help it. I know what I'm talking about, June. This is my greatest dream and worst nightmare wrapped up in one. Maybe I should go home and give you some time. Just please don't let anything happen to the book. Please leave your options open." Michael began walking slowly toward the door.

She couldn't believe he was walking out. "Why is it your worst nightmare?" she gasped.

Michael stopped walking, turned back around toward her, and said, "I don't want you to feel manipulated by me and I'm afraid you're going to feel that way unless I drop the idea of publishing this book. Maybe you underestimate yourself and cover up your higher goals with sarcasm and jokes. Why don't you think about that? I don't know what else to say about it tonight. So I better go."

With that he left and June heard the door close behind him. Her eyes had filled with tears again. She couldn't even see him leave. She stood there clutching the stupid book, unable to move. And on top of everything else, he had only had one lousy little 45 minute therapy session, and he's telling June that she covers up her real feelings with sarcasm. Well, fuck him. How could he walk out like that? He left her standing there, supposedly so that she could sort out the myriad thoughts in her head and make a life altering decision, about which she already clearly knew his opinion.

She certainly did feel manipulated by him. If she decided not to publish it, her relationship with Michael was on the line. He couldn't understand her perspective. He wouldn't even consider it. The years of studying, dissertation research, graduate school loans, attempts to gain the respect of her colleagues, and most importantly, to do difficult, often painful and frustrating work, in which the lives and happiness of others rested in her hands, all meant nothing to him. She could end up a laughing stock. How could he be so definite about something that could destroy her life if he happened to be wrong? "Oops, I'm sorry June. It looked good to me. You win some, you lose some." He had nothing to lose. She had everything. Maybe he didn't care so very much about her, if he could take the consequences of his misjudgment so lightly. She thought of Emily's warning. She supposed he knew he could always dump her like he did Amber before her, as others laughed and pointed at her, and he could escape untarnished.

And June didn't believe that there'd be anything near that amount of money. That sounded like the most unrealistic piece of all.

The other problem with this whole fantasy of Michael's was that, suppose the book were to be a popular hit. How would she be able to face herself in the mirror knowing the book was a sarcastic joke that foolish people were eagerly taking seriously? She didn't want to get paid big money to play a cruel trick on vulnerable people, who would be desperately looking for help to escape their depressions by reading her stupid book.

Then she'd have to go on interviews and book signings and pretend that she had seriously written this ridiculous book to help people in need. How would she face her colleagues, who had supervised her and referred to her over the years? They would see her as a traitor, making fun of their hard, serious work. How could she live with herself?

June was so unhappy to see this side of Michael. What had come over him? How could this idiotic book have come between them? Why hadn't she put it away that morning? That would have prevented this entire thing. How dare he read it without asking her first? She wouldn't have read a notebook of his if she'd found one lying around. How dare he? She felt infuriated with him for ruining the evening, not to mention their relationship. Her eyes were burning with rage. Their relationship would not hinge on an embarrassing book full of ridiculous scribblings that he thought were brilliant because he was having a job crisis. Why had she ever written it?

June had gone from having everything one moment to having nothing the next. Why had he left after making her feel so bad? She threw herself on the couch. The book crashed to the floor. She cried and cried and couldn't stop. She never should have believed that he loved her.

Chapter IX: Forgiveness

Forgiveness is the acceptance of another's limitations. A letting go of the angry, disappointed attitude that was held closely like a shield. True forgiveness is perspective, distance, and reduced vulnerability. It can strengthen the relationship while reducing its intensity, allowing for a less needy and more tolerant attitude. Forgiveness is never a black-and-white picture, but is always grey. It is often accompanied by sadness, the benefit of which is a clearer, more stable view of the other that allows room for judgment. Most importantly, forgiveness is always a compromise. (Be Happy, by June Gray, Ph.D.)

It was hard to believe that Michael was so focused on money that he'd imagine that June's silly writings could be a big seller. She hadn't thought that money was so important to him. He'd seemed to see it as a necessity but not a career focus. Why would he have gone into the low-paying publishing business otherwise? Unless he had some fantasy that he would become a bestseller finder, or write one himself. Maybe he believed that he'd have a rare talent for finding unknown, unsuspecting writers of small, ridiculous works that had the surprising potential to become blockbusters.

It was early morning. June's face was terribly puffy. Her heart had slowly dripped out all over the floor throughout the night. She fantasized that Michael and she would see one another that night, and the entire thing would never have happened. Commonly called denial.

In her attempt to eliminate Phil from her life, had June attached herself to an immature, unrealistic, greedy guy? Was her judgment that bad? She made her living trusting her impressions, intuitions, and judgment. Could she have made such a grave error in her own case? She couldn't figure out any other explanation.

She needed to get to work and get through the day, listening to the troubles of others, and offering them understanding and solace. She'd done it before in something like this state of mind. She was going to do it again. Life sucked. She wished she could have stayed home in bed. Instead, she found herself grabbing her briefcase and walking out the door before she knew what she was doing. As soon as she opened it to the empty hallway of the apartment building, June felt the first new disappointment of the day. Michael had not spent the night sleeping in front of her door. He wasn't waiting outside, contrite about his behavior. As she let the door close behind her, she caught a last glimpse of the book on the floor near the coffee table. The weapon implicated in the ripping out of her heart.

> *Children must feel safe in order to be able to learn and integrate information, to be curious about the world and to feel an eagerness to explore. Before issues of moral import can be addressed, there must be safety. A person who does not feel safe will not function adequately. He will be consumed with finding safety. He will not be able to feel motivated to better himself, pursue education, have ideals, philosophical thought, artistic expression. He will not be able to maintain relationships.*

June struggled through her day, forcing herself to attend to the needs of others. She kept hoping he would call her. She checked her answering machine at home repeatedly throughout the day, even though he would have no reason to call her there unless he was trying to avoid but still contact her. She worried that while she was checking, he might have been trying to reach her. So she would check again.

Why did she feel unable to call him? June thought about it, even decided to do it several times, but couldn't. He left her. He had to contact her first. She could not move past this idea. It was like a mathematical equation. What would she say if she called him anyway? "You shouldn't have walked out. You shouldn't have gotten so upset about my stupid book." She had nothing she needed to apologize for. But he had plenty to apologize for. Why wasn't he doing that?

June dragged herself home. It was not late, but she dreaded going home to her lonely apartment. What would she do now? Even more immediately, what would she do for the five or so hours before falling into bed? She couldn't imagine eating. She felt nauseated. She didn't want to spend the night crying again. She wasn't prepared to call Emily or anyone else to talk about her sad predicament. She couldn't face the possibility of either the smugly comforting attitude or the bluntly stabbing "I told you so." She couldn't concentrate, so reading was unlikely. Unless, perhaps, she read her own book. Maybe that would give June some perspective on it. She had never actually read it. She'd written it in spurts, but she had never really viewed it as a book.

That became the plan for the evening.

June walked through her apartment door with slightly more energy now that she had a plan, braced to not find Michael there. She entered the dark empty apartment and felt her heart sink nonetheless. She looked down for the book. She'd left it on the floor that morning, unable to go near it. She didn't see it, so she began to look around. Her heart started racing. She looked all around the living room. Where was it? She thought she had seen it when she left, lying on the floor, away from the couch. She panicked. Had Michael come and taken it? To publish it without her consent? To steal it? To take credit for it himself?

June had been scraping through the day, holding on by her fingernails, and this made her slip right off the ledge. She tore apart her living room area with a vengeance while enraged thoughts circled around in her head. He stole her book. How greedy could he be? She needed to get proof that she wrote it. They never should have exchanged keys so early in the relationship. How could she have been foolish enough to trust him?

Her book was suddenly turning golden in her mind. Yesterday she wanted to burn the damn thing. Today, because she didn't have it, it was the most valuable property she'd ever had. She was aware of the lack of logic, but she just couldn't help it. He must have been in her apartment. He had walked in, spotted it on the floor, grabbed it and left. As her blood boiled with rage, June couldn't help feeling excited that he'd been in her apartment. He had touched her doorknob when he opened the door. She couldn't help herself. She headed to the door, just to put her hand on the knob where his had been. She longed for him. If he could just be what she thought he was, she'd give him the damn book and let him do whatever he wanted with it. She would dedicate it to him. She wanted him back so achingly.

> *As the relationship intensifies over time, the risk of unconscious sabotage increases. Each partner reacts to the other, creating a push-pull dance, experiencing the painful vulnerability caused by the powerful longing and raw emotions, balanced by anxiety, anger, and fear of rejection. This is a time in the relationship rife with misunderstandings and disappointments as well as increasingly strong feelings of love and need.*

June pulled her apartment door open to have her ridiculous, desperate merger experience with the doorknob, and, to her shock and relief, Michael was standing there about to knock. He smiled, "Have you been watching for me?" As if she had been standing lookout through her peephole, which, thank God, she had not yet done.

June could feel her anger rising to the surface again. But she bit her tongue. Maybe he would apologize and seem sincere. She gave him a weak smile back and retorted, "I thought I heard something."

They stood there a moment awkwardly, until Michael said, "Is it okay if I come in?"

"I guess so," June faltered.

"Look, June. I don't know what to make of yesterday. You really hurt my feelings. I know you have the doctoral degree and all, but I had no idea how little respect for my profession and my abilities you have. You think that I don't know what I'm doing. How would you like me to have that opinion of you and your profession?"

June was floored. He felt that she had insulted him. She couldn't believe it. "You wouldn't be the first."

"You know that you wouldn't like it. You would feel hurt. I care about your opinion. You wouldn't even consider mine. You act like you know everything. I had to leave yesterday because you made me feel bad and I knew you wouldn't understand it, and I couldn't handle that. Just like right now. I'm sure that you don't understand. You're probably just putting some psychology label on me, analyzing my behavior. You don't even seem concerned about what I am telling you. The other reason is mostly personal and probably too complicated to explain, even if you did care to understand it."

June stared at him, trying to put it all together. She burst out, "Of course I care to understand it." Tears were coming to her eyes. How had this turned out to be her fault? Had she messed up? She thought it had been so crystal clear that he had. Of course, in couples therapy, it is always assumed that it takes two to tango. June felt dizzy. She noticed that they were still standing in the doorway. She heard herself say, "Please sit down. I'm sorry that I hurt your feelings. I would never intentionally do that. You took me by surprise yesterday and I panicked. Maybe we can just talk it out and see if we can understand one another better."

They sat on the couch. June looked up at Michael and could see vulnerability in his eyes. He looked a little relieved, but also uncomfortable about what else he had to say. In June's state of confusion, tears were rolling down her face. She felt anxious, guilty, and relieved that he hadn't abandoned her. He was there to work it out, if possible.

Michael whispered, "Why are you crying?"

June was not exactly sure why she was crying, so all she could respond was, "Just ignore it. It happens sometimes in emotional situations." Michael reached out and wiped off one tear with his finger and put it to his lips. It only made the tears fall more quickly.

"I'm not sure how to explain this to you, June, but I do respect your knowledge and ability in your field, so I'm hoping that you can understand it. I don't want you to think that I'm manipulating you in any way. I'm unsure sometimes about whether I do that without knowing it. I was accused of being manipulative by my father a lot when I was growing up. And in my field, it helps in making deals and marketing. But I don't want you to feel that I'm trying to do that to you. Yesterday, I was so impressed by your writing that maybe I got carried away. I couldn't judge myself."

As Michael spoke, June tried to take it all in. She tried to understand what he meant, how he was feeling, what his relationship with his dad must have been like, whether he had manipulated her, whether she was overreacting, whether he still loved her, all the while trying not to be distracted by her desire to hold him and kiss him. Had he tricked her? She was rolling it all over in her mind when he mentioned her writing and she remembered that the book was missing. Maybe he was manipulating her that very instant. Her head was ready to explode off her body and enter into orbit around the earth.

"You don't have to do anything that you don't want to do." Michael was on a roll. "But at least give me the chance to show you that I do know what I am talking about. And after that, if you still really don't want to publish the book, then you have the right to do that, of course..." Michael took a breath and looked closely at June, "I'm getting the feeling that you stopped listening to me," he said accusingly.

She had been trying to listen. She could see he was struggling to be clear. "Well, I..." she slowly began.

He interrupted her, "I know you think that I didn't hear what you said about your professional status, but I still think there's so much that could be helpful...that's not what's on your mind, is it?"

"Well, um, no. You see, I had left the book on the floor, here in the living room..." She responded slowly, so that he could interrupt her.

"Oh, right. I came by to get it because I wanted my colleagues to see it and give you their opinions."

"What?" June's heart was racing. She felt lightheaded. She was trying to remain conscious.

"I'll explain everything."Michael had a guilty look on his face.

"But you didn't ask me first." June heard herself speak, but felt dissociated from her body.

"I guess I felt like you wouldn't let me," he said looking down.

"Then that's how it would have been. You did something you thought I wouldn't have wanted you to do." She spoke slowly, felt sick saying it, but had to.

Michael looked upset. He spoke falteringly. "I needed to prove to you that my opinion isn't worthless, that I know my profession, that I'm good at what I do. If I had asked you, and I know I should have, and I'm very sorry that I didn't, I feel really bad about it. But if I had asked you and you had said no, then I would be stuck with you believing that I'm some kind of fool, or crazy, or grandiose, or money hungry or just inadequate, and I couldn't stand that. It wouldn't be fair. I don't feel that way about you. I didn't know what else to do. Maybe I'm sensitive about it because I'm a little younger than you. I don't know."

He made a good case against her. Was it manipulation or honesty? June felt so unsure of her own judgment that she wasn't sure what to say. Then it occurred to her that someone else, or other people, people she didn't know, were reading her embarrassing book. She felt ashamed. "You mean there are other people reading my book right now?" she cried out.

"Actually, they've already read it. I put a lot of pressure on them to do it quickly. I have the book upstairs. I should've brought it back down with me but then I would have had to explain right away why I had it. I guess I wanted to explain my feelings to you first. I know that I shouldn't have taken it. Do you want me to go get it?" Michael was ready to jump up and go.

"You mean they've already read it and told you what they thought? " June was mortified. "If we manage to work this relationship out, how will I ever be able to go to office parties with you?" She was thinking, or panicking, aloud. She looked up at Michael and was surprised to see panic in his eyes, too.

"What do you mean if we manage to work it out? What does that have to do with this? Why did you say that? You think because we have a disagreement you have to start thinking it won't work out?" Michael was absolutely beside himself. He looked like he was going to cry.

June started to cry again. "Yes. I don't know," she whimpered.

Michael said, "There's nothing in the world more important to me than you. I don't care what you do with the book. You can burn it and never discuss it again. That's not what I care about. I felt like you didn't think I was smart enough or knowledgeable enough. I needed to show you that I'm worthy of your respect. We can forget about the book if you want."

June filed Michael's passionate words away to be mulled over later. "I do respect you, Michael. I know you're very bright. I don't know anything about your profession really. I'm sorry if I seemed to disregard your opinion. It wasn't about you; it was about me. I know that I wrote a piece of junk, from my professional point of view. That has nothing to do with your opinion about whether it would be a popular piece of junk. I guess if it weren't junk there'd be almost no chance it could become popular. But I didn't look down on you in any way. I'm grateful for you. I love everything about you. I was crushed when you walked out of here last night. I thought you hated me. I was afraid, so I guess I assumed the worst so it wouldn't come crashing down on me like a bad surprise..."

At this point they were both crying. Somewhere in her ramblings Michael had put his arms around her and hugged her. Then they were both sobbing.

> Listening is a key to a couple's success. Each partner needs to allow the other to express his or her feelings. An empathic, or mirroring response is the next step, allowing the speaker to feel heard. Judgment and decisions should be held off until each person has spoken his or her mind and received supportive, caring feedback. After each partner has spoken, and has felt heard and understood, then the couple may proceed to the problem-solving part of the discussion.

June hadn't had much experience negotiating in her last relationship. The rule was that she was always wrong and Phil was always right. This was obviously going to be a lot more complicated. She could see that she and Michael were both sensitive about their careers and about whether they were worthy enough to be loved. They would probably have future misunderstandings. Somehow that thought gave her a warm feeling.

After they calmed down, Michael took her red, puffy face in his hands and said, "I want us to be a team. I want you to know that I'm the one person you can always trust and rely on. I'll be there for you, and I'll do my best to protect you from harm."

June smiled at him and said, "I feel the same way. Just don't walk out on me again."

"I won't," he said. "It was the worst night of my life." Michael paused and added, "there is just one other thing I need to tell you. You see, the two people who read your book...they were, well, I had asked them to meet us for drinks at 9 p.m. They frequently hang out at this place, so it was no big deal. If you want, I'll cancel. You can think about it or forget it. I just wanted you to hear their opinions. But I understand if you don't want to. I just need to call them and cancel." He got up to go to the telephone.

"Wait," June burst out. She surprised them both. "You already know what they thought of the book?" she asked.

"Yeah, but it doesn't matter." Michael responded.

"Why don't you tell me what they thought of it?" she gently asked.

"Oh, I can't do that."

"Why not?"

"I can't speak for them."

"But you know what they said."

"Well, not verbatim."

"Michael," June said, irritated, "just tell me if it was thumbs up or down."

"Would they be meeting us at 9 p.m. on a weeknight to tell you they didn't think your book is worthwhile?" Michael eyed her closely.

"I don't know. How would I know? Maybe as a favor to you they want to give me a lot of pointers so that I'll write better in the future. Or they're pretending to like it because they know I'm your girlfriend."

"You're a very suspicious person, June. Do you realize that? They have no interest in helping out anyone with no talent and they don't know that the author of the book they read is my irresistible girlfriend."

"Otherwise you would try to resist me. You're feeling trapped."

"See how you turn everything around?"

"I never denied that. But I was joking," she said, only half-joking. "Who do they think wrote the book, then?" She couldn't help the surging feeling of curiosity. Strangers had read her book. They had no personal interest in her, didn't even know who she was.

"We often read without knowledge of who did the writing. They didn't care until after they read it," Michael said, with a tiny smile on his face.

"Why did they care then?" June made an attempt.

"If you are so curious, why don't we meet them briefly for a drink. You can hear what they have to say. They'll treat you nicely. You'll have a good time. Then, no matter what you decide or even if you make no decision, we'll come home to my place and I'll show you exactly how I feel about you."

"That's a tempting plan. Especially that last part." June briefly had the fantasy that they could skip the first part and just go to his place. She felt relieved. They were all made up. But did she want to hear the serious opinions of his colleagues? What if they thought it should be published, too? What would she do?

> *The socially anxious individual feels inferior to others, and powerless in comparison. He feels likely to be rejected or ridiculed, that something secret and mortifying about him will be revealed inadvertently. The socially anxious person loses perspective, puts too much importance on individual interactions and may bring about his greatest fear, that his interaction will be awkward and will ultimately fail, leaving him open to the judgment of others.*

They cleaned themselves up to head outside. June felt lightheaded as they rode down the elevator, wondering if she should just stay on the elevator for the return ride back up to safety. She managed to make it outside into the fading evening light only because she was attached to Michael's arm. They had a fifteen minute walk over to this out-of-the-way place. It had an old, faded awning and a couple of tables outside. Inside was dark wood paneling, tiny candles, plastic flowers, a big dark wood bar and artsy-looking people. June had walked by it many times, never really noticing it before. It had no neon and a very small, simple sign above the door that read, "The Tin Roof." Inside, the ceiling was plastered with old metal sheeting stamped with intricately decorated squares. Hence the name. The place was not especially crowded on a weeknight at 9 p.m, but there were clusters of people, and conversation drifting around the room. The bartender, a woman with stringy blonde hair and a dirty apron, smiled at them as they walked in. Michael smiled back.

Maybe this was an old hangout of his. June wondered if this was where he used to meet women or if he'd dated the bartender, and then she forced herself to stop. Michael had his hand gently resting on her shoulder at this point and he used it to guide her across the room to the back wall where a man and a woman sat at a little round table having an energetic conversation.

The woman was 50ish, with well coifed blonde-gray hair, hanging stylishly over one eye, wearing a finely tailored suit. In the darkness, the color appeared to be a pinkish white. June assumed long legs and high heels below the table. The male looked a bit younger, had a rather disheveled look, but seemed powerful nonetheless. June immediately felt intimidated. They were not meeting her as potential patients might meet a therapist, eager to find relief from their problems. They were meeting June, the writer.

Were they planning on telling her that her little book was clearly a valuable piece of writing? That depression does seem to take only 10 steps to cure? That the work was a masterpiece? Was everyone here crazy but her? Michael nudged her closer. The two at the table had not yet noticed them because they were so wrapped up in their conversation.

When they got very close, Michael said, "Ed, Miranda, this is June Gray."

Miranda flipped her hair off her face. They both reached out to shake June's hand without getting up. She managed to choke out two "hello's" and shake their hands. Michael pulled out a chair for her and sat down next to her in the other remaining chair at the table. Just before June sat, Miranda said, "Sit," and waved her down into the chair.

June looked at the drinks on the table. Miranda had a martini and Ed had a beer. June could see that even ordering a drink would be a complex event for her that night.

Michael looked at her and said, "What can I get you?" Exactly what she had dreaded. There was an endless silence of a few seconds until the idea of a glass of white wine came into her head. It just popped in. She could have said gasoline, for all that she would taste it.

"I'll be right back," he said, smiling at June.

She had gotten past the drink decision hurdle, only to find herself on the precipice of a cliff of abandonment. Michael went to the bar. She was alone. She sat facing Miranda and Ed, knowing both were staring at her, sizing her up. She felt utterly embarrassed and at a loss for words. She finally managed to say, "I, uh, had no idea that you had read my book..." She didn't think either of them understood what she was saying, as they continued to look blankly at her. She felt herself flush and could not say any more.

After a brief moment, Ed brusquely jumped in with, "So, are you dating Mike?"

She stared at him, not having the vaguest idea what to say.

Miranda gave him a look and then said, "Don't pay any attention to him. We would like to learn a little about you. Have you been writing long? What do you do for a living?"

She really knew nothing about June. That would be easy to talk about until Michael got back to save her. So he was Mike at work. June filed that thought for later perusal. She cleared her throat. "I'm a psychologist in private practice. I don't, haven't been writing for long, except my dissertation and case notes. But..." She felt like she needed to apologize for the ridiculous thing that they'd read.

Miranda had more questions, and seemed interested in hearing her speak. Ed was staring at her like a hungry wolf the entire time. "How did you come to write about depression, dear?" Miranda asked with a smile.

They would have days of laughter at the office over her. Would she tell her the obvious? June thought not. Could she get up out of her chair and walk away? She was not yet that far gone. She would preserve what little self respect she could still muster. "I've been frustrated by the treatments used for it currently," she answered, "and it was a way to express my frustration." Not very well said, but she had not collapsed in tears yet.

Miranda nodded in encouraging approval. "Yes, your frustration with complexity is evident. But I am so curious as to how you devised your approach."

Like a smiling slap in the face, she had basically let June know that the book was simpleminded. It just ignored all modern advancements into the understanding of depression. She was speechless with shame.

Ed apparently found an opening in the silence and fired some questions of his own at June. He stared at her, as if in disbelief, and said, "Did you do a research study or a review of the current literature in the field? Did you use references? Where did you get your ideas from?"

Where was Michael? She took a deep breath and began her apology. What else could she do? How could he have allowed these people to read her stupid, foolish writing and leave her to be victimized by them? A glass of white wine wasn't going to do it for her. She needed a gun to her head. "I'm sorry, I..." she began. But at that moment, Michael returned with her glass of wine and his beer.

He looked at the three of them and laughed uneasily. "Have you two been giving her the third degree?" he asked.

Miranda pretended to look offended and retorted, "Of course not. We're only eager to understand the development of the book. We want to get to know June the writer." That sounded so sarcastic to June, she involuntarily caught her breath.

Michael looked at June carefully. He could see that she was extremely upset, but he had no idea why. He sat down, patted her leg under the table and said, "Have you given June your impressions of the book, or did you begin firing questions at her the moment I walked away?"

Miranda shot an irritated look at Michael and an apologetic one in June's direction. Ed shrugged. Miranda said, "He's giving you the wrong impression of us. And I have no idea why, dear. We are so eager to learn more about you because we think you have written a marvelous book." She looked at June with a maternal smile.

As she heard her say it, June nearly fell out of her chair. She actually did like the book. There was Ed, nodding away. June sat there, blank. Dumbstruck. How could that be? Did they read the book that she wrote?

Michael, still watching her, smiled. To him, this was all a joke, in which his brilliance triumphed, and was supported by other know-it-alls in his field. He didn't seem interested in the tremendous emotional pain that she was suffering. Even their positive response overwhelmed her. She felt like she needed to go hide in her bed with the pillow over her head.

June began to experience a dissociative state resulting from her intense anxiety. She was at a distance watching four tiny little people at a tiny little round table. She wondered when she would come out of it.

> *Money holds great psychological meaning. In psychotherapy, discussion of money is often avoided by the patient, more than issues of sex and fidelity. Money is symbolic of our self-worth, the size of our sexual member, our power, and so much more. We feel inadequate such that no amount of money can alter it. We become obsessed with the power of money, with its magical power, with its promise. We control others with it, care for others with it, and harm them, as well. A person's attitude toward money is a window into his soul.*

Apparently, June's state of mind didn't matter. When she mentally returned, the three of them were in an effusive discussion about the populations for which the book might be helpful. Miranda looked at her with a kindly expression and asked, "When you were writing the book, who did you have in mind?"

It would have been mortifying to tell her that it was written for herself alone. Under the current circumstances, that would have been a little too revealing. So June came up with a close-to-the-truth answer. "I wrote it for my patients, especially those who had been suffering with depression and depressive symptoms for many years." But immediately she regretted her response.

Miranda asked earnestly, "Did you use the concepts in the book with your patients? Is that how you came to see that these seemingly simple and almost obvious ideas had such a powerful effect?"

June paused. Then she said, "Yes."

She did it. She lied. She gave in. She'd been unable to attempt even to pick up her glass of wine. She felt like she had sold her soul, and climbed aboard a speeding train to Hell.

"So you came up with these ideas through your patient work? Is that right?" Ed asked, as though he were a reporter, or a crime investigator, or perhaps, a judge.

June tried to justify it to herself. She was often frustrated in her patient work, wanting to help people more than she'd been able to. She did have experience with depressed people. Could she have had all that in the back of her mind as she was writing the book? It was not such a farfetched idea. Again, she choked out a quiet, "Yeah, that's right."

Who cares where she got her ideas from? Why were they so obsessed with that? Were they fearful that she read a whole collection of pop psych books and plagiarized? If only they truly knew how she felt about this sort of book. She didn't want to offend them by stating her true feelings. How had she gotten into this predicament? Michael sat there quietly watching her lie. She felt manipulated by him. Why couldn't she have met an accountant or a lawyer in the laundry room of her building? Even a computer person. She immediately thought of Phil and the safety she felt with him, the predictability. She even felt a pang of longing for him and wondered how he was doing.

She looked up to find all three of them looking at her expectantly. She felt defensive. "You know, I'm a psychologist, not a writer. I don't really know what you want me to tell you. I'm not even sure exactly what I want to do with this book I wrote. Hardly anyone has seen it. I don't want to mislead you. I came here tonight because I was convinced that I should. I don't want to take up any more of your time..."

Michael continued to look calmly at June as if to demonstrate that he really didn't care about what happened to the book. He'd shown her what he'd wanted to show her, namely that his opinion was up there with the leaders in his field. Ed and Miranda looked surprised. Ed seemed to be smirking. Miranda seemed confused, a combination of perturbed and concerned.

Miranda looked at June closely. "We understand that you don't yet know who you want to manage this process for you. We want you to know that we're very interested. You're aware of our longstanding experience in the field. We all agree that your book would be very desirable to many people, that it would be helpful to many people." Miranda gave June an encouraging look. "As a psychologist, you must have had that in mind when you wrote it." She paused and when no one else spoke she added, "We're here tonight to tell you that we are very interested in it. You probably have an agent already. If I can be of help to you in any way through the process, if you choose to pursue it...with us..." she paused and looked around at all three of them, then added, "Please feel free to contact me."

June thanked her and Ed for meeting with her and shook their hands. Ed held on to her hand a bit longer than necessary and gave amused looks to Michael. June stood up and walked out. She had not touched her drink. Michael came up behind her as she reached the door. She felt overwhelmed to the point of being numb.

They left the place and walked down the block in silence until they turned the corner. He put his arm around her. She needed to be held despite her anger. She felt on the brink of coming apart at the seams and needed to be held together physically. He gently touched her hair and they walked a little further. Then he stopped walking and they turned to face each other. He looked at her with those shining green eyes and said, "You did great. You have a lot of integrity."

"I don't know what you are talking about, but I need a hug." He put his arms around her and held her tightly. She felt better immediately. She wanted to forget about the meeting they'd just had. It was too much to digest at the moment. She needed a few days to think it over. She was concerned that Michael would keep bringing it up. He'd want to know what she thought of them and their opinions.

Michael released June from the hug and they kept walking with his arm around her. He said, "Unless you want to talk about it, I'd just as soon not think about that meeting any more tonight."

"Why not?" she heard herself ask.

"I just thought maybe you needed some time to think it over. But if you want to talk about it, we can."

"No, I don't. Not really." But then she did feel like talking about it. Why didn't he want to discuss it? Maybe he felt guilty.

Michael said, "I think you have to figure out what you really want to do. I hope you know that whatever you decide is okay with me."

But June knew that he wanted her to publish the book. Why couldn't he have been honest? She needed to do whatever was best for her no matter what he or anyone else thought she should do. But what would be best? And could what was best for her also be what would be best for other people? Should she have believed that they all thought the book would be helpful to lots of people? It seemed so utterly farfetched.

As they walked back to their apartment building in the darkness marked by sudden spotlights from the street lamps, June got brief glimpses of Michael's face. He looked so attractive. Handsome features, aquiline nose, strong jaw line, and those eyes. He had a peaceful, calm look to him as they walked. He seemed thoughtful. Why did she doubt him so much? Why was she suspicious of his sincerity? Why did she fear that he was plotting to take advantage of her or hurt her in some way? In looking at him under the street lamps, and feeling his arm around her, June knew he was gentle and patient and a good person. But as the spotlights faded into darkness and she could no longer see his face, she couldn't maintain her faith in him. Was he just after money? Was that such a bad thing? Did he truly care about her, the real June, the neurotic, fearful, suspicious, socially uncomfortable, easily angered, and needy June? Was it possible for anyone to truly care about the real June? She had trouble doing it herself.

She sighed as they walked. Michael looked down at her and said, "I can tell you have a lot on your mind. The wheels are spinning. Would you like to talk about it?"

June felt tired and down. She knew that most people in this situation would be excited and flattered, overjoyed and ecstatic. Not her. She was anxious and fearful of becoming depressed. Did she really want to share all of that with Michael, whom she wasn't so sure she could trust? Wouldn't it just be a burden on him? What if he didn't understand what she was feeling but instead just became increasingly frustrated with her?

"Michael," June began, "I think I actually need to be alone tonight. I'm exhausted and confused. I do have a lot on my mind and I don't think I would make very good company tonight. I think what I need is to take the time to think alone."

Michael looked surprised and disappointed, and June saw him try to understand.

"You want to be alone?" he asked.

"Uh, yes," she faltered.

"Okay." Michael looked disappointed. The wheels seemed to be turning for him, too.

June felt extremely anxious as they entered the apartment building. It seemed awkward and strange for them to part ways on the elevator. But she couldn't change her mind. She got off, after kissing him goodnight quickly, and said she'd call him the next day after work. The door closed behind her, with him staring hard at her. She knew he was trying to understand her and couldn't. She was puzzled, too.

> *Trust, the foundation for true intimacy, is a slow process that can require years to truly develop. Many couples, in a hurry to feel close, develop a 'false intimacy' in which they find as many similarities and codes of relating as possible, all the while hiding their authentic selves from one another. If the false intimacy does not ripen into true intimacy over time, the couple will gradually become alienated from one another, rather than closer and more accepting. If they do not take the necessary risks and tolerate the vulnerability required for true intimacy, they will feel as though they have grown apart. They may look back feeling that they no longer know the partner they once felt so close to, when, in truth, they never formed the trust necessary to know each other in a truly intimate way.*

June walked into her lonely, dark apartment, turned on a light, and landed on her couch. She found herself reaching for the phone and punching in an old familiar number. She could hardly believe it, but she felt a need to talk to Phil.

He answered immediately, after one ring. She was shocked. She felt unprepared to say hello. The thought breezed through her head that she could just hang up.

"June!" Phil cried out, in an unprecedented show of emotion. "I am so glad to hear from you. I was just thinking about you. How are you?"

Just then June's mind seemed blank. Why had she called him? What was she looking to get from him? She gave a short answer and asked how he had been.

"It's been a rough road, June. I have missed you tremendously. I feel that I have grown and learned. I have been in twice weekly psychotherapy and have gained a great deal of insight into myself, and you, too. I have so much that I have been eager to tell you. I knew that you would call me eventually."

The thought had been dawning on her, and now it seemed as clear as the light of the midday sun, that she had made a grave error in calling Phil. She was glad to hear that he was in treatment, but she knew he was only just beginning to chip away at the very tip of the iceberg. Of course, he was still Phil, thinking that he'd already gotten to the bottom of things. And to think he would tell her that he had learned about her, too. Still so self-centered. What was she expecting?

June attempted to have a conversation. "I'm glad that you're doing so well. I called to say hello and also to talk to you about a situation in my life. But perhaps I shouldn't do that." She could barely believe what she was saying. She knew it was a bad idea, but she just couldn't stop. She needed to talk to someone, an outsider. He was always so logical and sensible and devoid of emotion, and he did know her, sort of.

June could feel his eagerness seeping through the phone line. "No. It's fine to call me for advice, although I should probably be encouraging you to try to be more independent."

He was still supercilious. She forged ahead, anyway. She told him about the book and the publishers' comments about it. She mentioned her own feelings about its value. She wanted him to give her some idea as to how firmly she should stand by her values regarding quality literature and psychotherapeutic treatment procedures, versus giving all that up because many people might feel better reading her book, even if it was total fluff.

But Phil was stuck on the publishers having such positive reviews. He couldn't believe it. He asked June to repeat their comments and he seemed upset, even irritated. He suspected that she'd heard them incorrectly, or that her own eagerness to do something impressive caused her to exaggerate their words. He suggested that this was perhaps all part of the little mid-life crisis she was evidently having. Finally, he was frustrated enough to blurt out that he had trouble believing her because he hadn't experienced her in the past as having anything special to say with regard to her work. June knew this meant that he didn't believe that she was bright enough to write something that would receive that level of praise.

Then he had an "aha" experience, right there on the phone, in which he realized that the publishers must be trying to pull June into some sort of shady deal in which she'd end up footing the bill. When he came to this conclusion, he calmed down and advised her to steer clear of the entire situation. He was then ready to move on to the more important issue of when to get together and rebuild, based on his newly acquired wisdom about them both.

The whole lecture absolutely enraged her, but she'd asked for it. What had she expected? She let Phil know that she couldn't make plans with him. This shocked him. She thanked him for his advice and got off the phone as quickly as possible, probably leaving him in a confused fog. He must have believed the conversation had been going along beautifully and that she'd be eager to learn from him what he'd discovered about them both in his therapy.

Amazingly, June really did seem to be beyond that. But, she had to question why she'd called him in the first place. Maybe she needed a dose of kick-in-the-ass proof to get him out of her system for good. He couldn't help her. This was going to be completely up to her. She'd have to take the risk and make a potentially life-altering decision on her own. She was beginning to feel more definite about what she wanted to do. She began to wish that Michael were there with her.

Just then the phone rang. June didn't immediately answer it because she assumed it was Phil calling back to argue that logically he needed to meet with her in order to dump his blame on her. But then she thought there was no way to avoid him really. She might as well get it over with.

She picked up the phone with an irritated, "Hello?"

But it was Michael. "I'm sorry to bother you. I know you said you wanted to be alone. But I realized when I walked into my apartment that I still have your book up here. And I know that you want it back. Should I bring it down or do you want to wait until tomorrow?"

"Oh, Michael. Please bring it down." June was so glad to hear from him.

"I thought maybe you'd want or need to look at it."

"I want and need to look at you." she said.

Michael was silent for a moment. She supposed he was surprised. He just said, "I'll be right there."

And he was in her apartment two minutes later. The book was on the coffee table and they were in each other's arms. Holding him felt so good. June looked into his eyes for a moment, and she saw a loving, sweet man who had real feelings for her. He thought she was intelligent, attractive, actually valuable. He seemed able to tolerate her craziness. She was so fortunate.

She felt a moment of guilt for having called Phil. Why had she needed to compare them? They were worlds apart. Phil would see her sunk in inadequacy while Michael had her flying far beyond her own dreams.

June was afraid. No, she was terrified. She could land hard with permanent damage. But it had to be better than never even trying to take off. She'd made up her mind. And she set it aside to be reexamined in the light of day. She decided to enjoy the moment with Michael. She'd have plenty of time to let him know what she'd decided to do and how she wanted to do it. She really didn't think he had the book on his mind right then, anyway.

In the morning June awoke to beams of light streaming in through the spaces in the blinds. She was in Michael's arms, feeling the warmth of his body next to hers, with the bedcovers over their naked bodies. She felt peaceful. The clarity from the previous evening was still with her. She did not have to live her life according to anyone else's expectations. If she even had half a chance at enjoying her life, she needed to begin by creating expectations for herself. No one else could say what she may or may not be capable of doing or being.

She felt for possibly the first time in her life that she could take chances and might just be fine, even if it ended in failure. She didn't have to be mediocre or feel inadequate. She didn't want her life to go by only to feel regret in the end. And here she was, with someone right next to her, encouraging her to do what made her happy. He had no plan for her life. No expectations regarding her behavior. He actually saw her as a separate human being. He loved her.

Michael was awakening. June felt him starting to move. He opened his eyes. He smiled at her and said, "I'm always so happy when I wake up and find myself with you."

She gave him a hug and said, "Me, too." She looked at the clock and realized that it was after 8:00 am already and her sense of peace evaporated. "We'd better hurry up."

"I don't want to." Michael said, holding onto her another moment. "What are you doing after work today?"

"I'll be home after 7:00. I was hoping we could see each other. I need to talk to you," she said.

"I'll cook you dinner. Come upstairs when you get home." he said.

"Okay." June started to get up. She loved that he cooked for her. She had to hurry because she had a patient to see at 9:30 am and couldn't afford to be late. She got into the shower, and he walked in behind her. He kissed her as water ran down their faces, and then they washed each other. The soap kept dropping. They were both laughing.

June ended up having to jump into her car with instant coffee in a travel cup. She felt more optimistic and happy than she could ever recall feeling before.

However, when she reached her office she found the irritating notice from one insurance company refusing payment for the 13th through the 15th sessions she'd had with a grieving woman, because she was no longer having panic attacks and suicidal thoughts. She had several other stacks of forms to fill in, on which she would probably be forced to exaggerate somewhat the symptoms of three other patients, so that their insurance companies would agree to give them the coverage that was due them and that they needed so desperately.

Why should a person have to be in crisis to warrant treatment? Why would anyone think it wise to terminate treatment immediately after a crisis started to subside? On top of the ethical nightmare of exaggerating symptoms on her paperwork was the gnawing issue of payment. Would June continue to meet with the grieving woman despite her insurance company's games, only to have her bills go unpaid? People were often grateful for her help, but at the same time, unable to extend that gratefulness to payment. And she didn't charge high rates. Especially when they were set at extra low levels for her by insurance companies.

June's good mood seemed to vanish, leaving in its wake irritation, outrage, and a general sense of hamster-in-a-running-wheel syndrome. She couldn't make her practice into what she wanted it to be, philosophically, ethically, psychologically, financially, or even esthetically. She plugged away, only to repeatedly encounter the same dilemmas, with no end in sight.

By the time her day at work was over, she had a painful headache. She had to drive her jalopy on the highway surrounded by trucks trying to break the sound barrier.

Her dingy, ugly office had looked worse than ever. The people, the paperwork, and the atmosphere had all taken their toll on her. June was in crabby mood.

She attempted to soothe herself as usual with loud music as she anxiously gripped the steering wheel with white knuckles, veering around the 18 wheelers, and madmen in sports cars. By the time she got home, she felt old and tired. These were familiar feelings. They were a nearly daily experience while she had been in the relationship with Phil, as well as after Phil, and now, even with Michael to come home to.

She just then remembered that he'd told her to come upstairs for dinner. That immediately made June feel better. She quickly changed clothes, left her datebook in her briefcase, grabbed her keys and shut the door behind her. What a relief. She didn't need to lead a life of misery and frustration. She had no obligation. She had not signed a contract or taken an oath of suffering. She could let go of it, leave it behind. She could be free of the constant daily pain, and live a more peaceful, happy life. Her destiny wasn't constant suffering, terminated only by her eventual death. She could think positively, like her little book said.

When Michael opened the door, he looked excited to see June. She found herself feeling surprised to be greeted with what looked like joy. He gave her a big hug and took her by the hand into the living room where they sat down on the couch. June noticed not for the first time that his apartment had a sense of relaxed, tasteful, warmth, a bit like the feeling June used to have when entering her therapist's office.

She looked up at Michael, into his green eyes, and said, "You seem so happy to see me."

"I've been waiting all day to see you. Don't even ask me what I did all day. All I remember is that I rushed home so that I could make you dinner. That's what I care about." Michael smiled.

That was both overwhelming and wonderful at the same time. June gave him a little kiss, and told him about her day. She also mentioned that as soon as she remembered that she was to come upstairs for dinner, she left the annoyances behind.

Michael looked pleased to hear that, and then took her hands and said, "I know you said this morning that you wanted to talk to me about something. Do you want to wait until after dinner, talk about it over dinner or right now?"

June smiled. It surprised her that he seemed to hear everything she said, and retain it. "I'm starved," she admitted. "I can't wait to eat. I love it when you cook dinner for me." She was hungry, and also felt that the moment was not right.

Michael jumped up and they headed over to his table, which was beautifully set with candles and wine glasses. "Michael, why have you gone to all this trouble?" she asked. She felt nervous and suspicious. She wondered whether something else was going on.

"Just because I love you, and I wanted to."

"Are you expecting this night to be something special?" she couldn't help nervously asking.

"I was hoping to make it something special," Michael said, looking unsure of what exactly she wanted from him.

Was he thinking that she'd made up her mind about the book, and they'd celebrate that? She couldn't ask him, but she resented how important it seemed to him. She looked up to see Michael standing still, staring at her, waiting for an explanation. Why was she so doubtful?

June realized right then that Michael wasn't braced for the worst, like she was, at all times. To the contrary, he actually planned his enjoyable occasions. He took control of the positive activities in his life. He didn't helplessly submit to the unpleasant occasions. He had an entirely different approach to life from her. She needed to leave hers behind and follow his lead. They could have a great time if they wanted to, regardless of whether or not she decided to tell Michael her news. He couldn't have been waiting for that, could he? Maybe he truly was happy to see her. Just glad that she was there.

This last realization was shocking. June had a habit of assuming ulterior motives around every corner. But Michael was a man without ulterior motive. Could she really feel safe with him? She looked up to see him watching her, and smiled. She felt incredibly lucky.

"Those wheels are turning in there again, June." Michael said, looking concerned.

She laughed. "I am trying to take in your wisdom."

"What wisdom? I am too simple to have any wisdom that you might be lacking."

"That's exactly the wisdom I mean." She smiled and added, "Is it time to eat?"

Michael looked startled for a moment and flew into the kitchen. He called out to her, "Have a seat. I'll bring out the first course."

He had made soup and salmon with red potatoes and steamed vegetables. They had wine and candlelight, fresh bread, and soft music. It was lovely. He'd obviously taken time to plan and arrange it all. June kept telling herself with a running loop of tape in her head that he did all of this to make them both happy. No other reason. He wanted to make her happy because he cared about her.

Everything was delicious. June thanked him and complimented everything. She kept thinking that no one had ever made efforts like this for her before. She'd never been treated so well. When she told this to Michael, he looked surprised and commented that he enjoyed doing it, and it didn't feel to him like a tremendous effort, although he was glad that she appreciated it.

One of the things June appreciated most about Michael was that he was interested in everything. Her own world was so limited to her profession and her own problems. But he could have a conversation about anything and everything. He got her thinking and talking about politics, his grandmother's childhood, books, and movies. They'd had energetic debates about books they'd read. Unlike Phil, he didn't pretend expertise. They had real discussions, no lessons, or corrections. They did spend a little time on her favorite subject—understanding other people. He told her about a coworker of his who was boastful about his ability to spot a best seller, although he hadn't actually worked with any bestselling authors.

June said, "Some people who feel insecure and inadequate need to try to impress others."

Michael thought about that and said that the guy didn't seem insecure at all.

June replied, "Not on the surface. But deep down. Otherwise, why would he spend time bragging? People who really are secure don't need to brag."

Michael thought about that and seemed to like the idea that sometimes what someone shows the world is the opposite of what's really going on inside them. Dinner and dessert flew by.

After they cleared the table together, they moved into the living room. June looked him in the eye, held his hands and said nervously, "There is something that I want to tell you."

Michael looked interested, and softly asked, "What is it?"

I want you to know…" she faltered. Why hadn't she planned exactly how she was going to tell him? "After a lot of thought," she continued, "I have decided to seriously look into publishing the book." She beamed.

But Michael looked a little disappointed and confused. "You want to publish it now?" he asked.

"You look disappointed." She couldn't help herself. Was she so dense that she didn't know what would and would not make Michael happy? She felt confused.

"No. I just thought you were going to tell me something else."

"What?"

"I don't know. I'm surprised you decided so quickly."

"What was it you thought I was going to say to you?" She couldn't stand that she'd disappointed him.

"I don't know," Michael repeated.

"Aren't you glad about the book?" June felt at a total loss.

"Yes. That's nice. I hope it turns out to be a good decision. What made you change your mind? You seemed so determined not to publish it."

Somehow June had turned a beautiful evening into a mundane discussion of her stupid book. Maybe he was expecting something romantic, a profession of great love, a passionate kiss. Instead, he got a self-centered, idiotic obsession with a book. He'd already told June that he didn't really care about what she did with it. He'd only wanted to prove his expertise to her. Once he'd done that, he actually must have stopped caring. She felt she'd ruined the lovely evening, in her egocentric view of the world, her relationship and herself.

She'd underestimated him again. He hadn't wanted her to give in to make him happy. He wasn't looking to control her. June wondered what was wrong with her that she couldn't see him clearly. She felt intense shame. Her sense of her own craziness was overwhelming.

And here was Michael, forever patient and generous. He might have been expecting something more romantic than a book discussion, but since she brought it up he was kind enough to ask her about it. What had she expected? That he would be ecstatically happy upon hearing about her decision to publish the stupid thing: 'Oh, June, this makes me so happy.' If he'd actually responded that way, she would have resented him, probably even thought better of it and changed her mind. Basically, she had no judgment.

June attempted to fix what felt irreparable. "Michael, I don't want to talk about that now. I just wanted to tell you, but I'd rather talk about it another time. Is that okay?"

"That's fine." Michael smiled at her.

She felt better. "I think I'd rather not talk about anything right now," she added.

"Really?" Michael moved closer.

"Except that I want to say one more thing. I must be the luckiest person on the planet." After that there was no more talking.

In the morning they were sitting across from each other at Michael's little kitchen table, the early morning sunlight bathing the room. June was drinking coffee and they were both looking through the paper. They both had to get ready for work, but today they had a little more time. It was a truly peaceful experience. June looked over at Michael. He looked so adorable in his bathrobe, intently reading an article on local politics.

The previous night when she'd been hoping to please him with her decision to publish the book, June had imagined that he would be eager to handle the whole project for her. Now he didn't seem eager at all. However, she had not the slightest idea how to pursue the whole thing. She didn't know what to do first, and having made her decision to forge ahead, she was impatient to do it. But she didn't want to seem overly self-involved. She had to find a way to bring it up in a matter-of-fact way.

"Michael, what would you suggest I do to get moving on the book?"

Michael looked up from the paper at June and said, "I'd call Miranda. She's probably the best person to work with."

"Okay," June replied, trying to sound nonchalant. She was surprised that he didn't offer to handle it. That would have been nice of him. He did know the business and started this whole thing about the book in the first place. Now he was acting like he couldn't be bothered.

Michael looked thoughtfully at her. "Why have you changed your mind? You felt so strongly."

June felt accused of hypocrisy. She was ashamed and irritated. "I became convinced that it could be beneficial to others, whatever my opinion of its merits happen to be."

"Are you still worried about how it might reflect on you professionally?" Michael continued his line of questioning like a good lawyer.

"Yes. But my job is to help people, and I wrote this book that looks like it could help a lot of people and I guess I'll have to take the risk and deal with it when it happens, whatever it is." June felt terribly self-conscious.

"Do you think I am a hypocrite, Michael?" she asked, fearing he did.

"A hypocrite?" Michael repeated, looking surprised. "No. I'm just surprised."

"You told me I had integrity the other night after the meeting. It meant a lot to me. But does that mean preventing the publication of a book that could potentially provide comfort for people, even if it makes me uncomfortable?"

Michael looked at June. "I meant that you had the integrity to voice your own opinion despite their flattery. But I also think it takes integrity to make a difficult decision." Apparently Michael was attempting to figure out what the hell she was talking about, but in a nice, supportive way.

"Michael, I don't want you to be disappointed in me." She mentally kicked herself for sounding like a small child.

"Why would I be disappointed in you?"

"Because I changed my mind so quickly."

Michael smiled and said, "It would take a bit more than a quick decision to disappoint me. But you still haven't told me what changed your mind."

"A bunch of things," she answered quickly. She realized that she didn't want to tell him that part of her change of heart was to please him. She was no longer even sure that it would please him. And it was more about risk-taking, optimism, setting fear and anxiety aside, things she had trouble finding the right words to convey to Michael. Also, she was having difficulty thinking clearly because she was feeling upset with herself for having created a neurotic dynamic between them in which she felt concern about his judgment. Her decision regarding publication of her book shouldn't have included concern over Michael's view. She should have assumed he'd support whatever decision she made, that he would have faith in her decision-making ability. Even if she didn't.

"Michael," June began, feeling she owed him some explanation, "I guess I thought it might be exciting and different and that maybe I take myself too seriously. I'm usually pretty risk-averse."

"Well, you took the risk of getting involved with me," Michael joked.

"The best decision I have ever made."

"Listen, June. I keep forgetting to tell you, because I guess I don't want to go. But I have to go out of town on Monday morning. I should be back on Thursday. I have to help promote a new book." Michael looked unhappy.

"I don't understand," she exclaimed.

"It's the beginning of a big book tour. I usually go for the first few days to get it rolling," Michael explained.

"What book is it? Where are you going?" She felt panicky.

"June, it's only a few days. The book is a how-to book for married couples."

"Really?" June interrupted. "How to what?"

"Actually," Michael laughed, "how to keep their sex life exciting."

"You're kidding me."

"No. It's got potential to become a best seller."

"Where are you going?"

"It starts in LA. So, I'll be going there for three days as long as there are no problems. And there shouldn't be," Michael added for June's sake.

"Who's the author?" She couldn't help herself. How could he have left this to the last minute? Why was she so upset? She needed to calm down.

"Her name is Gloria Valentine. You may recognize the name from some of her other books, like, "The 48 Hour Getaway - Breathing New Life into Your Marriage," and "Games Married People Should Play."

"No, I don't read books like that. Is she married?"

"Divorced." Michael and June both laughed. June couldn't help it.

"I wish I could go with you," she said.

"That would be great sometime, but not this time. Gloria is a very touchy person. She requires a lot of care. I think she'd be insulted if I had any distractions along with me."

"She sounds very narcissistic." June knew she had reverted to her psychological intellectualizing so as not to feel irrationally threatened by this Gloria Valentine.

Michael nodded in agreement. Then he added, "We still have this weekend. Or some of it anyway. Why don't we plan to do something fun on Saturday? I'll probably have to go to the office on Sunday to do last minute things for Monday."

"Okay." June was having so many feelings, she decided that the safest thing to do at this point was to say as little as possible. "I better get going." She got up to head for the door as quickly as she possibly could.

June felt as though she were being abandoned. How crazy. A few days in LA with someone named Gloria Valentine should mean nothing. June so badly wished she were able to trust Michael entirely. She couldn't help having fantasies that they would have a fling in some sunny, palm-tree studded hotel. She wondered what he meant when he said she was touchy. Irritable? Sensitive? Wanting to be touched? Touching him? Zero to sixty in a flash. She needed to find a way to get through the week without jumping out a window. What else could Michael possibly do to reassure her that he truly cared for her? What did she want from the poor guy? And if she got it, would it truly reassure her? Perhaps she couldn't be reassured. She was a hopelessly self-sabotaging person.

June suddenly wondered if she were to get her book published with his company, would he accompany her on a trip like that? Would she have to give talks and readings all over the country? She hoped not. It would be intolerable. She'd be promoting a book like Gloria's - pop psych drivel, and would have to pretend that it was valuable. She'd be an official hypocrite. That would clinch it. June realized like a slap in the face that she couldn't go through with it. She couldn't possibly do a book tour. And what about her patients? She'd have to abandon them for the several weeks of tours and lectures. She'd have to pretend to believe in the book. That was the most difficult part to swallow. She didn't think she could do it.

She felt stunned. Did she think she could publish a book, pocket the cash and walk away classified in the Gloria Valentine category of writers? She couldn't go ahead with it. She wouldn't be able to live with herself.

All of this swirled through June's head as she swirled through the highway traffic on her way to the office. By the time she arrived, she'd decided against publication, and had such a negative, superior attitude about Michael's publishing company and the drivel that it produced and promoted she could hardly concentrate on the real-life problems of her patients.

She found even after a hard, frustrating day of work, that as she left the office, all the feelings and thoughts rushed back at her. She resented the existence of the Gloria Valentine's of the world. She hated her. She'd never even seen her picture. June imagined her as a desperate, flashy divorcee, as done in stereotype on a television sitcom. She felt angry at Michael for catering to her touchiness. A couple of weeks ago she'd gotten a mailing about an all-day conference at the Center for Psychoanalytic Studies to be held on Saturday on the impact of early sibling psychodynamics within the adult couple. She considered going, if only just to reimmerse herself in the real stuff and get away from all of the pop psych trash.

When June got home that evening her mind had just about come to a boil. She felt out of control. Feelings of betrayal, resentment, anger and disgust all overwhelmed her. She called Michael's place and got his answering machine. Good. He must have been working late, preparing for his exciting trip. After the beep she left him a message, "Hi, Michael, It's June. I know we discussed making plans on Saturday because you're going away, but I am afraid that I have to cancel. I forgot that I have an all-day continuing education meeting to attend that day. And it sounded like it would be impossible for you on Sunday, so, I guess I'll have to see you when you get back. Bye."

She hung up and immediately felt like crying. Something was seriously wrong with her. Crazy thoughts kept circling through her head. Did she want him to feel rejected? Cancel his trip? Realize how completely irrational she was? Was she so angry that she didn't want to see him? Was she feeling any legitimate betrayal at all? He wasn't protecting her like she needed him to. Didn't he see the terrible position she'd be placed in by having to promote a book that she didn't believe in? It would be an ethical and moral nightmare. Maybe he just didn't care about her as much as she needed someone to care. Maybe it wasn't humanly possible for anyone to truly care about her. June could see where all of this was heading and was not feeling eager for another plummet into dark depression.

If she'd been her own patient, she would have advised herself to peel herself off the floor, out of the puddle of pity, shake it off, and take responsibility for her own actions and needs. Why was she leaning so hard on Michael, and then avoiding him? It was becoming uncomfortably clear that she did have intimacy problems of her own. It had not been all Phil's issues. Wonderful epiphany! Maybe it would be best to have some time apart from Michael to regroup.

Perhaps June did need to handle this whole book dilemma without his assistance. Then, no matter how it turned out, it would always have been her own doing. No one to be angry with or proud of but herself.

She peeled herself up off the floor and got determined. She would call Miranda on Monday morning and give her the chance to convince her to publish the book. If she failed, that would be it. June would put the book away and feel a tremendous sense of relief. Maybe she'd be a bit disappointed. If she somehow found a way to convince her to go ahead, despite June's numerous reservations, an unlikely scenario, then June would go ahead with it and not look back. Either way, it would be her decision entirely. No influence from Michael, who apparently didn't care, anyway.

She felt better. She had a plan. She also decided that right then would be a good time to read over the book, and get a more objective view. It would better prepare her for the meeting with Miranda. She sat down with the book, which had been sitting on her coffee table ever since Michael had returned it. It was just a black-and-white, lined notebook, worn from a lot of handling. She opened it to the first page, and saw to her surprise, that she had actually outlined the entire book at the beginning. Her memory of it was apparently not very good. She started to read.

June jumped out of her seat after what must have been a half hour or so, startled from the knocking on her door. She'd been completely absorbed in the book. It was full of emotion, but also comfort. For a moment she sat still, stunned that she'd been so involved, and also slightly alarmed by the knocking. She got up, put the book back on the coffee table and walked to the door. She desperately wanted it to be Michael and it probably was, and she felt angry that she wanted to see him so badly, and that he could just go away for most of a week. Maybe it wouldn't be Michael, it would be some stranger with a big frying pan, to whack her over the head and put her out of her misery.

It was Michael. June felt completely grateful to see him. He gave her a hug and a kiss and then shut the door behind him. He said, "If I can't see you tomorrow, then I have to spend all of tonight with you. And I'll find some time on Sunday, too, since I'll have Saturday to get work done. Unless you don't want to see me." Michael looked at June expectantly.

"Of course I want to see you. I'm upset that I won't see you all week. I'm jealous that you'll be taking care of some other extremely needy woman instead of me."

Michael thought for a moment, then said, "That's just my work. You are my passion."

"Good answer."

"It's true," he said seriously.

They had dinner in a little romantic place nearby and walked around the city afterward. June told him about a patient she was struggling with, who didn't seem to want to face his feelings of loss. It was challenging but frustrating to work with him. Michael asked about how she tried to help the guy and she explained that it involved trust and his ability to learn to tolerate his own feelings. Michael asked about June's conference the next day, and what kind of information it would cover, and how she could use it. She explained that, when a conference was successful, she could apply new insights from the cases that were discussed to her own patients' issues. She frequently found herself thinking about them during the presentations.

They talked about what Michael would be doing in California and about how in general he worked with an author from start to finish, adjusting his own behavior to build up relationships with the various difficult personalities he encountered. June said that explained how successful he'd been with her. Michael emphatically disagreed, confirming her sense that she was correct. She knew she was a difficult personality. She'd never before realized it so crystal clearly. She continued to feel painfully grateful to Michael, and annoyed with herself for her excessive degree of gratitude. And she didn't mention either to him.

They returned to his place for the night. June absolutely couldn't keep her hands off him. He didn't seem to mind. The only satisfactory explanation for the intensity of June's feelings that she could come up with was that they had to have some chemical basis.

> *Sibling rivalry, an often overlooked aspect of development, impacts later relationships in many ways. Partners in a couple reenact early parental expectations, disappointments, and behaviors with one another. What often remain unexplored are the competitive and entitlement conflicts that stem from sibling interactions, expectations, and roles within the family.*

June attended the conference the next day. It ran from 9 to 4. She regretted it early in the morning when she had to leave rather than stay in the wonderful warm bed with Michael. She also felt that she couldn't back out now, without looking manipulative or insincere. She had to go. It would be good for her, anyway. She tore herself away, but once she left, she felt happy. Why not? Michael was the greatest thing that could ever have happened to her. She'd had a great night with him. She was heading to a psychoanalytic conference, which she usually found to be stimulating and interesting. They had agreed that they would see each other that night and then again on Sunday night, but that Michael would work most of the day on Sunday. June felt satisfied with the plan.

The conference was good overall. There were periods in which June's mind wandered, or the topic became obscure or unrelated to her work. What was surprising was the amount of time she spent thinking not about her work with patients, but about herself and her relationship with Michael.

She had felt a lot of sibling rivalry with her brother. He was the clear favorite of both of her parents. She couldn't really get their approval the way he did. Everything had always come so easily to him. He was smart, popular, good looking, and athletic. And he ignored June most of the time. She must have been irritating to him, because to some small extent she did manage to interfere in her parents' relationship with him. She recalled, sitting at the conference, surrounded by a hundred other people, that she'd wanted her brother's attention as a child, too. She remembered her mother telling her how much she had admired him and followed him around. She'd give him her toys and candy. But she never got much attention from him that was positive.

June couldn't avoid the connection between her brother and Michael. She had felt jealous at times of Michael, even though she knew it was ridiculous. She desperately wanted his attention. But the important difference was that he actually did give it to her, and he wasn't her childhood brother, but an adult man. He was unlike her brother in that he clearly cared deeply for her, and didn't have the kind of jealous or intensely competitive feelings toward her that a brother would have. This was no small revelation for June.

After the conference June had the usual dazed, head-spinning experience walking out. She had thoughts about her patients and herself, and how sibling rivalry is so obviously a component of the relationships between couples. She had renewed faith in her own ability to sort through her feelings in her relationship with Michael, as well as new awareness about her relationship with Phil, which was, in retrospect, a repetition compulsion. She'd never before understood it all so clearly.

She'd run into colleagues she hadn't seen in ages, who were happy to see her. She had easily found people to sit with at the luncheon, and enjoyed talking to them, and had felt overall, more comfortable at a conference than she could ever before recall. She had bolstered her identity as a psychologist. She was glad she went.

Would these friendly, open, not especially judgmental people reject or shun June if she published her depression book? She had a moment or two in which she could imagine their being impressed and/or excited for her rather than cold and harsh. How could she make that view last?

That night June told Michael all about the conference. He was interested in the theory and how she might apply it to patients. She didn't feel ready to share her more personal revelations. He was just happy to be with her. They had another great night together.

On Sunday, June felt sad that Michael had to work and then leave the next day. She used the time to do chores and to read her book. After finishing it around three p.m., she put it down and realized that it had been absorbing. Her outlook was more optimistic. She'd done a better job writing and getting ideas across than she would have believed without rereading it. Where had she gotten those ideas? The one that struck her just then was that avoiding the judgment of others causes us to miss out on the experiences that might make us most fulfilled and happy. How had she come up with that back when she'd written this? June was currently struggling with her concern about how others would react to this book. She should have been attending instead to her own reaction.

She liked it. It wasn't brilliant; there wasn't much real theory. Mostly it was full of reassurance and common sense and probably came from her own wishful thinking. But it was not trash. She wasn't giving advice on how to play games in the bedroom, or flirt or avoid certain foods in order to diet, or anything else that seemed ridiculous or trendy. Mostly it seemed to be advice she wished someone kind and loving had given her that she could have absorbed for her own use.

She felt pretty good after reading the book. She could live her life, make it what she wanted it to be, enjoy herself, and set the harsh, self-directed judgments aside. She didn't deserve them.

June felt determined to have a great time with Michael that evening because she had no reason not to. They were a terrific couple, lucky to have found one another. And it wouldn't hurt for him to think about what a great time he'd had with her just before leaving for LA.

Monday morning June awoke in Michael's arms to find him watching her sleep. When he saw her open her eyes and look at him, he said, "I'm going to miss you, especially when I have to sleep alone in a hotel room." He brushed her mess of wavy brown hair out of her face and kissed her.

"I'm going to miss you, too. Will you call me a lot?"

"Of course."

"Will you really come back on Thursday?"

"Of course, unless there is some problem. But most likely."

"What if this has all been a dream?"

Michael rolled over on top of June and said, "I am as real as it gets." He rolled off and got out of bed. He began to rush around getting ready to go. June threw on her clothes, made his bed and after a long hug and kiss, headed downstairs to her place. She had to go to work. She felt lonely and anxious. She was worried that something could happen to him. And she'd be alone again.

The uncomfortable experience of anxiety can push people into blindly making difficult decisions too quickly, avoiding necessary thought and emotional exploration. These same impulsive decision makers can feel such a high degree of self-doubt that they do not believe they have the ability to mull over and tease out the best decision. Mistakenly, they can feel less responsible for the outcome if they avoid truly making an informed decision.

During June's lunch break she called Miranda, who actually called back only twenty minutes later. June hadn't actually expected to talk to her that day. She was friendly and eager to meet. Wednesday was a light day for June, so they planned to meet then. She readily understood that June had given this project serious thought and now felt ready to discuss it. She spoke of planning to have an offer and a contract ready. June wasn't absolutely sure what she meant, but supposed there would be plenty to negotiate and discuss.

She got off the phone in time for it to ring again immediately. To her shock, it was Emily, sounding out of breath and frantic, begging to stop over June's place later that evening, very unlike herself. She was never flustered, never frantic, never called June at her office in the middle of the day, and never stopped by on a weeknight. Otherwise known as a school night. She wouldn't tell June what it was all about, only that it was extremely important. June was somewhat alarmed. Since Michael was out of town, the timing worked for her to stop by at 7 p.m.

June decided that she wouldn't tell Michael about the Miranda business until he returned. She knew that he'd be busy managing everything in LA. They spoke briefly Monday afternoon after Emily's call. He sounded tired. June was relieved that he'd made it there safely. She made him describe the hotel room and his dinner. He told her some amusing stories about Gloria Valentine's difficult personality and her complaints about the lighting at the bookstore, the lack of adequate seating, and her expectations that the bookstore or the publisher should provide her with a gold fountain pen for signings. He told June he couldn't believe how much he missed her. She actually believed him. She knew she loved him. And she knew he felt the same way. She also knew that later she would go to bed alone, but would feel peaceful and happy. But she had to meet with Emily first.

June felt nervous. She and Emily hadn't been talking much since she'd verbally attacked June about Michael. They'd exchanged some phone messages and emails, but June really had no idea what had been going on with her.

At seven she was at June's door, out of breath as if she'd run all the way from the suburbs. Her face was not the usual picture of perfect hair, light makeup, and upbeat expression. It was puffy, as she'd clearly been crying. Her hair was in disarray. June pulled her in, gave her a hug, and sat her down, realizing how much she'd missed her.

Emily put her hands to her face and began to cry as soon as she sat down. June put her arm around her and wondered if she'd ever actually seen her cry before. They sat on the couch, June's arm around her, her shoulders shaking, for a long while. Finally she began to slow down. She took her hands off her face, grabbed some tissues and wiped her face slowly. She turned to look June in the eye, and said, "He's been cheating on me."

Emily's husband, Ed, the ever reliable, good-natured, easygoing, calm and logical (but not like Phil who used logic as a weapon) guy who June couldn't even imagine actually making love to Emily, was having an affair. She hadn't known what to expect, but this hadn't even been a possibility.

"How do you know?" June blurted out.

"The bastard admitted it today. It's been five months."

"Five months!" June couldn't believe that he'd had a five-month affair. She started to have images in her head of five months going by with Ed feeling that passionate, longing, chasing love one might feel in an illicit affair.

"He's lied to me for five months. He cared more about this woman than about the kids and me. There were signs but I guess I didn't want to see them."

"Like what?"

"He was working late, distracted, checking his phone constantly. He seemed tense and excitable, like his personality had changed. He kept claiming that it was all stress at work. I was too stupid to even consider the possibility. Then, I accidently opened his cell phone bill. He always takes care of it. I was about to put it back in the envelope for him, when I noticed the same number over and over again. It wasn't one I recognized. I went back in our files and found several old bills with the same number on it repeatedly. So I confronted him. He didn't even try to cover it up. I feel so betrayed. Why did he do it? He can't even tell me why?"

June felt so bad for her. By cheating on her, Ed had destroyed the life Emily had tried so hard to create. She needed the perfect relationship, along with the perfect home, and perfect children. As they sat on the couch, June knew that it wasn't just that she was hurt and felt betrayed by Ed. Her whole life had crumbled. June wasn't sure Emily could tolerate the imperfect life she'd now have. Even if she and Ed worked it out, there was no going back.

June couldn't help thinking that Emily's extremely negative attitude about Michael had been somehow related to the huge relationship problem with Ed. June had felt throughout her relationship with Emily that she always needed to be better off. Maybe she had been aware of a problem, at some deeper level, in her own marriage, but was projecting it onto June's relationship with Michael. Was Emily competitive with her? June would have to mull that one over later on. Meanwhile, she couldn't help but forgive her. It really wasn't about Michael, after all. She needed June to be there for her and she would be.

They talked late into the night about her feelings and her options. Ed was ending the affair and claimed to want to work on the marriage. She knew it would be a long road.

June's conversation with Michael on Tuesday night was similar to Monday's. She filled him in on what was happening with Emily, and Michael listened and responded. She could tell Michael had struggled through a long and frustrating day. He seemed tired and a little irritable. But June was proud of herself for recognizing that it had nothing to do with her. She didn't want him to be unhappy, but she had to admit that she didn't mind that he was not having the most terrific time. He would be happy to come home. And he said as much on the phone.

June's meeting the next day with Miranda felt like a whirlwind. She had actually had a contract made up for June to go through and sign. Miranda must have felt kindly toward her, or perhaps sorry enough for her to let her know in all her ignorance that people often show their contracts to a lawyer or agent before signing. June stupidly asked why. She couldn't give her a good reason. She showed June the dollar amount being offered for the book, as well as the foreign rights, paperback release and film options. All of that looked complicated, but June's mind became total mush when she took a look at the dollar amount. And apparently, it was only the initial amount, before the figures for all of the other things that she didn't understand even got estimated.

Miranda said something that indicated that she assumed that June would be shopping the book around and she was letting her know that she felt strongly about its potential success and the dedication of this publishing house to June and her writing. They were also interested in optioning her next book. June's brain shut down. She couldn't process any of it. The numbers kept blinking on and off in her head like a neon light in the blackest desert. Nothing she had ever done or could ever imagine doing would or should be worth six hundred thousand dollars. Perhaps it was a typo. June felt like she'd won the lottery. Who would she tell? Her parents? The doorman? She felt like her life had just been altered in some basic way. Suddenly she was careening down a new path with no breaks. Six hundred thousand dollars? She had never had more than twenty thousand to her name at any one time before, and until this moment, that had felt like a lot.

June was so entirely blown away that she couldn't actually read the contract that she signed. She was only wondering what a check for six hundred thousand dollars might actually look like. What would the bank teller say when she handed it to her to put in her puny account? She could get a new car. Michael would be absolutely shocked. Her parents might finally be proud of her. Her brother might be impressed with her for the first time in her life. Emily could help her shop for new furniture. June had lost her mind.

Chapter X: Risk

A mid-life crisis occurs when a person cannot tolerate his knowledge that the life cycle comes to an end. To avoid painful feelings of loss, he makes sudden, impulsive decisions. This risk-taking may bring feelings of hurt and loss to those around him. If, however, the risks taken ultimately lead to relationship improvements or other successes, the crisis becomes an opportunity for growth and positive change. (Be Happy, by June Gray, Ph.D.)

With her head in a fog, June went to work on the Thursday of Michael's return. Fortunately she had only a few sessions that day: A light day with some cancellations would normally have made her feel like a frustrated failure. All she could feel was relief, and inadequate to the task of handling the few souls who did make it in to see her.

Annabelle's session began with her dramatic announcement that she'd begun dating a new guy. "Dr. Gray, I'm sure that this will come to nothing because of course I'm a loser and I deserve nothing." Long dramatic pause.

"What will come to nothing?" June asked with trepidation.

"This new guy named Dave. He's divorced four years now and has no kids. I know you're going to get all excited and say that sounds promising. He's not still married, not burdened by having to take care of kids. He's actually available."

"You're right. I might be thinking all of that."

"Well, he isn't rich or sophisticated or cultured. I'm not sure I'm actually interested in him. But we went out to dinner and talked for four hours. He was very nice and considerate. At least he has manners. He and I like the same movies. He didn't try to sleep with me afterward. And, he did pay for dinner."

"Okay."

"That's it? Okay? Aren't you going to try to convince me to hang in there and see if maybe he's the one for me? My one true love."

"You know, Annabelle, you are so tough on us both."

She looked at June in surprise. "What do you mean?"

June tried to say it as clearly as she could without triggering Annabelle's anger. "You assume that I'll make some inane comment about hanging on to him, which I'd like to think underestimates me."

"Okay."

"But, more importantly, you don't give yourself any room. You don't have to be madly in love right away. He may not be the one for you. But he may be worth getting to know, slowly, patiently. Or, he could do or say something that makes you decide he isn't worth getting to know. You can't possibly know yet."

"Dr. Gray, are you trying to tell me to be patient?" Annabelle smiled at June this time. "You know that I'm not very good at that."

"I've heard."

"I'm just afraid he might be too boring for me."

"Boring isn't always a bad thing. You have definitely had a hard time with excitement often followed by big disappointment."

"True." Annabelle sighed. "Maybe I don't know if he'll stay interested in me. Why would he?"

"Because you are an interesting person."

"I have no reason to believe he's going to think that. I don't think that."

"That's what I mean. You're very judgmental about yourself. I guess, for him to find out that you're an interesting person, you'd have to take some risk and let him get to know you a little."

"But then he can reject me."

"You're right. You could get hurt."

Annabelle's eyes welled with tears. "That scares me. What if I can't handle it? I've been hurt a lot. I'm not sure I can take even one more rejection."

"I'm sure you can handle whatever happens, although I wonder whether it would be scarier to have him think you are interesting." The room was quiet as June allowed the thought to sink in. "Either way, I'll be here."

"Thank you. That means a lot to me. You know, I am afraid that he might be interested in me. Then, I might have to deal with a relationship. I don't really know how to do that. What if I get dependent on him?"

"I think you're jumping the gun. Take it slowly and we'll deal with whatever feelings come up for you."

"See. You do want me to date him." Annabelle smiled again.

"You trapped me." June laughed. The session felt like a bit of a breakthrough. Afterward, she felt somewhat rewarded for her own hard work and patience. Of course, she had to wait to find out if Annabelle could hang in there.

June could barely believe she'd handled her appointments with patients as well as she did. Her own changing life and relationship were on her mind. Her heart was racing all day like it had somewhere important to go. She could hardly speak. She could not eat. The world looked different: the colors were brighter and the spaces were bigger, as if June had been freed after a long jail sentence. The blue sky was a deep and penetrating blue, the trees and grass glowed with life, people looked interesting and friendly. She had unbelievable energy. It felt like a combination panic attack and manic episode. She felt fear and glory simultaneously. She couldn't wait for Michael to come home and calm her down. She was banking on the fact that he dealt with people going through this kind of thing on a regular basis.

Once home, June paced around her apartment. The limo, after dropping what's her name off, was to drop Michael off. The message he'd left claimed that he'd be back around 8 p.m. June was relieved to know he was returning that day after all, but she was pacing like a caged tiger and it was 8:15 p.m. Could she take another few minutes of this? She might explode.

When she finally opened the door to him at 8:27 p.m. according to her blue digital clock, she was practically in tears. Michael looked immediately concerned. He came in, dropped his bags, and shut the door. "What's the matter?"

"I'm overwhelmed. I feel like I've been waiting for you for days."

Michael breathed out and looked relieved. "Well, you have."

"No, I mean, I have, you're right, but it's only really been a little while today.

Um, you were supposed to be here at 8," June blurted out, too confused to explain herself.

"Gloria took a very long time to leave the limo. She had to talk to me about the many important issues on her mind, all the way from the airport, and still had not quite finished when we pulled up in front of her home..."

"I need to tell you some news," June interrupted.

"What is it?" He sounded all concerned again.

"I don't know where to start or how exactly to say this. I'm a wreck. I thought I was happy, but I'm a nervous wreck."

"About what?"

"I signed a book contract with Miranda."

Michael was silent. He looked shocked. His mouth was slightly open and his eyes were wide. Finally, he said slowly, "You signed? Already?"

"Yes."

"I was only gone four days."

"I was very impulsive," June blurted out. She felt like crying. "...I realize in retrospect," she added.

Michael was silent again. June could see that he had questions and didn't know where to start. "Tell me about it" was what he finally came up with.

"Well, I met with her on Wednesday. She had the contract all made up already. It was very generous."

"Very generous? What do you mean?"

"Very, extremely, generous."

"June, no one signs a contract in a day. I'm afraid you..."

"Six hundred thousand."

That stopped Michael in his tracks. He was dumbstruck. Finally, he choked out, "Six hundred thousand dollars?"

"Yes."

"Oh." He stood there looking like he'd forgotten how to speak English. It seemed like a long time. June tried to wait patiently. She'd been wrong. He had not taken it in stride. She stood there waiting.

Finally, he recovered enough to speak. "Six hundred thousand dollars?"

June confirmed it. Perhaps she was making the entire thing up, or she'd dreamed the whole book deal thing. She became unsure of her accuracy. She thought about getting the contract out and going over it with him. But she didn't want to leave him standing there, in case he were to fall over in a faint. So she waited some more. This was not at all what she'd expected or hoped for. He was supposed to be the calm, supportive one, there for her. That was why she had paced so impatiently around her living room area, counting the seconds in each minute until his arrival.

Michael blurted out, "Six hundred thousand for the whole thing, or just the book deal?"

"Book. We haven't done the rest yet."

June decided to get all the shocking over with. "By the end, Miranda says she thinks I'll make about one million dollars, depending on sales and other things, I guess."

Michael sat down on the couch. He actually fell onto the couch and managed to sit, and then echoed her words, "one million dollars."

"I don't think my little book is worth all that either, but it's not really up to me." June tried to speak lightly to snap him out of it.

There was a long silence.

"I know this is a big surprise," June said, "and I know you must be exhausted from your trip and all, but I need you to make an effort to share with me what is going through your mind. Your silence is making me nervous."

Michael looked at June. She walked over and sat down next to him and took his hand. He attempted a smile, took a deep breath and gave it a try. "June, I don't know what to say. I feel happy for you, very surprised at the amount. I, uh, don't know exactly what you signed, but I can't imagine Miranda wanting to make a bad impression on you, or wanting to cheat you in some way. I guess this changes your life in some ways..." Michael's voice trailed off at this point.

"My life? You're happy for me? I was hoping you would just be happy period. Why are you happy for me?"

"Because you have this chance to change your life." Michael spoke in a monotone and looked crushed.

"My life? Why are you making me upset, Michael?"

"I'm sorry. When someone gets that much money at once...well, in my experience, when people earn a lot suddenly, they are able, or want to... they sometimes make big changes or do things they always dreamed of. I've worked with a lot of people..." Michael spoke haltingly, like he couldn't bring himself to say all that was on his mind.

June was finally beginning to understand. She felt hurt, and tried to tell herself not to. He was insecure. It was one of the things that made him lovable. She told herself not to experience this as a lack of faith in her. The thought flew through her head that if he had just gotten a million dollars, she would feel unbelievably insecure. She'd assume that he'd no longer want her. He'd have a much larger selection of interested women as a result of the money, June would undoubtedly conclude. She would probably go nuts. She felt glad that it was her instead of him who won the lottery, so to speak. She knew she could trust herself, at least.

June smiled at Michael. She had missed him so much. She looked into his green eyes and said, "Do I seem like the limousine, fluffy, bleached hair, fur coat, chunky jewelry, fancy dinner type to you?"

Looking more unsure than June had ever seen him look before, he said, "You haven't...I hope not."

"I'm not. So you don't have to worry about my turning into a Gloria Valentine."

"I know that," Michael tried to convince them both.

"And furthermore, Michael, you and I both know that I'd never have even bothered to think about publishing this book I wrote if it weren't for you."

"Someone eventually would have convinced you."

"Stop it." June was losing her patience. He was so distant and cold, like a total stranger. Maybe he'd planned to come in and tell her it was all over, that he had decided that he did not love her anymore. She worked very hard to push that thought out of her head before it could grip her too tightly and start a nasty downward spiral.

She took a breath and tried to stay calm. "What is mine is yours. I consider this ours, like anything else I have. I feel the same way about you. Nothing has changed." As she spoke the word, "ours" she felt a little nervous. She was saying she trusted him completely to not take advantage of her. She wanted to believe it. Did this mean she was saying they were committed to each other? Did it speed the whole process up between them artificially? Would they now have to go out and buy a place to live with the money? Did she just propose to him? June felt herself starting to perspire and feel nauseated.

Michael moved a little closer to her on the couch and looked into her eyes and said, "My feelings for you haven't changed, either. And I know you're a good person and you have values like mine, but I have to admit I am afraid. I know it might not make sense but I'm not sure that I'll ever be able to think of that money as ours. I want to share my life with you, and I would do anything for you, but I don't want to feel like you're supporting me or that we aren't equals because of all this money you'll have. I don't know if you can understand what I'm saying. Maybe if you reversed the situation, you might see how I feel more easily."

June jumped in to say, "I do know what you mean. I have thought about it. I would feel like you'd want to leave me behind. I'd feel as though your having so much money would make you value me less. But I also know that I'd think all of that based on my own feelings, not yours. You'd still be the same sensible, wonderful, loving person to me, whether you suddenly got a million dollars or not."

"That's true." Michael seemed to brighten up.

"That's how I feel. I don't want it without you. Do you understand that? I love you. I'm crazy about you. I'm scared too. I need you to help me get through this. I'm not actually sure what I have signed up for. I can't think straight. I've been waiting to see you so that you might help me figure all of this out."

Michael was actually smiling authentically for the first time since he had entered June's apartment that night. She felt so relieved that she started laughing. So did he. They both felt a bit giddy. They were laughing with tears rolling down their faces. In the middle of it all June said, "Can you picture me sitting there with Miranda seeing the figure $600,000 and agreeing to sign without being able to read because I was so overwhelmed. I was afraid that if I didn't sign it would turn out to be a mirage, and vanish before my eyes, or they would find the extra zero typo."

When they finally calmed down, Michael pulled June over to him and kissed her hard, and held her close. He whispered in her ear, "You are too good to be true."

"Likewise," she said. They decided that Michael needed some food. June cooked pasta for him, one of the few things she felt entirely competent to make. After his dinner, he suggested that they take some time to sit down together and read the contract she'd signed. June felt tired, and could see that he was exhausted, so they decided to do it Friday night, after she got home from work. He was planning to go into his office to deal with the week's mail and messages, even though he wasn't obligated to go in; and he was planning to leave early and do whatever errands and chores he had to do the next day.

They went up to his apartment to sleep that night so that he could unpack and listen to his messages and feel like he had returned home. June preferred sleeping there, anyway. She just wanted to be in his arms, feeling safe and secure now that he was back, and their lives were on the brink of what could be a whole lot of big changes.

> *In family therapy, the goal is to bring about a change at some point within the family system. The exact nature of the change is less important than the ultimate shake-up it causes in the dynamics of the family. Once the family has altered in some even barely perceptible way, the door is thrown open for more meaningful shifts and changes that can then lead to healthier family interactions.*

Miranda referred to it as minor, but to June it seemed like a mountain of editing she'd have to do over the next few months. However, she also felt that for that kind of money, she would be willing to make whatever changes they wanted. They knew better than she did what might make it sell and recoup some of that money. June had guilt about the money. She knew she didn't really deserve it. She had no idea whose it was, but she felt obligated to be a good investment.

She and Miranda met several times and sent tons of pages back and forth over email. June began to appreciate Miranda's editing skill. She made ideas clearer, tightened up June's points and her suggestions were generally valuable. She was direct and didn't mince words. June actually enjoyed their time working together, finding it at times educational and also comforting. Clearly, Miranda thought the book was worth putting effort into. And she seemed confident that it would work out. June admired her confidence and was eager for the reassurance.

Several months went by in which Michael and June gradually got used to the idea of having some money, and they also had to get used to the fact that June was spending a lot of time - all her free time – rewriting. She was so far from the mindset she'd been in when writing the book that she had to remember how down at the bottom of a well she'd felt. That was difficult now that she was so happy. The rewriting finally ended and the book was turned in. Soon after, the move to a beautiful, new, larger, windowed-all-around apartment left them disorganized and adjusting for a while. Michael could still walk to work, and June did get herself a new, not too big, but extremely reliable car. That transition was exciting and not nearly as difficult or frightening as they had both expected.

June remembered wishing for change way back before she met Michael. Now she had it, but it meant other changes she didn't want. She couldn't alter the fact that Michael was younger than she was, and had career needs of his own. It worried her. And, as time passed, she could feel that he was dissatisfied. He didn't talk about it, but she could sense his frustration. And she knew that her success served as pressure for him to prove himself, to achieve more success for himself. Their lives became completely work focused at times.

June noticed messages from strange area codes for Michael on their answering machine. Unexpectedly, she found that her eyes would well up with tears. But she also secretly wished that one of those area codes would be an opportunity for him. He had become impatient and restless and she feared, unhappy. She felt responsible. She knew what he needed. She was torn between wanting to have her own needs met and wanting to make sure that his needs were met.

She loved him, with a closeness and comfort she had never before felt with anyone. They could say anything to each other. Almost. Of course, she'd force him to process everything ad nauseum. Between June and his weekly therapy, he could do that in his sleep at this point, and June believed that sometimes he did.

Michael was working hard in his therapy. One day he reported that he realized for the first time in his life that he tended to be a caretaker.

June said, "What do you mean?" But she already knew.

"I think I can be so supportive that I don't always take care of my own needs."

"Any needs in particular?"

"I'm starting to look at jobs. You know I'm stuck where I am. There's one in San Francisco... They're eager to meet me. I am thinking that I have to consider it." Michael spoke haltingly.

They had processed June's success half a million times, talking in circles, contradicting themselves and ending up right where they had begun. Michael needed more from his career to be truly happy and fulfilled. They both knew it. June had felt the same way until recently.

During the next several weeks, in between his phone interviews, and his flight to California to meet everyone, they discussed the pros and cons. June wanted him to be successful but not leave. He needed to leave to be successful in order to stay with her.

Finally Michael made plans. One day they stood in the kitchen that not so long ago they had decorated together, where he cooked his French toast and she made her simple pasta dishes. They stared at each other. She could feel his decision. It was pressing hard on her heart. He felt excited, but he didn't want to hurt her, and he knew he'd miss her. June knew that too, but it still hurt. She knew it was unhealthy to assume she could read his mind. Still a psychologist after all, she forced them to speak.

"You took the job offer." Their eyes were still locked.

"You know it's just for one year. You could come with me." He knew that was not going to happen.

"I can't just leave my practice. You know that."

"You could leave it altogether if you wanted to. You don't really need it anymore."

June's practice had gotten smaller and more manageable, especially because she had limited all the managed care. But she wasn't going to give it up altogether. It was an important part of her identity, the meaning in her life. "I don't want to do that."

"You know I need to do this." Michael looked at June with those green eyes.

"I know."

"You know it's the best thing for us. You know we'll see each other frequently. I'll come home, and you'll visit me out there. It'll be fun."

They both struggled not to fall into that cloudy, paralyzed silence that could make them weak and sleepy and unable to think or speak.

"That's a long time. What happens after that?" June's voice echoed, bouncing off tile and counter top.

"We'll figure it out together." His eyes were sad and loving.

She knew that they would. But again, she heard herself sounding like a child under water, "Do you still love me?"

He moved toward her, through the clouds and fog until his arms engulfed her and she knew that they'd be okay. For as long as he held her, anyway.

Then it felt like only a few days later, but it had been more like two months. Their lives had become about Michael's leaving. The faint lines of predawn light shone through the blinds and June could hear the birds beginning to chirp. She could barely breathe. The day had finally arrived. She felt completely unprepared. He ran around getting last minute things together. They stood and hugged silently for a long time.

As the door swung shut behind Michael and his two suitcases full of belongings with a loud, final note, June felt a sudden jolt of her old, long buried, desperate, aching loneliness. The ground under her feet began to shift and waver, her legs became loose and then numb, and her heart was gripped into a tight fist. What had she agreed to? How could she let him leave? He was the only source of her sanity. She wouldn't be functioning if not for him. She wasn't before him. It wasn't that long ago. She remembered it clearly. He gave her self-worth, he valued her thoughts, he desired her.

She knew it was selfish, but she resented his need to take the new job, now that it had become real. She couldn't really comprehend what a year in California would do for him that was more valuable than remaining here with her. And the possibility that he could choose to stay there immediately brought tears to her eyes. Why couldn't it have been New York City? Maybe it would have been better if he resented her and she didn't have to do all of the resenting.

California was warm and sunny, with palm trees blowing in the breeze and beautiful women everywhere. Maybe there'd even be one who'd make him realize that love can be easy, and life can be fun. June could become a little speck of history with some wiry grey hairs, far away. He could avoid the neuroses that make simple things difficult, the neediness, the crying, the red puffy face.

Why the hell would he ever want to come back? Maybe he'd just go ahead and leave the country altogether so that he'd never have to deal again with the burden that was June.

She'd taken this ride before on many occasions. Usually it flipped her over and left her gasping on familiar shaky ground. Could she crawl back up without his help? She wasn't sure. It would be a year in which she'd be busy promoting her book and trying to work on the next - if she could figure out what else to write about. It would be a year of growth for both of them. If they could withstand it, then they'd know they had what it takes to stay together. That sounded good. It sounded great. If it was really so great, why couldn't June stop crying?

Mostly, she did think she'd be fine. After a week of walking around in a dream, not feeling completely present, thinking she'd forgotten something somewhere, wondering who she was again, staving off depression by distracting herself, numbing her feelings, and not sleeping well, she was on her way to fine-ness. Just fine. Perfectly fine.

They'd talked for an hour the first night, both crying and frightened like little children in a thunderstorm. June hid under her blankets and hugged his pillow. As the week progressed, Michael became busy with his new job, and settling into his new place, meeting new people and not having much time for her. Their phone calls got shorter, more distant, some even perfunctory.

June felt unplugged, untethered, drifting at sea. And ugly, or at least plain and fading away. She'd forget what day it was, or what was supposed to happen next in her life. She'd walk into the kitchen and not have the energy required to prepare food or eat it. Or look at it or smell it. She had trouble sustaining herself.

As the second week began to drift by, she realized, due to her sharply honed therapeutic skills, that she was depressed again. At first she felt frightened by the realization. Who would save her? Would she just dissolve away until she was nothing? How pathetic was she? Michael couldn't save her. She didn't even want him to know what she was experiencing. It would have made no sense to him anymore. He was busy squinting into the bright sunlight. He would no longer comprehend the language of black and grey, frail and sad.

And then June realized, on the third day of the second week, that she was angry as hell. Why had a stupid new job taken him away? What kind of idiotic decision had he made? Was he so shallowly competitive that he had to threaten their relationship? And how strong was it if she felt it was being threatened?

The stabbing pain in her chest was shame. Had she made another bad decision? Chosen another person who would never really be able to love her enough or take care of her? Had everyone really been right about him? Could she trust her own judgment? Ever?

Or, was this a matter of being patient, the prize at the end being that they would have conquered the distance and time with their everlasting love? Does love actually work that way? Or was it more like a fire that needed to be tended constantly for fear that it would go out? Did love burn down to embers and then fade out?

It was never a good sign when June started to ask this many questions.

The anger she felt was like a surge of long lost, inaccessible energy. She woke up. Her life was going to be important, too. Whether Michael and she worked out or not, she deserved to have a life. Why should she shut down, turn off, and stop functioning right at the moment that everything had become new and exciting?

She needed to explore the possibility that she could be happy on her own. She needed to stop needing so desperately, so pathetically. Once again, she was mixing up the old, burdensome, baggage with the new. Some serious sorting needed to happen fast. At least this time, it looked like she would figure out how to pick herself up and dust herself off more quickly than she had while it was ending with Phil. And then the book came out.

PRESS RELEASE

Dr. June Gray, best-selling author, and expert on depression, will be answering your questions and signing copies of *Be Happy* on May 15th at the Barnes and Noble Book Store on Omega Square. Plan to arrive early, as large crowds are expected.

Seated at a small table in the corner of the bookstore, Dr. June Gray, depression specialist, in more ways than one, anxiety riddled, first time fraud author and hypocrite, signs her book. A runaway best seller, Be Happy, has turned the field of mental health upside down. Hoping the time will pass quickly, allowing her to remain in a semi-dissociated state, June stares at the long line of probably depressed, yet reverently hopeful and excited looking people, snaking out the door and down the street. Miranda has abandoned her to negotiate with the manager about providing water and coffee for June, as well as enough books to sell for the hordes of people storming the store.

The huge glass windows at the front of the store provide June with an uninterrupted view of those hordes approaching, pouring down from the parking lot like rain, increasing her desperate need for escape. Her left leg has fallen asleep, resulting in pins and needles in her foot. She allows herself to stand briefly as if looking for Miranda or water, but really to evaluate the location of the nearest emergency exit and the possibility of escape before Miranda's return. But Miranda appears as if summoned, cheerleader face on tightly.

June sits back down, a prisoner who smiles and signs. Many of the people on the line have already read the book. Some have several copies, to be endorsed to various friends or family members who need to have their depressions lifted like magic. Many arrive eager for a quick comment from the now semi-famous Dr. Gray, to alleviate all pain.

She attempts to look wise and empathic, nods as though listening to their quick attempts to tell her their tales of woe, shakes her head at the pity and recommends her book. Miranda stands proudly by, dollar signs glowing in her eyes. Time passes, as June's writing hand gets cramped and then altogether numb. Just like her brain. Short breaks are taken, failed attempts to achieve privacy in the ladies room, stretches to un-cramp the signing hand, and then back to the little table.

June was watching herself sign books from across the store and had no idea who Dr. June Gray was. She was responding on autopilot, a smile, a sympathetic look, an interested expression, but not too interested or Miranda subtly shooed her poor, depressed reader away. She felt trapped in purgatory, and would be taking the down elevator to

Hell any time now. She was looking forward to the ride. At least the sensation would return to her feet. She deserved to be there. She hated the hypocrite she felt she'd become.

She looked up to see the next face, made brief eye contact, smiled and signed, when to her shock and mortification she saw Phil approaching in the line. He looked the same although many months had passed. He saw June spot him, and had probably been looking relentlessly at her until she did. He waved. She waved back. At least she observed her arm move up and down in a waving motion. What in Hell would she write in his book? "Please leave me alone. June." Or "Have a nice life." Or "You're the reason I wrote this book. I hate you." Or "If you continue to stalk me, I'll call the police." She felt herself starting to choke. She needed water. Fortunately, Miranda had arranged for a glass right nearby. She gulped some down and planned how to cope with Phil as she smiled and signed away.

Thank goodness she'd had no time to really obsess over it. When Phil got to her, she gave him a big welcome, half stood for a half hug. He congratulated her and said he was looking forward to reading her book. When she actually took the risk and looked him directly in the eye, she knew it was over. Really over. She hardly knew him. She signed his book, "Best wishes, June." Generic. She helplessly shrugged, suggesting how she was sorry that she couldn't speak with him as so many people were waiting in line. He saw the logic, held her hand for a moment too long, and then vanished.

When she looked up about twenty minutes later to see her parents walking over, not waiting on line, June was unsurprised. Her mother looked as proud as she had ever seen her. Both parents hugged and kissed her as if they commonly exchanged dramatic shows of affection. In an overly loud voice her mother said sympathetically, "Honey, how are you holding up?"

June watched as people waiting in line nearby whispered to each other, her mother's desired effect. Then when June responded with a smile and "Fine," her mother added, "Can we do anything for you?" as if it were routine for her to take care of June's needs. Maybe she was offering to take her place and sign some books. Again June smiled and shook her head no.

"June, honey, we'll wait til later to have you sign our copy." This was exceptionally loud. Miranda noticed the hold-up in line and headed over. June immediately introduced her to her parents. She gave them an overjoyed to meet you look and expertly steered them away, chatting with them secretively about how wonderful the book and their daughter were. She was impressive.

June's brother, with his entourage in tow, showed up shortly afterward. They all came directly over, the wife and kids grinning as if they all had tremendous fondness for one another. Gerry shook June's hand, giving her an impressed nod. His wife air kissed her with expertise and flair and the girls became interested in a teddy bear and jelly bean display nearby. They soon joined June's parents and Miranda, who, with Houdini-like skills, escaped from them soon afterward. Her parents, brother, and family stood together talking for another half hour as she sat signing away before letting her know that they had to leave. The kids needed to be fed. They said their goodbyes.

> *Some people have either a compulsion to be completely honest even when it could be detrimental or a compulsion to lie when there is no logical reason to lie. The latter may have sociopathic tendencies. The compulsively honest person feels tortured by anything less than total disclosure, as lies of omission are as unacceptable as outright lies. He may, when forced to lie, develop symptoms of anxiety that can be attributed to his unconscious fear of punishment.*

Somewhere in the mix, June's patient, Annabelle, appeared. She had read the book already and had many opinions about it. June had to point out to her that a huge line of people waited behind her, but they'd discuss her opinions another time, as June very much wanted to hear them. Annabelle was able to agree to that without apparently feeling insulted. She did lean in while June opened her book to sign it, and whispered, "It's obvious that our work together greatly influenced your book." So, June signed it with, "Thanks for such a marvelous learning opportunity." Annabelle immediately read it, smiled at June, held her book tightly to her chest, and walked away.

Another couple of patients appeared as well, each eager for a little bit of personal attention. Both looked terribly excited for June. Perhaps they were also proud that their therapist was getting notoriety. Fortunately, it went smoothly. It hadn't occurred to her during the previous night of anticipatory sleeplessness that any of her patients would think to show up at her local signing. She had been lying awake imagining how she would hide the fact that she felt like a total fraud. That was a lucky thing, or she would have wasted hours imagining the worst and slept even less. A couple of colleagues also showed up and offered supportive, encouraging comments. Whether they truly meant them or were secretly horrified by June's book, they were polite and kind. That meant a lot to her.

The crowd finally began to thin. The sun was setting over the parking lot, reflecting golden, glowing windshields. June knew her hand would never un-cramp. She'd have to apply for disability; job-related injury. Would she get Workmans Comp? She looked up and saw Emily waiting on the line patiently. She grabbed Miranda and asked her to go get her. She gracefully introduced herself and brought Emily up to the front of the line. They gave each other real hugs. June felt so glad to see her. Emily explained that she had purposely come late in the hopes of having a little time to talk afterward. They agreed that she would wait for a half hour in the hope that June would be all done by then.

About forty-five minutes later, she was done. Emily had waited. They headed over to the coffee bar at the store and ordered cups of coffee. Emily listened politely as June whined quietly about the signing. When she finally finished, and felt calmer, June asked Emily how she was doing. She let June know that she and Ed had been in couples therapy, and that it was helping them. They had decided to try to make it work again. She had learned that she had been taking him for granted and that their communication skills had been pretty pitiful.

She smiled at June and said, "Relationships are harder than I thought."

June smiled back, grateful for the acknowledgment. "They don't seem to get easier with time, either."

"No. If anything, they require more attention."

It felt like Emily and June were discussing their relationship as well as her marriage. June told her what had been going on with Michael, and to her relief, Emily had no judgment to make. She was even encouraging. Emily felt that they should continue to communicate about their feelings, see one another when they could, and plan for the future. She made it sound like it wasn't such a desperate situation, after all. When they left, the sun had almost completely set. They hugged again and walked to their cars. June felt so glad to have her connection with Emily back.

Late that night, June got a call from Michael, sounding excited about all the hype he was hearing about her book. He was clearly proud of her. That felt good. They made plans for him to meet her at the California stop on her book tour since she'd have a few days off before the next one. They could have a mini-vacation. June had something to look forward to.

As it turned out, June had signed up unknowingly for a tremendous amount of promoting. Not just your usual book signings where you read a few pages and sign cleverly for an hour or two or four. She had inadvertently signed up for the talk show circuit. She could never even tolerate watching talk shows. She abhorred the so called professionals who would go on these shows and act like they had all the answers, give advice and say quick-witted, clever little quips in response to public suffering on the part of the severely exhibitionistic people who would agree to go on the show to pour out all of their personal pain to the widest possible audience. She found it offensive and horrifying for so many different reasons, from so many different perspectives, and would now be a part of it.

She was tortured by the thought of having to be one of those snide, falsely warm-hearted professionals. But she'd signed an agreement to do it. And she'd already spent a bit of the money she was getting for it.

She felt troubled about promoting her book in any way. She still had mixed feelings about its effectiveness. The book jacket lauded it for being far-reaching, but for June to say that same thing was clearly a different level of what seemed to her to be manipulation. Passively putting it on the book jacket is not the same as claiming it aloud to the masses. That terrified her.

As she sat in the mirrored, well-lit make-up room, June realized that she'd been dissociating. Someone was fussing with her hair, while another person was applying make-up. She realized it when the make-up girl, maybe 19 years old, with tight, revealing, clashing clothes in black and white patterns, and excessive make-up, shook her by the shoulder.

"Are you okay?" She was staring at June.

She wasn't. "Yes. Why?"

"You didn't seem to be hearing me when I was telling you to move your head a little and tilt your face up."

"I'm sorry. I guess I'm nervous."

The young woman's upper lip curled up and she squinted her eyes. A look of pity suffused her face. "Just do what I say. I don't have tons of time for you. I have other people to take care of."

"I guess I was lost in thought. I'm sorry."

"Look up and stop talking," she snapped.

June couldn't believe she had checked out so completely. "I'm sorry. You know make-up much better than I do. Why don't you do what you think is best, and maybe go light." She felt panicky. If the make-up girl paid any attention, she would notice that her whole body was trembling.

The make-up girl made a face that seemed to convey that June had severely limited intelligence. She leaned in a little too close and spoke in an exaggerated and slow way. "I said stop talking. You don't know anything about stage make up. If I go light, they won't be able to see you."

One of June's worst nightmares had materialized into real life. In thirty minutes, she'd be talking to Sandy Saunders, the national, daily talk-show host, in front of a live audience as well as millions of viewers. Her publicist, Stacy Clapp, and her entourage of encouraging young women had stepped out for coffee and cigarettes. They had not been having a lovely morning. Stacy kept trying to make June relax and smile. She couldn't help how she felt. She knew she was heading for humiliating doom. The conveyor belt she was strapped to kept moving closer and closer to the swinging pendulum's razor-sharp saw. So it was difficult to smile in a carefree way.

How would she discuss the book without being a complete hypocrite? It's one thing to make supportive comments to a group of eager-faced listeners at a big chain bookstore. It's another thing to go on national television and pretend belief in what had begun as an angry, sarcastic joke. Routinely, Stacy grabbed June's hand and looked in her eyes with the most sincere face she could muster and exclaimed, "Your book is helping millions of people. They read it, follow your advice and they FEEL LESS

DEPRESSED!" She repeatedly stressed the last three words as though they should make June see the light.

She met Sandy Saunders briefly and quickly went over what they would talk about. It seemed pretty basic. June's plan was to stick to the book and maybe even discuss the pros and cons of some of the advice, in a secret effort to be less hypocritical.

She had begun focusing on the time at which it would all be over. Her freedom and relief were one hour away. If people were really feeling better as a direct result of reading the book, was it fair to take that away from them? Was feeling better enough? What about self-understanding? There were many ways in which people might make themselves feel better: love, money, religion, medication, alcohol, illegal drugs, sex... June's brain was racing along making irrelevant lists. Would her colleagues laugh at her? Or worse, forever dismiss her as just another sellout? Sandy had mentioned something about listening to a few audience members' stories of their depression and then discussing some interventions. Would June insist on good old plain talking therapy? Or would she tell them to wear bright colors, add fun to their lives, leave encouraging notes lying around?

She looked up to find herself alone. The make-up girl had left and June hadn't even noticed. The hair girl was long gone. The publicist and her two girlfriends blew back into the room with big smiles on their faces.

"Ten more minutes, June. You look great." Stacy's friends nodded on cue. "How are you feeling?"

"I'm just fine."

"Oh, good. Don't forget to smile. Always let Sandy lead the conversation. Don't say anything too long or drawn out or complicated.

"Okay." How was that?

"You'll be great. Isn't she great?" More big nods and smiles.

The set looked like a three-sided living room with a sea of faces looming on the fourth side. The lights were bright and hot and a strong feeling of unreality overcame June. Michael flashed through her head. She wanted him to hug her. But instead he had abandoned her and it was his fault that she was there.

She waited offstage until she heard music and her name being announced. Someone guided her to the edge of the set and told her to go ahead and smile. June walked across the stage and was overwhelmed by the sound of clapping. She made herself smile and got to her chair without falling down. Sandy grabbed her hands like she was her favorite person. As she did, she said, "Dr. Gray, it is such a pleasure to have you on the show today. Isn't it?" With that she turned toward the audience and the applause shook the place all over again. June even heard some yells and cheers.

At that moment, June had the relaxing realization that she would be whoever Sandy wanted her to be. She'd be doing an acting job. A tidal wave overtook her. She heard herself say, "It's a pleasure to be here, Sandy." June had become a talking mannequin.

"We have a special surprise today. We've chosen a studio audience member to tell her story," Sandy said. "Then we'll see up close how Dr. Gray works her magic."

Of course June felt a twinge of pressure just then from that comment, but mostly she was feeling relieved. The studio audience member would take the focus off her for a while. Somehow she'd make some generic comments afterward. She'd memorized a few.

A beautiful young woman was ushered onto the stage. She looked June in the eye and smiled widely in an eerie way. She had a familiar look to her, but June had that sense frequently with people because she had a terrible memory for faces. She had lovely, shiny brown hair, cut similarly to June's, and was dressed in a flattering suit. She was very thin. Possibly eating disordered. June thought this might all work out okay, after all. Like the other viewers, she was eager to hear her story. Sandy made her feel comfortable. The two of them spoke briefly. Sandy turned back to June and smiled encouragingly. "Doctor, if you have any questions or need for clarification as Miss Cleaver tells her story, please feel free to jump in."

June thanked her. The spotlight went on, the room became silent, and Miss Cleaver began.

"I've had depression ever since I can remember. I just don't feel happiness. I have no joy in my life. When I do have moments of joy, they get taken away from me. I don't have much appetite. I have to force myself to eat; and whatever I eat tastes like cardboard. I don't sleep well. I have no interest in other people. I've been so hurt by people over the years. I have been in the same low-level job for years, even though people say I'm smart. I don't know why I'm alive." She bowed her head dramatically.

Sandy looked over at June. She was supposed to ask a question. She complied. "Have you had any relationships?"

Out of the corner of June's eye, she saw the camera man give Sandy a cue.

Miss Cleaver's head shot up and she glared at June. "I did have one boyfriend. He was the greatest. He did make me happy. But some bitch stole him away from me."

At this point, Sandy jumped in to announce a commercial break. As soon as the cameras were off, she whispered about language use and then made some sympathetic and calming comments to the guest.

June was experiencing a sickening jolt of recognition. It was like electricity shooting through her veins. The guest. She had dyed her hair and dressed up. She'd only seen her once before. Had she actually trapped June on national television? Her body was paralyzed in the seat. The camera guy was holding up two fingers. Sandy was smiling and complimenting June's question.

They were back on the air. June hadn't looked at the young woman during the break. She could see her from the corner of her eye trying to make eye contact. But she wanted to do it on the air to have the greatest effect. She didn't want to give it away at the commercial break and risk being removed from the show. It had to be a surprise. June could see the plan. She was terrified.

Suddenly, she realized what she had to do. She took a deep breath to steady herself.

Miss Cleaver looked at June with a challenge in her eye. She knew that June recognized her. June gave her a sympathetic smile. Miss Cleaver looked away, toward Sandy, with a changed expression, at once pleading and eager to please.

"My boyfriend was madly in love with me. He spent all of his time trying to please me. I was happy and felt loved for the first time in my life. I felt complete." A tear worked its way down Miss Cleaver's cheek.

June felt sick, unable to avoid picturing Michael attending to Amber's every need. In her mind, those needs were sexual. She was sinking.

"We were devoted to one another, planning our life together, when a selfish, older woman lured him away. He's so sweet and innocent that he didn't recognize what was happening to him. I tried to warn him."

June's head had begun to swim. Her mouth was dry and she was sure Amber was about to make an announcement. She wouldn't seem delusional at all. June would be the evil cougar to the millions of viewers. She plastered a sympathetic look on her face.

Just then Sandy forcefully interrupted Amber. "So, when he abandoned you, you became depressed. Tell us what that was like for you."

Amber nodded, whimpering, with tears streaming down her face now. "I was destroyed. I couldn't eat or sleep. She tore away all of the joy in my life."

Sandy cut in again, "How are you feeling right now?" Sandy looked over at June who nodded vigorously, like she'd never wanted to hear anything more than exactly how Amber was feeling at that very moment.

Amber wailed, "I'm depressed. My life is ruined. It's all her fault." She turned toward June.

June could see her struggle with whether she could finger point on television. Somehow Dr. Gray began to talk. "You need to try some of the solutions in my book." Sandy nodded and smiled at her now. June was eager to continue. Anything that took the focus off of Amber.

Out of the corner of her eye June saw Amber's frustration as she realized she would look crazy, as if she had a fantasy that June had actually had some role in her life. She seemed to be about to make a last ditch effort to ruin her, anyway. She turned toward June, raised her arm and opened her mouth.

Sandy cut in just then, to discuss with June, the doctor, various ways to cope. Amber looked completely deflated. Sandy had no idea. June was suddenly more eager than ever to suggest that she dress more colorfully, and take care of herself. She felt completely comfortable taking the suggestions from her book and serving them up to Amber. Sandy artfully manipulated her, so that she even appeared grateful for the help.

When it was all over, June shook Sandy's hand, offered very brief sympathetic and encouraging comments to Amber within Sandy's earshot and dashed off to the dressing room to safety. Her heart was pounding. She needed a big drink.

Later, from the much greater safety of their bed, June called Michael to process the appearance on Sandy's show. At first, Michael couldn't fully believe that Amber had actually meant to do June harm. As much as this irritated June, she did her best to convince him that there was no other rational reason for Amber to disguise herself and describe how Michael's current girlfriend ruined her life, to June, his current girlfriend. On national television. But what really concerned June was Amber's comment that rang endlessly in her head, about his spending all of his time trying to please her. When she mentioned that to Michael, he tried his best to convince June that they were much better suited for one another and that he found it a joy to please her. Not to mention how pleased he felt by her. June tried her best to believe him from a few thousand miles away.

Other talk show experiences weren't as traumatic, but each was its own personal horror for June. She didn't agree to help people directly on the set anymore. They could write letters and she'd answer them aloud. She was eager for her final appearance on the talk show circuit.

And then there she was, one bright, sunny morning, being powdered and prepped for a five minute spot on a local morning talk/news show. It had a wide audience. June was trapped on the usual speeding train to Hell. It had begun to feel like her regular commute. The people prepping her were telling her not to mention her book. The host would handle that. She was there to answer general questions about depression and the various cures being offered. June was relieved to hear this. She had gotten good at toning down her usual judgmental, jaded view, and she'd been able to do what they'd asked for the most part. She knew the many so-called cures for depression out there. She learned not to say that those in her book were the best. Let the reader decide.

The room in which she was to be interviewed was not a room at all, once again. It was a third of a room, on a platform, with orange carpet and intense lighting. It was a living room set, or an interview room set, to be more exact. Cameras pointed at them from several locations. June was surprised to find that she didn't feel especially nervous, but there wasn't much of a real audience to bring out that feeling. Overall, the whole thing felt artificial and unreal.

The interviewer, Dan Nelson, briefly greeted her and indicated that he'd truly enjoyed her book. The feeling of being flattered went through her, although she knew he hadn't bothered to actually read the small book. He had a handful of questions for her, prepared by someone else. She was offered coffee and danish. Someone brushed her hair and put make-up on her.

By the time they finally began the interview, June was feeling like she'd just had a day at the spa. She felt pretty relaxed, reassured by many friendly, complimentary faces and comments. Dan Nelson may not have read her book, but apparently quite a few of the support staff in the studio had read it and felt the better for it. This took her by surprise each time she heard it, first, that many people had already read it, and second, that the response was quite positive. Several people told her about specific issues addressed in the book that really made a difference for them, making June feel good and guilty at the same time.

The lights came on, the cameras were rolling. The music faded in and out. Dan smiled at June on cue and welcomed her to This Morning. Out of June came a confident, professional sounding, "Thank you. I am glad to be here."

Dan made some innocuously positive comments about the book, and then with an innocent twinkle in his eye, he said, "So, Dr. Gray, have you yourself benefited from any of your own advice in this book?" His tanned and coated face looked expectantly at her, as if this had been one of the prep questions they'd discussed earlier.June had been advised that they would talk about depression in general, types of depression, vulnerable groups, treatment options, all of which she felt absolutely prepared to discuss. To make up for the superficiality of her popular little book, she'd learned all she could about depression. If she was an expert on depression, she'd better have done all she could to deserve that title.

She'd also reread the book she'd written over and over in order to be prepared for specific questions from her interviewers and audience members. If she had to go through the hell of mass media production and marketing, she would do so in as professional and knowledgeable a manner as she could. She'd work to improve the image of psychologists in the media, since she was a psychologist forced into the media. She'd show the world that theirs could be an informed, intelligent, ethical, and caring profession. She'd show the public that most psychologists are dedicated, hard-working people motivated to improve the quality of life for as many people as possible.

She would work to change the common image of psychologists, and all other psychotherapists, as manipulative, greedy, crazy quacks who want to get control over weak, suggestible people when they are at their most vulnerable. If she was going to have to do this distasteful thing, she was going to do it right, and walk away proud of herself.

The only thing she felt unprepared for was a direct exposure of her own mental health struggles. She had not agreed to disclose personal information about herself to a huge anonymous television audience. She felt her heart racing, sweat gathering in the usual places, and her face flushing deep red. This last symptom of her panic upset her the most because it bluntly revealed her loss of cool to the mobs of viewers.

June had no idea what to say. She stared at Dan. There was a moment of awkward silence, when Dan gave her a phony smile meant to cajole her into baring her soul. He followed it up with, "You have helped so many people to finally climb out of their depressed states and lead more satisfying lives. Your book has been such an inspiration to so many. I'm certain that many of your loyal fans would feel all the more inspired if they could learn whether you yourself have struggled with the dreaded depression, and if so, how you climbed out of the darkness. Did you follow the advice in your own book? Is that how you developed the enlightening approach you use?"

Dan gave June a smiling "Well?"

She began slowly, "I'm not certain how to answer that question. I do understand that it would be inspiring for me to share my own struggles and triumph over depression. It's just that I've never spoken about it in a forum so public before. I'm not sure that I am prepared to do it today in this interview."

Dan looked at June, nodding like a bobble head toy, and then, without missing a beat, he moved on to the questions they had actually prepped for. June was so relieved that she just spouted facts and research data. They got along perfectly well, and the whole thing was over quickly. It would probably turn into a five minute segment on the air, if that.

It took June the rest of the day to calm herself down. She paced around her apartment. She called Emily. She called Michael ten times. She couldn't concentrate on anything for more than a moment. The thought kept repeating in her head "Millions of people now know that I have struggled with depression. The smiling, plastic man got me to admit it on television. I publicly labeled myself mentally ill!" She was in shock. From now on she might as well walk around with a tattoo on her forehead that read "Mental Illness: Depression". She felt that it must be the end of her career as a therapist and as an author. Who would go to a mentally ill therapist?

> *Because a real separation is necessary at termination of treatment, many feelings arise for the patient. Early abandonment fears, feelings of dependency and helplessness, and disappointment are common. There is tension between the feelings of hopefulness, independence, and optimism reflected by the patient's newfound understanding and abilities, and the feelings of sadness, loss, and fear about the separation. This ambivalence must be made conscious, and then gradually tolerable to the patient, until she can accept that painful feelings of loss are a permanent part of the human condition.*

June was getting a distinct feeling that her struggles with depression were far from over. Perhaps she was on the precipice of a new episode.

As she was bemoaning her pitiful state, standing in the middle of her living room, with tears rolling down her face, the phone rang. It was Miranda, overjoyed that she had reached June, who was mortified to hear her voice, silently berating herself for having answered the phone at all. She'd been so eager to hear from Michael. It hadn't occurred to her that anyone else would call her, least of all Miranda. Maybe there was some mental illness clause in their contract, and she wanted the money back.

She said in the most bubbly voice June had ever heard emanate from Miranda, "June, we have gotten a most interesting response to your interview."

June moaned.

Miranda interrupted the moan as if she hadn't even heard it, and continued, "The station has been bombarded with requests from viewers to have you back to tell your story and suggestions that you write your own story in book form - your struggle to overcome depression."

Miranda paused. When she got no response, she added. "So, what do you say? It will be big. I can feel it. How about coming down to talk it over with me?"

June had the distinct sense that her head had popped off her body and had rolled across the living room and banged into the wall. As that feeling faded she realized that Miranda was going to make her another big book offer. She would become known as the depression expert who overcame depression. She supposed worse things could happen.